KU-544-987

Further titles available in Arrow by Jean Plaidy

The Tudors
Uneasy Lies the Head
Katharine, the Virgin
Widow
The Shadow of the
Pomegranate
The King's Secret Matter
Murder Most Royal
St Thomas's Eve
The Sixth Wife
The Thistle and the Rose
Mary Queen of France
Lord Robert
Royal Road to Fotheringay
The Captive Queen of Scots

The Medici Trilogy
Madame Serpent
The Italian Woman
Queen Jezebel

The Plantagenets
The Plantagenet Prelude
The Revolt of the Eaglets
The Heart of the Lion
The Prince of Darkness

The Battle of the Queens
The Queen from Provence
The Hammer of the Scots
The Follies of the King
The Vow on the Heron
Passage to Pontefract
The Star of Lancaster

The French Revolution
Louis the Well-Beloved
The Road to Compiègne
Flaunting, Extravagant
Queen

**The Isabella and
Ferdinand Trilogy**
Castile for Isabella
Spain for the Sovereigns
Daughters of Spain

The Victorians
The Captive of Kensington
The Queen and Lord M
The Queen's Husband
The Widow of Windsor

Red Rose
of Anjou

Jean Plaidy, one of the pre-eminent authors of historical fiction for most of the twentieth century, is the pen name of the prolific English author Eleanor Hibbert, also known as Victoria Holt. Jean Plaidy's novels had sold more than 14 million copies worldwide by the time of her death in 1993.

For further information about our Jean Plaidy reissues and mailing list, please visit
www.randomhouse.co.uk/minisites/jeanplaidy

Praise for Jean Plaidy

'Plaidy excels at blending history with romance and drama'
New York Times

'Outstanding'
Vanity Fair

'Full-blooded, dramatic, exciting'
Observer

'Plaidy has brought the past to life'
Times Literary Supplement

'One of our best historical novelists'
News Chronicle

'An excellent story'
Irish Press

'Spirited ... Plaidy paints the truth as she sees it'
Birmingham Post

'Sketched vividly and sympathetically ... rewarding'
Scotsman

'Among the foremost of current historical novelists'
Birmingham Mail

'An accomplished novelist'
Glasgow Evening News

'There can be no doubt of the author's gift for storytelling'
Illustrated London News

'Jean Plaidy has once again brought characters and background vividly to life'
Everywoman

'Well up to standard ... fascinating'
Manchester Evening News

'Exciting and intelligent'
Truth Magazine

'No frills and plenty of excitement'
Yorkshire Post

The Red Rose of Anjou

JEAN PLAIDY

arrow books

Published by Arrow Books 2009

2 4 6 8 10 9 7 5 3 1

Copyright © Jean Plaidy, 1982

Initial lettering copyright © Stephen Raw, 2008

The Estate of Eleanor Hibbert has asserted its right under the Copyright, Designs and
Patents Act, 1988, to have Jean Plaidy identified as the author of this work.

First published in Great Britain in 1982

The Random House Group Limited
20 Vauxhall Bridge Road, London, SW1V 2SA

www.rbooks.co.uk

Addresses for companies within The Random House Group Limited can be found at:
www.randomhouse.co.uk/offices.htm

The Random House Group Limited Reg. No. 954009

A CIP catalogue record for this book is available from the British Library

ISBN 9780099532972

The Random House Group Limited supports The Forest Stewardship
Council (FSC), the leading international forest certification organisation.
All our titles that are printed on Greenpeace-approved FSC-certified paper
carry the FSC logo. Our paper procurement policy can be found at
www.rbooks.co.uk/environment

Typeset by SX Composing DTP, Rayleigh, Essex
Printed and bound in Great Britain by
CPI Cox & Wyman, Reading, RG1 8EX

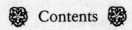

Contents

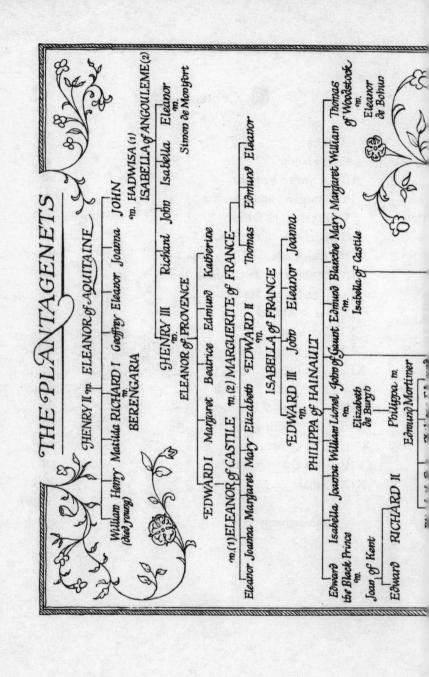

THE PLANTAGENETS

HENRY II m. ELEANOR of AQUITAINE

William Henry Matilda RICHARD I Geoffrey Eleanor Joanna JOHN
(died young)   m.   m. HADWISA (1)
                         BERENGARIA   ISABELLA of ANGOULEME (2)

HENRY III Richard John Isabella Eleanor
m.   m.
ELEANOR of PROVENCE   Simon de Montfort

EDWARD I Margaret Beatrice Edmund Katherine
m. (1) ELEANOR of CASTILE   m. (2) MARGUERITE of FRANCE

Eleanor Joanna Margaret Mary Elizabeth EDWARD II   Thomas Edmund Eleanor
                                       m.
                                       ISABELLA of FRANCE

EDWARD III John Eleanor Joanna
m.
PHILIPPA of HAINAULT

Edward Isabella Joanna William Lionel John of Gaunt Edmund Blanche Mary Margaret William Thomas
the Black Prince   m.   m.   of Woodstock
m.   Elizabeth   Isabella of Castile   m.
Joan of Kent   de Burgh   Eleanor
                                                                                                  de Bohun
Edward RICHARD II   Philippa m.
                                      Edmund Mortimer

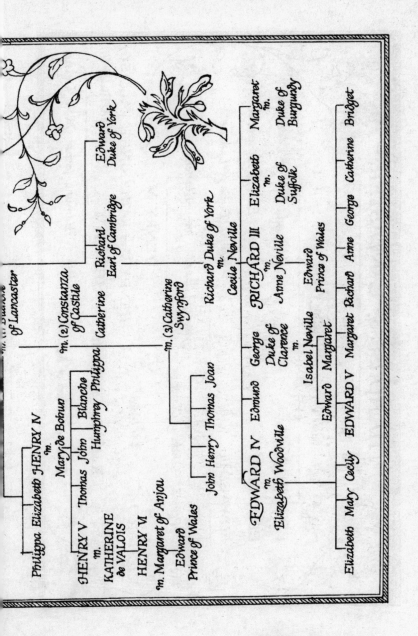

THE HOUSE of LANCASTER

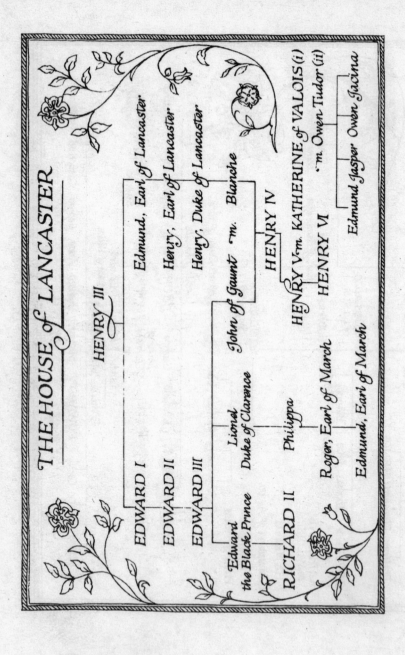

HENRY III
- Edmund, Earl of Lancaster
- Henry, Earl of Lancaster
- Henry, Duke of Lancaster — Blanche — m. — John of Gaunt
  - HENRY IV
    - HENRY V — m. KATHERINE of VALOIS (i)
      - HENRY VI
      - ⌐ m. Owen Tudor (ii)
        - Edmund   Jasper   Owen   Jacina

EDWARD I
EDWARD II
EDWARD III
- Edward the Black Prince
  - RICHARD II
- Lionel Duke of Clarence
  - Philippa
    - Roger, Earl of March
      - Edmund, Earl of March

family. May God preserve them. Oh, Agnès, my child, there are terrible things happening in France at this time. I often think of those poor souls in Orléans.'

'We must hope and pray that succour will come to them soon.'

'God seems to have deserted us. You don't remember, Agnès, but when I was young there were not these troubles. Life was peaceful. Then it started. First it was the Armagnacs against Burgundy.'

'It still is,' said Agnès.

'But our real enemies are the English. They are the ones who are tearing this country apart. It is because of the war . . . because they say we are defeated that I have to make over my lady Yolande's little things for this new baby.'

'There could be worse troubles,' suggested Agnès.

She returned to her sewing, but Theophanie, nurse to the five children of the King and Queen of Anjou and now transferred to the nursery of their second son René to take charge of his offspring, was in a reminiscent mood.

'He was always my favourite . . . René,' she mused. 'A lovely boy he was, and a lovely man. He was one for the poetry . . . for the singing of the troubadours. He was more interested in that than in doing all those fancy tricks on his horse. His mother Queen Yolande used to fret about it a bit. His father was rarely in the castle. "René likes reading books better than shedding blood," she used to say. "Admirable but books won't hold his estates together if someone casts a greedy eye on them." "Oh, don't you fret, my lady," I used to tell her, "when the time comes my lord will know the right way to act."'

'That is all any of us needs,' said Agnès, 'to know the right way to act when the time comes.'

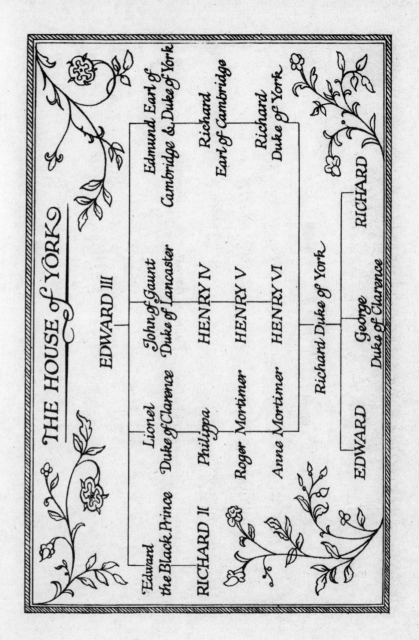

THE HOUSE of YORK

2

✤ Chapter I ✤

RENÉ

Bleak March winds buffeted the walls o
Château Keure and the two women wl
together in the large draughty room hu
closer to the fire. They were both busily sewing.

The elder of the two paused suddenly and held up
garment. 'I never thought,' she said, 'that it would
this. A child to be born and here am I hard put to i
clothes worthy of it. Who would have thought that a s
King of Anjou would ever be in such straits?'

Her companion lifted a strikingly beautiful face
work. Her expression was of a serenity unusual
young.

'The whole of France must be prepared to accep
ferences, Theophanie,' she said.

'Oh, 'tis all very well for the young,' was
'Remember I was with the King and Queen of An
until I came here. I brought the children up . . .
them.'

'Well, you have not really left the household.

'No . . . no . . . Here I am with my lord Rer

I

Theophanie regarded her steadily. She had come to look on the girl as one of her charges. Agnès had been sent by her family to be brought up in a noble household as so many girls of good family were. One could not help liking her. She was quiet, unassuming and ready to make herself useful. She was fond of the children and as they were so young Theophanie was glad of her help in the nursery. John was not yet four and then there was Louis who was three and Yolande not much more than eighteen months. She had had a twin, Nicolas, who alas had died a few weeks after his birth. It was a pleasant little clutch, thought Theophanie; and my lady was young yet. My lord was away a great deal as all noble lords were, but they managed somehow to accumulate families. Theophanie sometimes thought the good Lord very obligingly made such ladies especially fertile so that the long absence of their lords did not hold up the filling of the nurseries.

The lady Isabelle was very young still and already this new child would be the fourth – and would have been the fifth but for the death of poor little Nicolas.

She looked about the room with pride. This was one of the finest castles in Lorraine and was part of the lady Isabelle's dowry. René had done well in his marriage, Theophanie considered. He had married a strong-minded young woman. In fact all the women in the household were of a forceful nature – more so than the men. Theophanie often thought it should have been the men who stayed at home and the ladies who went into battle. René would have been a wonderful companion for his children; he would have patiently initiated them into the delights of poetry and music. As for the lady Isabelle, one could imagine her leading her troops into battle.

'Is this one of Your little jokes, Lord?' Theophanie asked.

Her faith was simple and she often conversed with God, treating him as though he were human like the rest of us – a sort of King above the King of France of course, but not without his foibles, and as her role in life was that of a nurse she was sometimes apt to adopt her nurse's manner to her Lord.

Of course it was a privilege to work for the House of Anjou. She greatly admired the lady Isabelle just as she had the lady Yolande. The lady Yolande was the daughter of the King of Aragon; and her daughter Marie, sister of René, had married the Dauphin of France.

'Mind you,' said Theophanie to Agnès, 'the Dauphin is a poor creature by all accounts. Sometimes I pity poor Marie. A good girl she was and deserving a better fate. Poor Marie . . . we thought she would be a Queen and what is she now . . . married to a Dauphin . . . one who should be King and they are calling a little English baby the King of France. It's pitiful when affairs get to that state, Agnès.'

Agnès bent her head over her sewing. She wondered about Marie and how she felt in the midst of such conflict, for although his mad father had accepted the English and allowed his daughter Katherine to marry the King of England, the Dauphin did not agree with him and put up a resistance, although in a rather feeble way. But perhaps it was those about him who resisted and used him as a figurehead.

What would be the outcome? It looked gloomy; more bleak than the cold March winds which swept across Pont-à-Mousson and angrily hit the walls of the Château Keure.

There was a tension throughout the country. Orléans, the key to the Loire, had been under siege since October. If it fell there would be little hope for France to extricate herself from

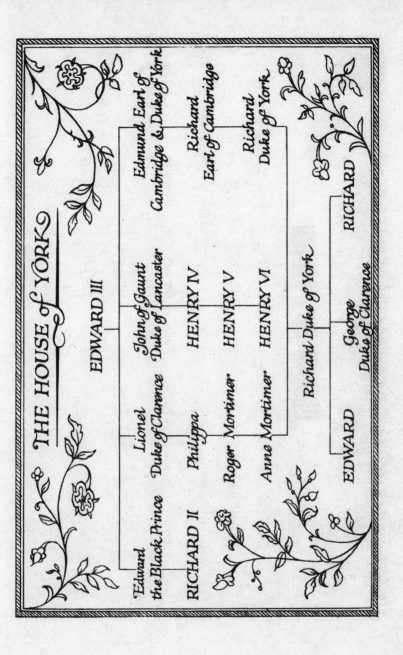

THE HOUSE of YORK

EDWARD III

Edward
the Black Prince

RICHARD II

Lionel
Duke of Clarence

Philippa

Roger Mortimer

Anne Mortimer

John of Gaunt
Duke of Lancaster

HENRY IV

HENRY V

HENRY VI

Edmund Earl of
Cambridge & Duke of York

Richard
Earl of Cambridge

Richard
Duke of York

Richard Duke of York

EDWARD

George
Duke of Clarence

RICHARD

🏵 Chapter I 🏵

RENÉ

Bleak March winds buffeted the walls of the Château Keure and the two women who sat together in the large draughty room huddled closer to the fire. They were both busily sewing.

The elder of the two paused suddenly and held up a small garment. 'I never thought,' she said, 'that it would come to this. A child to be born and here am I hard put to it to find clothes worthy of it. Who would have thought that a son of the King of Anjou would ever be in such straits?'

Her companion lifted a strikingly beautiful face from her work. Her expression was of a serenity unusual in one so young.

'The whole of France must be prepared to accept these differences, Theophanie,' she said.

'Oh, 'tis all very well for the young,' was the reply. 'Remember I was with the King and Queen of Anjou for years until I came here. I brought the children up . . . every one of them.'

'Well, you have not really left the household.'

'No . . . no . . . Here I am with my lord René and his little

I

family. May God preserve them. Oh, Agnès, my child, there are terrible things happening in France at this time. I often think of those poor souls in Orléans.'

'We must hope and pray that succour will come to them soon.'

'God seems to have deserted us. You don't remember, Agnès, but when I was young there were not these troubles. Life was peaceful. Then it started. First it was the Armagnacs against Burgundy.'

'It still is,' said Agnès.

'But our real enemies are the English. They are the ones who are tearing this country apart. It is because of the war . . . because they say we are defeated that I have to make over my lady Yolande's little things for this new baby.'

'There could be worse troubles,' suggested Agnès.

She returned to her sewing, but Theophanie, nurse to the five children of the King and Queen of Anjou and now transferred to the nursery of their second son René to take charge of his offspring, was in a reminiscent mood.

'He was always my favourite . . . René,' she mused. 'A lovely boy he was, and a lovely man. He was one for the poetry . . . for the singing of the troubadours. He was more interested in that than in doing all those fancy tricks on his horse. His mother Queen Yolande used to fret about it a bit. His father was rarely in the castle. "René likes reading books better than shedding blood," she used to say. "Admirable but books won't hold his estates together if someone casts a greedy eye on them." "Oh, don't you fret, my lady," I used to tell her, "when the time comes my lord will know the right way to act."'

'That is all any of us needs,' said Agnès, 'to know the right way to act when the time comes.'

Theophanie regarded her steadily. She had come to look on the girl as one of her charges. Agnès had been sent by her family to be brought up in a noble household as so many girls of good family were. One could not help liking her. She was quiet, unassuming and ready to make herself useful. She was fond of the children and as they were so young Theophanie was glad of her help in the nursery. John was not yet four and then there was Louis who was three and Yolande not much more than eighteen months. She had had a twin, Nicolas, who alas had died a few weeks after his birth. It was a pleasant little clutch, thought Theophanie; and my lady was young yet. My lord was away a great deal as all noble lords were, but they managed somehow to accumulate families. Theophanie sometimes thought the good Lord very obligingly made such ladies especially fertile so that the long absence of their lords did not hold up the filling of the nurseries.

The lady Isabelle was very young still and already this new child would be the fourth – and would have been the fifth but for the death of poor little Nicolas.

She looked about the room with pride. This was one of the finest castles in Lorraine and was part of the lady Isabelle's dowry. René had done well in his marriage, Theophanie considered. He had married a strong-minded young woman. In fact all the women in the household were of a forceful nature – more so than the men. Theophanie often thought it should have been the men who stayed at home and the ladies who went into battle. René would have been a wonderful companion for his children; he would have patiently initiated them into the delights of poetry and music. As for the lady Isabelle, one could imagine her leading her troops into battle.

'Is this one of Your little jokes, Lord?' Theophanie asked.

Her faith was simple and she often conversed with God, treating him as though he were human like the rest of us – a sort of King above the King of France of course, but not without his foibles, and as her role in life was that of a nurse she was sometimes apt to adopt her nurse's manner to her Lord.

Of course it was a privilege to work for the House of Anjou. She greatly admired the lady Isabelle just as she had the lady Yolande. The lady Yolande was the daughter of the King of Aragon; and her daughter Marie, sister of René, had married the Dauphin of France.

'Mind you,' said Theophanie to Agnès, 'the Dauphin is a poor creature by all accounts. Sometimes I pity poor Marie. A good girl she was and deserving a better fate. Poor Marie . . . we thought she would be a Queen and what is she now . . . married to a Dauphin . . . one who should be King and they are calling a little English baby the King of France. It's pitiful when affairs get to that state, Agnès.'

Agnès bent her head over her sewing. She wondered about Marie and how she felt in the midst of such conflict, for although his mad father had accepted the English and allowed his daughter Katherine to marry the King of England, the Dauphin did not agree with him and put up a resistance, although in a rather feeble way. But perhaps it was those about him who resisted and used him as a figurehead.

What would be the outcome? It looked gloomy; more bleak than the cold March winds which swept across Pont-à-Mousson and angrily hit the walls of the Château Keure.

There was a tension throughout the country. Orléans, the key to the Loire, had been under siege since October. If it fell there would be little hope for France to extricate herself from the yoke the English had put about her neck. And how could it be saved? It was asking for a miracle.

'But You could do it, Lord,' Theophanie admonished. 'It's not past Your powers. I thought You could move mountains. Well, if You can do that why don't You drive the English from Orléans?'

So there was waiting throughout the country and waiting in the Château at Pont-à-Mousson.

In the castle they were rewarded before the people of Orléans.

That very day when Theophanie and Agnès sat sewing over the fire, the lady Isabelle's pains started. And on the twenty-third day of March she gave birth to a healthy girl.

She was called Margaret.

Times might be hard but the baby must be given a worthy christening. Theophanie brought out the elaborate christening robes which had been worn by generations of the House of Anjou and in the Cathedral of Toul, Margaret was baptised. Her sponsors were René's elder brother, Louis King of Naples, and her maternal grandmother, the Duchess of Lorraine, after whom she had been named.

Margaret, blissfully unaware of the importance of the ceremony, accepted it with serenity and in due course was carried off to her nursery in Theophanie's waiting arms. René was paying one of his rare visits to the château. He had just acquired the title of Duke of Bar on the death of his great-uncle and this had contributed in some degree to his income and importance, particularly as with the Dukedom came the Marquisate of Pont-à-Mousson. Before this as a younger son he had had nothing but the little county of Guise.

He talked earnestly with Isabelle of the change in his fortunes.

'I may now be able to do a little towards helping Charles,' he said.

Isabelle nodded. Like everyone in France she was looking to the future with a great deal of hope. What had happened at Orléans had indeed seemed like a miracle. Isabelle was not sure that she believed in the special powers of the peasant girl who had been guided by Voices from Heaven. The fact remained that this girl had marched into Orléans and somehow defeated the English, thus saving the city and as a result Charles was now going to be crowned at Rheims.

It would not have seemed possible a few months ago. But the fortunes of France had really changed and strangely enough so had those of the family. René was a man of some importance now. He would have the means to raise men and arms; and naturally he wanted to place himself beside his brother-in-law and help him to regain all that had been lost to the English.

He had proclaimed himself an Armagnac supporter – which of course the Dauphin was – and this meant that he was the enemy of the Duke of Burgundy, whose actions in allying himself with the English must be deplored by all true Frenchmen.

'I can only hope that we do not antagonise Burgundy too strongly,' said Isabelle.

'Burgundy would consider us beneath his notice,' René re-assured her.

'Let us hope so, but it is my belief that he is aware of every Armagnac and regards him as an enemy.'

'Burgundy will be changing his tune ere long; it would not surprise me. Things have changed, Isabelle. Changed most miraculously.'

'René, you have become bemused by this Maid like so many others.'

'You would be impressed if you saw her, Isabelle. They jeered at first but gradually they began to see her in a different light. I trust my mother's judgement. She at first was sceptical but when she examined the Maid she changed her mind and persuaded my sister to do the same – not that Marie needed much persuasion. She too began to believe in the Maid.'

'And the King's wife and mother-in-law persuaded *him*.'

'Yes, but he too quickly realised that she had some power within her . . . something divine . . . and you see it worked. She frightened the English . . . there is no other way of describing it. And although defeat was staring us in the face at Orléans we turned it into victory.'

'I can only rejoice. And now Charles is to be crowned. I am glad of that. After the ceremony he will no longer be known merely as our Dauphin but our King.'

'Life will be different, you will see, for France . . . for us . . .'

'Perhaps it will mean that you can be with us more. Perhaps when this war is over people will be able to settle down with their families. But it is not over yet, René. The breaking of the siege of Orléans and the crowning of the King do not mean that the war is over.'

'Indeed not,' agreed René. 'But who would have believed a few months ago that we should have achieved such success.'

It was true. But Isabelle was more realistic than her husband and she knew that the English would not be driven out just because of one French victory – spectacular though it was.

There was bustle throughout the castle as René made his preparations to leave for Rheims. Even the children were aware of it and young John wanted to know why his father was with them.

'He'll not be here for long, my lord,' Theophanie told him. 'He'll be off again soon. He's going now to put a golden crown on the King's head.'

'Why?' asked John.

'Because he's the King of course.'

'I want a golden crown.'

'You can't have one, my little master, and that's flat, and I can't say I'm sorry about that. Crowns,' muttered Theophanie more to herself than the child, 'they never brought much good to anyone as far as I can see.'

John was inclined to whimper until Agnès took him into her lap and explained to him that crowns could be heavy things that sometimes hurt the head that carried them. He should not crave for one. Those who had them had to wear them and sometimes did not very much enjoy it.

John went to sleep and as she sat holding him Agnès wondered about the King. What she had heard of him had not been very flattering. He had made a bad impression on the people and few had any hope in him except the strange peasant girl who was supposed to have had instructions from Heaven to have him crowned and to win France back for him.

'His father was mad,' people said. And yet there were some who said he was a bastard and no son of the mad King after all. He was now about twenty-six years old. 'But he looks all of forty,' was another comment. 'It's the life he lives. They say the ladies of the Court won't look at him – Dauphin though he is and true King you might say – so he contents himself with serving-maids who welcome him to their beds for the sake of the royalty he brings with him.'

Agnès was wise enough to realise that these stories must be exaggerated – and on the other hand there was possibly a grain of truth in them.

'His mother told him he was a bastard . . . not the King's true son. They say that has upset him more than the loss of his kingdom.'

Poor Charles, thought Agnès.

He was a husband though and a father. Surely he found some comfort in his family.

'His lips are thick and he has hardly any brows and lashes; he was born with an exaggerated Valois nose which is bulbous and most disfiguring in his blubbery face . . .'

Oh no, thought Agnès, he cannot be as bad as all that. The Lord René was fond of him, and extremely happy because he was going to his coronation. Perhaps I shall see him one day and judge for myself, and as I am prepared for a monster I might have an agreeable surprise.

Theophanie came in and took the sleeping John from her. 'A crown indeed. God preserve you from that, my precious,' said Theophanie kissing the sleeping face.

René was ready to leave and the whole household was in the courtyard to wish him godspeed on his journey to Rheims.

Theophanie was there beside him – the specially privileged nurse who remembered the days when she held him in her lap and taught him his first tottering steps.

'Now you take care, my lord René, and don't you get caught up in any of these troubles. Keep well away from those Burgundians . . . a nasty lot them . . . going against their own country. And tell Marie I'm thinking of her and not to forget to keep her temper. Tell her she's a Queen now . . . in very truth. Tell her that Theophanie wants to be proud of her.'

René smiled at her and kissed her hand. Dear René, the best of the bunch – always so kind and courteous, a real gallant knight. She only hoped he would be able to look after himself if he came into contact with those wicked Burgundians or the even more wicked English.

Two years had passed since René went riding to Rheims to assist at the coronation of Charles the Seventh. The war was not over as so many people had optimistically prophesied it would be. The Maid had been captured by the Burgundians and sold to the English who had burned her in the square at Rouen. That brief glory was over – but not quite. Joan had made her impact. The fortunes of France had changed and although there were still English in France – and in dominant positions – Orléans had been saved, several towns had been recaptured by the French and there was a crowned King of France. The English had wanted to bring the little King of England over to crown him and they had done so, but not at Rheims. Oh, no, that was still in the hands of the French. They had had to be content with Paris and everyone knew that a crowning at Paris was not the same as one in Rheims.

René was often with his family at the Château Keure. They were wonderful days when he came to the nursery and played with the children and told them stories. He was far more gentle than their mother and they all adored him. Even two-year-old Margaret waited for his coming and shouted with delight when he appeared.

René said to Isabelle: 'This is the life for me. How much happier I am with my family than attending Court.'

'You are happy to be with your sister though.'

'It is good to see Marie. She is well able to take care of herself.'

'And Charles, too, it seems.'

'Well, she and my mother have a strong influence on him. He has changed, Isabelle. The coming of the peasant girl from Domremy had a marked effect on him. It is said that she assured him he was the King's legitimate son.'

'A mixed blessing,' commented Isabelle. 'To be the son of a mad father and have every right to the crown or to be free of taint and no right at all. A difficult choice to make.'

'Not for Charles. He is convinced now that he has a right to wear the crown and it seems of late that he is rousing himself from his previous lethargy. He is really giving his mind to freeing his country and bringing prosperity back to it.'

'Perhaps he will do it . . . with your sister to help him.'

'Don't forget my mother.'

'Ah yes, indeed. Well perhaps there are better days ahead for France.'

Occasionally René left on some military exercise. Then there was gloom in the château; but when he returned the joy of reunion was so great that, said Theophanie, it was almost worth the sadness they had suffered through his absence.

One January day two months before Margaret's second birthday, messengers arrived at the château.

They brought sad news. Isabelle's father, the Duke of Lorraine, had died.

Isabelle's grief was tempered by the sudden realisation that she, as her father's heiress, should inherit the Dukedom of

Lorraine. The possession of this rich territory would make all the difference to them. René would of course take the title and this would mean that Lorraine and Bar would be united and that René instead of being a not very affluent nobleman would become a wealthy and influential one.

Her assumption proved to be correct. The Duke's estates passed to his only child and the family fortunes changed overnight.

The first step would be to leave Pont-à-Mousson for Nancy. There they would take over the late Duke's château and live in a style afforded by their new position.

'This,' said Theophanie, 'is more like it. This is how it should be for my lady Yolande's son.'

There was great excitement in the nurseries when the children realised they were to leave for Nancy. John plied everyone with questions and Louis and Yolande listened wide-eyed to the answers. Even baby Margaret was aware that something was afoot. Theophanie was very glad of the help that Agnès gave her.

'That one is so good with children,' she commented to the lady Isabelle. 'I rely on her. She will make a good mother when her time comes, mark my words. The Lord intended her to be a mother.'

'She is a good girl,' said Lady Isabelle, 'and now that we have the means we shall look to finding a husband for her.'

'I'll ask the Lord to find her a good one,' said Theophanie. 'She's worthy of the best, that one.'

It was all very pleasant while it lasted. Everyone was enchanted by the château in Nancy and all the new treasures they were able to acquire. They hadn't realised until now how shabby everything had been in the Château Keure. Nancy was very grand.

'Little more like what we had when I was with my lady Yolande,' commented Theophanie. 'My lord René would remember.'

Lady Isabelle might have commented that she had been brought up in grand surroundings also and that indeed they owed their new good fortune to her side of the family.

But disaster was lying in wait.

One day travellers arrived at the castle. As René and Isabelle watched their approach they felt a twinge of alarm for they recognised the colours of the Duke of Burgundy.

He was not present himself. They would not have expected the great man to call without some herald warning them first; and in any case, he was one of the enemies. He had made it known that he had deeply deplored René's arriving with his men to help the Orleannese at the time of the siege.

The visitors were received with the customary hospitality, and while they were drinking wine in the great hall they came to the point.

The fact was that René and Isabelle were being asked to leave the château as soon as they could conveniently do so and René must also give up his title of Duke of Lorraine. In accepting this and Isabelle's believing herself to be her father's heiress, they had overlooked one important point. The Salic Law prevailed in France and that meant that *she* could not inherit her father's estates. The title and estates of Lorraine in truth belonged to the late Duke's eldest nephew, Antoine Count of Vaudémont, who was the nearest male heir.

'That is not so,' cried Isabelle. 'I am my father's daughter. He meant everything to go to me.'

'My lady,' was the answer, 'the Count of Vaudémont does not agree with this. Nor, I must tell you, does the Duke of Burgundy.'

'The Duke of Burgundy! This is not his affair.'

'He disagrees.'

René was deeply depressed. His brief respite was over. He knew what was in Burgundy's mind. This was punishment for supporting the Armagnacs. It was more than that. Burgundy wanted his way in Lorraine. Burgundy wanted to control the whole of France.

Isabelle's eyes were flashing with fury. 'You may go back and tell your masters that Lorraine is mine . . . ours. We will not give up one part of it.'

'My lady, I would ask you to consider carefully . . . My lord Duke is determined.'

'Go back to the Duke of Burgundy and the Count of Vaudémont,' cried Isabelle. 'If they want Lorraine, tell them to come and take it.'

Thus it was that the idyll was over and the battle for the estates of Lorraine began.

Theophanie shook her head over the turnabout in their affairs.

'My lord René had no heart for it,' she told Agnès. 'If it had been left to him he would have handed it all back to that Vaudémont. There's a saying, Agnès my dear, that if you want to live in peace keep friendly with Burgundy.'

'I have no respect for a Frenchman who works against Frenchmen.'

'It goes back a long way, my dear. The Duke's father was murdered by the Dauphin's men . . . That started it. Well, more or less, but before that the Duke of Orléans was murdered by Burgundy. It's these family quarrels. I never did like them. If I was the Lord I'd just pick up that Burgundy and

Armagnac and give them a smart smack where it hurts most.'

Agnès laughed, visualising such nursery tactics from the Almighty.

But there was disaster in the air, she knew. She had become interested in their nation's affairs since the coming of Joan of Arc. She liked to hear how the Maid had restored his confidence to the Dauphin. But this was of course a private quarrel – a battle for Lorraine. 'They should amend this Salic Law,' she said to Theophanie.

'Of course they should,' agreed the nurse. 'When I think of the women in my family . . .' She meant of course that of Anjou in which she had served since she was a girl. 'Well, when I think of our women, I'll say this, Agnès, they'd do as well in battle as any man . . . and bring more sense to it too if you ask me. The Lord saw it when He sent the Maid. Look what she did. What if they'd started talking about this Salic Law to her, eh?'

'It would scarcely have applied to her,' Agnès pointed out.

'Salic Law,' went on Theophanie. 'As if the lady Isabelle hasn't got every right to what her father left her. And what has it to do with this Burgundy? That's what I should like to know.'

The days passed. The lady Isabelle was clearly anxious. She would go to the topmost turret and there look out for signs of René and his men returning, she hoped victorious from the battle to uphold their rights.

She did not have to wait long. The battle had been over quickly and it was decisive.

She was in the turret watching when she saw several men riding fast and making for the castle. Hurrying down she was in the courtyard before they arrived. One look at them was enough to tell her that her worst fears were realised.

'My lady,' gasped the leader of the band. 'Ill tidings. We

were completely overcome at Bulgnéville. We put up a brave fight but none could withstand Burgundy's troops. They were everywhere and we were outnumbered. Vaudémont would not have succeeded without the help of the great Duke.'

Isabelle cried impatiently: 'My lord . . . René . . . Oh God help us they have taken him. He is dead . . .'

'No, no, my lady. He lives. But yes, they have taken him. He was badly wounded . . . but he lives . . . in the hands of the Burgundians.'

Isabelle closed her eyes. Theophanie was beside her. 'There, my lady. The news is not that bad. He lives . . . that is what matters most. The rest we'll sort out.'

'A prisoner . . .' murmured Isabelle. 'Burgundy's prisoner . . .'

'The good Lord won't let that wicked man keep a good man like Lord René long. I know that. He'll be back, my lady. You'll see. Here, Agnès, take my lady's arm. Let's get her to her chamber. This has been a great shock for her.'

Isabelle smiled wryly. 'Oh stop treating me like one of your children, Theophanie.'

Theophanie said, 'You're right. You're not one of my children. You'll know what to do, my lady. Don't I always say it's the women who manage these things best?'

So they went into the castle and the soldiers were housed and fed and later on more came, with more news, news of how René had fought bravely and it was only when most of his force had been destroyed and he himself was badly wounded by an arrow on the left side of his forehead which had half blinded him, that he had allowed himself to be taken.

But accounts of his bravery could bring little solace to his family. He was a prisoner in the hands of the enemy.

16

Isabelle was not one to sit down and accept disaster. She was not going meekly to hand over to her cousin the estates which she considered were rightly hers.

She knew what she was going to do. She was going to raise an army and she herself would lead it against the Count de Vaudémont. What of the children? She sent a messenger to her mother the Dowager Duchess Margaret, the godmother of little Margaret, and begged her to take charge of her children while she set about releasing her husband from captivity and keeping what her father had left her.

The Dowager Duchess, as strong-minded a lady as her daughter, immediately came to the rescue. She would take over the care of the children while Isabelle set about working for her husband's release.

Isabelle had been greatly upset by the fact that it was her own cousin who had acted in this way. They had known each other as children and she was surprised, for he had always appeared to have been amiable and reasonable and she had thought would have been a good friend to her.

It suddenly occurred to her that she would see him. Perhaps she could arouse some pity in him, some sense of honour.

Her mother was uncertain whether it was wise for her to go. She was after all placing herself in the hands of the enemy. Let someone go for her, suggested the lady Margaret. But Isabelle thought that only she could shame her cousin and was determined to make the journey herself.

Her mother knew that it would be useless to attempt to dissuade her. In her daughter's place she herself would have done the same. They were neither of them women to cower behind the might of their husbands. It had been they who had made decisions in their families, for women such as they were invariably gained the ascendancy over their men. So Isabelle set out and in a short time was confronting her cousin.

She was pleased to see that Antoine de Vaudémont was a little ashamed of himself.

'It surprises me,' she told him, 'that we should be facing each other as enemies.'

'A sad affair, I grant you.'

'And brought about by your greed,' Isabelle reminded him. 'You know full well that my father wished his estates to pass to me. It was always understood.'

'My lord of Burgundy thinks otherwise.'

'It is not the affair of the Duke of Burgundy.'

'He believes that the affairs of Lorraine are his.'

'I am surprised, Antoine, that you allow yourself to be his creature. He is a traitor to France.'

'Have care what you say, cousin. If those words were to be repeated . . .'

'Oh, save your fear of that man for yourself. I will tell him what I think of him if I ever have the misfortune to come face to face with him. But I have come to talk of my husband René.'

'Alas, he suffered bitter defeat. He has recovered from his wounds though. You need have no anxiety on that score.'

'Then we will talk of my other anxieties. I want him released.'

'That is out of the question.'

'Why? Have you forgotten, Antoine, that we are cousins? Our fathers were brothers. There must not be this strife between us. Release René. Forget this greedy claim of yours.'

'My dear cousin, if I wished to release René I could not. He is not my prisoner. He is in the hands of the Duke of Burgundy.'

'Why so! Why did you hand him over to that man?'

'René was captured by Maréchal de Toulongeon, the commander of the forces Burgundy sent to Bulgnéville.'

Isabelle felt limp with dismay.

'Then what can I do?'

Antoine shrugged his shoulders. 'Burgundy will make terms, I doubt not.'

'And those terms will doubtless be that I give up my estates. Where is René?'

'He is at Dijon. I hear he is a prisoner in the castle there.'

Isabelle covered her face with her hands and briefly gave way to her emotion. Then she faced Antoine steadily. 'It surprises me that you can behave in this way. I am sure my father will curse you from Heaven. His great concern was for my welfare and that of my family. Think what you have brought on us, Antoine.'

Antoine said sullenly, 'The Salic Law prevails in France.'

'A curse on the Salic Law! My father's estates should go where he wished them to and that was to his daughter. Antoine, your conscience must be sorely troubling you.'

She had hit the right note. His conscience was troubling him.

'Isabelle,' he said, 'please understand that there is nothing I can do. This is in the hands of the Duke of Burgundy. But perhaps after all there is one thing . . .'

'Yes?' she asked eagerly.

'I could call a truce . . . say for six months.'

Six months' respite! she thought. That was something.

She would accept that for she could see she could get nothing more from her cousin.

Isabelle returned to her family. Six months. It was a very short time and what could she hope to achieve?

But she was not the woman to sit down and brood. There must be some action she could take and when she had decided what was the best thing to do she would do it.

Then the idea came to her. René had shown friendship to King Charles. He had gone to Orléans at the time of the siege and had taken with him a troop of men to fight for the town – a small one it was true but it had been all that he could muster and Charles had known that and been grateful. He had assisted at the coronation. He had always been loyal to the King and now that the country was emerging a little from the English yoke perhaps Charles would do something for René and his family.

She would go to the King.

She called Theophanie to her and told her that she planned to make a trip to Vienne in Dauphiné where the Court was at this time.

'I shall need time to get the children ready,' said Theophanie.

'You are not coming, Theophanie, nor are the children . . . except the girls.'

Theophanie stared at Isabelle in amazement. 'You are taking the little girls, my lady?' she said. 'Why my lady Margaret is only two years old.'

'I know well her age, Theophanie, but I am taking her and Yolande and I want you to look after the boys while we are gone.'

'Of a certainty my boys will be safe with me but have you

thought, my lady, that it is no easy task to take two little girls . . . no more than babies . . . on such a long journey?'

'I have considered and decided,' said Isabelle coldly. She was not so much inclined to accept Theophanie's familiarity as René was. Theophanie had not been *her* nurse. And, Isabelle often thought, it was time she was reminded that she was no longer René's. But she was so good with the children and Isabelle really could trust them with her. René's mother had said that Theophanie was an excellent nurse and it was wise to keep such people in the family.

'The point is,' went on Isabelle, 'that I shall need someone to look after Yolande and Margaret and I have decided to take Agnès.'

'Oh, Agnès is a good girl. You'll not be disappointed in her. It's the poor little mites I'm thinking of . . . going all that way . . .'

'There is no need to concern yourself with them. Find Agnès and send her to me. I will tell her what preparations she should make.'

Isabelle went back to her chamber. She wondered what good it would do. It must do something. She was pinning her hopes on the King's gentle nature and the possibility that he would be moved by the sight of Yolande and little Margaret. They were such charming children.

Agnès came to her. A beautiful graceful creature, Isabelle thought. And useful in the household, Theophanie had said.

'Agnès,' said Isabelle, 'we are going on a journey. Did Theophanie tell you?'

'She mentioned something. I was not very clear about it.'

Isabelle decided to explain to this serene and sensible girl.

'You know the terrible plight of my lord René,' she said.

21

'He is the prisoner of the Duke of Burgundy. I am going to the King to ask him to help me.'

'Oh, my lady. I do hope that he will.'

'I shall talk to him and explain and try and persuade him. It is a hope . . . perhaps a forlorn one . . . but I think the sight of my two little girls without a father might move him to act. But I must hope, Agnès. Our situation here is desperate. Now I want you to come with us and help look after the children.'

'With the greatest pleasure I will do that, my lady.'

'I thought so, Agnès. Now you must make your preparations.'

Agnès listened. So she was to go to Court. She would perhaps see the King and Queen. She had thought so much about Charles at the time of the coronation and how the Maid had been so loyally devoted to him. She could not believe he was really as unattractive and as helpless as people represented him to be.

At last she would see for herself.

'You're dreaming, Agnès,' said Isabelle sharply. 'I suppose like most girls you want to go to Court. I can tell you ours will be a somewhat sombre visit and I doubt that even now the Court will be the least bit what you imagine it will be.'

Agnès was thoughtful. 'I shall be prepared for anything,' she answered.

So they set out.

It was an exhausting journey, but the children, under Agnès's supervision, were too excited by the novelty of everything to complain.

In due course they reached the Court and Isabelle had no

difficulty in gaining an audience with the King. Charles was depressed. He was recognised as the King at last after that miraculous crowning at Rheims, but events had not moved very fast since then.

He was so tired of everything. He almost wished he were a country nobleman and could retire to his estates and have done with all the troubles which surrounded him.

Joan of Arc was on his conscience, and often that strange episode would intrude on his thoughts and try as he might he could not forget her. Luxembourg, Burgundy's man, had captured her and had sold her to the English. It was the English who had burned her as a witch but his remorse must be as great if not greater than theirs – for he had done nothing to save her. He should have fought with all his might . . . and he had turned away. He had rejected her; he had tried to tell himself that she was after all some sort of witch.

He hated war. Bloodshed was revolting. He had to admit it brought gain to some. He thought of Harry of England at Agincourt. But where was Harry of England now? And if the war had brought misery to France how had England fared? They were still struggling for the crown of France. They were groaning under taxation to pay for the war and there was many a widow in England mourning her husband, and children grieving for a father who had gone to France and would never return.

Oh for peace! thought Charles.

And now here was Isabelle of Anjou come to ask something from him. He was sorry for René. He liked René. He was especially fond of René's mother who was his own mother-in-law. She was one of the most enlightened and interesting women he knew. He found pleasure in her society and regarded her advice with a greater respect than that which he felt for many of his ministers. Yes, he would like to have helped Isabelle. But how could he, against Burgundy? How he hated Burgundy. Burgundy was the bogey of his life.

Her little girls were adorable. Isabelle was a beautiful woman and she pleaded most eloquently, but as he had told his mother-in-law Yolande, there was nothing he could do against Burgundy. The Duke's resources were far greater than his own; and much as he would like to he could hardly involve even what he had in a private quarrel between two families.

He was desperately sorry. He would have liked to help. Yolande understood. Isabelle must.

Oh, what a wearying business it was being King of a country that was in such a dire state as France was at this time!

He liked to walk alone in the gardens about the castle. One day as he sat down under a tree brooding in his melancholy way, he saw a girl. She was walking through the gardens and stopping now and then to admire the flowers. He watched her for a few moments before she was aware of him. She was unlike any other girl he had known. She was of the Court he supposed but he had never seen her before. He would have remembered if he had, because there was something so distinctive about her.

He called: 'Well a day, my lady. Are you enjoying the gardens as I am?'

She paused and smiled at him.

'They are very beautiful, my lord.'

It occurred to him that she could not know who he was because she showed no sign of the great honour he did her by speaking to her.

'Would you care to sit awhile and talk?' he said.

She came and sat beside him. The purity of her features

startled him. He admired beauty, he admired women. He guessed by her clothes that she was not a lady of high rank. She could not be for if she was he would surely know her. She was not a serving-woman either. His adventures with women had been many. He had never hesitated to indulge himself, and because of that sense of inferiority which his mother had inspired in him those of the lowly kind attracted him. With them he had been able to feel superior. He despised himself and often wished he did not know himself so well. This was different though. He admired her beauty but had no desire for a quick seduction this day and to forget her by tomorrow.

'I have not seen you at the Court before,' he said.

'It is not surprising since I am lately come,' she answered.

'And what think you of it?'

'It is a sad Court in a way. The threat of the English invaders hangs over it still.'

'Ah yes,' he sighed. 'But it has improved has it not? In the last two years there has been change.'

'A slow change,' said Agnès.

'And you think it should be quicker?'

'But of course, my lord.'

'The King should bestir himself, you think?'

'Aye, that he should. He should rid himself of ministers who impede him, and act for himself.'

'You are not of the Court, but lately come, you say, yet you tell the King's minsters how they should act.'

'Not his ministers. But I think the King should rouse himself. He should take the governing of the country in hand. He should be a King in truth.'

'Which he is not at the moment?'

'As you said I am a simple girl from the country, but I listen,

I think; and I know what has happened. We had a brief glory when the Maid came and drove the besiegers from Orléans and had the Dauphin made King at Rheims . . . and then . . .'

'Yes, my lady, and then?'

'Then it stopped.'

'There were no more miracles, you mean. The Maid lost her powers and then the English burned her as a witch.'

'They should never have been allowed to.'

'Nay, you speak truth there. And do you think that is why God no longer seems on the side of the French?'

'He is not on the side of the English either.'

'In fact He has shut the gates of Heaven and is leaving us to our own devices.'

'I think . . .'

'Yes, my lady, what do you think?'

'I think that God would help France again if France helped herself.'

She stood up.

'So you are going now?'

'Yes, I must return to my charges.'

'Who are your charges?'

'The children of the Duchess of Lorraine. Yolande and Margaret.'

'So you are in that lady's train. Shall you be in the gardens tomorrow?'

She looked at him steadily.

'I would be here, if you wished it.'

'That is gracious of you.'

She laughed then. 'Nay, all would say it is gracious of you. I know who you are, Sire.'

He was amazed. She had not behaved as though in the

presence of the King. And all the time she had known him!

She was quite unabashed by her own temerity. 'I have known you long,' she said. 'I thought of you often . . . during the difficult days. I should have been very happy to have been at Rheims on the day they crowned you.'

'You are a strange girl,' he said. 'What is your name?'

'It is Agnès Sorel.'

'Agnès Sorel,' he repeated. 'I have enjoyed our talk. I shall see you again.'

She saw him again. He was attracted by her. She was in the first place outstandingly beautiful, and in a serene way, quite different from the flamboyant beauties of his Court. She cared about the country. That was what amazed him. There was no sign of coquetry. She must have thought him extremely ugly, which he undoubtedly was, and old too, for he appeared to be older than his years and she was very young. He was astonished by how much she knew of the country's affairs.

By the end of the second meeting he was more fascinated than he had been at the first. Her frank manner, her complete indifference to his royalty enchanted him. He could not stop looking at her. He discovered she was more beautiful every time he saw her. But chiefly he discovered a peace in her company which he had never known before.

He talked to the woman he admired more than any other. She was his mother-in-law Yolande of Anjou who was a frequent visitor at the Court and who had been one of his closest friends ever since he had known her. He was closer to her than to his wife. He was in fact glad that he had married Marie because the marriage had brought him Yolande.

'Do you know the young girl who travelled in your daughter-in-law's train? She is in charge of the little girls.'

'Oh, Agnès, you mean. She's a delightful creature is she not?'

He was relieved that his mother-in-law shared his views.

'I find her so,' he said.

'You have made her acquaintance . . . personally then?'

'Yes. But not as you might think. She is not the sort of girl for a quick encounter today and to be forgotten tomorrow.'

'I would agree with that.'

'Her conversation is amazing in one who has lived her life in the country.'

'She has a bright intelligence and a rather unusual beauty.'

'That was my opinion.'

'Have you . . . plans concerning this girl?'

The King was silent.

'I find myself thinking of her often but not . . . in the usual way.'

'I see,' said Yolande thoughtfully. She was thinking that it would be good for him to have a mistress of good reputation. If Charles were ever going to win the respect of his people he would have to change. He would have to develop confidence in himself; he would have to act more forcefully; he would have to be extricated from ministers whose one aim was to enrich themselves. He was fond of women; he listened to women. Yolande regarded that as a virtue. She believed that if Charles could be surrounded by wise people, if he could be aroused from his lethargy, if it could be brought home to him that he had the makings of a great monarch in him, he could become one.

She went on thoughtfully: 'I think the girl would be an asset to our Court. She has a certain grace. I noticed it myself. She could become a member of Marie's household. I will speak to her.'

'As always you are my very good friend.'

'Leave it to me,' said Yolande.

It may have seemed strange, she ruminated, that she should introduce into her daughter's household a young girl who was very likely destined to become the King's mistress. But Yolande was far-seeing. How much better for the King to have one good woman to whom he was devoted than a succession of furtive fumblings with serving girls which was ruining his health in any case as well as undermining his dignity. Yolande looking into the future could see the day arrive when Charles could be a great King. She must therefore allow no obstacles to stand in his way. He needed guidance until he found the way he must go; and he would succeed, Yolande believed. She knew men; she knew how to govern; she herself had acted as Regent of Anjou for her eldest son Louis who was in Naples trying to keep hold of the crown there. In her wisdom she believed that Charles needed as many steadying influences as could be found. And it seemed to her that this beautiful and wise young girl could well be one of them. She could mould Agnès, become her friend. Charles was not the only one who sensed rare qualities in this girl. It was worth giving the matter a try.

Isabelle, realising that no help could be obtained from the King, prepared to return to the palace in Nancy where her own mother was in charge.

When she went she left Agnès Sorel behind. Agnès had become Maid of Honour to the Queen of France.

Meanwhile René was finding a certain amount of enjoyment in captivity. He had never been one to care for battles. His position forced him into a situation which his inclination would have been to avoid if there had been a choice. Yolande had seen that he had been brought up to reverence the laws of chivalry, and these often made heavy demands on a man.

However, at Dijon, he had leisure and he was free of making war. The laws of chivalry demanded that he must be treated with the utmost respect which resulted in the fact that, strictly confined as he was, he was more of a guest at Dijon than a prisoner.

Although he was closely guarded he could go where he liked within the castle and he found pleasure in the chapel where there was a great deal of glass some of which had been decorated with exquisite paintings. René was a painter of some ability; he was also a poet and a musician; how often had he deplored his inability to devote himself to these activities which he loved. Now here was a chance. He had so much admired the paintings in the chapel that he would like to paint on glass himself. Glass was found for him and paints provided and in a short time René was passing the days of his captivity in a very pleasant fashion.

Time flew. He had completed a portrait of the late Duke John of Burgundy, who had been known as the Fearless; and so pleased was he with it that he did another of the Duke's son, the present Duke Philip.

He then painted miniatures of other members of the family and looked forward to each day when he could continue with his work.

When he heard that the Duke of Burgundy had announced his intention of visiting Dijon he scarcely heard the news; he was so intent on getting the right texture for the hair of the subject of one of his paintings.

Duke Philip arrived and expecting to find an abject René of

Anjou begging for his release was surprised to find the captive intent on his work.

The Duke looked at the painting. 'Why it is beautiful,' he said. 'I had no idea you were an artist.'

'Oh,' said René modestly, 'it passes the time.'

He talked of the way he mixed his paints and the subjects who pleased him most.

'You seem to have found an agreeable way in which to spend your captivity,' said the Duke.

'An artist,' explained René, 'can never truly become the captive of anything but his own imagination.'

'So an artist can be content wherever he is.'

'While engaged in the act of creation most certainly.'

'It seems to me you do not find all this in the least irksome.'

'At times, yes. I should like to be with my family. My children are growing up, you know, and it is always a joy to see them changing. But while I paint my work engrosses me. It is so with artists.'

The Duke was amazed. There could not be a man less like himself. It was not that the Duke was not a highly cultured man. He was. He loved beautiful things, but first and foremost he was the Duke of Burgundy and his main object in life was to uphold his power and increase it.

But he was greatly impressed by René's work and when he saw the pictures which his prisoner had painted of Duke John and himself he declared that they were very fine indeed and should be placed in the window of the chapel.

'You embarrass me,' he said. 'I do not care to hold an artist such as you captive.'

'There is an easy remedy for that,' said René with a smile. 'Let me go free.'

'Now you know that is not possible. There are conventions to be observed in matters like this. If I freed you without conditions I should have every prisoner I take claiming to be an artist.'

'That is a matter, my lord Duke, which could be put to the test.'

'The appreciation of great art is an individual matter. I should be told that my prisoner was a great artist but of a different school from that which I admired. You see my difficulties.'

'I do, my lord.'

'On the other hand,' said the Duke, 'I would discuss terms with you. You were captured in battle. The dispute over Lorraine has to be settled. Who has the prior claim – you as husband of Isabelle or Antoine de Vaudémont? Are we to enforce the Salic Law or not? I can see an easy settlement to that dispute.'

'I should be glad to know it.'

'You have a daughter, have you not?'

'Two. Yolande and Margaret.'

'It is of the elder I would speak.'

'That is Yolande.'

'My dear man, Antoine has a son, young Ferri. Why should not these two be betrothed? In time Antoine's son and your daughter would inherit Lorraine. Would you agree to that? I ask you this, but at the same time I must remind you that you will remain a prisoner until you do.'

'It seems a fair enough solution,' said René.

'Then that will settle the main dispute. But naturally there must be a ransom. Certain castles shall we say?'

'Which?' asked René.

'Clermont, Châtille, Bourmont and Charmes?'

'You strike a hard bargain.'

'And twenty thousand gold crowns.'

'Twenty thousand gold crowns! Where shall I find them?'

'You will have time to find the money. I should advise you to agree. Ransoms have a habit of increasing with the years. I am being lenient. You must admit. It is because of the respect I have for an artist.'

When the Duke had gone René considered the matter. He wanted to be with his family. He longed to see the children. It was true that little Yolande would doubtless be expected to join the Vaudémonts. Well, that was the sort of thing that happened to girls.

He agreed and very soon after was speeding on his way to join his family.

After René had been warmly greeted by his family both Isabelle and her mother considered the terms of his release and declared that they were very harsh.

In the nursery, Theophanie was fuming.

'A nice state of affairs,' she said. 'A little mite like my Yolande to go off and live with strangers. Her cousins they may be, but it's not right. It's not right at all. And Agnès. Who would have believed that? A Maid of Honour eh, to the Queen. I reckon she'll be pining for her nice place in my nurseries before very long. Agnès at Court! I can't see it. I can't see it at all.'

But the real tragedy was of course the departure of Yolande.

It was a mercy, she muttered to herself, that the child was so young . . . too young to realise. She was only four years old, poor mite. She was asking a great many questions about her new home.

'As if I could tell her,' mourned Theophanie.

Margaret looked on with wide eyes.

'Why is Yolande going away?'

'Because she's going to be betrothed.'

'What is betrothed?'

'Married, in time.'

'Theo, shall I be betrothed?'

'You certainly will, my lamb.'

'Is it a good thing to be?'

'It's sometimes very good . . . for others,' added Theophanie bitterly.

The boys were interested. *'You'll* have to go one day, Margaret,' they taunted her.

Yolande was half sorrowful, half proud. She was after all the centre of the activity. She had to have new clothes and was given special lessons on how to behave.

It was particularly hard that she should have to go now that their father was home. When Margaret pointed this out to Theophanie she said somewhat mysteriously: 'Well, it's just because . . .'

And try as she might Margaret could get no more out of her.

In due course Yolande went away and Margaret missed her very much although her father was with them again and that made life very pleasant. He had changed. There was a scar on the left side of his forehead which was where the arrow had struck when he had been captured by the Maréchal de Toulongeon which was the reason why Yolande was no longer with them.

René was very different from their mother. He liked to be with them. He would paint and sing and read poetry and that was very interesting. He talked to them all about how he had been captured and had painted on glass in the Château of Dijon; he was entirely frank with them and he was giving them all an interest in music and poetry.

'It is well enough,' said the Dowager Duchess Margaret who was with them. 'They will be cultivated; but we must not forget that they must learn other things besides an appreciation of the arts.'

Margaret was fond of her son-in-law but she was now and then exasperated with his attitude. He was a considerable artist it was true; his poetry and music gave pleasure to the entire household and even the youngest pages would listen entranced when René sang his own compositions in the great hall after dinner.

'But what of this ransom?' demanded the Dowager Duchess of her daughter. 'Fine poetry and paintings are not going to pay that, are they? And will Burgundy wait much longer?'

There was an additional disaster. The Maréchal de Toulongeon had added his claims to those of his master Burgundy.

He was the one who had actually captured René. He was therefore claiming a further eighteen thousand crowns as his share of the ransom.

'There you are,' said the Dowager Duchess. 'Time is passing and nothing is being done.'

'I don't think René gives it a thought,' said Isabelle. 'He is so happy to be here with his family and to pursue those pleasures which are such a delight to him.'

'In that way he is merely putting off the evil day. It is more than two years since he returned and nothing has been done except to send Yolande to the Vaudémonts. Believe me, Burgundy will not wait much longer and now that Toulongeon is adding his demands René will find himself in great difficulties. Something must be done,'

'I will speak to René,' said Isabelle.

Margaret shook her head. 'That is no use. I will speak to the Emperor of Germany.'

'Sigismund?'

'Why not. He has great power. He might be able to persuade Burgundy to be more moderate. There is just a possibility that Burgundy would listen to him.'

'It is worth trying,' said Isabelle. 'No harm can be done.'

The more the Dowager Duchess considered this the more pleased she was with the idea. She would send messages to the Emperor who, as he was her brother-in-law, could scarcely refuse to help her. She was getting old, she said, but thank God she could still make decisions.

'On the day I could not do that,' she told her daughter, 'I would wish to depart this life.'

'My dearest mother,' said Isabelle, 'you have always been a woman of power. Sometimes I think the women of our family should have been the ones to govern. Everywhere we are cursed by this ridiculous Salic Law.'

'It is an added obstacle for us to overcome, my dear. Now we will see what Sigismund can do for us with Burgundy.'

It was some time before she discovered. The messengers had to reach Sigismund and he had to decide how to act. He wanted to help and sent messengers to the great Duke to tell him that he considered the terms he had arranged with René were too harsh. They must in the name of reason be modified. He knew the state of René's affairs and that he was not in a position to meet demands such as the Duke had made.

A few months passed. The pleasant life continued. René

asked nothing more than to be with his sons and little daughter; and his only regret was that little Yolande had had to go away. He could blissfully forget that he must find the ransom and that Burgundy's patience might be getting exhausted.

The Dowager Duchess was feeling very pleased with herself. She had received a message from Sigismund to say that he would do all he could to make Burgundy see reason and had already approached him. She was congratulating herself on her ability to solve her son-in-law's problems far better than he could himself when she had an unpleasant shock. Emissaries from the Duke of Burgundy arrived at Nancy.

Their message was that the Duke was incensed that René should have had the temerity to appeal to Sigismund. As for the Emperor, he would do well to mind his business. As a result of this meddling, Burgundy would negotiate no longer. René must return to captivity and this time bring his two sons with him as hostages.

René was astounded. He did not know what Burgundy meant.

He expressed his bewilderment to his wife and mother-in-law. 'I do not understand what Burgundy is talking about,' he said. 'Sigismund! What has he to do with it?'

The Dowager Duchess had turned pale. She put her hand to her heart. Isabelle laid an arm about her shoulders and whispered: 'You must not upset yourself. It is bad for you. You were only trying to help. René will understand.'

Margaret shook her head. 'It is my fault,' she said. 'Oh René, how can you forgive me? I could not bear to see you doing nothing and it was I who asked Sigismund to help.'

'Ah,' said René slowly. 'I see now what has maddened

Burgundy.' He shrugged. 'You must not reproach yourself, my lady. I know all you did, you did for me and Isabelle. Well, it is an end to our life here at Nancy but only for a while. All will be well in time.'

'René,' said Isabelle, 'stay and fight. Let us see if we can defeat this arrogant Duke.'

'With what?' asked René. 'We cannot pit ourselves against him. I must perforce go and take the boys with me.'

'René . . . stay. Let us find some means . . .'

But he shook his head. 'The laws of chivalry demand that I honour my commitments. I was taken in fair battle; I must therefore pay the ransom demanded or remain a prisoner.'

They could see that it was impossible – he being René – for him to take any course but the honourable one.

'When you take the boys with you,' said Isabelle, 'there will only be little Margaret left to me.'

René took her face in his hands and kissed her.

'She is a beautiful child. You will find great comfort in her.'

Within a few days Isabelle, with little Margaret on one side and the Dowager Duchess on the other, waved goodbye to René as he rode off into captivity.

It was a sorrowful household. The Dowager Duchess was wrapped in gloom. She could not forget that she had brought this about and she could not forgive herself.

'Sometimes I think,' she told her daughter, 'it is better to be as René. He reviews his captivity with calm and without shame. If they will supply him with paints he will be happy.'

'Dear Mother,' replied Isabelle, 'you must stop grieving. You are making yourself ill. You were right to do all you could. Who would have believed that Burgundy would be so angry that he takes his revenge in this way?'

'I think Sigismund must have approached him without tact. I should have thought of that. But for me René would be here now and although you are poor and without the means to extricate him from this humiliating position, at least you were together.'

There was nothing Isabelle could do to comfort her mother. Each day the Dowager Duchess grew more pale, wan and listless. Her appetite had deserted her and she could not sleep at night thinking about the havoc her interference had caused.

When August came it was stiflingly hot and she was obliged to take to her bed. Within a few days Isabelle had grown really anxious. The old lady had lost that tremendous verve which had made her seem immortal and because she had lost it, Isabelle knew that she was very ill indeed.

As the month progressed she grew steadily worse and on the morning of the twenty-seventh when her women came into her bedchamber they thought she was sleeping peacefully and did not disturb her, but before the morning was out it was realised that she was dead.

Isabelle knelt at her bedside and thought of all this vital woman had done for her. She could not believe that she would never see her again. Devoted mother, great ruler, affectionate, clever . . . how fortunate she had been to have been born to such a woman!

I must be like her, thought Isabelle. I must be strong and particularly so since I am married to a man who is scarcely that.

Deeply she mourned her mother but there was little time for mourning. This was going to mean changes. Margaret Dowager Duchess of Lorraine would be greatly missed. She had been popular with the people and that had been of great use in the fight against Antoine de Vaudémont. Isabelle was going to have to take over much of the work her mother had continued to do until her illness overtook her. Yes, there was little time for grieving.

She must plan. Here she was, without the support of her husband and her mother. She had to get her sons back; she had to free her husband; and she had to rule over Lorraine and prevent Antoine de Vaudémont taking it from her.

Her mother had been a power throughout Lorraine. What would happen now she was dead?

Isabelle was going to need all her resources to keep hold of what she had until René and her sons returned.

Messages came from René's mother, the redoubtable Yolande of Aragon. She understood the predicament in which her daughter-in-law found herself; she admired Isabelle, seeing in her a strong woman such as she was herself. The only kind for a man of René's gentle nature, and she was grateful to her daughter-in-law.

Now she wrote to her:

'You have a great task before you. The only child left in your care is Margaret. She will be five years old now. If you would agree to send her to me I should be glad to take charge of her education. Theophanie could bring her back. I promise you I would do my duty by the child.'

Isabelle was greatly relieved to receive the letter. She had been wondering what she was going to do about Margaret. With her father gone and herself unable to give much time to the child, she had been anxious. Moreover Margaret must have sorely missed her brothers after having lost her sister some time before.

It was a good plan.

Little Margaret was alarmed when she heard she was to go to live with her paternal grandmother but Theophanie was delighted.

'It will be like going home again,' she said. 'We'll be in that very nursery where I nursed your father and his brothers and sisters.'

There was no doubt of Theophanie's pleasure and it made Margaret feel less apprehensive.

❀ Chapter II ❀

YOLANDE

Margaret quickly became absorbed in the life of the castle where her grandmother reigned supreme. The child had become accustomed to feminine dominance. Her mother had been far more important than her father in Nancy; and here of course all the men of the household bowed to the will of her indomitable grandmother.

Yolande, handsome, young for her years – she was in her fifties – was a woman who could command immediate obedience, and for good reason. Under her rule the Duchy of Anjou prospered as well as any state could with the constant threat of invasion. It was true that the French were gradually winning back territory which the English had wrested from them, but the English were still a danger and there must be constant surveillance lest they should come raiding the country.

Yolande had watchers at every point and was constantly on the alert.

She received her little granddaughter with affection restrained by dignity and tempered by a certain sternness. Margaret was to be brought up to become as strong a woman as her grandmother.

Yolande had no patience with those ladies who remained ignorant of everything outside the domestic needs of a household and who were merely objects of ornament. Women should be able to rule when the need arose and Yolande was of the opinion that very often they made a better job of it than the men.

At the same time her granddaughter must be brought up to enjoy the arts and to practise them if she had any ability to do so. Secretly she hoped she would not have too much talent, as her father had. Yolande often sighed over René. René had taken to his artistic instruction with greater enthusiasm than he had to training in outdoor accomplishments. René had too many talents in the artistic fields. He could paint like the finest artist; he could write poetry and music to compare with any troubadour. Oh yes, René had been talented in many directions, except the one which he most needed to hold his estates together in these troublous times.

So she was very anxious that René's daughter should be brought up in a fitting manner. The best teachers should be provided for her and she could trust faithful old Theophanie to be a good nurse to her.

During her first week at the castle Margaret had two interviews with her grandmother. They were more like audiences and were conducted with a certain amount of ceremony.

During them Yolande stressed the importance of Margaret's absorbing all she would be taught. She must learn to appreciate fine arts which was what her father would wish. She must at the same time give due attention to her academic studies. She must practise obedience. She must in fact grow up to be worthy of her grandmother.

Five-year-old Margaret, bewildered after being taken from her family, still mourning the loss of her brothers and above all her kind father, tried to understand all that her grandmother endeavoured to impress upon her. She looked upon Yolande – who seemed very very old to her – as a goddess in her temple, all powerful, all seeing, all knowing, one who must never be offended and always obeyed. Everyone in the household paid the greatest deference to her and Theophanie spoke her name in that special hushed voice which she used when speaking of the Virgin Mary.

Yolande thought it well that the child should understand the true state of affairs, young as she was.

'Your father is a captive of the Duke of Burgundy,' she explained, 'and you are his fourth child. As the Duke of Bar and Marquis of Pont-à-Mousson he would have had little standing in the country even if he were free. He is deeply in debt and there is a ransom to be paid. So you see your position is not a very glorious one.'

Yolande was determined that the child should learn humility. She must not think because she was the granddaughter of Yolande that in herself she was important. She had been taken into the household as an act of charity because her mother was so busily engaged in trying to hold together her father's impoverished possessions that someone else must take charge of her daughter.

Margaret looked suitably ashamed and Yolande went on: 'Never forget that you are my granddaughter. We do not know what lies in store for you. It may be that one day you will be called upon to govern as I have been, and as your mother has been. You must be ready for it.'

Margaret said that she would do her best.

Yolande dismissed her and was thoughtful for a while. Poor child, she thought, what hope will there be of a grand marriage for her? René will never regain his estates and if he did would he be able to hold them?

If Margaret had not been so young she would have explained to her that she, Yolande, was the Regent of Anjou because her eldest son, Margaret's uncle Louis, was away in Naples trying to make good his claim to that crown. She was a woman who had much to occupy her for she was also on excellent terms with the King himself who was her son-in-law. She had little time to spare for bringing up a child – and the youngest daughter of a second son at that. Still, she had done right in bringing her here. Isabelle, capable as she was, would be too deeply caught up with holding René's estates and trying to get his ransom together. These were difficult times.

Theophanie was in a state of delight, much as she missed Margaret's brothers. She often talked of little Yolande and hoped the Vaudémonts were good to her.

'She will have forgotten about us by now, I doubt not,' she said to Margaret, fearing and half hoping that she would. Poor little mite, to be torn from her home.

Theophanie hoped they would not be making a match for Margaret . . . just to settle some of their differences.

'You've let them take the others, Lord,' she reproached. 'At least let them leave me this little one.'

The days began to pass slowly at first and then not so slowly as Margaret grew more and more accustomed to living at Saumur.

She began to develop a taste for music and poetry. She read the works of Boccaccio with great delight; her teachers discovered that she had an aptitude for learning; she was becoming pretty and her long lustrous blondish hair with a hint of red in it was her greatest attraction.

She missed her home, most of all her father; but she was remembering him even less with the passing of every day. She liked excitement and was even glad on those days when the castle was in a state of alert because there were English in the neighbourhood. Her grandmother had everything in readiness in case they should be besieged.

One day she was summoned to her grandmother's presence. These summonses were rare and they must herald some important event, so Margaret went to the meeting in a state of excitement mingled with trepidation.

She curtsied to her grandmother aware that those alert eyes watched every movement and that it would be noted if the curtsy was anything but perfect.

'Come here, child,' said Yolande, and when Margaret approached, she took her hand and bade her sit on a stool at her feet.

'I have bad news,' she said.

Margaret wanted to cry out for she thought of her father at once, then almost immediately afterwards of her mother and brothers and sister.

'Your uncle Louis is dead.'

Great waves of relief swept over Margaret. Uncle Louis was a vague figure. She had never met him. She merely knew that he was her father's eldest brother.

'As you know, he was in Italy fighting for the crown of Naples which is his by rights.'

Margaret said: 'Yes, my lady.'

'He died of a fever. He had a wife, Margaret like yourself, and the daughter of the Duke of Savoy, but they had no children. Do you see what this means?'

Margaret knew that it was something to do with the crown

of Naples. It was always some crown or castle which was the cause of controversy when someone died. So she guessed this was too.

'It means that the crown of Naples will go to . . .' began Margaret.

'His nearest of kin. You are right.' Yolande nodded with approval. 'And who is the nearest of kin as he has no son and his wife cannot inherit? It is your father, René. Your father is now the King of Naples, Jerusalem and Sicily.'

'But . . . he is in prison . . .'

'That makes no difference. Your mother will now have to assert your father's claim to Naples as he cannot do it himself.'

'But he has not got it. He has to fight for it.'

'You will learn that most things in this life have to be fought for, my child. What you have to understand is what this means to *you*. You are the daughter of a King now instead of being merely the daughter of a Duke. You are a Princess, Margaret.'

'Oh,' said Margaret overawed.

'Pray close your mouth,' said Yolande, 'and always remember that you are royal.'

In spite of becoming a Princess, Margaret found that life went on very much as it had before. She saw little of her grandmother who spent her time between the castle of Angers and that of Saumur. Margaret herself now and then travelled between these two castles for Angers was less than thirty miles from Saumur and easily accessible. Both castles were magnificent fortresses and if the English were to attempt to take them could withstand a long siege.

Margaret was growing into a handsome girl. She was not tall

but well formed, very slender and her features were well defined. She had beautiful blue eyes and a firm mouth.

'It'll not be difficult to find a husband for her,' Theophanie confided to one of the attendants. 'A Princess and even if her father has yet to regain his kingdom, she has looks enough to make some gallant young suitor forget that.'

She was clever, too, said her teachers. She had a sharp wit and was growing up (Theophanie again) to be another such as her grandmother.

Some would have liked to see her grow taller but Theophanie was not so sure. Petite women often had a way of getting what they wanted more easily than their larger sisters. They could be feminine and appealing when the need arose. Theophanie reckoned that Margaret had the best of both sides of the coin. She was going to be as strong-willed as her mother and grandmother and with her dainty looks she was going to appeal to the masculinity of the men she had to do battle with.

All things considered, mused Theophanie, she would not have had her Princess any other than the way she was.

Margaret had passed her ninth birthday when a great occasion occurred.

She was at her lessons, as she was every morning, when a clatter in the courtyard announced the arrival of visitors. They must be friendly or the alert would have been given. There were always men on the watch towers to look out for the approach of the English.

Without waiting to ask permission she ran from the room and down to the courtyard. A small company of men were there and as her eyes fell on one of them she gave a shriek of delight. She could not wait for ceremony. She flung herself into her father's arms. There was no mistaking the kindly smile, although he had aged considerably, and there was the scar livid as ever on the left side of his forehead.

'My dearest child,' cried René. 'Why . . . a child no longer. How you have grown! What a fine lady they have made of you!'

'Oh my father, dearest *dearest* father . . .'

They clung together. And there was Yolande standing in the courtyard watching them.

René released his daughter and embraced his mother.

'This is good news,' she cried. 'René, my son. You are free.'

'Free . . . but with much to tell.'

'Rooms must be prepared and orders given in the kitchens. How delighted I am to have you with us. You have already seen Margaret.'

Margaret could not remember anything that should be done on occasions such as this. She could only think that her beloved father was with her once more. She just stood with him, her arms encircling him, and even Yolande could not hide her emotion.

They went into the castle. There was bustle everywhere and very soon appetising smells pervaded the place.

There must be a banquet in honour of this son who, since the death of his brother, was Yolande's eldest.

There was indeed much to tell and it did not all make good hearing. René had insisted that Margaret be with them. He could not stay long and he wanted as much time as possible with his daughter.

'When must you go?' asked Yolande.

'I must not stay more than three or four days at the most.'

Yolande, to Margaret's surprise, made no attempt to send her away so she heard all that had been happening to her father.

'So you are really free,' said Yolande.

'Completely,' replied René. 'The ransom has been paid. Isabelle has been wonderful in raising the money.'

'You should be grateful to your wife,' said Yolande.

'I am. Make no mistake about that. She is a wonderful woman . . . as you are, my lady mother. She has come from the same mould.'

Yolande graciously inclined her head. She never denied anything in which she believed. It was true that dear weak René had been blessed with a strong wife and a strong mother.

'And Burgundy?' she asked.

'You may be sure he struck a bargain. John is betrothed to his niece Marie of Bourbon.'

'Indeed,' said Yolande. She was resentful that a match should have been made without consulting her.

'Burgundy's niece,' said René. 'And therefore a good connection. Besides, he was adamant. Those were his conditions.'

'Well, at least it shows that he still thinks well enough of you to want the connection. How old is John now?'

'Twelve years.'

'Well, old enough I dare swear. And where is Louis?'

'With his mother in Naples. Whither I must go with all speed. But I could not resist coming to see my mother and my daughter.'

'My dear René, may God preserve you and give you strength.'

'I shall need it,' said René. 'I know it does not go so well in Naples.'

'How happy you must be to feel free again.'

'To be with my family, yes, but I have been treated well

during my captivity. I have been painting a great deal and it is astonishing how quickly that passes the time.'

Yolande smiled at him fondly. Painting when he should have been considering means of ruling his possessions, and first of all getting some of them into his hands.

Ineffectual René. But dear René all the same. None could help loving him.

It was a sad day when he rode off. He was longing to join Isabelle but it was clear that his heart was not in the fighting that would have to be done to gain the crown of Naples.

Each day Margaret waited for news of her father, but the months passed and there was nothing. There was less danger now of the English raiding the land, for fortune was favouring the French and the situation was very different from the way it had been when Joan of Arc had come from her village to talk to the King.

One year passed and then another and still no news from Naples.

'A crown is not easily gained,' said Yolande. 'Your father is short of money and I do not believe he is the greatest general in the world. If only he were half as good a soldier as he is a painter it might be a different story.'

Then there was exciting news, but not of René.

The King had sent word that it was long since he had seen his mother-in-law. He was, if she would receive him, thinking of paying her a visit.

Yolande was beside herself with delight; and almost immediately apprehensive. A royal visit! It must be conducted in a fitting manner and that meant that they must begin to prepare at once.

It should take place at the castle of Angers which would be more suitable than Saumur. She would see her dear daughter again but Margaret sensed that the one she really cared about was the King.

For several weeks there was no talk of anything but the coming visit. The castle was cleaned from the tallest turret to the lowest dungeon although as Theophanie grumbled it was hardly likely that the King would go there. She herself would be glad to see young Marie again, but she reckoned she had changed a lot since nursery days. All those children she had had and a Queen too. Oh, she expected to see changes in Marie.

It did her good though to see the lady Yolande so pleased with life. Just of late she had imagined that my lady was getting a little tired, feeling her age. If she did it would be the first time in her life that she had — but that was what worried Theophanie.

There must be new clothes for them all. Margaret must stand still while rich materials were fitted on her. She had never felt so grown up in her life before.

Then came the great day.

The watchers on the tower gave the signal. The cavalcade was sighted. Everyone was to be ready now to greet them, to let them know what a great honour this was.

Yolande stood at the gates of the castle, Margaret beside her. The heralds blew their trumpets and there were the King and the Queen and a brilliant company of ladies and gentlemen.

The King dismounted. Yolande went on her knees, and Margaret did the same.

'Rise, rise, my lady,' said the King. 'It does me good to see you. I have missed your company.'

And there was the Queen, Margaret's aunt Marie. She

embraced Yolande, and then Margaret was presented to her and the King.

She was too nervous to look at them closely and too busy remembering all she had been taught she must do, but she did have time to glance at the King and she thought he did not seem very much like a King. He was not very handsome. His nose fascinated her; it seemed to hang right over his mouth. However, he spoke very gently to her and she believed that in spite of his unprepossessing appearance he was kind.

And then as Yolande was about to lead them into the hall she noticed someone else. Her hand was taken and held firmly. She turned and looked up into a beautiful and half familiar face. For a moment she was unsure and then she murmured: 'Agnès.'

'Yes, it is Agnès. Oh Margaret, how you have grown.'

'You have changed too.'

A strange look came over Agnès's face. 'Yes,' she said. 'I have, have I not?'

There was no time for more talk as they followed the party into the hall.

It was a visit Margaret felt that she would never forget. She had never known such entertaining at Angers before. But of course she had not. She had never known what it was like when the King came to visit. Yolande had said that there should be all the splendour of the past in Angers on the occasion of the King's visit and she had certainly kept her word about that. The banquets, the balls, the players who were called in, the singing, the dancers, it was one spectacle after another. Yolande threw herself into the arrangements with such enthusiasm that at the end of the day she could scarcely stagger to her bed. Margaret knew this, for one night she had gone to her room to take her one of Theophanie's possets. 'I used to give it to the children now and then,' the nurse said. 'My lady will know what it is. She's doing too much, that she is.'

Theophanie was right because when Margaret went to her grandmother's room she found her stretched out on her bed, her eyes closed and a look of utter weariness on her face. She was not pleased with Margaret and made that clear. It was not, as she said, because it was unseemly of her to do a servant's work, it was because she hated her granddaughter to see her exhaustion.

It was true that Yolande was feeling her age. She could tell herself that she had become too excited, had thrown herself too energetically into the task of entertaining the royal party, but a few years ago these activities would have provided nothing but stimulation.

Sixty! It was a great age. And Yolande had till now unconsciously believed herself to be immortal.

How much longer was left? There were things she would like to see before she died. René settled. Well, she had given up hoping for that. She knew René. He was greatly loved but he was somehow ineffectual. She often wondered how she could have given birth to such a son. No, she was a realist. She must not hope for the impossible. What she wanted more than anything was to see France free and she wanted Charles to bring about that happy state. Some strange instinct within her had always known that he could do it. There had been a time when that would have seemed absurd to some, but it never had to her. She had been drawn to the King when as Dauphin he had married her daughter. He had felt similarly attracted to her. It was a strange relationship having in it none of the elements which the King usually felt towards women. It was an abiding friendship, a rare devotion. If she had been younger perhaps she should have been his wife. No, it was better so. She had watched his progress from afar and she had rejoiced, and she felt that she had had some small part in the surprising advance which he had made.

She was determined to have a private talk with Agnès Sorel because she felt that she could learn a great deal from her, but first she wished to speak to her daughter.

It was not like Yolande to feel uneasy about her actions. She was almost always certain that she was right and that she had been in this case was proved. The change in Charles had been little short of miraculous and Yolande had a shrewd idea of how it had been brought about.

She was on the point of sending for her daughter when she remembered that even she did not send for the Queen of France. Instead she requested her daughter to come to her.

Marie came at once. Like her husband she had the greatest respect for Yolande.

'Dear child, I will forget you are the Queen for a time and remember only that you are my daughter,' said Yolande. 'It is so rarely that I have a chance to be with you alone. Tell me, Marie, how are the children?'

'In good health, thank you, Mother.'

'And Louis?'

The Queen lifted her shoulders. 'Louis will always go his own way.'

'Something of a trial to his father,' said Yolande.

'Poor Charles, he has troubles enough without a rebellious Dauphin.'

'It is a pity,' agreed Marie; but Yolande had not brought Marie here to speak of the Dauphin's behaviour. She went on:

'Charles has become a different man. That gives me great pleasure.'

'Oh yes. France is emerging victorious all over the country. We shall soon have driven the English out.'

Yolande nodded. 'And how do you feel about . . . Agnès Sorel?'

Again that lift of the shoulders. 'Charles has always had mistresses,' said the Queen.

'Agnès is perhaps . . . different.'

'Oh yes,' said the Queen, 'quite different. In fact one might say the King no longer has mistresses. He has a mistress.'

'Agnès is a good girl, Marie, do you agree?'

'I do.'

'And you, Marie . . . you are her friend.'

Marie smiled. 'I know what you are thinking, my lady mother. You decided that Agnès should be at Court when you saw he was taken by her. And you are wondering what I his wife think of my mother who should introduce him to such a mistress. Do not forget, my dear mother, that it was you who brought me up. Life was wretched before. You know how we lived when his father gave Katherine to the King of England and promised that King his throne on his death. Charles was cast out. Even after his father's death he was just the Dauphin when he was in truth the King. We had no money . . . nothing. I had to sell jewels to provide us with food. And he did not care . . . He went whichever way he was guided. It was humiliating. And then the Maid came. We both believed in her, did we not, and we made him believe and he did. She saved Orléans and had him crowned at Rheims and even after that he was still listless. He has never really forgiven himself for letting her be burned as a witch.'

'Poor poor Charles, he needs looking after.'

'He has someone to look after him. He has his queen . . . his mother-in-law . . . and most of all his mistress.'

'Ah, I knew Agnès would be good for him.'

'He loves her, my lady. I never thought he could rouse himself from his lethargy to love. But he loves Agnès. She is a good woman. I think he had to persuade her rather forcibly to share his bed and bear his children. She loves him too. In spite of his looks there is something lovable about Charles.'

Yolande agreed with that. She loved him herself. She said, 'Then it was right not to take Agnès away.'

'Agnès has done more for him than anyone. He roused himself to gain her good opinion. She changed him and in doing that changed France. Dear Mother, ease your conscience. I am his wife but I rejoice in Agnès.'

Yolande's conscience was now clear on that point. She sent for Agnès.

Agnès came and stood before her. How beautiful she is! thought Yolande. Even more so than when she was a maiden in Isabelle's household. She has gained with maturity.

Agnès guessed that Yolande wished to speak to her about her relationship with the King and since Yolande was the mother of his wife, she expected some reproaches.

Yolande bade her sit.

'You have changed since I last saw you, Agnès,' she said, 'but you are more beautiful than ever. And happy, I trust.'

'Yes, my lady, I am happy as any can be in these troublous times.'

'Growing less troublesome though since the King roused himself and decided to be a King.'

Agnès did not answer; she lowered her head but Yolande caught the smile of satisfaction.

'Agnès, I hear Charles has built a château for you in the forest near Loches. The Château de Guerche I believe.'

'That is so, my lady. The King has been very kind to me.'

'I believe you have been very kind to him.'

The delicate colour in Agnès's cheeks deepened slightly.

'My lady, I did not wish to find myself in this position.'

'I know, I know. He fell in love with you and you wished to escape from him. You had no ambition to be a King's mistress. I believe that, Agnès, so would all who knew you. But you were at his Court and he would not let you go. You were not a young girl who would fall in love for love's sake. Charles was hardly the sort to inspire that, was he? You resisted him and you told him that he was indolent, that he was destroying his country, that you could not admire a King who behaved as he did. Is that so, Agnès?'

'Perhaps I implied that. A maid of honour to the Queen could scarcely be so bold to the King.'

'But you were bold, Agnès, because you had this effect on him. He changed his ways to please you. He sought you out. He talked to you. And you were always a clever girl. Rarely is one so blessed with beauty and wisdom and when God bestows these He expects them to be used. I brought you here, Agnès, to tell you that I and the Queen are thankful to you. We believe that you have done as much for France as the Maid did. She showed him the way to victory but you led him there. I want you to know, Agnès, that both I and the Queen are grateful to you . . . as the whole of France should be. You love him now.'

'It would be impossible not to. I am so often with him. We talk of the affairs of France.'

'He listens to you.'

'I am no general, my lady. I am no statesman. But I do know that the King must bestir himself. He must rule. My lady, he does rule now.'

'Yes, he does indeed. And see what results it is having. The English lost Henry and then the Duke of Bedford. That was good for France, particularly as we regained our King. I wanted you to know, Agnès, that we are with you . . . the Queen and I. France will be with you . . . if not now one day. It surprises me that France must be grateful to two women, Joan the Maid and Agnès Sorel.'

'Others too, my lady. Yourself. The King sets great store by your opinion. And there is the Queen, too.'

'And your little girls are well? There are three of them are there not?'

'Yes. The King loves them dearly.'

'May God preserve you, Agnès . . . you and the King and your family.'

When Agnès had left her Yolande went to her bedchamber to rest. Again that humiliating tiredness had come over her, but she felt relieved and happy.

She had done right in bringing Agnès to Court.

Margaret, too, was able to be with Agnès for a short time. Although Agnès had grown into a woman and was clearly quite an important one, Margaret felt able to talk to her as she was to few others.

She wanted to hear what Agnès had done when she joined the French Court and what it was like to be a lady in waiting to the Queen.

Agnès told her. She spoke to Margaret of her own little girls. 'Charlotte is growing up now,' she said, 'and Agnès is not far behind. Then there is the baby.'

'Your children, Agnès? I did not know you had a husband.'

Agnès hesitated. Margaret was eleven years old. She might well hear gossip. It would be better for her to hear the truth from Agnès than from others.

'They are the King's,' Agnès explained.

'But I thought you had to have a husband to have children.'

'You should,' Agnès explained, 'but sometimes it does not happen so. People understand.'

'I suppose,' said Margaret with a certain wisdom, 'it is all right because it is the King.'

'Yes, I think that might explain it,' answered Agnès.

'Agnès, shall you always stay at Court?'

'I hope to.'

'The King loves you very much, does he not?'

'Who told you that?'

'I saw it in his eyes when he looked at you.'

Agnès was pleased. 'Yes,' she said, 'the King loves me and I love the King and that makes everything right.'

'I was very little when you went away. But I do remember you. I suppose it is because you are so beautiful. I feel I can talk to you . . . as I can't talk to anyone else. One cannot talk to Theophanie about some things and no one could ever talk to my grandmother. I could to my father but he is not here.'

'Of what things, Margaret?'

'Oh . . . I am a little frightened sometimes. You see my sister Yolande went away to the Vaudémonts when she was a very little girl and now my brother John is going to marry Marie de Bourbon. One day they will find someone for me to marry and I shall be sent away.'

'And that frightens you?'

'It makes me wonder what will become of me.'

'Dear Margaret, we none of us know what will become of us. That is in God's hands.'

'Yes, but we can wriggle out of them if we don't like what He plans for us . . . sometimes.'

'Whatever gave you that notion?'

'Well, they say that the King who was weak and dissolute has now become kingly and rules his country well. If God meant him to be a great King why did He make him a foolish one for so long? I heard my aunt Marie tell my grandmother that you and the Maid had led him out of his despondency and awakened the desire in him to be a King.'

'Well, perhaps that was God's will.'

'It seems to me,' said Margaret, 'that anything can be said to be His will. But it was the Maid and you who actually did it, wasn't it? I think you make up your mind what you wish to do and do it, and if it turns out to be wrong say, "That was God's will", and if it is right you did it yourself."

Agnès laughed. 'You have a clever way of reasoning, Margaret. It is unusual in one so young. Where did you learn that?'

'From my grandmother. I intend to be exactly like her when I grow up for if I am it will not matter to whom they marry me. I shall be the one to say what has to be done.'

The royal visit was over and in due course Margaret and her grandmother went back to Saumur. After all the revelry the castle at Angers needed a thorough sweetening.

Margaret noticed how the journey – although it was less than thirty miles – tired her grandmother. When they arrived at Saumur she stayed in her bed for two days which was something she had never done before.

When she arose she was as energetic as ever and life settled down to the normal routine.

Two years passed. There was no good news from Naples. In fact there was rarely any news at all. Yolande had come to believe that René would never succeed. There were no longer the scares that the English might come and attempt to take the castle. The English were being turned out of France and a peace party under Cardinal Beaufort was formed in England.

'What they will try to do is to marry the young King to one of Charles's daughters.'

'That would be a good way to finish the war,' said Margaret.

'I doubt not that is what it will come to. A French Princess for Henry. Yes, these alliances are always a good way of settling differences. I hear that he is a good young man, religious, eager to do what is best. Of course, his kind always seem to lack strength. What he needs is a strong wife, a woman to lead him and the country.'

Margaret smiled. Yolande had always believed firmly in the power of women. She had taught Margaret to believe the same.

'We shall have to find a suitable match for you, Margaret,' said Yolande. 'But for your father's exploits in Naples it would have been done long ago.'

'I am content to wait awhile.'

'It cannot be much longer. You are thirteen, are you not?'

'Yes, my lady.'

'Then it is time.'

A little while before such talk would have made Margaret uneasy. Now she was not so sure. She knew what influence Agnès Sorel had with the King; he was in some measure guided by the women about him. She knew what a power her grandmother was and so was her mother. If success came in Naples it would be due to her rather than to René.

Margaret sometimes dreamed of marriage and of being the wife of some man whom she would be able to lead to greatness.

That this matter occupied the thoughts of her grandmother was obvious because in spite of the fact that she was becoming increasingly tired Yolande decided that she would go to Court and take Margaret with her. It was only right, she said, that Margaret should visit her aunt and there would always be a welcome for them, she knew.

The preparations for such a visit were lengthy. Margaret must be adequately dressed, and Yolande was constantly reminding her of Court etiquette which Margaret absorbed with ease.

Her grandmother was delighted to see what a success the girl was. It was due to her upbringing and Yolande took the credit for that. Margaret was a handsome girl. A pity she was not a little taller, but she was well made and had an air of daintiness which was appealing and somehow in contrast to her sparkling intelligence which was obvious when she conversed.

Agnès was delighted to see Margaret and her aunt Queen Marie expressed her pleasure too.

'Now that you are growing up,' she said, 'you must be with us more often.'

There was a great deal going on in Court circles at that time. For one thing the English Cardinal Beaufort was there.

'He has come,' Yolande told her, 'to try to arrange peace. He is a wise man, this Cardinal. He knows that to continue the war can ruin his country.'

'I am sure the King will agree with him,' said Margaret. 'In that case this must mean we shall soon have peace.'

'The Cardinal unfortunately does not represent the whole of English opinion. You have heard of the Duke of Gloucester, brother to King Henry the Fifth and the Duke of Bedford. He is for continuing the war.'

'Then he must be exceedingly foolish.'

'I believe he is. He has done great harm to the English cause. He nearly brought about a quarrel between Burgundy and the English.'

'That would have been a good thing.'

'For France yes . . . for England disastrous. However, it is indeed good to see the Cardinal here. He is an extremely cultured man and one, I believe, who serves his country well.'

Margaret was presented to the Cardinal. He appeared to be very interested in her. She talked a little about the affairs of her country and he listened to her with the respect he would have shown to one of the King's ministers.

He remarked afterwards that the daughter of the King of Naples was a most interesting young lady. Moreover a very good-looking one.

'I see,' said her aunt Marie, 'you have captured the attention of my lord Cardinal. What did you say to him that impressed him so much?'

'Oh, we talked a little of the war and its effects.'

'That must have amused him . . . coming from one who could know very little about it.'

'Oh, I do know something, Aunt. I have kept my ears open. In any case the Bishop seemed interested in my views.'

The Queen laughed. 'Well, my dear Margaret, it seems that you are being a success at Court. Your parents would be proud of you, I am sure. I am going to ask your grandmother to allow you to come again soon. You are getting too old to be shut away in the country all your life.'

'Thank you, my lady,' said Margaret fervently.

When they returned to Angers life certainly seemed a little dull. Yolande noticed the change in Margaret and commented on it. She was not displeased. The girl was meant to take part in affairs. She had a lively brain. There must be more visits to Court and perhaps someone would be so impressed by her that he would think her a possible wife in spite of the fact that she would have no dowry to speak of.

Yes, Yolande was determined that there should be more visits to Court.

In the summer they went again. It did Yolande good too. She loved to be with Charles and she was delighted by the change in him. She spent a good deal of time with her daughter and with Agnès. The visits were stimulating.

'I am glad I have lived long enough to see the coming change,' she said. 'France will be great again. If the English had any sense they would get out now.'

'They would,' said Charles, 'if it were not for Gloucester and his faction. I believe Beaufort will succeed though. The English must be tired of paying for a war which is bringing them nothing but defeat. You'll see. We'll have peace soon.'

'What think you of my granddaughter?' asked Yolande.

'Margaret? A beauty and she has a sharp wit, too. Do you know I think she is going to be another such as her grandmother and that is the highest compliment I can pay her.'

Yes, the visits to Court were certainly very agreeable.

That winter was harsh. The snow came early and was piled high about the walls of the castle. It was difficult to keep warm in spite of the large fires. Yolande seemed to feel the cold more than usual. Perhaps this was because she was no longer able to move about with her usual vigour. There was no doubt that she was ailing.

At the beginning of December she took to her bed. Theophanie was in despair. 'It is so unlike her,' she kept saying. She made posset after posset and had them sent up to Yolande's bedchamber. But Yolande needed more than possets. She had led a very full and energetic life and the plain truth was that it was nearing its end.

On the fourteenth of the month, completely exhausted, she died peacefully in her bed.

The youngest of her sons, the Duke of Maine, arrived at the castle and took charge of the arrangements for her funeral. She had always wanted to be buried with her husband in his tomb which was in front of the high altar in the Cathedral of Angers.

Margaret had little time to think of anything until the ceremony was over and then she had to face the fact that there would be a big change in her life.

Her uncle Charles of Maine discussed the situation with her. She was now thirteen which was considered to be of a certain maturity.

He said: 'It will be impossible for you to remain here now that your grandmother is dead. I have sent word to your father and I have no doubt we shall soon be hearing of him.'

'Yes,' said Margaret. 'Perhaps my parents will come here now.'

'It would be wise to,' replied Charles. 'I believe the Naples adventure has proved disastrous. You should stay here until we receive definite news from them.'

66

'Yes, I shall do that,' replied Margaret.

The Duke was satisfied. Margaret had been brought up in the right way by her grandmother and would therefore be able to deal with a situation such as this one.

Charles of Maine was right about René's return. He and Isabelle were already at Marseilles having abandoned the Naples adventure. They would come to Saumur with all speed.

The anticipation of the reunion did a good deal to assuage Margaret's grief at her grandmother's death. Indeed it took a long time for her to realise that the old lady had gone. She had been such a dominating character and her household had been run under such disciplined order that it continued working in the same way after she had gone.

Each day Margaret watched for her parents' arrival and it was not long before their approach was sighted by the watcher in the tower.

Margaret was at the gates of the castle waiting to greet them.

❀ Chapter III ❀

A STOLEN PORTRAIT

The meeting was ecstatic. It was long since Margaret had seen her mother. Eight years, Isabelle reminded her. It was four since her father had been in Anjou.

Although it was such a joyous reunion, René had a sorry story to tell. When he had arrived in Naples he had been warmly welcomed by the people but as soon as his rival, Alfonso of Aragon, had started to invade it became clear that René was no match for him. He had quickly realised that if he wanted to go on living he must get out of Naples. He had no money with which to continue the fight; he hated the war; he had no great desire for the crown. Even his wife Isabelle realised that they were fighting a losing battle.

'When a Genoese galley was available we took it and were brought back to France,' said René. 'And, my dearest daughter, how glad I am to be with you.'

There was so much to talk about, and family matters were so much more absorbing to René than the quest for a crown. He was titular King of Naples still, even if he could not stay there and win the crown, and Margaret was a Princess, a fact which she knew would be important when the time came to find a bridegroom for her.

Margaret wanted to know so much. How was John now that he was married to Marie de Bourbon? Had they heard how Yolande was faring at the home of her betrothed, Ferri de Vaudémont? When was Louis joining them? It was wonderful to be once more with her parents.

It occurred to Margaret that they could have been together all the time, for what good had any of René's attempted conquests done them? He was wise perhaps after all. It was only the opinion of the others and the need to submit to the laws of chivalry which had sent him out to fight. If he had obeyed his own inclinations he would have stayed at home, painting, writing music, singing to delighted audiences and building roads and bridges which he had always wanted to do. His great idea was to turn his towns into seats of culture, to which people came from all over the world to see fine paintings and hear good poetry and music.

He had plans for Angers which would need a great deal of reconstruction as would the whole of Anjou when it was finally taken out of the hands of the English.

They went to the castle of Angers and from there to Tarascon for René was also the Count of Provence and he had responsibilities in that part of the country as well as in Anjou.

For a few months Margaret felt she could forget everything but the joy of being united with her parents. But there were sorrows in the world which could not be ignored.

Her brother Louis had died suddenly of dysentery. The news was a shattering blow for they had been planning that he should come and join them.

It was a household of mourning. René became more and more absorbed in his painting. Isabelle decided that it was no use trying to persuade him to set out on any more ventures which would inevitably end in disaster.

Life went on quietly until emissaries from the Duke of Burgundy arrived at the castle.

After a long consultation with the messenger from the Duke of Burgundy René and Isabelle sent for Margaret. This concerned her and she was old enough now to be prepared for what must be inevitable.

That René was uneasy was obvious. Isabelle was less so but then she was always more politically minded than her husband.

'Margaret my child,' said René, 'as you know our visitors have come from the very noble Duke of Burgundy and he has put a certain proposition before us.'

Margaret's heart began to beat rapidly. She guessed what the proposition must be.

'The Duke has suggested an alliance which would certainly be good for us.'

She waited for him to go on and he hesitated. He had no desire for such a union. Isabelle might say it would be advantageous and in any case they dared not offend the Duke of Burgundy, but René did not want to see his daughter married to an old man. Margaret should have someone young and beautiful like herself.

He sighed. He must not be foolish. He had been foolish so many times.

'He suggests that you should give your hand in marriage to his nephew Charles, Count of Nevers.'

'I see,' said Margaret.

'He will be a good husband. He has already proved that to his first wife. It will be good for us to form such a close alliance with the House of Burgundy and the great Duke himself wishes the match to take place. In fact it is he who has proposed it. I think we should rejoice in this. Your marriage has long been a subject which has absorbed your mother and myself. Now here is the solution.'

He was looking at her anxiously, wanting her not to be upset by the proposal. She knew this and she smiled at him reassuringly although she was feeling very uneasy.

She had often thought of marrying, but a middle-aged husband did not fit in with her dreams. She had visualised someone young and handsome, someone who needed her to lean on, someone like her father – clever, charming, pleasant to be with and yet at the same time needing her care. A middle-aged Count, a nephew of great Burgundy, did not fit in with her dreams.

'It is really a very good match,' said René.

'Yes, my lord, I suppose it is.'

'What an important lady you will be. Countess of Nevers.'

'I am a Princess already.'

'A Princess . . . Yes, your father is a King. It is rather a hollow title but a King nevertheless. They are asking a dowry of fifty thousand livres.'

'You will never be able to pay that!' cried Margaret with a hint of relief.

'Oh, we will think about that when the time comes,' said René with customary abandon.

So it seemed that Margaret was destined to marry the Count of Nevers.

❀ ❀ ❀

It was a few days later when there was a visitor at the castle of Tarascon. He came with two manservants only. He had ridden far, he said, and craved a bed for the night.

Such travellers were never turned away and this one proved to be an entertaining gentleman.

He was Guy de Champchevrier, a gentleman from Angers. He entertained them as they sat at the table with his stories of the war in which he had served for some years until he had been captured and taken prisoner. He had been held to ransom by an English soldier, Sir John Fastolf. Did they know of him? They would have heard of the Battle of the Herrings outside Orléans. He had been the hero of that little adventure.

'His one claim to fame,' said the visitor. 'Unless the other was capturing Guy de Champchevrier . . .'

He had been in England for some time and had been at the Court there. He had conversed with the King of England, who had seemed to take a fancy to him. 'He liked to hear me talk of France,' he said.

'And what manner of man is this Henry of England?' asked René.

'A good man . . . very religious. Handsome in a way, though not like the Plantagenet Kings with their long legs and their yellow hair. He does not bluster or swear, nor does he make sport with the women. I would say that first of all Henry of England is a good man.'

'They will be seeking a wife for him soon,' said Isabelle.

'Oh yes, my lady, negotiations are going afoot. It will be a daughter of the King . . . or a daughter of the Count of Armagnac. A French marriage. It will be a seal on the peace.'

'There is nothing like a marriage between two enemies to make a peace,' said René.

'Yet Henry the Fifth married Katherine of France and there was nothing but war after,' Margaret reminded them.

'That was a shameful marriage,' said her mother. 'Our poor crazy King gave away France at that time.'

'Well, we're winning it back,' said Champchevrier, 'and a marriage will put an end to war. I know that a painter has been sent to the Court of Armagnac for the express purpose of painting the Count's daughters. There are three of them and they say the King will take the one most to his taste. I know the painter well. A Dutchman named Hans who has a deft hand with the brush. He has had instruction that they shall be painted in simple garments just as he sees them and in no way is Hans to think of making pretty pictures, but to paint exactly what he sees.'

'Ah, it seems as though the King is serious. And he will take the one he likes best.'

'It's humiliating,' said Margaret. 'If I were one of the Count of Armagnac's daughters I should refuse to be painted.'

'What, my lady, and deny your chance of being Queen of England?'

'If it meant submitting to such a test, yes.'

'My lord, you have a spirited daughter,' commented Champchevrier. Then he went on to delight them with stories of the Court of England and it was a very agreeable evening.

He left early next morning with many protestations of gratitude. It was a few days later when René discovered that a picture he had painted of Margaret was missing.

It was a charming portrait of the girl in a simple gown with her lovely hair falling about her shoulders and showing to

73

perfection those reddish tints. It was one of René's favourite paintings.

His anger quickly passed and he became highly amused.

'Do you know,' he said, 'I think that rogue Champchevrier stole the picture of Margaret. He must have been very much impressed by her.'

Guy de Champchevrier was congratulating himself on the manner in which he had achieved what he had set out to do. The King would be pleased with him. It was a delightful picture; and what was more important than the King's approval would be that of my lord of Suffolk. William de la Pole, Duke of Suffolk, was, after the Cardinal, the most powerful man in the land; the great enemy of both the Duke and the Cardinal was the Duke of Gloucester and every day the latter was becoming more and more ineffectual.

No, it was the Cardinal who ruled England with Suffolk close on his heels and so it would be for although England had a King and he was now past twenty years of age he was not meant to be a ruler. He was too gentle to his enemies; he hated the sight of bloodshed; he never wanted to harm his enemies; he liked to be with his books and he was constantly engaged in prayer. He showed no interest in the ladies of the Court many of whom would not have hesitated to indulge in a little frolic with the King and when he had seen some of them, as he thought, immodestly dressed he had turned shuddering away crying 'For shame.' His strongest oath was 'Forsooth and forsooth', and 'By Jove'. He would have made a better priest than a King, thought Champchevrier.

And as he was riding along he suddenly realised that he was

being followed. He called to his servants to move faster and they broke into a gallop, but it was not long before they were surrounded.

Champchevrier protested but he was told that he was arrested in the name of the King.

'The King of France . . .' cried Champchevrier.

'Indeed the King of France. What other King could there be on French territory?'

Champchevrier said: 'I can explain.'

'That you are an escaped prisoner. We know that already. It is on that count that you are now under arrest.'

There was nothing Champchevrier could do but submit.

But when he reached the Court he managed to assure his captors that he was engaged on a mission of some secrecy and one which he could only divulge to the King himself.

'You are mad if you think the King will see you,' he was told.

'You will be in trouble if you refuse to take my message to the King. I come from the King of England.'

After some preamble Champchevrier's claim was put before the King and Charles, intrigued, agreed to see him.

Champchevrier bowed low before Charles and begged that he might speak to him in private for the nature of his mission was very secret.

Those about the King were suspicious but Charles insisted that he would hear the man and his guards retired to wait at the door and Charles said: 'Well, proceed.'

'Sire, I am on a very private mission for my lord Duke of Suffolk and the King of England. It is true that I was taken in battle by Sir John Fastolf and the ransom demanded has not been paid.'

'Then you have offended against the laws of chivalry and I must hand you over to Sir John.'

'Let me explain, Sire. I have had conversations with the King of England for I have been treated most honourably in England. I am a native of Anjou and have on several occasions seen the fair daughter of King René. The Lord Cardinal has also seen her. You may know, my lord, that there are negotiations going on for a marriage between the King and one of the Count of Armagnac's daughters. The Duke of Gloucester wishes this marriage but the Cardinal and my Lord Suffolk do not believe that such a marriage will help to bring about a peace.'

The King nodded. 'I think I agree with that.'

'My lord Gloucester wishes that marriage to take place because he is all for prolonging the war. He is a man of unsound judgement, my lord.'

'There you speak truth.'

'The Cardinal was much impressed by Margaret of Anjou.'

'I begin to see what this is all about,' said the King with a smile.

'Yes, Sire. Being a native of Anjou, I know the country well. I was able to add my opinion of the lady Margaret's beauty to that of the Cardinal. Sire, you know what a delicate matter this is. The English do not wish the Count of Armagnac to know that the King is looking elsewhere. It is disastrous that having completed my mission I should be arrested. As I saw it, the only solution was to put the case to you.'

'And what was your mission?' asked the King.

'To secure a picture of the Princess Margaret, my lord. Her father is a fine painter. It seemed likely that he would have made a portrait of his beautiful daughter.'

'You procured it?'

'Stole it, Sire. I am on my way to show it to the King of England.'

'You have it with you? It would prove your story.'

Champchevrier brought the picture from a pocket in his cloak.

The King took it and studied it intently. 'A beautiful child,' he said. 'I think her father has painted her well. I am fond of her father. I was very fond of her grandmother. I liked the girl, too. She made quite an impression at my Court.'

'Sire, it is bold of me to ask but your sympathy and understanding tempts me to. Would you approve of a match between Margaret of Anjou and Henry of England?'

The King was silent for a moment. Then he said, 'I think it would have pleased her grandmother.'

He was very sad thinking of Yolande. He had suffered a terrible blow in the loss of her. Of course Yolande had been old and he should not have been surprised at her death but that was no consolation.

But what was this matter? Champchevrier stealing a portrait of Margaret and getting caught with it, and Sir John Fastolf getting angry because his prisoner was at large, and demanding that he be handed back to him.

Sir John would be disappointed. It would pay him back for the Battle of the Herrings which had been such a disgrace to the French. Besides, a marriage between Margaret and the King of England might be very advantageous to France.

And how pleased Yolande would have been. She had often fretted about the lack of Margaret's chances. And here was an opportunity which was too dazzling for Yolande ever to have dreamed of.

Charles said: 'I give you permission to travel freely through France. You shall be released at once to return to the King of England. Guard the picture of my niece well. It is a very fine one and exactly like her. I think Henry might like that well.'

René was uneasy. He could not concentrate on his painting and that was a sure sign that something weighed heavily on his mind.

It was Margaret's marriage. He really did not want her to go to the Count of Nevers. She was far too young; and far too dominating a character for a match like that. He knew that Nevers would expect a docile young girl whom he could mould to his ways and whose only important task would be to bear him children.

Margaret was an unusual girl. It was not merely because she was his daughter that he thought so. She was like her mother and his mother. They were strong, dominant women – and there were signs that Margaret was the same.

Why had Champchevrier stolen the portrait? It was quite clear that his arrival at the château had not been an accident. He had had some purpose. To steal Margaret's picture. For whom? That was the question.

There was gossip that Champchevrier had been arrested, that he had been taken to the King himself and that Charles had given him permission to go on his way even though he was in fact a prisoner for whom a ransom was being asked.

It was all very mysterious and René had a shrewd idea that the mission had been to procure a picture of Margaret surreptitiously so that no one would guess for what reason.

And she was to go to Nevers.

He could not stop the match. Nor did he wish to until he was sure there would be a better; but he could delay matters.

Nevers – and Burgundy with him – was eager for a contract to be signed and the Count had sent word that his emissaries would be arriving very shortly.

I must do something, thought René.

Then he had an idea. His daughter Yolande was to marry Ferri de Vaudémont and there would be a dowry to provide for her.

He must consider this very carefully. All he had to offer was promises. They must know how impoverished he had become. His only asset of any worth was his daughters.

Although he could not cancel the contract with Nevers without arousing the fury of the House of Burgundy he could introduce a clause which would make the contract distasteful to someone, and he would have to work through the Vaudémonts. He agreed that Margaret's children should inherit Sicily, Provence and Bar excluding any children Yolande and Ferri might have. He added that if Yolande married again any male of the second marriage would come before Margaret's children as far as Bar was concerned.

This was, as René had known it would be, construed as an insult by the Vaudémonts and they protested. They were going to take the matter to parliament, they declared. They were going to set it before the King and see what he thought about such injustice.

All well and good, thought René. Delay . . . delay . . . that is always a good policy.

'Why have you done this?' Margaret asked him. 'You must have known what the result would be.'

'I did it for that reason.'

'But why, Father?'

'May I ask you a question. Do you want to marry the Count of Nevers?'

Margaret considered calmly. 'I have to marry someone,' she said.

'But you can imagine someone younger . . . someone more romantic . . . than a middle-aged Count, perhaps?'

'Why, yes, of course.'

'Then you don't want to marry him? You would rather wait awhile. Who knows what gallant suitor might come forth? Is that so, dear child?'

'Yes, Father. I do not want to marry the Count of Nevers.'

'So I thought,' said René. 'Now we will settle down to wait.'

Chapter IV

MARGARET AND HENRY

The King was riding from St Albans to Westminster. He was waiting impatiently for the return of Champchevrier. The thought of this young girl whose father had become impoverished through a series of misadventures appealed to him. Henry was always sorry for the failures. Perhaps it was because he sometimes felt he was a failure himself. He often wished that fate had not made him a King. Sometimes he imagined what he would have been if he had not been born royal. He might have gone into a monastery where he could have spent his days illuminating manuscripts, praying, working for the poor. He would have been content doing that and he would have done it well.

But he was the son of a King, a King in his own right, and as such was burdened by responsibilities which he could not endure.

He had not been formed to be a King – and a Plantagenet King at that. He did not belong with those blond long-legged giants who only had to wave a banner to have men flock to them. They had imposed their iron rule on the people – or most of them had – and the people had accepted it, almost always. Edward Longshanks; Edward the Third; his own father, Great Henry the Fifth. They were all kings of whom England could be proud.

And then had come Henry, a King at nine months old, surrounded by ambitious men all jostling for power. No, he was apart. His ancestors in the main had been lusty men. They had scattered their bastards all over the country. But he was different. He believed in chastity and the sanctity of the marriage vows. He was acutely embarrassed when women approached him seeking to tempt him, as they used to. They did not do it so much now because they knew it was useless; but there would always be women who would be delighted to become the King's mistress. Never, he had said, and turned disgustedly away.

He remembered one occasion when some of his courtiers had arranged for dancers to perform for him and they came before him, their bosoms bare. So horrified had he been that he had quickly quitted the chamber muttering the nearest expletive to an oath of which he was capable, 'Forsooth and forsooth.' And then 'Fie, for shame! You are to blame for bringing such women before me.' And he had refused to look at them.

It needed incidents like that to assure those about him that he really was a deeply religious man of genuine purity.

Very laudable in a priest. But a King!

All he wanted was to live quietly, in a peaceful household; he wanted no more of the conflict in France. Did he want to be King of France? He did not want to be King of England even! His great uncle Cardinal Beaufort had assured him that with the death of his uncle Bedford the hopes of retaining a hold on France had ended. Everything had changed since the glorious days of Harfleur and Agincourt. Then England had had a great warrior King and had he lived doubtless France and England would be one by now. But he had died and Joan of Arc had come forward and changed the war. She was dead now . . . burned as a witch and he was still horrified by the memory of that deed. He had seen her once when he was a boy and had peeped at her through an aperture in the wall and looked into her cell; he had never forgotten her. He was certain now that she had been sent from Heaven. It was a sign that God wanted France to remain in the hands of the French. Henry wanted it too.

The great Cardinal on whom he relied had said that the time had come to make peace with the French – an honourable peace before they had lost too much.

Heartily Henry agreed with that. Others did too. There was one notable exception: Henry's uncle Gloucester. Henry disliked and feared his uncle Gloucester. He was nothing but a troublemaker and his wife was now a captive in one of the country's castles because she had indulged in witchcraft in an attempt to destroy Henry's life.

For what reason? So that Gloucester could be King as he was the next in line.

No, Henry would never trust Gloucester. He did not want him near him. He had given orders that he must have extra guards and if ever his uncle Gloucester attempted to approach him they must watch most carefully.

It was the Cardinal who had suggested that a marriage with Margaret of Anjou might be a good thing. A French marriage was necessary. The King of France was disinclined to offer one of his daughters. 'At one time we could have insisted,' said the Cardinal, 'but times have changed and the sooner we take account of this the better. Margaret is the niece of the Queen of France; she is a Princess even if René is only titular King of Naples. She is young and could be taught. It seems to me, my lord, that Margaret would be a very good proposition.'

He had agreed as he invariably did with the Cardinal and the fact that he knew his uncle Gloucester would be against the match made it seem doubly attractive.

And because of that he had sent Champchevrier to France to bring to him, secretly, a picture of Margaret, for it must not yet be known that a match was being thought of. He wanted to make sure that his prospective bride was indeed a young pure girl. He wanted no brazenly voluptuous woman, but he would like one who was beautiful; he had a great love for beauty, usually in painting, poetry and music, so his wife must appeal to his aesthetic tastes. He planned to live with her as a good husband and if she would be a good wife to him they would remain faithful until death parted them and in the meantime give the country the necessary heir.

The Duke of Gloucester was in favour of a match with one of the daughters of the Count of Armagnac. Armagnac was not at this time friendly with the King of France and the last thing Gloucester wanted was peace with France. Henry was not sure whether Gloucester wanted the conflict to persist because he saw himself as a great warrior like his brother Henry the Fifth and had dreams of bringing the French crown to England or whether he wanted the match because the Cardinal was against it. But any match that Gloucester would arrange for him could never please Henry. He had, however, diplomatically dispatched Hans to the Court of Armagnac, telling him there was no need for haste, and at the same time had sent Champchevrier out in secret and in all speed.

The Cardinal had seen and conversed with Margaret and had reported that not only was she a beautiful girl but she was an intelligent one.

When Champchevrier returned he would first make his way to Westminster and Henry wished to be there when he came, to save delay. It was for this reason that he was now on his way.

As he approached the capital he was recognised and cheered by a few people. They were not wildly enthusiastic for he was not a man who could inspire that frenzied admiration in them which they had accorded to some of his ancestors and it was always difficult in any case for the living to compare favourably with the dead.

Coming into Cripplegate something stuck on a stake caught his eye. He looked at it in puzzlement not recognising it for what it was. Then he turned to one of his attendants and said: 'What is that revolting object?'

'My lord,' was the answer, 'it is the quarters of some wretch who has been punished for treason to yourself.'

Henry covered his eyes with his hands. 'It disgusts me,' he said. 'Have it taken away. It does not please me that my subjects should be so treated for my sake.'

'This man was a traitor, my lord. Proved to be so.'

'Traitors should die mayhap, but not in such a way. Have that rotting flesh taken down at once. I never want to see the like again.'

His orders were obeyed but he knew they were asking themselves, What manner of King is this?

On to Westminster. Champchevrier had not yet arrived. Henry settled down to wait with patience.

He had so much to absorb his interest at this time. He was deeply involved in plans for founding colleges at Eton and

Cambridge. One of the greatest joys in life was learning and he wanted to do all he could to promote it. The planning of these colleges pleased him more than anything at this time and he dearly wished that he could give more time to such projects instead of the continual preoccupation with continuing the war in France. He saw quite clearly that no good could come of this war. It had been going on for a hundred years and still nothing was resolved. It was like a seesaw, first England was in the ascendant and then dashed down to the ground; up went France and then down . . . It would go on like that and it meant nothing but bloodshed for the men who went to France and excessive taxation for those who remained behind.

There was no joy in war. He would like to end it as soon as possible and this French marriage would be a step towards it.

He was delighted when Champchevrier finally arrived in Westminster with the picture. He had pilfered it from the castle of Tarascon, he explained, where by strategy, posing as a traveller, he had spent a night.

Henry seized the picture eagerly. A pair of gentle blue eyes looked at him out of a heart-shaped face; the brow was high, indicating intelligence, the expression serene and her hair hung about her shoulders – fair with tints of red in it.

'My lord, you like the picture?' asked Champchevrier.

'By St John, yes I do.'

It was the nearest Henry could come to an oath but it meant that he liked what he saw – he liked it very much.

The Cardinal Beaufort was riding to Westminster. He had urgent business with the King but before he went to Henry he wished to sound the Earl of Suffolk, for the Cardinal had selected the Earl as the most suitable of all the English nobles to conduct the business ahead of them.

The Cardinal was thoughtful. He was getting near to the end of a full and very satisfying life. Born bastard son of John of Gaunt and Catherine Swynford he had been legitimised by his father and had enjoyed many honours. He had played a large part in the government of the country since his half-brother Henry IV had taken the crown from poor ineffectual Richard and so set up the House of Lancaster as the ruling one.

At one time it had seemed that the dream of capturing the crown of France would be realised. And so it would have been if Henry the Fifth had lived. Henry had a genius for war and when he married the French Princess and it was agreed that he should have the throne on the death of mad Charles it seemed that the war was virtually over. But change comes quickly and unexpectedly especially in the history of countries at war. Who would have believed twenty years before that the crown of France should have been saved for the French by a peasant girl and that Charles the Dauphin, indolent, careless of anything but his own pleasure, listless, indifferent to the fate of his country, should become one of the most astute Kings that France had ever known?

There was one truth which had been apparent to the Cardinal for a very long time and that was that England had lost the war for France and that the sooner this was realised and the best terms made, the better.

But there was certain to be differing points of view and the Duke of Gloucester, in spite of everything that had happened, was still a force to be reckoned with.

Gloucester did not want peace with France. He still dreamed that he was going to win spectacular battles like

Agincourt. He really believed he was a military genius like his brother. Even Bedford had not been that, great soldier though he had been and wise administrator too. There was none to compare with Henry the Fifth. His kind appeared only once in a century. And Gloucester thought he could achieve what his brother had! It was contemptible.

It was a pity Gloucester had not been found guilty of practising witchcraft when his wife had.

But for some reason Gloucester was popular with the people. It was some strange charismatic quality he had. Many of the Plantagenets had it – it was a family gift, though it missed some. For all his excellence Bedford never had it. Henry the Fifth had had a double dose of it. And oddly enough, Gloucester, who had a genius for backing the wrong causes and made a failure of everything he tackled, who had married a woman far beneath him socially who was now charged with sorcery . . . all this and the people still retained a certain tenderness for him. So in spite of everything Gloucester still had to be reckoned with.

And Gloucester wanted to continue this disastrous war.

Therefore there must be a certain secrecy about these arrangements for Henry's marriage. A Princess of Anjou was the best they could hope for. It was no use trying to badger Charles for one of his own daughters. England alas was not in a position to make demands any more. A marriage with Armagnac would be tantamount to a pledge to continue the war, so that was the last thing they needed. Charles might be pleased to permit the marriage of his niece – she was in fact his wife's niece – and he might consider that it was a very good match for Margaret of Anjou, which it was. She would be Queen of England and if that was not a dazzling prospect for the younger daughter of an impoverished man who was only titular King of Naples, Beaufort did not know what was.

He had selected the man who should be the chief ambassador to the Court of Anjou and he was going to see him before he went to the King. Indeed, he thought they should go together without delay to the King so that the negotiations could be put into practice immediately.

When the Cardinal arrived at Westminster he went at once to the Earl of Suffolk's apartments before seeking an audience with the King.

Suffolk was delighted to see him while at the same time he wondered if this might mean trouble or some unpleasant task for him. He and the Cardinal worked closely together; and they were both sworn enemies of Gloucester.

William de la Pole had become the Earl of Suffolk when his elder brother was killed at Agincourt. He had had a distinguished military career and after the death of Henry the Fifth had served under the Duke of Bedford. He had been with Salisbury at the siege of Orléans. He had seen the mysterious death of Salisbury and the coming of the Maid.

He knew, as the Cardinal did, that those English hopes which had seemed so bright before the siege of Orléans had become depressingly dim. England should slip out of France and try to keep as many of her old possessions as possible. Only hotheads like Gloucester would disagree with this.

Since his marriage he had formed a connection with the Beaufort family for his wife was the widow of the Earl of Salisbury and she had been Alice Chaucer before her marriage. Catherine Swynford – the mother of the Beauforts – had had a sister Philippa who had married the poet Geoffrey Chaucer and so there was a family connection.

His long military career made him feel very strongly that peace was necessary and he and the Cardinal had often discussed the best way of achieving this.

Now the Cardinal thought he had found a way.

'A marriage with Margaret of Anjou could be a stepping stone to peace,' he told Suffolk when they had exchanged the customary pleasantries.

'And the King, will he agree to marriage?'

'He wants it. He knows he has to marry sooner or later. It is his duty to provide an heir and though he has little interest in women he will do his duty. We can count on him for that. In fact he has sent a secret messenger to France to find a picture of her and he is delighted with what he sees.'

'The pictures of Princesses have been known to flatter.'

'Well, what would that matter? He would be half way in love with her before she arrived and that can do no harm. Moreover, I have seen her. I found her good-looking, intelligent and vivacious. In fact, everything that Henry needs in a wife.'

'And of course there are the marriage terms to be arranged.'

'What we need is a peace treaty. I want this marriage to mean that we abandon our claim to the crown of France.'

'And do you think the people will accept that?'

'They have to be convinced it is best.'

'They are intoxicated by victories like Agincourt and Verneuil. They do not understand why we don't go on providing them with glorious occasions like those.'

'The people will accept what has to be done. Give them a royal wedding and they will be happy.'

'They do not like the French.'

'They loved Katherine of Valois.'

'She came in rather different circumstances. When she married Henry it was in victory. He had won France they thought, and was taking the French Princess to make a happy solution for both countries.'

'What is wrong with you, William? It almost seems that you would put obstacles in the way of this match.'

Suffolk was silent. Then he said: 'I have a notion that you have decided that I shall go as the King's proxy to Margaret of Anjou.'

'Who would be better?'

'I knew it. It is why you wished to speak to me.'

'You are a man of maturity and wisdom, William. It is clear to me that you are the one to go to Anjou to treat with the King of France, for that is what it will mean.'

'You know, Cardinal, that the King of France is a shrewd man. It is not the old Dauphin we have to deal with. Whenever I think of Charles of France I say to myself: "There is Joan of Arc's miracle."'

'Yes, Charles has changed. There are such changes. I remember my own nephew, Henry the Fifth – a profligate youth who filled us all with misgivings and then once the crown was on his head he became the hero of Agincourt.'

'I shall have to barter with the King of France.'

'It will certainly come to that.'

'And we shall have to sacrifice something for Margaret. And it will be land, castles . . . you can be sure of that.'

'But of course.'

'And the people are not going to like the sort of sacrifice for which Charles will ask.'

'Nevertheless the sacrifice will have to be made.'

'And they will blame the one who made it. Not the King, not

the Cardinal, but their ambassador Suffolk. I can imagine what Gloucester will make of that.'

'So that is what holds you back.'

Suffolk was silent for a few moments.

'I feel that the people will not like a French marriage and when they hear we have had to sacrifice territory won in battle they will blame the one who made those concessions, that is the King's ambassador, otherwise Suffolk . . . if he goes.'

The Cardinal moved closer to Suffolk.

'But have you thought how grateful the new Queen will be to the man who brought her to England and so skilfully arranged the necessary details for her marriage? The man who has the Queen's favour will be fortunate indeed. The King is not a very forceful character, is he? I can see him relying on his Queen and then the one she favours will be in a very happy position indeed.'

Suffolk was thoughtful. There might be something in that but there were too many conditions attached. No, he would prefer not to be involved in anything like this. He was getting too old. He would be forty-eight in October. Not that he wanted to disengage himself from politics, but at least he did not want to run into anything that might be uncomfortable or even dangerous.

'I would rather not be the King's ambassador on this occasion,' he said.

The Cardinal shrugged his shoulders.

A few days later the King sent for Suffolk. He wanted him to undertake a delicate mission and Henry was sure he was the best man for the task.

He did not have to ask. He knew the nature of the order. He was to go to France, leading an embassy to arrange terms for the King's marriage to Margaret of Anjou.

It was on a windy March day when the embassy landed at Harfleur. Still uneasy, Suffolk congratulated himself that at least he had the King's assurance that no charge should be brought against him if he ran into danger, which meant that he should not be blamed if this proved to be an unpopular move.

They joined the Duc d'Orléans at Blois and from there sailed down the Loire to Tours where the Court was and in due course Suffolk was presented to Charles at his château of Montils-les-Tours.

Suffolk was amazed by the change in the King of France. Here was a shrewd and resolute monarch, and it was an astonishing fact that the change had been brought about by women. First the Maid and then his wife and his mother-in-law Yolande of Aragon; and now, it was said, Agnès Sorel.

That the new Charles was going to drive a hard bargain was apparent. He would not give Henry one of his own daughters which he could easily have done; but Margaret, he implied, was good enough for Henry. She was a French Princess and the French were no longer in the position they had been in when Katherine the present King's sister was given to Henry the Fifth.

Charles was not inclined to agree to a peace treaty. Why should he, with everything going in his favour? He would agree to a truce, of course; but he implied that the only thing which could bring about peace was for England to give up all claim to the French crown.

René of Anjou expressed himself dubious. Could he give his daughter to one who had usurped his hereditary dominions of Anjou and Maine?

This was an indication of what terms would be demanded.

Suffolk was relieved to escape from the conference and return to his wife. He was glad he had brought Alice with him for he could talk to her as he could to no one else.

'I like not this matter,' he said. 'I can see what will happen. The French will make great demands and the King will accept them because he wants peace and Margaret. And later when it is realised what we have had to pay for her, the people will blame me.'

'You have the King's assurance that no blame shall be attached to you.'

'The assurances of Kings don't account for much in matters like this.'

'What can you do?'

'I cannot agree to give up Anjou and Maine, of course. I don't know whether a truce will be acceptable when peace terms were required. I have achieved very little advantage for ourselves.'

'And what is Margaret's dowry to be?'

'There again, they seem to set a high store on this young girl who has only recently acquired the status of Princess and even then her father has nothing more than a hollow title.'

'Alas,' said Alice, 'it shows how low England has fallen when you remember it is only a little more than two years ago when it was England who was calling the tune.'

'Which brings us back to the Maid of Orléans who brought about the change. Charles is a different man from the Dauphin.'

'They say it is Agnès Sorel who has changed him.'

'It is amazing that women should have had such an effect on men.'

'It often happens,' retorted Alice, 'although rarely so

spectacularly. Perhaps it is because Charles is a king that it is so noticeable. But what will you do, William?'

'I can see only one course of action. I shall return home and put the proposals before the council.'

'Very wise,' she commented. 'Let it be their decision not yours. It is well in such matters to be only the ambassador.'

So they travelled down to the coast and set sail for England.

Suffolk faced the Parliament. He had already laid the proposition before the King and the Cardinal. The French were asking a great deal but the King was becoming more and more enamoured of the idea of marriage with Margaret of Anjou and the Cardinal saw it as important to peace and although the demands for Maine and Anjou had startled them at first, they were wavering and were coming to the decision that anything was acceptable which would bring about the marriage.

To make matters worse, Margaret's dowry was to be the islands of Majorca and Minorca which were of no value at all, for although René claimed to have inherited them from his mother, Yolande had had no jurisdiction over them. In fact all René had to offer was titles. There could rarely have been a man who had so many titles and so few possessions.

The Duke of Gloucester stood up and loudly opposed the marriage.

It was humiliating, he said, for the King of England to contemplate marrying a lady without possessions whose title to Princess was suspect, who demanded everything and gave nothing. He and his party – which was quite significant – opposed the match. He would do everything in his power to prevent it. It was giving way to the French; it was playing into Charles's hands. They could be sure their enemies were laughing at them. Forget this marriage with Anjou. Let the King take one of the daughters of the Count of Armagnac and then let them prosecute the war and win back all they had lost because of the weak policy they had followed since the death of his brother the Duke of Bedford.

The Cardinal rose to oppose Gloucester. The enmity between them which had lasted for years was as strong as ever.

The Cardinal pleaded for peace. The country needed peace. Those who thought otherwise had no knowledge of what was happening in France.

Gloucester was on his feet. He was a soldier, he reminded them, a man who had conducted campaign after campaign.

'With considerable failure,' commented the Cardinal.

Gloucester, red in the face, almost foaming at the mouth, spat out at his uncle, 'And you, my lord, you man of the Church, what do you know of military campaigns?'

'I know, my lord, whether they succeed or not and we cannot afford more failures. The people will not agree to go on being taxed for a war that brings us no gain.'

'My brother the King . . .'

'Your brother the King was one of the most successful generals the world has known. Alas, he is dead, and his victories have gone with him. Times have changed. The French are in the ascendant. To carry on a war in France with all the attendant difficulties of transport and supplies is impossible. We need peace. And if the French will only give us a truce let us take it.'

The Parliament had grown accustomed to listening to the Cardinal. The late King and Bedford had relied on his judgement. He was known to be a man who served the Crown well, whereas Gloucester, popular as he might be in some quarters, was renowned for his rashness.

And the King clearly wanted the marriage.

The Parliament was therefore persuaded that the marriage with Anjou would be good for the country and it was agreed that the terms for a truce would be accepted and the question of Maine and Anjou should be left open to be discussed at some later date. So Suffolk was sent back to France to arrange the marriage by proxy.

For his services in this matter he was awarded the title of Marquess.

Theophanie was in a state bordering between bliss and sorrow. She was going to lose her charge and yet the young girl, who had so little in possessions to offer a bridegroom, was going to make a brilliant marriage, for although she was going to marry the enemy she would be a Queen and a real Queen at that. Not like her father and mother who called themselves King and Queen and had no country to rule.

Oh, she was proud of her Margaret. So would her grandmother the lady Yolande have been if she could see her today.

Margaret herself did not seem greatly impressed.

'You don't seem to want to be Queen of England,' Theophanie complained.

'England has been our enemy, Theophanie. Have you forgotten how we used to watch out for the soldiers and how alarmed everyone was when they were near?'

'Young ladies like you were born to end these wars. I always reckoned you did more with your pretty looks than the men did with their cannons and cross bows.'

'You mean alliances. I am just a counter in the game, Theophanie.'

'Oh, you're more than that. You're like your mother and your grandmother. You're going to be one of those women who do the ruling. I've always seen that in you.'

'It will be strange to be in a foreign country away from you all.'

Theophanie was saddened and put up her hand to knock away a tear with a degree of impatience. 'It's always the same with us nurses,' she said. 'We have our babies and then they are snatched away from us. Kings and Queens and noblemen lose their daughters when they become ready for marriage. It's only the poor who can keep their children with them. You'll have to promise me never to forget old Theophanie and what she taught you when you are Queen of England.'

Poor Theophanie, she felt the parting deeply. Margaret did too. It was the end of her girlhood. She was going to a new country and a husband. She wondered a great deal about Henry.

Her parents were to escort her to Nancy where the proxy ceremony would take place. The King of France would attend, for her marriage was of importance to France. She knew that. She would see her aunt Marie and Agnès again.

Her father talked to her about the marriage as he painted, for he was loth to leave the picture he was working on.

'It never seems the same when one comes back to it,' he said. 'When people produce works of art they should live with them, stay with them night and day until they are completed.'

'Dear Father,' she replied, 'I am sorry my marriage is taking you away from the work you love.'

'I was joking,' he said. 'Of course I want to be at my daughter's wedding. Do you realise what you are doing for France . . . for us all by this marriage?'

'Yes,' she answered.

'You will be in a place of authority. You will be able to guide the King to act in favour of your country.'

'Do you think a King of England would be guided to act against his own country in favour of France?'

'Not really, of course, nor could we expect him to. What I mean is a little gentle persuasion eh, when some matter arises.'

'I shall have to wait and see what matters arise.'

'You will delight him I know. And he must want this marriage very much to consider giving up Maine and Anjou for it.'

A few days later her father was disturbed. Since her betrothal he had taken her into his confidence. It was as though he regarded her as already Queen of England and if she were going to work for the good of France she must be kept cognisant of affairs.

'The Vaudémonts will attend the wedding and they say that it is high time that your sister Yolande and Ferri were married. Yolande is older than you and yet you are to be a bride. They want a double wedding.'

'It will be wonderful to see Yolande again.'

'Margaret, I always intended that this wedding should never take place. Yolande . . . my daughter . . . to marry my great enemy.'

'But it was the terms of peace, Father. You agreed to this marriage.'

'Because I was forced to.'

'But it was for this reason that you were released.'

'Yolande was only a child then. I was determined that the marriage should never take place. I am still determined. And now the Vaudémonts will be coming to your wedding and they are making plans for Ferri de Vaudémont to marry Yolande at the same time.'

Margaret was astounded. She was very uneasy when she saw the look of determination in her father's face and she wondered whether he was planning some wild action to prevent the marriage of Yolande and Ferri de Vaudémont.

Margaret said a sad farewell to Theophanie, who was in tears knowing that it was highly improbable that they would ever meet again, and with her parents set out on the journey to Nancy.

The whole neighbourhood was *en fête*. This was going to be the grandest wedding they had seen for a long time. It was true the bridegroom would not be present and there would be a nobleman of high rank to stand in for him but the King and all the Court would be there, among them the famous beauty and counsellor of the King, Agnès Sorel, who, it was said, he loved more than his life.

There would be festivities which would last for days and already the traders in the neighbourhood had profited by all the work this had brought them.

Crowds of people were converging on the town of Nancy from all over France and the people even cheered the English delegation.

When Margaret appeared riding between her father and mother the people went wild with joy. 'Long live the beautiful bride!' they shouted; and Margaret was thrilled for the first time by the acclaim of the people. It was then that she realised the importance of the occasion. She was going into a new country as its Queen and silently she vowed that she would never forget her native land.

The King and the Queen were already in the castle. Margaret sank to her knees and was lifted up by the King and warmly kissed. Her aunt Marie glowed with affection too and there was Agnès standing beside the King, dazzling as ever with that rather unearthly beauty of hers.

They were making a very important occasion of it.

Then she was presented to the English embassy headed by Suffolk. He introduced her to his lady to whom she immediately took a great fancy. She liked Suffolk too. There was a kindliness about him and he had such a protective air.

The King told her that jousts and all sorts of entertainments were being planned to celebrate her nuptials.

'Dear niece,' he said, 'this is going to be an occasion you will never forget.'

'I suppose, Sire,' said Margaret, 'that few forget their wedding days.'

'This is but a proxy marriage and there will be the official ceremony when you get to England. I want you to remember this as your last ceremonial occasion as a Princess of France.'

He placed his hand over hers and patted it. She sensed that he was very pleased with the wedding.

It was a great delight to see Yolande again.

At first the sisters did not recognise each other, which was natural since it must be twelve years since they had been together. They both remembered though vaguely the upheavals in their lives which young as they were had made a deep impression. There was that journey undertaken when Margaret was two and Yolande three to go with their mother to plead with the King. They remembered how shortly afterwards Yolande was taken away to go to live with the Vaudémonts.

'And now we are both to be married,' said Yolande.

'You too?' asked Margaret.

'Ferri is determined on it. He has said we have waited overlong. Every time it is suggested our father makes some excuse why it should not take place.'

'You want to marry then, Yolande?'

'But of course,' said Yolande. 'Ferri and I have grown up together. We have always been good friends. It is different for you, Margaret. You have never seen your bridegroom.'

'The Marchioness of Suffolk tells me a great deal about him. She says he is handsome though gently so . . . if you know what that means. In fact, everything about him is gentle. He is kindly and hates being cruel to anyone even his enemies, and he is a great scholar and interested in poetry, painting and music.'

'That should suit you,' said Yolande, 'and if you are anything like our mother and grandmother — which I suspect you are — you will be able to tell him what he ought to do.'

'The more I talk of him the less apprehensive I become. What of Ferri?'

'Ferri is bold and romantic and I would not have him otherwise. I am fortunate not to be going to a man I do not know.'

'But I feel I already know Henry through Alice.'

'Who is Alice?'

'She is the Marchioness. I call her Alice. She asked me to. She is a very pleasant woman. I have taken a fancy to her and I think she has to me.'

'Most people would be ready to take a fancy to their Queen.'

'I have no doubt, but I do feel friendship for Alice. She is different from any woman I have met. Perhaps it is because she did not descend entirely from the nobility. Her father, she tells me, was Thomas Chaucer, the eldest son of Geoffrey Chaucer who made a name for himself with his writing. He married a sister of Catherine Swynford who was John of Gaunt's third wife. You see the connection.'

'Ah, she climbed into the nobility.'

'Her father was a very rich man. He was Speaker of the House of Commons and the Marquess of Suffolk is her third husband.'

'What a lot you know about her.'

'We talk and it comes out. She was an only child and I suppose she had a fortune. She was married to the Earl of Salisbury before she married Suffolk. I like her very much. In fact I like Suffolk too. I feel in them I shall have good friends in my new home.'

'You are excited about this marriage, Margaret. I wish mine could be settled. Father is going to stop it again, I believe.'

'Perhaps if you spoke to him . . .'

'I have done so. He hates the Vaudémonts, Margaret.'

'I suppose it is natural. They were really the beginning of his troubles. If they hadn't claimed Lorraine . . .'

'They had a right to,' declared Yolande. 'The Salic Law does exist and their claim for Lorraine comes before his.'

'You will never get our father to see that.'

'But he agreed to the terms . . . marriage for Ferri and me.'

'I am sure Father will relent. It would be pleasant to have the two marriages together.'

'We are going to insist on it.'

'Then I am sure it will take place.'

But René was adamant when it was suggested.

'There is so much that has to be arranged first,' he insisted.

But those who knew him well fully understood that this was another example of his procrastination. The fact was that he did not want his daughter to marry into a house which he considered an enemy. That he had promised, that the marriage had been one of the terms of an agreement did not worry him. René was accustomed to waiving an agreement when it suited him.

But he had reckoned without a hot-blooded, romantic lover. Ferri was making plans and if he could get no satisfaction from his prospective bride's father he intended to carry them out.

The dark November weather had no effect on the ceremonies. In fact it accentuated their brilliance and crowds witnessed the proxy marriage of Margaret with the Marquess of Suffolk standing in as her bridegroom when the Bishop of Toul performed the ceremony in the church of St Martins in Nancy and in the presence of a most illustrious assembly presided over by the King of France.

The King had said that this should be an occasion to be remembered and he was determined to make it so. René was nothing loth. He was eager that no expense should be spared – even if it was the expense of others – and with the King of France giving the orders it was very grand indeed.

There must be a tournament in honour of the new Queen of England and all the most famous champions of France must perform in it. Margaret could not help being thrilled by the sight of the pavilions flying their pennants and the numbers of chivalrous knights who wore the daisy. She had chosen this symbol because her name was Margaret which meant a daisy and she had always loved the flower because of that. From now on it should be her emblem and this exhibition of chivalry should be the Field of Daisies.

She sat with the two Queens – her mother and her aunt Marie of France – and watched the jousting. The King himself took part more than once and René also rode into the lists.

Margaret had never seen anything like it in the whole of her life and the fact that it should all be in honour of herself – a fifteen-year-old girl – was overwhelming.

There must be eight days of revelry the King had decreed, and each day should be better than the one before. There was one occasion when a figure clad in armour set with jewels appeared at the tournament and when the visor was thrown back the most beautiful face in France was revealed. Agnès Sorel had appeared thus at the request of the King who wished the whole of France to know how much he revered her.

Charles rode round the field with Agnès and even the Queen joined in the applause.

It was while this was happening that there was a sudden commotion around the royal loge where the ladies were seated. Ferri de Vaudémont had stepped up to Yolande and taking her hand had walked with her across the field. Intent on the glittering Agnès and the homage done to her by the King, few had noticed. And then Ferri had set Yolande on a horse and himself mounting behind her, with a company of five or six friends, began to gallop away.

René was the first to notice. He shouted: 'After them!' And several of his men gave chase.

The King was astonished. Instead of admiration for his beautiful Agnès there was a tittering in the crowd and everyone was agog to know what had happened.

He ordered that a troop of guards be sent out to see what the disturbance meant and to bring back the fugitives.

Ferri's attempt to abduct his bride was short-lived; perhaps he had intended it should be so and his motive in making it had merely been to call attention to his case. Within a few hours he was brought before the King.

'What did you mean by behaving in such a way at my tournament?' demanded Charles.

'Sire,' replied Ferri, 'I had to call your attention and that of others to the situation in which King René has placed not only me but his daughter. Yolande was sent to us as a child. We have grown up together. She wants to marry me as I do her and yet again and again the ceremony is put off simply because the King of Naples does not wish to honour his agreement.'

'I will speak to the lady,' said Charles and ordered that Yolande be brought before him.

'You have been the victim of an abduction,' said Charles. 'How do you feel about that?'

'I was very willing that the abduction should take place, Sire.'

Charles began to laugh. 'And doubtless planned it with your abductor?'

'You are right, Sire.'

'And you want to get married. You are a year older than your sister, eh, and she is now marrying. Is that what you feel?'

'It is, my lord.'

'For my part I see no reason why we should not have a double wedding. Perhaps I should speak to King René.'

The two young people fell on their knees and kissed the King's hands.

'Enough,' said Charles. 'I know you will be grateful if I persuade René to allow the marriage to take place. So, let me see what I can do.'

He sent for René. Agnès was with him when René arrived.

'So your daughter was abducted?' he said.

'It is an outrage. It changes everything. It releases me from my bond. I shall take my daughter back with me.'

'Nay, nay. You go too fast. In the first place it does not release you from your bond. The marriage was at the root of the agreement you made with the Vaudémonts when you were beaten in battle by them. You must remain faithful to the laws of chivalry, brother-in-law.'

René was silent. He had always prided himself on keeping those rules.

'Be reasonable. The marriage must take place if you value your honour. The young people are eager for it. Why delay?'

'There are certain matters which have to be arranged.'

'Oh come, René, how many years have you had to arrange those matters?'

Agnès said: 'If I may say it, my lord, it would seem to me that much expense would be spared if Yolande and Ferri were married now. Margaret could share her celebrations with those of her sister.'

Charles laughed inwardly. Trust Agnès to find the right answer.

René was wavering. The expenses of a daughter's wedding were great. He was deeply in debt everywhere. Of course if the wedding took place now Charles would be paying for everything.

He said: 'To abduct her in that way . . .'

'Poor young man. He was desperate.'

'You must forgive him,' said Agnès gently. 'Remember it was for love of your daughter.'

'Well,' said René, 'since it appears to be your wish, Sire, and yours, my lady . . .'

'Let us send for the happy pair and tell them the good news,' said Agnès.

So Yolande and Ferri were married and the jousts and the entertainments continued.

Charles talked to Agnès about the alliance of Margaret and Henry. He was sure it was a good thing for France.

'It is an indication of the change which has come about since his father married a French Princess. The Fifth Henry had the daughter of the King of France. Our dear Margaret is a very minor Princess – in fact some would say no true Princess at all.'

'Well, her father *is* the King of Sicily and Naples.'

'Poor René, do you think he will ever see Sicily again?'

'No, but it gives him some satisfaction to call himself King.'

'And it has brought a crown for his daughter. I doubt she would have been considered if she had not borne the title of Princess . . . minor though it is.'

'I hope the dear child will be happy.'

'She will rule Henry, I am sure of that. He is a weakling, you know, and she is the sort of woman to rule. I shall never forget her grandmother . . .'

Agnès put her hand over his. 'I know how dear she was to you.'

'She was such an extraordinary woman. I was sad to lose her. Thank God I had you, Agnès, then.'

'I shall always be beside you.'

'It must be so,' he said. 'It would be too hard for me to live without you.' He was thoughtful for a while. Then he said: 'It is very good for France to have a strong Frenchwoman Queen of England.'

'Remember she is very young.'

'I do. But she is clever, and I think she will remember her duty to France. I will send for her and talk to her, and then you shall tell me if you think she will be good for France when she is in England.'

Margaret was pleased to be summoned by the King. She had become very fond of him. He was always kind and treated her as though she were his daughter. He had made a great effort to give her a splendid wedding and, although she knew that this was to impress the English, at the same time he had delighted to please her. Moreover he had brought about the marriage of Ferri and Yolande, for if he had not made it his business René would have found excuses to put it off again.

He received her informally and kissed her tenderly. Agnès did the same.

'So,' said the King, 'we now have before us the Queen of England. How does it feel to be a Queen?'

'I am scarce that yet.'

''Tis true you have not seen your bridegroom and have had to take old Suffolk in his stead.'

'The Marquess of Suffolk has been a good friend to me, as has the Marchioness.'

'It is well that you make friends. You may need them when you get to your new home. So you have taken a fancy to the Suffolks. And the Talbots too, I believe.'

'I have found them to be very kind to me.'

'So they should be . . . to their Queen. It is going to be a difficult path you have to follow. Sometimes it is necessary to pursue a devious policy. You are very young and there are those who will seek to exploit your youth. You will have to be watchful, Margaret.'

'I know that it is not going to be easy . . .'

'But you are a clever girl. Often I see your grandmother in you and your mother has always had my greatest admiration. You are another such as they are, and I can tell you you will find the King easily led. Margaret, make sure you are the one to lead him.'

'Do you think he will listen to me?'

'Of a certainty he will. You will be the nearest to him. He is a gentle person, they tell me. He does not care for brilliant ceremonies and all the pomp of kingship. He is a good young man. You will have no difficulty with him. It is those around him of whom you will have to be watchful. You must influence him in the choice of those close to him and let me tell you something I have learned: walk very warily at first. Let them see you as the young girl . . . the child . . . a little bewildered by her new home, anxious to please. But all the time you will be watchful. Make sure you are friendly with those closest to the King. At the moment he is ruled by them. One of whom you will be particularly careful is the Duke of Gloucester. He was against the marriage, and he will be unfriendly to you. He will try to prove that it was a mistake. Watch him but do not be afraid of him. If you are clever there will be nothing to fear from him. He is popular – for some odd reason – but his wife was accused of witchcraft which she was using to destroy the King. He is losing his power, but watch him.'

'I will do as you say, dear uncle. I can see I shall have to learn a great deal.'

'Then you have made the first step. Is that not so, Agnès?'

'Yes,' said Agnès, 'the first lesson is always learning that there is much to be learned.'

'It is never wise,' went on the King, 'to give too much power to the nobles. Then they will vie with each other. It sets up rivalries between them. It is better to give posts of authority to those who come from less exalted beginnings and have shown by their talents that they can excel in them. Above all, dear child, remember that you are French. Never forget your native land.'

'I could never do that. I shall always love France. England will be my adopted country but France is my own.'

'That is right,' said the King. 'And your marriage has brought about a truce between us. They wanted a peace but they shall not have that until they withdraw all claims to the crown of France. In the meantime they are holding on to Maine and Anjou. Margaret, they must give up these provinces and in particular Maine. Only when Maine is in our hands can we be certain of driving them out of France. You must persuade the King to give up Maine.'

'You could not take it?'

'At great expense of life and money and then perhaps not succeed. No, I want them to give it back to us in exchange for peace.'

'I will do what I can . . . for France,' said Margaret.

'Bless you, my child,' said the King. 'Our love and faith go with you.'

It was time to leave and her father very solemnly handed her over to the Marquess and Marchioness of Suffolk. The King was present and he was seen to wipe away a tear when he took his niece into his arms and kissed her tenderly.

He whispered to her as he held her against him, 'Remember us. Remember France.'

And she replied: 'I will. Oh, I promise I will.'

When the cavalcade went out from the castle, the King rode with Margaret for two leagues and then he said he must take his last farewell of her. They embraced and they were both weeping.

'You are going to one of the greatest thrones of Europe, my dear niece,' said Charles, 'but it is scarcely worthy of you.'

'I will try to do what is right,' she told him. 'And I shall always love you and France.'

The King was genuinely moved and after one last embrace turned and rode sadly back to Nancy.

René and Isabelle rode on with her. The parting with them would come later; and as they rode along it occurred to them that their daughter was very young and that they were placing her in the court of intrigue in a country which was not entirely in favour of receiving her.

They reached Bar where they were to part and when the moment came they could not speak – not one of them. They could only look mutely at each other lest their pent feelings should escape and they give way to grief.

As she rode away, not daring to look back at her father, Alice brought her horse to ride beside her. She said nothing but her sympathy and this gesture touched Margaret deeply. It meant that she had said goodbye to her family but she still had friends.

There was a long way to go yet. Her party consisted of the most important people in England, led as it was by the Marquess and Marchioness of Suffolk and the Earl and Countess of Shrewsbury. The Earl of Wiltshire was also there with the Lords Greystock and Clifford. The English were as determined as the French had been to make a good impression and had sent not only guards but all the servants which the young Queen might have need of on her journey; and besides knights and squires there were carvers, grooms and servants to perform any task which she might require of them. The wages of these people in addition to the food which had to be provided for them had cost the King of England more than five thousand pounds which had to be found from a very depleted exchequer and showed, said those who knew the state of his finances, how very eager he was for the French marriage.

When the party arrived in Paris the people were out to cheer and there was a meeting in the streets between Charles Duc d'Orléans and the Queen. The people were delighted and cheered madly. The Queen was so young, so appealing, so beautiful. Our little Daisy, they called her and everyone carried daisies – some of which were made of paper; and it was all in honour of the little Queen. There was a service in Notre Dame where a Te Deum was sung and there was great rejoicing in the street for the people saw in this marriage a prospect of peace; and that was what they longed for more than anything.

When the party left Paris the Duc d'Orléans rode with it to Pontoise. This was an important point of the journey because it was at the border between the French and the English possessions in France. And there waiting to welcome her was Richard, Duke of York.

This was her first meeting with a man who considered himself as royal as the King. He was descended from Edward the Third by both parents, for his father had been the son of Edmund Langley, the King's fifth son; and his mother was the daughter of Roger Mortimer, grandson of Lionel Duke of Clarence. He had come to join the party and conduct her to England.

He was immensely proud and although he was courteous, Margaret thought him arrogant and she did not like him as she had the Suffolks and Shrewsbury. However, he was a man of great importance in England and must be close to the King. She remembered what her mentor the King of France had told her and tried to win the friendship of the Duke of York.

At Pontoise she must say goodbye to the last of her personal attendants, also to her brother John and the Duc d'Alençon who had accompanied her so far. She was now entirely among the English.

In a barge decorated especially for her with a fine display of daisies she sailed down the Seine to Rouen and there she was received with great acclaim.

She was taken into the city in a litter lavishly decorated with more daisies. The Marquess of Suffolk, who had stood for the King in the proxy ceremony, rode ahead of her litter, and the Duke of York and the Earl of Shrewsbury were on either side of her. The other members of the party followed behind.

She must rest awhile in Rouen and therefore perform the ceremonies which were expected of her.

Alice proved to be a good friend for Margaret was very soon in difficulty over money. René, always financially pressed himself and with many debts which he could never hope to settle, had not been able to provide her with the money she would need to defray the cost of the journey which it was her responsibility to pay.

When Alice told her that it was the custom in Rouen for royal brides to give to the poor certain articles of clothing according to her age, she was bewildered.

'Clothing,' she cried. 'What sort of clothing?'

'A gown of some sort and a pair of shoes . . . the shoes are very important. You must give these. The people expect it.'

'But how many garments and pairs of shoes must I provide?'

'As many as the years you have lived. In your case it will be fifteen. Oh, do not worry. We have arranged everything and the gowns and the shoes are all ready. They will be handed over as soon as they are paid for. The people of Rouen never trust anyone . . . even Queens.'

'I can see they are a wise people,' said Margaret a little grimly, 'for frankly, Alice, I cannot pay for these things. If I do I shall not be able to continue the journey. There are other expenses yet.'

'Your father will pay, I doubt not.'

'Alice,' said Margaret slowly, 'my father can never pay. He is deeply in debt now and has been for as long as I can remember.'

'I shall have to lend you the money,' said Alice.

'I will put some of my silver in pawn with you. You shall hold it until I can pay you back.'

'There is no need . . .' began Alice.

But Margaret silenced her. 'I do not want to build up debts,' she said firmly. 'I do not want to be careless with other people's money. I fear my father has always been like that and see what has happened to him. He is always warding off some creditor. Not that he minds. He is sublimely indifferent to such matters. Oh, he is the dearest man, the finest man . . . I love him very much, but he does have this characteristic . . . and I do not want to be like that.'

So Alice took the silver and found the money for the garments and shoes, and more also for there were all sorts of people to pay on the way and the Queen could not begin by making a bad impression by not paying her dues.

At last they came to Harfleur where two ships lay in the bay awaiting them. One was the *Cokke John of Cherbourg* in which Margaret and her immediate entourage were to sail and the other, *Mary of Hampton,* was for the rest of the party.

It was a short journey across the Channel for the strong south-east wind blew them over, but it was exceedingly uncomfortable and almost as soon as they had left the shore Margaret was dreadfully sick.

Most of the party were ill but not as violently so as Margaret. Alice, feeling dreadfully ill herself, tried to minister to her but Margaret could only murmur: 'I never before felt so ill. I just want to die.'

It was a great relief to all when land was in sight.

Alice bent over Margaret and whispered: 'We have arrived. This sickness will rapidly pass once we are on dry land.'

All the same she went to call her husband for the Queen seemed to her to be suffering from something more than the effects of the sea.

There was great consternation for spots were beginning to show themselves on Margaret's face. Alice opened her gown and saw that they were also on her chest.

'God help us,' she cried. 'The Queen is suffering from a plague.'

The Marquess told his wife to wrap the Queen in a blanket and he would carry her ashore. Alice did as she was bid and taking the Queen in his arms Suffolk waded through the sea with her to the beach. From the town came the sounds of revelry and many people having seen the ship lying off the land had come down to greet her.

There was a hushed silence as Suffolk placed her in a litter and took her with all speed to a convent in the town of Portsmouth. This convent was known as Godde's House, and there the doctors attended her and under their instructions the nuns nursed her.

There was great consternation for it was believed that the Queen was suffering from the dreaded small pox which would almost certainly mean her death or at best her disfigurement, so it was with tremendous relief that after a few days Margaret appeared to be suffering not from small pox but a mild form of chicken pox and the spots began to disappear without leaving any mark behind them and she herself, under the care of the nuns, began to recover.

Meantime Henry, all impatience, came riding to Southampton and immediately sent for Suffolk to hear the latest news of the Queen.

'She is recovering, my lord,' said Suffolk. 'We have all been so anxious, but the Queen's illness was not what we feared. There is nothing but a minor outbreak of some pox and she is recovering fast.'

'I wish to see her. Does she know I am here?'

'I think not, my lord. But you may rest assured she is as eager to see you as you are to see her.'

Fearful that he might find her hideously disfigured and might not be able to hide his revulsion, Henry said on impulse: 'I will not come to her as the King. I wish you to tell her that I am a squire who has brought a message for her from the King. Then I may see her as she is . . . naturally . . . without ceremony, you understand.'

'Perfectly, my lord. I will tell her that the King's squire has brought a letter from him.'

Margaret was seated in a chair. She was pale and wan and had a rug wrapped round her. Suffolk came to her and told her that the King had sent one of his squires with a message for her. Did she feel well enough to receive him?

'But I must receive the King's squire,' she said.

'Then I will bid him come to you.'

Vaguely she saw a slight young man, simply dressed, with a self-effacing manner. She scarcely looked at him as he knelt before her and presented her with a letter. She took it while he watched her as she read it.

'Is there an answer, my lady?' he asked.

She shook her head. 'I will write to the King when I feel a little better,' she said.

When the squire had gone she lay back in her chair and Alice came in to her.

'I understand,' said Alice, 'that a squire brought a letter to you. What did you think of him?'

'The squire?' cried Margaret. 'I scarcely noticed him.'

Alice began to laugh. 'You have no idea then who that squire was?'

Margaret continued to stare at her.

Alice went on: 'It was the King. He was so eager to see you and he did not want to disturb you by a formal visit so he came as a squire.'

'The King!' cried Margaret aghast. 'My husband. But I allowed him to stay on his knees!'

'Serve him right,' said Alice. 'If he comes as a squire he must expect to be treated as one.'

'Oh Alice,' cried Margaret, 'you ask what I thought of him. I wonder what he thought of me!'

Henry was meanwhile writing to the Archbishop of Canterbury. He had seen the Queen in private and he was delighted with her. She was all that he had believed her to be but it was clear to him that she was still very weak and forsooth they must wait awhile before the marriage could be celebrated.

The marriage was to take place on the 22nd day of April in the Abbey of Tichfield and the Bishop of Salisbury would perform the ceremony. Margaret was quickly recovering from her malady; she was young and healthy and the fact that her indisposition had not been that dreaded one which at first had been feared was a sign, said those about her, that she would be fortunate in her new land. Alice could not help commenting that it would have been even more fortunate if there had been no illness at all, but she did not say so to Margaret who in her weak state of health was happy to be assured of good omens.

She thought a great deal about the humble young squire who had knelt before her; she greatly wished that she had taken more notice of him; but she did know that he had a gentle face and that made her feel reassured.

Henry was thinking a great deal of Margaret. She had seemed so young and frail wrapped in her rugs and he had been overwhelmed by tenderness. She was also very pretty in spite of being pale but that somehow made her vulnerable. He was delighted with what he had seen and he was looking forward to their marriage with an enthusiasm of which he would not have believed himself capable before he had seen her.

He prayed earnestly that the marriage would be a happy one. He was, as ever, desperately in need of funds for a wedding was necessarily an expensive matter and he had been forced to raise money on the crown jewels to pay for it. He had had the wedding ring made from one of gold and rubies which had been given to him by his uncle Cardinal Beaufort. It was his coronation ring. His uncle had so often during his reign come to his aid with the money he would need. The Cardinal seemed to have inexhaustible coffers into which he could plunge in an emergency, and Henry often wondered how, without this uncle, he would have survived all the difficulties which beset him. Now he was going to use the Cardinal's ring for Margaret.

Presents were arriving for the Queen – one of them was rather extraordinary and rather difficult to handle. It was a lion, which after it had been duly admired had to be sent to the menagerie at the Tower.

So the wedding took place. It was not as grand as the proxy wedding in France had been but as the bride and bridegroom held hands they ceased to be afraid of each other and they realised that affection was already beginning to grow.

Solemnly they made their vows and as they listened to the Bishop's address they both inwardly vowed they would do their duty.

'Blessed is everyone that feareth the Lord; that walketh in
  his ways.
For thou shalt eat the labour of thine hands; happy shalt
  thou be and it shall be well with thee
Thy wife shall be as a fruitful vine by the sides of thine
  house; thy children like olive plants round thy table.'

They were young; there were many years before them. It was their duty to produce heirs to the crown. They both vowed they would not be found lacking.

For Margaret Henry was the perfect husband. Gentle, courteous, eager to be loved and to give her the utmost devotion. She recognised his weakness and that endeared him to her. She wanted someone to lead, to guide, to take care of. And she sensed that Henry was just the man for that.

And Henry saw in Margaret the young girl who was lovelier every time he looked at her and he could not forget the small fragile-looking creature he had first seen wrapped in rugs. He had begun to fall in love with her then.

Thus the marriage appeared to have a successful beginning.

For the first few days after the ceremony the royal pair were lodged at the Abbey. They had an exhausting programme ahead of them and Henry felt that after her short convalescence and all the ceremonies of the wedding Margaret needed a rest.

They were pleasant days getting to know each other, Henry revealing his feelings slowly, Margaret becoming more sure of herself as the hours passed.

They would have to go to London for her coronation, Henry explained, and that was to take place at the end of May.

'But first,' Henry told her, 'we must make our progress through the country. Everyone will want to see you. I am anxious to show them what a beautiful bride I have.'

Feeling stronger every day Margaret was growing excited at the prospect of her life as Queen of England. She was realising how dull it had been until now when she had been a background figure – a younger daughter of a King who was not quite a King and was always trying to find some way of avoiding creditors.

She had developed a taste for attention when she had become important in the marriage business and the King of France had seen her as a means of recovering Maine and Anjou. Now she had a country of her own. She had a husband who was already beginning to adore her, to respect her, to talk to her and listen to her opinions. The King ruled the country and the Queen would rule the King. It was a very pleasant prospect.

Alice brought her down to earth sharply.

She had been looking through her wardrobe. 'I had no idea,' said Alice, 'that you had so little with you. What of the clothes you will need for your ride to London? The people expect a show of splendour from a Princess now a Queen.'

'But I have no more than those you see.'

'Those with which you travelled through France. You can't mean that you plan to wear those again. Besides . . . they are not fine enough. Where is the wardrobe your father must have provided for your arrival in England?'

'He provided none.'

Alice sat down on a stool and covered her face with her hands. After a few seconds she stood up. 'I must see my husband at once and he must see the King,' she said.

'But Alice, what a fuss to make about a few clothes!'

'A fuss? By no means. You must make a good impression on the people. They are not very fond of the French you know and they must not have a chance to criticise. They will welcome you because you represent peace. But you must look like a Queen.'

Alice remembered ceremony enough to ask leave to depart. She went at once to her husband who immediately saw the King.

Consternation reigned when the situation was explained, but within a few hours Suffolk's valet John Pole was riding as fast as he could to London and he was commanded to bring back with him – with all speed – a certain Margaret

Chamberlayne who was one of the finest dressmakers in the City.

Within a very short time Mistress Chamberlayne arrived and with her were bales of very fine materials. Several women were immediately found to work to Mistress Chamberlayne's instructions and gowns were made which would be considered suitable for the Queen's progress to London.

Henry, who never cared very much about his own clothes, was delighted to see Margaret splendidly arrayed. Margaret herself was delighted. She was liking England more and more every day.

So the journey to London began. It was a triumph. Margaret was beautiful in her magnificent new garments, her abundant golden hair glowing reddish in the sunshine, streaming about her shoulders; a circlet of gems was on her head, and her blue eyes were alight with excitement; a faint colour glowed in her cheeks, and she looked every bit the fairy Queen as she rode through the countryside with her husband. The fact that she was small and rather fragilely built added to her charm for the people. She looked so dainty. Everywhere she went the daisy was displayed and people who came to see her pass all carried the flower – most of them fabricated – waving them ecstatically.

'The war is over,' they said. 'This marriage means peace.'

So they cheered and the cheers were for peace as well as for Margaret; and when they shouted 'Long Live the Queen' they meant also 'Prosperity is coming'.

It was a warm welcome and it was for her. They made that clear. It was time their King married and gave them an heir and here was the bride – a bride from France to settle the war. Now there would be a coronation and then a royal birth. And no more war. Good times were coming.

At length they arrived at Eltham Palace and there stayed for a few days to prepare themselves for the journey into London. Margaret knew that now the important ceremonies were about to begin. But Henry's devotion to her was growing every day and she felt complete confidence in her power to charm his people as she had their King. She had not met anyone so far who had not expressed delight in the marriage; but she did know that there were some who were opposed to it. The powerful Duke of Gloucester was one and she must be ready for him when he appeared, as he most certainly would.

From Eltham the royal party set out for Blackheath and there coming towards them was a procession consisting of all the high dignitaries of London. The mayor, the aldermen and the sheriffs of the city made a colourful spectacle in their scarlet gowns while the craftsmen who accompanied them were in vivid blue with embroidery on their sleeves and hoods of vivid red. They had come hither, the mayor told her in his welcoming speech, to conduct her into the City of London.

Margaret responded graciously and was exceedingly glad that Alice had noticed how ill equipped she would have been to face such a brilliant assembly. She could never be grateful enough for Alice's care – nor for that of the Marquess. I shall insist that they are duly rewarded, she promised herself. Henry will be willing to do anything that I ask him to.

Another party had arrived at Blackheath. This was led by a man of great importance. She could not help but be aware of that. It was apparent in the looks of almost near reverence in the faces of those about her. They were astonished too. He was old but handsome in a raddled way; he was most splendidly attired and the livery of his attendants was dazzling.

He rode up to the Queen, bowed low and made a fulsome speech of welcome.

Margaret was responding with her usual grace when the King said: 'My lady, I should present you to my uncle the Duke of Gloucester.'

The Duke of Gloucester! The enemy! She could see the wise old face of her uncle Charles; she could hear his voice: 'You will have to beware of the Duke of Gloucester.'

She was too young to have learned to hide her feelings. This was the man who had done everything to oppose her marriage. He was going to try to undermine her. His wife was in captivity because she had made a waxen image of Henry with the purpose of destroying him. The enemy indeed.

'I thank you, my lord, for coming to welcome me,' she said coldly and turned away.

Everyone about her was aware of the snub to mighty Gloucester and knowing he had inherited his share of the famous Plantagenet temper, they awaited developments in an awed silence.

Gloucester however did not appear to notice the slight. He was very gracious and when he wished to be, in spite of his ravaged looks, he could be charming.

'What a pleasure,' he said, 'to find our Queen so beautiful. The King is a man to be envied for more than his dominions.'

'There are always those to envy kings,' said Margaret. 'It is to be expected, and accepted as long as they do not attempt to replace them.'

Margaret had always had a ready tongue and it was something she had never learned to control. In her grandmother's household she had never been seriously provoked; but she had heard so much about Gloucester's opposition to her marriage and she was too young to hide her resentment.

'Ah,' said Gloucester, 'that is wisdom indeed. But who, my lady, would not wish to be in the King's place now that he possesses such a blooming bride?'

'You are gracious.'

'My lady, I would welcome you to the country, which I am sure you will rule well . . . with the King.'

He had turned so that his magnificently caparisoned horse was side by side with hers.

'It would give me great pleasure,' he said, 'if you would rest at my Palace of Greenwich for some refreshment before proceeding into London. The people are going to love you so much that they may impede your progress with their cheers and their pageants. They all wish to show you how delighted they are that you have come to us.'

Margaret was about to say that she was in no need of refreshment and had no intention of resting at his Palace of Greenwich when the King said: 'That is gracious of you, uncle. The Queen will enjoy seeing Greenwich.'

There was nothing she could say after that but she did not glance at the Duke riding beside her and she wondered that Henry could be so affable to one who, everyone said, was his enemy.

The Duke riding beside her was smiling gaily. He talked to her about Greenwich and how fond of the place he had become since it had passed to him through his Beaufort uncle. Not the Cardinal whom she had met but his brother Thomas, Duke of Exeter.

'I was granted a further two hundred acres in which to make a park. I have done this so we have some good hunting there. You like the chase, my lady?'

'I do.'

'Then you will find great pleasure in some of our forests. I always say we have the best in the world. When I was granted the land I had to agree to embattle the manor, and make a tower and a ditch ... and all this I have done. So I shall proudly welcome you to Greenwich.'

She rode along in silence, her colour heightened, her head held high.

So they paused at Greenwich and afterwards made their way through Southwark and into the City of London. The pageants so astonished and delighted her that she forgot the unpleasant encounter with Gloucester. London had surpassed itself. The citizens revelled in pageantry and this show they were putting on to welcome the Queen was a prelude to all the rejoicing that would take place at the coronation.

All the tableaux and scenes which were enacted were for the union of Henry and Margaret and the theme was that for which they had all been longing. Peace. It was true they had all believed that peace would come with the conquest of France. There had been a time some twenty years before when that dream had seemed to be at hand. And then Henry the Fifth had died suddenly, cur down in his prime, and since then the scene had changed.

Well, if this was not great victory, it was peace and peace would mean an end to the exorbitant taxation which had been crippling trade and making them all poor.

At the bridge at Southwark the pageant represented Peace and Plenty. There was one puppet display with Justice and Peace as the figures. These approached each other and after much juggling met in the kiss of peace. Then Saint Margaret appeared; and there were dancers and children reciting and in the hair of every girl was a daisy.

It was a great triumph. Henry was delighted with the impression she had made on the people and refused to have his spirits lowered by the knowledge that they were cheering a peace which had not yet been made. The marriage had taken place, yes . . . but the only concession which had been agreed on was a truce. We must have peace, Cardinal Beaufort had said; and Henry agreed with him.

'My brother would rise up and curse you if he could,' was Gloucester's comment. 'Peace. Never. We are going to fight on until we put the French crown where it belongs: on the head of the King of England.'

Gloucester was hot-headed. He always had been. But why had he come to Blackheath and been so affable? And Margaret had shown her contempt for him. He must explain to her.

He did.

'I could not understand,' she told him, 'how you could have been so gracious to him. He is no friend of yours.'

'That I know well. I don't trust him. I always double the guards when he is near. I am sure he would do me some harm if he could.'

'And yet you behaved as though he were your very dear uncle!'

'He was playing a part, Margaret. I had to play one too.'

'I could not hide what I felt.'

He smiled at her tenderly. 'You are so good, so honest. But, my dearest, Gloucester is a dangerous man. He has his followers. He has always been a favourite with the Londoners.'

'Then the Londoners are false to you.'

'Indeed not. You saw their welcome. They are powerful, you know. They stand on their own at times . . . If they express their disapproval we have to be wary.'

'And you . . . a King.'

Henry laughed. 'Dear Margaret, you are wise and clever. But you have something to learn.'

She did not answer but she thought: 'I will never accept those who are my enemies. I will not pretend to love them.'

Meanwhile Gloucester was discussing the Queen with the Duke of York. There was a bond between them. They both believed they had a claim to the throne. Gloucester would have to wait for his nephew to die; but York descending on both sides of the family from Edward the Third and through his mother from the Duke of Clarence, who had been older than John of Gaunt, secretly believed he had a higher claim than Henry himself. So Gloucester felt he could be sure of York's agreement.

'She slighted me,' said Gloucester. 'I wonder I did not ride off right away. The impulse to do so was there. But I restrained myself.'

'You restrained yourself admirably. We were all astounded. You seemed as though you positively admired the girl.'

'She is pretty enough, I grant you. But there is a strong will there. I can see our Henry will be as wax in her hands.'

'Then it will be the Queen with whom we have to deal.'

Gloucester clenched his fist. 'I will think twice before I submit to the will of a woman . . . and a French one at that. This is a disastrous marriage. We have given away so much and gained what? A French Queen! Mark my words, we shall be called upon to give away more. We should be waging war on France, not making a marriage with her.'

'We have gained little, it is true. Minorca, Majorca! Empty titles! And they are after Maine . . . ?'

'I tell you this,' said the Duke of Gloucester, 'I shall not allow the daughter of so-called King René to insult me with impunity.'

'The little girl will have to learn her place,' agreed York, 'and that means that although she is allowed to sit on a throne and wear a crown on her pretty head she will have to take account of her noble subjects.'

'Ah yes, our dainty little Queen has much to learn.'

At the end of May the coronation took place. It was a splendid occasion and the people crowded to Westminster to have a share in it. There was rejoicing throughout the capital and in spite of the fact that the royal exchequer had to be drained to its dregs to provide for it, all seemed very satisfied.

Wine flowed from the conduits in the streets of London; the people danced and sang.

'This marriage means peace,' they declared. 'Peace at last. Long live King Henry and his pretty little Queen.'

They would not remain for long in this state of euphoria.

Chapter V

MYSTERIOUS DEATH

Margaret was happy. Henry was all she could have wished and he was devoted to her. He had had her emblem of the daisy shown in every possible place; it had even been enamelled and engraved on his plate.

'The young fool is besotted by the French wench,' commented Gloucester.

He would have his revenge, though. He would be equal with them all. He had never managed to outwit that wily old bird the Cardinal, nor Suffolk; but he would have done but for that unfortunate matter over Eleanor and the waxen image. He often wondered not how such a clever woman could have become involved in such practices but how she could have been so careless as to have been caught. She had been working for his advancement, of course. She had wanted to see him on the throne.

He would have been there but for people like the Cardinal and Suffolk. They thought they were clever arranging this French marriage but they had not seen the end of that yet. All they had was a temporary truce, and the French would soon be making further demands. He could see it coming.

Meanwhile Margaret revelled in her role as Queen. She dazzled Henry with her prettiness and her quick wit. She visited the Cardinal at his mansion of Waltham and there she was received with great pleasure.

The old man delighted in her youthful charm. She was such a dainty creature and he was amused to think that such a delicate-seeming person could conceal a woman of strong will which she undoubtedly was.

But she was willing to submit that will to him.

'I know,' she told him, 'that there is so much I have to learn and I want you to teach me.'

This seemed the utmost wisdom to the Cardinal for in spite of the adulation she was receiving she realised her short-comings and she could not have sought a better teacher.

His old eyes misted over as he watched the beautiful young creature and she raised her blue eyes to his and said: 'I shall never forget our first meeting. I knew then that you would be my friend.'

'You are so young and yet from the first I saw your latent wisdom,' said the Cardinal. 'There is no one on earth I would rather see than you beside the King on the throne.'

'I hope I may come and see you often now that you do not always find it easy to come to Court.'

'What a plague old age is when a beautiful Queen invites a man to Court and he is too infirm to take advantage of the honour. My dearest lady, whenever you come to see me I shall deem it the greatest honour that could befall me.'

Margaret enjoyed such compliments, particularly coming from this old man of the Church who was, she had quickly sensed even now, the most important man in England.

He talked to her of affairs in England. He said that what

England needed was peace and he was sure the King realised this. She was heartily in agreement with that because it was exactly what her uncle the King of France wanted. The trouble, she knew, was that he wanted it on certain terms which the English might not be prepared to give.

He talked of Gloucester. His hatred for the Duke was in every inflection of his voice, every gesture, every expression which flitted across the old face.

'Gloucester has been at the root of all our trouble. In his first marriage he offended Burgundy when Burgundy's friendship was of vital importance to us. He was a menace to his brother Bedford, as fine a man as ever came out of England and almost as great a soldier as his brother the late King. 'Twas a pity Gloucester was not strangled at birth. He has caused nothing but trouble in this realm.'

'I hate him,' said Margaret vehemently. 'So does Henry. He doubles the guards when he is around.'

'You must be wary of him. He hates your marriage. He wanted the King to have one of the daughters of the Count of Armagnac. He does not want peace. He wants to continue the war.'

'Did his wife plot against the King?'

'Yes, she made waxen images with a witch and some sooth-sayers. They got their just deserts. She has been a captive ever since.'

'Why was Gloucester allowed to go free?'

'He was not suspected of plotting against the King's life.'

'I feel sure he was involved. Henry thinks so.'

'Well, that is Gloucester. Be careful of him. He will harm you if he can. You have a good friend in the Marquess of Suffolk.'

'I have, and the Marchioness is my dearest friend.'

'Cling to them. And the Shrewsburys. Kings and Queens have many enemies.'

'They will not get the better of me,' said Margaret.

When she next came to Waltham the Cardinal showed her a chamber he had had prepared for her. He called it the Queen's Chamber and the Cardinal had gone to great expense to furnish it elaborately with hangings of cloth and of gold from Damascus.

Margaret was delighted with it. She felt that with such friends as the Cardinal and the Suffolks she cared nothing for her enemies. And she was not going to put up any pretence of liking them. She would make it very clear to the Duke of Gloucester that she regarded him as an enemy.

Margaret was delighted with the friends who rallied round her. With such as them what had she to fear from a few enemies? She was already assembling what was known as the Court Party, and she insisted on Alice's being in constant attendance.

Alice was delighted, but she was wise enough to know that the joyous feeling which at the time prevailed throughout the country could not last. Her husband was worried, too.

'It is only a truce, that's what they don't realise,' he said. 'There has to be a reckoning soon and then the question of Maine and Anjou will arise again. When the people know what price we have had to pay for peace they will blame me.'

'They must not do so,' cried Alice. 'What have you done but what you consider best for England?'

'My dear, one's intentions get little consideration. If one is successful one is a noble hero; if one fails, a villain.'

'Oh come, William,' said Alice. 'You are strong enough to stand against them.'

'I fear Gloucester.'

'He has not the same power these days.'

'He could always make trouble and now his friendship with York is growing.'

'York. What is his grievance?'

'That he doesn't wear the crown.'

'Why this is a nonsense.'

'It would seem so. But he reckons *he* comes nearer through Clarence than Lancaster does through John of Gaunt.'

'That is going back a good way.'

'That matters not. There is a certain reason in it.'

'Oh, no, it is too far back.'

'As you say, it is far back and there are closer matters with which to concern myself. I have to face the Parliament. Well, I can tell them that the delegation will be coming to England to discuss the truce and that in the meantime I am advising the strengthening of the frontiers round Maine.'

'That should please them.'

'For the time being. But the reckoning is coming. I want them to know that whatever is arranged it is none of my doing.'

Alice looked at him a little dubiously. She did not remind him that when a man set out to guide a country's policy, to be the most important minister in the land, he would surely be blamed if anything went wrong.

'The Queen settles in happily, it seems,' she said to change the subject.

'Is she really beginning to lead the King?'

'I can see it coming. She was born to lead and he to be led so the outcome is inevitable.'

'Alice, try to restrain her a little.'

'It is difficult. She is honest by nature. She finds it hard not to speak her mind. She lets it be known that she regards Gloucester with something like venom. She is sure that he is plotting to destroy the King.'

'She is probably right but she should not say these things. Gloucester will show his hand if she goes much farther. At the moment he is pretending to support the marriage – which we know full well he did everything he could to prevent. I distrust him in this mood.'

'Margaret does not yet understand the devious ways of statesmen.'

'She must learn to, Alice.'

Alice lifted her shoulders. 'She is a lady of very strong views. She will go her own way, I think.'

'If anyone can influence her, you can.'

'She is fiercely loyal. She is affectionate. But she will not prevaricate. No matter what one tried to make her she would always be Margaret of Anjou.'

'And the King?'

'He thinks that the words which fall from *her* lips are pure wisdom.'

'She has managed to enchant him.'

'He loves her strength. It appeals to his weakness. And she is very pretty but small and that seems to make her especially attractive to a man like Henry. He feels protective when he looks at her, knowing all the time that he will rely on her to protect him.'

'Well, Alice, we must pray that we can extricate ourselves from this situation with skill so that we are not blamed for any of the demands which will have to be made.'

It seemed that he might do so, for when in the Parliament he explained that although there was no real peace with France, only a truce, that the frontiers of Maine and Anjou were being strengthened and that a delegation was coming to England, he was applauded.

The Commons congratulated him on the manner in which he had conducted affairs, and when the Duke of Gloucester moved a motion to the same effect in the Lords, he felt he had come through very well indeed.

But very quickly he became more uneasy than ever. When Gloucester complimented him he ought to be very wary indeed.

It was, he knew, only a respite.

The French Embassy had arrived in England.

From the City they came by barge to Westminster where Henry, with Margaret, was waiting to receive them. With them were the Duke of Gloucester, the Duke of Buckingham and the Earl of Warwick. Margaret was very interested to meet this last nobleman for Henry had told her a great deal about his tutor, the Earl of Warwick, and he appeared to have had a great affection for that stern old man. This was not that Earl of Warwick, however, but a very ambitious young man of about seventeen or eighteen, a certain Richard Neville who had come to the title through his marriage with old Warwick's daughter Anne Beauchamp. Also present were the Archbishops of Canterbury and York. The French Embassy was headed by the Counts of Vendôme and Laval and the Archbishop of Rheims.

It soon became very clear that there was only one condition

which the King of France would consider in making peace and that was the surrender of Maine. It was the great issue. He knew, and the English knew, that once that province was surrendered the English hope of claiming the French crown would be over.

When they were alone Margaret discussed the matter with Henry.

'You want peace,' she said. 'You should give up Maine. I know my uncle well. If he says that is the only condition, he will insist on it. He means it.'

'Oh, he means it,' said Henry. 'I have no doubt of that. If it rested with me alone I would say: Take Maine, let us have no more war. No more loss of life. No more high taxation. But the people . . . what will they say? My father gained so much. They have come to expect victories.'

'They have had very few of late.'

'No, not since the Maid came. But they believe that will pass. This war, you see, has been going on and on and up and down. It is down now but they think it will go up again.'

'And yet they protest about paying taxes for it.'

'People always protest about paying taxes. They want the war to end . . . but victoriously for us.'

'Henry, the English are beaten.'

'The English are never beaten until the last battle.'

'Do not have any more battles. They are useless, Henry. They bring you no good.'

'I know. War is waste of men and materials. People should be enjoying the beauties of life. But what can I do?'

'Give up Maine,' said Margaret softly.

Gloucester was gleeful. The Cardinal was a sick man and had had to retire from affairs. One enemy the less, thought Gloucester.

He now concentrated his attack on Suffolk.

Suffolk was a friend of the French. He had brought the Frenchwoman over. He was going to sell English possessions in France to the French just to buy the King a pretty French wife.

Were the people going to stand by and allow this to happen? Gloucester knew how to set up a whispering campaign. He was going to bring Suffolk down and perhaps the King and Queen. Who knew what would happen then? Perhaps his dream would be realised. He was the next of kin.

York believed that he had a chance. York before Lancaster! He was a very ambitious man. During the negotiations for the marriage of Margaret and the King, York had been in correspondence with the King of France trying to arrange a marriage for his eldest son Edward with one of Charles's daughters. Young Edward must be about three years old. Oh yes, York was ambitious all right and he had his eyes firmly fixed on the throne.

All very good. He would be a good adversary of Suffolk.

Gloucester went to see York. He was getting friendly with him. So it was when men had a similar aim, although the goal might not be the same for they were both after the crown.

'What think you of this conference?' he asked York.

'The French are asking for the return of Maine and Anjou.'

'And what say you as a soldier to that?'

'That it is tantamount to saying goodbye to the crown of France.'

'So say I. But we have married our King to a French

Princess, have we not, and this is the price asked for her. The price of peace and Margaret.'

'We already have her. Maine is for peace.'

The two men fell silent, then Gloucester said: 'Our little Queen is very partial to Suffolk.'

'She would be. She looks upon him as the maker of her marriage.'

'*Very* fond of Suffolk.'

'And his wife.'

'But particularly Suffolk.'

'You don't mean . . . ?'

'Why not? She is young and lusty and I doubt Henry can give a good account of himself.'

'Nay . . . Suffolk is devoted to Alice Chaucer and Alice is Margaret's dear friend.'

'What has that to do with the matter? This devotion to Suffolk can be for only one reason.'

'Suffolk is an old man.'

'Some girls like a little maturity, particularly when they are saddled with a young boy.'

'The King is hardly that.'

'In manners he is.'

'I can't believe it.'

'How explain this devotion then?'

'Well, he brought her over. He arranged her marriage. He was the first Englishman she had contact with . . . He and the Cardinal. She is devoted to the Cardinal too.'

'I believe there is a special relationship between Suffolk and Margaret.'

York shrugged his shoulders. He was a little impatient. Gloucester had always been a fool, always plunging into wild adventures. Now he was letting his imagination run away with him.

Nevertheless within a very short time the scandal was being whispered in the taverns. 'Have you heard . . . ? Well, it must be true. I heard it from someone at Court. Yes . . . the Queen and whom do you think . . . Suffolk!'

The Queen Suffolk's mistress! It was incredible. Could it be believed? She looked so young and innocent. 'But,' it was said, 'you know the French. After all she *is* French. She is one of the enemy.'

'They say the French are demanding that we give up all King Henry gained. He would turn in his grave.'

'But we won't. We can't. The Duke of Gloucester will see to that.'

The people were becoming convinced that something had been arranged while the French Embassy was in London, and it was being kept from them.

The Queen was persuading the King to agree to the French proposals. Of course she was. She was one of them. She was the enemy.

People no longer carried the daisy. Something was very wrong, and they blamed Margaret.

You could never trust the French, they said. Margaret's brief popularity was at an end.

When Suffolk heard the rumours he knew without a doubt who had set them in motion. He was aware of the friendship between York and Gloucester. They were working up a case against him and the fact that they had brought Margaret's name in showed clearly that they were trying to turn the King against him.

It was no use delaying. It was quite obvious that Maine would have to be given up. The Queen was persuading the King and the King wanted to please her and bring about peace.

It had to be. Suffolk would have agreed at once if he had not feared the effect on the people, knowing that they would make him the scapegoat. Gloucester would see to that. That he was already working his mischief was clear.

Suffolk came to see the King. It was not difficult to play on his fears, and he was always ready to believe the worst of Gloucester. That matter of the Duchess's involvement with the Witch of Eye and the others had had a marked effect on Henry. He believed that one day his uncle would stage a coup, murder him and take the throne.

Therefore it was simple.

Gloucester had made a long speech in Parliament urging that the truce be violated. He was working up feeling against the French and that meant the King's marriage.

'You see, Sire,' said Suffolk, 'we have to take some action. We know well that he is in collusion with York. Gloucester at least may be plotting against your very person.'

'It would not surprise me,' said Henry. 'His wife did it once and I believe he may well have been with her. He is waiting his chance to try again.'

'Sire, in my opinion we should call him to face the Parliament and answer certain charges against him.'

The King hesitated. It was a pity that the Cardinal had retired to Waltham. He could go and see him, of course, but the old man was quite aloof from politics now.

Henry had to make his own decision.

'Where is Gloucester now?' he asked.

'I have heard, my lord, that he is in Wales.'

'In Wales? What would he be doing there?'

'Stirring up trouble, doubtless. I have heard that he is getting together an army.'

'To come against me! Oh, I am weary of this uncle of mine. He has been nothing but a menace for as long as I can remember.'

'Bring him before Parliament and let him answer to the charges brought against him. Parliament will be meeting at Bury on the tenth of February. Is it your wish, my lord, that Gloucester be summoned to attend?'

'Yes,' said the King, 'that is my wish.'

So Gloucester was summoned to Bury to attend the Parliament and answer certain charges which would be brought against him.

Gloucester was dead. The country was stunned. They knew, of course, that he had been murdered. In the towns and the countryside they talked of it.

The news spread rapidly. He had been riding through Lavenham to Bury. Many had seen him – just the same as usual, splendidly dressed, smiling and acknowledging the cheers of the people, certain of his popularity. Many of them knew that he was something of a rogue but they liked his roguery. The King was a saint, they said. Everyone could not be that and saints were uncomfortable people. Yes, they liked a rogue and for all his debaucheries and follies Gloucester had kept his place in their hearts. His marriage to a woman who was humble compared with him, his devotion to her, was appealing. It persisted and even now he was trying to obtain her release. Yes, Gloucester was a popular figure.

And what had happened? Riding to Bury he had been intercepted by the King's guard, ordered to return to his lodgings and after a few days it was announced that he was dead. He had fallen sick and died. The people simply did not believe that he had died from natural causes.

The weather was bad, of course – many people had died of cold – it had been the worst winter many remembered; the Thames had been frozen and so had almost every river in the country. The Duke had lived too well for the years not to have taken some toll of him. But sudden death? No.

The day after his death his body was exhibited. The lords and the knights of the Parliament and the people flocked to see it. There was no sign of foul play. There were dark hints about Edward the Second who had died mysteriously in Berkeley Castle. They had inserted a red hot poker into him, destroyed his internal organs, and there had been no sign of foul play on his body except that expression of agony on his cold, still face. It was all very well for his enemies to express their grief and send Gloucester's body to be taken in pomp to St Albans to be laid in the fair vault which had been prepared for him during his lifetime. It was not good enough. The people would not believe that he had died by natural causes.

Moreover the servants of his household had been arrested. They were accused of plotting to make Duke Humphrey King. Gloucester's illegitimate son known as Arthur was arrested with them and he, including four others, was condemned to die the traitor's death.

Henry was very unhappy. He could not help feeling relieved that that arch-troublemaker Gloucester had been removed but at the same time he hated the thought of men being subjected to the horrible traitor's death.

'They have plotted against you,' Margaret reminded him.

'If they have done so it was at Gloucester's orders,' said Henry. 'He was the one to be blamed.'

'Well, he has paid the price now.'

'What do you mean?' asked Henry quickly.

'I mean that God has taken him in the midst of his iniquities.'

'I hope a priest was with him at the end.'

'Oh Henry,' laughed Margaret, 'will you always love your enemies?'

Suffolk came to see them. He did not want to talk of the rumours which were growing. They were too embarrassing. It was quite absurd to link his name with Margaret's. Alice could laugh at the idea. Others might not.

But he saw that if the members of Gloucester's household were condemned it would be tantamount to saying that there had been a plot, and if there had, it would seem that Gloucester might well have been murdered.

He laid the matter before the King. 'The Duke of Gloucester died as he acted throughout his life,' he said. 'By which I mean he died to cause the most inconvenience to those around him. I do not believe there was a plot against the crown. If there was, people will say that Gloucester was murdered . . . without trial. That is not so. If there was no plot then it seems very probable that Gloucester died a natural death which would be the happiest solution. My lord, I think our best plan is to free these servants of the late Duke.'

Nothing could please Henry better. Now he would not be disturbed by the revolting things that would be done to those men. He grasped at the idea.

'Let us free them,' he said. 'They have been punished

enough by contemplating a terrible fate. Yes, let them go free. There was no plot. My uncle died of his years and the strain he had put on them by a life of debauchery.'

So they were freed. But that did not stop the rumours.

The people still adhered to the story that Gloucester had been murdered. He was the enemy of the Duke of Suffolk, and the Queen had shown that she hated him.

The Queen had helped plan the murder, they whispered, and if she had not actually carried it out she was as guilty as those who had.

So Margaret, who had ridden through the streets of London to the acclaim of the people and the waving of daisies, was now branded 'Adulteress. Murderess. And French!'

Margaret found it difficult to understand the change in the attitude of the people towards her. When she rode out she was greeted with sullen stares. They did not abuse her. They whispered as she passed by, and she looked in vain for the daisies.

Bewildered and hurt, she demanded of Alice: 'Why do they blame me for Gloucester's death?'

'They will always blame someone,' Alice consoled her. 'They blame William, too.'

'It is true that I hated him,' said Margaret. 'But others must have done so too.'

'The people always look for scapegoats in high places,' Alice reminded her.

'It makes me unhappy and . . . uneasy.'

Yes, thought Alice, it should do that.

She said: 'You will have to act very carefully now. You must not show your pleasure in his death.'

Margaret shrugged her shoulders. She found it very hard to hide her feelings and she could not but feel relieved by the death of Gloucester.

She went to Grafton to see the Cardinal. He would have advice to offer her.

She was horrified to find him in his bed. He looked very ill – far worse than when she had last seen him.

She felt she could not burden him with her troubles. In any case he seemed too ill to listen to them. He was pleased to see her though and she sat by his bedside and tried to be cheerful.

He must get better, she told him. She needed him.

'You will do well,' he said. 'You will look after the King.'

Only once did he mention Gloucester. 'That trouble-maker has gone,' he said. 'Well, it was a fitting end. Do you know I have been told that some have accused me of having a part in his death.' His face creased into a smile. 'You see me in no fit state to do murder.'

'They will say anything . . . anything!' cried Margaret vehemently.

'Indeed it is so. But these things are quickly forgotten. They look round. "Who was Gloucester's enemy?" they say. "Oh . . . the cardinal." Everyone knew of the enmity between us. It had been there for years. I always saw what a menace he was to the crown, to England. A pity others did not see it also. His brother Bedford did. Well, he has gone now. He can make no more trouble here on earth. And you, dear child, forgive my temerity in speaking to my Queen thus, but you are to me a very dear child and I love you and have great faith in you. You can be exactly what our King needs. He loves you. Who would not? You must guide him always, dear lady. Care for the King always . . . He will need your care. He is surrounded by enemies . . . but the greatest of them is dead now. Take care of him . . .'

'I will, I will,' said Margaret fervently. 'But you talk as though you are going to leave us. You are not. I forbid it. You will stay with us. I need you.'

'God bless you,' said the Cardinal.

She sat by his bed but she could see how tired he was. He tried to struggle up when she left but she would not have it. She bent over and kissed him.

'I shall come to you again . . . soon,' she said.

But she did not for within a few weeks the Cardinal was dead.

Her grief was great. She had lost her worst enemy she believed and so soon after her best friend.

❧ ❧ ❧

Alice was very worried. She did not like the rumours which were circulating about Gloucester's death. She spoke to her husband about it.

'You worry unduly,' he assured her. 'Gloucester's death is the best thing that could happen to us.'

'Yes, it would have been if he had died without mystery.'

'The mystery will be forgotten shortly. In the meantime there is much to gain. Gloucester was rich and what will happen to his estates? His wife, a captive suspected of plotting against the King's life through witchcraft, can claim nothing. There will be his estates to dispose of. We shall do not badly out of that, I promise you.'

'I was not thinking of estates,' said Alice.

'As I said you worry yourself unduly. All will be well.

Margaret will have some of the estates but we shall have our share.'

Alice shivered.

'What is the matter with you?'

'Nothing. If you say all is well, all is well.'

He looked at her seriously. He was very fond of Alice and had never regretted their marriage. She had given him two sons and a daughter and it had been a very successful union. She was wise, too, and she did communicate a certain element of her apprehension to him. He admitted it at length.

'Gloucester was my enemy,' he said, 'and Gloucester was a fool.'

'Exactly,' replied Alice. 'You know now what I have in mind.'

'There will be another enemy . . . less foolish perhaps.'

Alice nodded. 'And you know who that will be.'

Suffolk replied in one syllable: 'York.'

'He will not be so reckless or so foolish as Gloucester.'

'If the King could get an heir that would make it less easy for York.'

'York will still be there. There is a purpose in him. He will bide his time.'

'But if the Queen produces a son the people will love the child. Margaret will regain some of the popularity she has lost.'

'If she gets a child.'

'Is there no sign then?'

'None. She would tell me if there were. I know that she is impatient and frustrated because she does not seem to be able to conceive.'

'A child will make such a difference. The people might even take to wearing daisies again.'

'We must pray for a child.'

'With fervour. We need that child. In the meantime don't fret about York. He must bide his time.'

'And he will,' said Alice.

'In the meantime there will be a child. There must . . . and why should there not be? They are both young and healthy. The King dotes on her and she is fond of the King. It will come. It is because they are over anxious that they fail.'

Alice laid her hand on his arm. 'We must be watchful of York.'

Her husband nodded.

It was a few days later when he came back to her obviously in very high spirits.

'News, my love,' he said. 'I think you will find it good.'

She looked at him expectantly.

'York is to be banished to Ireland.'

'Banished?'

'Well, it is tantamount to that. He has been appointed to be the King's Lieutenant there for ten years. That will put him out of the picture for a while.'

'He must be furious.'

'He is. But what can he do? He cannot say: I want to stay in England and make an attempt on the crown, now can he? He must submit with a good grace. I have an idea that he will delay his departure for as long as he can. Never mind. He must go to Ireland.'

'Henry agreed?'

'I only had to tell him it was a good thing and Margaret helped as I had previously explained everything to her.'

'It seems that one must go to the Queen before the King.'

'Well, that is true. Margaret means to rule, and Henry is

only too pleased to let someone else take over the role that he never really wanted.'

'It is very good news indeed.'

'There is more to come. There are some weighty titles coming our way. I already have the Earldom of Pembroke.'

'From Gloucester's estate?' added Alice quietly.

'Well, yes, and not only that but Chamberlain and Constable of Dover and Lord Warden of the Cinque Ports. I am to be Admiral of England as well. What do you think of that?'

'I am overwhelmed and so must you be with so many honours.'

'And in addition, my lady Marchioness, how would you like to become a Duchess?'

'So . . . that as well.'

'Behold the Duke of Suffolk.'

'The King must be very pleased with you. He must love you well.'

'The King,' said the new Duke of Suffolk, 'and the Queen as well.'

Chapter VI

NICHOLAS OF THE TOWER

Henry was happier than he had ever been. He was delighted with his marriage. He believed he was surrounded by good ministers headed by the Duke of Suffolk, but he was grieved that his great-uncle the Cardinal had died. That had been a sadness and Margaret had felt it deeply. She had dearly loved the old man and she was very touched that he had left her all the fine scarlet damask and the bed which he had had made specially for her on her visits to Grafton.

'I shall always treasure them,' she said but she wept bitterly and was sad every time she saw them.

She was recovering from her grief though, and she was interested in Henry's plans for building. They visited the work frequently. He had enjoyed showing Margaret the College of the Blessed Mary of Eton beside Windsor. He had explained to her how interesting it had been studying the plans for the building and what a boon it would be to scholars. They would go on from the college to the one he was building at Cambridge. He was going to call it College Royal or King's College to Our Lady and St Nicholas.

Margaret was very interested. She said she would very much like to found a college herself.

Indeed she should, said Henry, and he thought how much pleasanter this was than the perpetual negotiations and plans for war.

Together they went to Cambridge and there Margaret met a certain Andrew Doket who was the rector of St Botolph's there. He was very gratified by the interest of the King and Queen because he had already laid the foundation stones and he was seeking help in bringing about the building of a college. It was his greatest ambition but a lack of funds was a tremendous handicap to progress, but in view of royal interest his hopes were soaring and since Margaret wished to found a college why should she not work in conjunction with Doket?

He had intended to call the college The College of St Bernard as before he had become rector of St Botolph's he had been the principal of the St Bernard Hostel. But he was ready enough to change the name in order to get the college built and it was decided that it should be called Queen's College of St Margaret and St Bernard.

Thus Margaret had a project to equal that of the King and they spent many happy hours glowing with enthusiasm, discussing plans and visiting sites. They had literature in common too. Margaret was very fond of Boccaccio's work and she and Henry read this together. Then there was the hunt to occupy her. Henry did not follow her quite so enthusiastically in this but Margaret loved to ride for after a few hours over her books she found the chase invigorating. She loved to ride ahead of the rest of the party, to be the first in at the kill. That was something Henry liked to avoid, for bloodshed, even of animals, was abhorrent to him.

When Margaret discovered that certain of the courtiers had been hunting in the royal forest she immediately gave orders that the game should be preserved absolutely for her use. Henry had never given such orders and the fact that Margaret did so without consulting him indicated her imperious nature. Why should she have consulted Henry? she would have asked. He would agree to give her what she wanted. And that was the truth. Henry was living in a state of blissful happiness. He had a beautiful Queen whom he loved and who loved him. The foolish war with France was petering out. He had made peace by his marriage and Margaret and he with their books and music and founding their colleges were happy.

They had no child as yet and that was a source of regret; but it would come. Margaret was very young and he was not old.

When their child was born, they would have reached perfection.

He deeply regretted the death of the Cardinal but then as though to balance that, Gloucester was dead also. York was to go to Ireland – although he was taking a long time to set out. Everything could be safely left in the capable hands of the Duke of Suffolk and Henry need only concern himself with his happy life.

And it *was* a happy time. He and Margaret made a tour of the country's monasteries. They went to the Austin Friary at Lynn and as far north as Durham.

In the midst of all these mutual pleasures Margaret received letters from France; among them was one from her father. There had been great delays, he complained, and he begged her for the good of England, he said, as well as for that of France, to urge the surrender of Maine to the King of France.

Margaret thought of the matter a great deal. She knew that the

English were clinging to Maine as one of the most important of their possessions in France. They should give it up. It belonged to France and if it were returned to that country her father would profit, for it would be restored to the House of Anjou.

She wrote to her father. 'I will do your pleasure as much as lies in my power as I have done already.'

She and Henry had had a happy day. They had been to the colleges and had indulged in a little friendly rivalry which delighted Henry.

She was so amiable, so amusing and so very beautiful. He was singularly blessed in his marriage, he told himself.

When they were in their apartment she sat at his feet with a book on her lap. She would read aloud to him; but after reading for a while she laid aside the book and said: 'Oh, I wish we could have absolute peace. I think if I could have a child and peace between our countries I would know perfect happiness.'

'The child will come,' said Henry. 'And peace . . . well, there is no active war at this time.'

'We have a truce!' she cried. 'What is a truce? It means that war can break out at any moment.'

'Yes,' he agreed solemnly.

'And it could be ended at once.'

Henry shook his head.

'Yes,' she insisted. 'Maine. That is all that stands between us and an end to this war.'

'If I thought . . .'

'Yes?' she asked eagerly. 'If you thought that giving up Maine would end the war you would give it up?'

'Yes,' he cried. 'Yes, yes.'

She rose and coming close to him put her arms round his neck.

'Then it is done,' she said.

He shook his head. 'The Parliament . . .'

'The Parliament. You are the King. Oh Henry, I cannot bear it when you let others rule you. You are the King. It is for *you* to say.'

'Yes, it is for me to say,' he repeated.

She brought pen and paper to him. 'Henry, write this. Say that you will give up Maine . . . for peace.'

Henry hesitated but only for a moment. She was so earnest and so beautiful. She was clever too. Far more so than he was. And he did want to please her.

Moreover he desperately wanted peace.

She was triumphant. It was done. The King had agreed to surrender Maine.

So Maine was to be surrendered and Edmund Beaufort, Duke of Somerset and nephew of the Cardinal, was in France with Adam Moleyns, Bishop of Chichester, to arrange peace terms.

The King of France was not eager to make peace unless he achieved what he wanted and he knew that it was impossible to get the English to agree to that. What he wanted was to clear the English out of France and to make them give up their claim to the French crown for ever. They would not be ready to concede that – but the surrender of Maine was a very good piece of good fortune to be getting on with. All that had been agreed to was an extension of the peace for two years.

The Parliament was very uneasy. They should not have surrendered Maine and yet on the other hand they were not in a position to continue the war. The French were becoming prosperous under the King who in his youth had seemed so hopeless. The English had a King who did not care for war and had no skill in conducting it. England was in no condition to continue the war but on the other hand they must get out of it with some advantages.

The surrender of Maine was a great mistake and for it they blamed the Queen and Suffolk.

Well, there was a truce and that might give them time to build up the army, to raise taxes – if the people did not revolt and refuse to pay them. It was a waiting time, but the uneasiness was growing.

Then disaster struck. Francis l'Arragonois, one of the English captains, seeing the build-up of French arms and knowing that attack would come sooner or later, forestalled them and marched into Brittany, took several fortresses and captured the town of Fougères.

It was a foolish action for it gave the French the very chance they wanted. The English had broken the truce. Very well, that meant it was over. There was nothing to stop them now. They were ready. In a very short time they had captured Normandy.

The loss of Normandy demoralised the English. So it had been long ago in the reign of King John. Normandy had been brought to England with the Conqueror and had been part of the English heritage since the Conquest.

The people were aghast. What had happened to the glorious victories of Henry the Fifth? It was little more than thirty years ago when the bells were ringing and the country was rejoicing in Agincourt.

And now . . . disaster. The surrender of Maine had meant the beginning of surrender to France. And they had let it happen. Not the King . . . he was too weak to do it. He had been forced into it. By his ministers, by the grand Duke of Suffolk and the

Queen. The Duke of Somerset was a fool. He had been defeated in France and he and the Bishop Moleyns deserved to be hanged.

There was uneasiness throughout the country.

Henry's idyll was rudely shattered.

They were losing France. Very well, let them lose it. He was content with England. He wanted to see the people happy. He wanted to encourage the artists. He wanted his people to appreciate fine music and art, to have colleges in which to study. War was the last thing he wanted. Let them abandon France . . . the whole of France if necessary and let them give their minds to being happy in England.

Suffolk came to Windsor to see him. A new Suffolk, a worried man this. His self-assurance was crumbling.

'My lord, my lady.' His eyes were on the Queen. She was the one who understood these matters better than the King. 'Bad news.'

'No more losses,' cried Henry. 'People should give more thought to prayer.'

'Prayer will do little to save Moleyns now. He went down to Portsmouth to pay the sailors for their work in carrying the troops to France, and he lodged there at the hospital called God's House.'

Margaret put her hand to her wildly beating heart. He is afraid to tell us, she thought. That is why he is hesitating.

'My lord,' she began. 'William, tell us the worst. We have to know it.'

'Well, my lady, the sailors began to quarrel about their payment. They said it was not enough and accused Moleyns of taking it for himself. Moleyns replied with some disdain, I gather, that they were behaving foolishly. Therefore they began shouting "Normandy. You have lost Normandy for us." And then they fell upon him.'

'Forsooth and forsooth,' cried the King. 'They did not . . . harm him . . .'

'They killed him, my lord. They so mishandled him that a short while after he was dead.'

Margaret looked at Henry. He had turned very pale. The thought of violence unnerved him.

'It was the mob,' she cried. 'I hate them. They act without reason . . .'

Suffolk said slowly: 'It shows the way the wind has begun to blow.'

He was right. His enemies were gathering. Maine had been surrendered, Rouen lost. Somerset might in some measure be to blame, Moleyns had paid the penalty, but the leader was Suffolk and now it was his turn.

Very shortly after the murder of Moleyns Suffolk was committed to the Tower.

Alice, Duchess of Suffolk came to the Tower and begged to be allowed to see her husband.

When she was shown into the small chamber where he was seated she ran to him and was swept up in his arms.

'William,' she cried, 'how could this happen? How could they . . .'

'I am the scapegoat, Alice.'

'Something must be done,' she cried. 'They will never allow this to go on. The King . . . the Queen . . .'

'I doubt either will have the power to stop it, Alice.'

'What have you done but ever serve your country?'

Suffolk was silent. He had served his country, it was true, but he could not deny that he had served himself rather well at the same time.

He sat down and covered his face with his hands.

'It is like a prophecy coming true. Do you remember years ago a soothsayer telling me that if I could escape from the Tower I should live? If I did not I should die.'

'A safe prophecy for any man,' said Alice scornfully. 'But put such foolish notions from your head. What will happen? You will have a hearing and how then could anyone bring charges against you?'

'They will accuse me of giving Maine to the French.'

'But that had to be. It was the price of peace.'

'But it did not buy peace. They will accuse me of losing Normandy.'

'You were not there. Somerset was in charge.'

'That matters not. They want to bring these things against me and they will do so. They have accused me of many things.'

A silence fell between them. Yes, the people had accused him . . . of Gloucester's murder, of being Margaret's lover.

Any accusations which could be thought of would be brought against him. When a man was down anything could happen to him.

'We shall not despair,' said Alice. 'I shall see the Queen.'

'Take care. They hate the Queen. Do not let us involve her in this more than she is. It can do us no good and it can bring harm to her. Be patient, Alice. I have to face the Parliament and I can give a good account of myself, I promise you.'

'But if they are determined to find you guilty . . .'

'They have to prove it, my dear. I tell you I did not reach

this position from which so many want to tear me down by being reckless or without guile.'

'I know. I trust you, William. You will pull through this as you have through other things. It is just that to see you here . . .'

'It is the Tower. It has that effect. So many cruel things have happened in this grim fortress. While one is here it seems impossible to escape from them. But I shall come through these troubles. Once let me get out of the Tower and all will be well.'

'I believe you,' said Alice.

She had to. She could not bear to contemplate the alternative.

He stood before his peers and listened to the charges against him.

They declared he had conspired to secure the throne for his son John Pole by contracting for him a marriage with Margaret Beaufort, the daughter of the first Duke of Somerset. The child had been two years old only when her father had died and she had been taken into Suffolk's house, there to be brought up until that time when she could be married to his son. This was nonsense. He had had no such thought. There would be many to claim the throne before Margaret Beaufort. The real grievance was the loss of Maine and Anjou which had been surrendered to the French. Suffolk was accused of working for the French and it was said that this was the reason why he had given over these important provinces. Moreover he had failed to supply adequate forces and arms to the army serving in France and was thus responsible for the present débâcle. These were the main charges, but in addition evidence was brought out that there had been some maladministration in property and money and that Suffolk had come far too well out of too many transactions for the good of the nation.

They were determined to condemn him and he knew it. But he also knew his own powers. He would not be easily defeated. He could give a very good account of himself.

He was taken back to the Tower.

Alice came to the Queen. She threw herself at Margaret's feet and seizing her hand begged her to help her.

'They are going to condemn William,' she said. 'They have made up their minds. They are all against him.'

'Not all,' said Margaret. 'We will save him. I promise you, Alice. Come to the King at once. He will give an order that William shall be freed from these ridiculous charges.'

Alice kissed the Queen's hand. There were tears in her eyes. 'Oh my lady, I knew you would be a good friend to me.'

'Of course I am your friend. Do you think I shall ever forget how you looked after me when I was so young and apprehensive? You and William are my first friends in England. Of course, Alice, we shall not allow these wicked men to harm William. They shall withdraw their charges at once. Come, we will go to the King.'

Henry was as grieved as Margaret. William was his good friend. He relied on William.

'You must order them to free him from the Tower at once,' said Margaret.

He looked at her rather sadly. There was much that Margaret did not understand. He was the King, yes, but he was to a large extent governed by his Parliament and he could not order the release of a man whom they had condemned.

'It will not be as simple as that,' he explained. 'The Londoners are against William and the Parliament is always afraid of the Londoners. You see the people don't understand that we had to give up Maine for peace. They blame William for the loss of Maine.'

Margaret did not meet Alice's eyes. She could not. Was it not she who had persuaded the King, because her father and her uncle had wanted the surrender of Maine? She had helped to bring about this situation and was partly responsible for the disaster which had befallen her friends.

'The war could not have gone on,' she said quickly. 'We had to have peace. If we have lost almost all the whole of Normandy that is not William's fault.'

'The people will have their scapegoat,' said Henry.

'And they have settled for William,' added Alice.

There was silence for a while and then the King said: 'I cannot order him to be released. There would be riots all over the country if I did. I can order him to be banished. Yes, that is the answer.'

'Banished,' cried Alice.

'Yes, my dear. He can go abroad for a time and you can join him. In due course he will come back.'

Margaret looked at Alice. She could see the dawn of hope in her eyes.

The King had given the order of banishment. Suffolk was to leave England for five years.

Alice came to see him in the Tower.

'Don't you see, it is a reprieve,' she said. 'Oh, William, I have been so miserable, so much afraid. But Margaret and

Henry are our friends. Henry does this because it is the only way of fighting your enemies.'

'To be banished from the country I have served . . . from my home . . .'

'Hush,' said Alice. 'Be thankful and rejoice. They were after your life. Remember what they have done for others. They would have had your head but for the intervention of the King. The Queen was wonderful. She is a true friend . . . a loyal friend. She insisted that the King act and you know he does all that she tells him. You will go to France. There you will stay . . . perhaps not five years and I shall join you there. And perhaps the children . . .'

'They will confiscate our estates.'

'We'll get them back, William. Be thankful. They have made you the scapegoat for inevitable defeat. But rejoice that you have escaped thus easily.'

They sat silently together. Then he said: 'You are a great comfort to me, Alice, and always have been.'

He was in better spirits when they parted and settled down to prepare to leave his prison.

The cool March air was exhilarating after the confinement of the Tower. Alice was right. All would be well. The walls of the Tower were enough to unnerve any man when he found himself a prisoner within them. In six weeks' time he was to leave England. He would not be safe until he had done so, but those six weeks could be spent on his estate in Suffolk. There he could be surrounded by his family. He could put his affairs in order.

One of the guards of the Tower came to him as he stood

looking over the river inhaling the fresh morning air.

'My lord,' he said, 'you must ride quietly out of the town. It would be unwise to go with your company. The people are muttering against you. Slip away quietly with one servant only. It may be then that you will not be recognised. Your attendants can follow later.'

'God help me,' said Suffolk. 'Have I not suffered enough?'

'You know what the mob can be like,' was the answer.

He knew it was wise to take the advice so he rode quietly out of the town with one servant beside him as two friends taking a journey together.

He realised what sound advice that had been when he saw the gathering crowds and listened to their murmurings. He was however unrecognised and came safely to the country. The men of his company were less fortunate. As soon as his livery was recognised they were set upon.

'Where is the Duke?' the people cried. And it was clear what his fate would have been if they had laid their hands on him. Several of his servants were injured, but when it was discovered that the Duke was not with them they were allowed to pass on, while the crowd went to the Tower to wait for the Duke to emerge.

Meanwhile riding eastwards he realised what a lucky escape he had had.

He spent a rather melancholy six weeks in Suffolk. He could not forget that he was an exile but those weeks passed quickly and it was soon time for his departure.

Alice had not left his side and she constantly assured him that they would not be parted for long. She would soon be with him.

'I am going to write to our son, Alice,' he said. 'I know he is only eight years old but there are things I must say to him in case I never see him again.'

'Of course you will see him again. It is only for five years and perhaps I can prevail on the Queen to make it less. I am sure she wishes to help us all she can and the King loves us too and he will do what the Queen asks him. Yes, write to little John and keep in good heart. Be thankful that you have escaped from the Tower. Remember the soothsayer. If you can escape from the Tower you will have a long and prosperous life.'

'God bless you, Alice,' said the Duke. 'Now I will write to our son. And in the morning we leave for Dover.'

It was a good sailing wind and the air was clear. He could see the outline of the coast of that land which would provide him a refuge from his enemies. It was so near and yet it would be so far because he could not leave it until the period of banishment was over. How often he would gaze with longing across that strip of water.

But Alice would come to him. They would plan . . . and who knew, she might prevail upon the Queen to get the banishment curtailed. The King would not do it unless prompted to. Poor Henry. He was a good and loyal friend, a good and saintly man, but he lacked the will and the power to act.

In his heart Suffolk knew that he had been wrong to rejoice in a weak King because such a King meant power to his ministers. The country needed a strong King like the First and Third Edwards and the Fifth Henry. Hard, stern men all of them. It was no use putting a gentle scholar on the throne and expecting strong rule.

He had been at fault. He had made the most of the situation.

He had enriched himself. What man wouldn't? He had wanted riches and power for his family.

It was too late now to regret.

But I'll come back, he told himself. I have escaped from the Tower.

He went aboard. There was an accompanying ship and a pinnace. He began to wonder what his reception would be in Calais and decided to send the pinnace on to discover if there would be anyone there to greet him and whether he could expect hospitality or hostility.

Then they set sail.

They had not gone more than a few miles when he saw a ship bearing down on them.

They were hailed and the master of the ship invited Suffolk to step aboard.

Suffolk did so and as he climbed on to the deck a shiver of apprehension ran through him for he saw the ship's name painted on the side. *St Nicholas of the Tower.*

It was the word Tower which had haunted him all the time he had been in that formidable fortress because he could not forget what the soothsayer had said.

No sooner had he stepped aboard than there was a cry of 'Welcome, Traitor.'

Then he knew that his worse fears were realised. His enemies had determined not to let him go.

The Captain spoke to him. He said that those who believed in justice had no intention of allowing him to escape to banishment. He had been tried and condemned and his last hours were near.

They were Christian folk however and would give him the rest of the day and a night in which to shrive himself.

He knew it was useless to appeal. This was the end.

He asked for writing materials which were given him for men such as these did not want to deny the last requests of a man condemned to die at their hands. He wrote to the King protesting his innocence.

He thought of Alice and his little son John. He was glad he had written to him; and he thought how fickle fortune was to raise a man to the heights of power and then as easily dash him down.

The Tower. He had not thought of any other Tower. But here it was and the prophecy was true. He was here, a condemned prisoner in the Tower ... *St Nicholas of the Tower*.

He faced his executioner, an Irishman with a cruel countenance which betrayed his delight in the deed he was about to perform.

Suffolk looked at the rusty sword in the man's hand and prayed that death would come quickly.

It took six strokes to sever his head from his body and when the deed was done, both body and head were taken back to Dover and thrown on the beach there.

The whole country was talking of the Duke's murder. Many called it execution for he was judged guilty. He had worked for the French, it was said. He had surrendered Maine; he had enriched himself; he was a traitor to his country; he was the lover of the Queen and had been conducting an adulterous intrigue since her arrival in England. He, with her, had murdered the Duke of Gloucester who now, for no reason but that he was dead, had become a saint.

Any ridiculous charge which could be brought against

Suffolk was brought; his death was used to increase the unpopularity of the Queen.

The King still kept the regard of the nation. He was good, he was a saint, he was deeply religious, he founded colleges and he hated bloodshed. Yes, they still loved the King. But he was weak and he was the slave of a wicked woman . . . an adulteress, a murderess . . . a French woman . . . and were not the country's greatest enemies – and always had been – the French?

Alice was heart-broken. The Queen tried to comfort her and Alice was relieved that not all the calumnies uttered against her husband reached Margaret's ears.

Henry did show a certain strength when Suffolk was attainted in an attempt to make his execution legal. The *St Nicholas of the Tower* was a royal ship and it was certain that the captain and crew had acted on orders from someone in a high position.

There was a whisper that Richard Duke of York was involved. He was in Ireland, it was true, but he had his supporters all over the country. He had been a great enemy of Suffolk. But then Suffolk had had so many enemies.

Margaret kept Alice with her. The Queen was seething with hatred against those who had murdered her friend. She wanted to arrest the captain of the *St Nicholas* and have him die the traitor's death.

Margaret was fierce in her denunciation of those whom she considered worthy of the most dire punishment. Her feelings went deep whether they were engendered by anger against her enemies or loyalty to her friends. She grieved with an intensity which matched Alice's own.

But it was useless. That would not bring Suffolk back.

The King however refused to agree that Suffolk was a traitor and ordered that his body should be taken for honourable burial to Wingfield. A stone effigy was placed above it; and the King and the Queen, with Alice, continued to mourn.

Chapter VII

JACK CADE

In his Manor House in the county of Sussex, Sir Thomas Dacre was seated at the long trestle table in his spacious hall entertaining his guests. It was summer and they were all tired after a long day's hunting. The smell of roasting meat came from the kitchens behind the screens and serving-men and -women were scuttling to and fro with steaming dishes.

Jack Cade, the Irishman, was giving orders. He was the sort of man who liked to give orders. He had started here in the Manor as an ordinary scullion but he had quickly shown his abilities and it was not long before the cooks were giving him special duties. He was in charge of the serving-men and-women; it was his task to make sure the dishes arrived hot at the table and to decide who should carry them.

He was quick and clever; it was said that he had a little tucked away which he had managed to save here and there. He would ride into market and buy stores that were needed and everyone knew that he took a little profit on that. Never mind. A blind eye was turned to these transactions. Jack Cade was a clever fellow. Even Sir Thomas Dacre had said that if he had been better born he could have done well for himself.

John Cade undoubtedly did well for himself in Sir Thomas Dacre's household. He was a man to be reckoned with, a little Caesar, a man who was outstanding in his world.

If he had a weakness it was for women, and he had little difficulty in satisfying his desires in that quarter. He was an outstanding man, good-looking, debonair, fond of fine clothes, often his master's valet gave him some garment of which Sir Thomas had no need and which would not fit the valet. He was forceful, powerful; and eager that everyone should recognise his power. He often hinted that he was of noble birth – his father was a duke who had got him on a serving-girl and had then failed to acknowledge him. That was his story. He was not going to say who the duke was. There were not all that many and that would be fining it down a bit. Suffice to say that he was part noble birth and part humble and this combination had made of him the very fine fellow he was.

On this occasion he was a little uneasy. There was one of the serving-girls who was giving him some trouble. The silly young creature had become pregnant and wanted him to marry her.

Why couldn't she have gone to the witch in the woods nearby who had a very good way of dealing with unwanted babies? Some of the more accommodating girls had had their babies and smothered them at birth, burying them respectably in some secret place; others had the little bastards and accounted it just a way of life. But this one – she had to shout and threaten. He would never have started with her if he had known what she was.

Willing enough after a time, a shy sort of wench, she had needed a lot of persuading. And now . . . she was threatening to go to Lady Dacre to tell her all and ask her to force Jack Cade to marry her. It really was disturbing, because although he had no intention of marrying the girl it would be very awkward if Lady Dacre insisted on his doing so.

The girl was there in the kitchen now turning the sucking-pig on the spit. The cook wanted it hot and succulent by the time it was required to carry to the tables. That would be in fifteen minutes' time, after they had worked their way through the partridge pie and the beef and mutton.

She caught his eye as he was about to pass her, and there was that in her expression which made him pause. It was half pleading, half threatening. He knew from experience that it was those quiet ones who were capable of strong action. He had to go carefully with her.

'What's wrong with you?' he muttered.

'You know well, Jack Cade, and 'tis of your doing.'

'I reckon you played your part in it, eh.'

'We both did and we both should have our part in what's coming.'

He gave her a playful push.

'Come on. You was willing enough.'

'Talk like that if you will, Jack Cade. I shall go to my lady.'

'Now listen. You go too fast. I want to talk to you. I've got plans.'

'What plans?' He saw the hope springing into her eyes.

'Listen. When they're served and lolling over the tables listening to the minstrels, slip out to the shrubbery. See you there. I've got something to say to you.'

'All right, Jack. I'll be there.'

He was thoughtful. What could he say to the girl? He was not going to marry her. That did not fit in with his plans at all.

She would be no good to him. He was going to get on in the world. When he married it would be the daughter of some gentleman of standing. That was the way to get on in the world and Jack Cade was going to get on in the world. Let no one make any mistake about that, and he was not going to do it by marrying one of the lowest serving-girls in the Dacre household.

It was very unfortunate that this girl had got herself with child. She was a determined little piece, too. He hadn't liked the look in her eyes when she had said she would tell Lady Dacre. It would not be the first time her ladyship, who believed in forcing morality on the poor, had insisted on a marriage. He wanted to stay at Dacre Manor. He was doing well here. He was not ready to pass on yet. He had found a profitable way of life with the tradesmen.

And now this slut threatened to spoil it all.

He would have to find a way of dealing with her.

When he went out to the shrubbery she was already there.

'Jack,' she cried, and flew at him, full of affection now, thinking that he was going to give in.

'Now listen here,' he said, 'you've got to get one thing straight. There's going to be no marriage. You've got to go off to the old witch. She'll give you something . . . and then in a little while you'll be slim and straight as a virgin.'

'It's too late, Jack. You know what happened to young Jennet. She left it too late and it was the end of her.'

Would to God it would be the end of you, he thought.

She was looking at him pleadingly. 'Well, what then?' she asked.

'Well then . . . you've got to have it, that's all. What's one more little bastard in the world?'

He was unprepared for the blow he received at the side of his face and staggered under it. The girl had strength.

He seized her arm and their faces were close, glaring at each other.

'Don't you talk about your baby like that,' she said.

'That's ripe, that is, from someone who a minute ago was talking of doing away with it. Besides, how do I know it is mine?'

Her eyes glinted at him. She looked murderous. Here was one he would have to handle very carefully.

'It's your baby and it's mine,' she said, 'and it's not going to be a bastard because I'm going straight to Lady Dacre to-morrow and she'll make you see where your duty lies.'

'You'll not go to Lady Dacre.'

'I will. I promise you, Jack Cade, I will.'

She would. Yes, there was no doubt of that. He gripped her arm and twisted it behind her. She continued to look at him in spite of the pain.

He released her suddenly and as she was about to run from him, he caught her. He shook her. 'You'll not go to Lady Dacre.'

'I will,' she cried. 'I will. I will.'

It had all happened in a few moments. His hands were at her throat. She opened her mouth to protest and then was silent. Her eyes seemed to be coming out of their sockets; her face was growing purple . . . and suddenly she was silent.

When he released her she slid to the ground.

'God help us,' he ejaculated. 'I have killed her.'

He stood still for a few seconds looking down at her. His problem was solved. Lady Dacre could not now force him to marry her.

He was a man who acted quickly. It was one of the reasons why he had come so far. He could bury the body. How long could that remain hidden? She would be missed. There were people who knew that he had been friendly with her. There might be some who knew she was carrying his child. If she disappeared they would wonder where. They might start making enquiries.

There was only one thing he could do. It was the very thing he had fought against. He must leave this profitable nest which he was feathering so lucratively and find some other outlet for his talents.

He hid the girl's body in the shrubbery and crept back to the house. There he collected the money he had amassed, put his clothes into a knapsack and chose the opportunity to leave the house unseen.

The Dacre episode was over. He had to find fresh fields to conquer.

He made his way to the coast. He was making plans. He would go to Dover or Sandwich and wait there until he found a ship which was going to France. There were always ships going to France carrying troops and ammunition. He could join one of those and seek his fortune as a soldier of war. Soldiers were always welcome in this perpetual war against France.

It would be well for him to get out of the country for a while.

He was right. It was not difficult to join a ship at Dover. As many men as possible were wanted to fight the French. He had taken the precaution of acquiring a tin box, putting most of the money he had amassed in it and burying it in a wood near the coast. So he crossed the sea and thought of that little incident back at the Dacre estate as closed.

It was a pity. It had been profitable but it would have been the end of ambition if he had been forced to marry and knowing Lady Dacre he was certain that would have been the outcome. It was a pity he had been driven to murder. But the girl had been a fool. It occurred to him that he could have got away like this without murder. However it was done and he was now putting it behind him.

It seemed a wise precaution to change his name. He had always liked to imagine he was of noble birth and he thought Mortimer was a good name. It had royal connections. He became Jack Mortimer and let it be believed that he was related to the Duke of York – on the wrong side of the blanket maybe, but the blood was there.

Free of servitude in the Dacre household he began to assume a certain air. He was careful not to overdo it, to learn gradually, to ape those of noble birth; and within a few months no one questioned his right to the name of Mortimer.

He began to be rather pleased at the manner in which life had changed for him. He did not dwell on the Dacre incident but he did occasionally wonder who had found the girl's body. They would suspect him, of course, because he had fled and the girl was pregnant. Still, better to have fled than have stayed behind to face it. Doubtless if he had he would be hanging from a rope by now.

He had dreamed of sacking towns, acquiring great trophies as he did so, but the war was going badly for the English, and there was little booty to be found.

The army was proving less profitable than the Dacre household had been, so he decided that he would return to England.

If he changed his name and settled in another part of the country, assuming a different personality, he would have nothing to fear.

He deserted from the army and decided to find some quiet village where he could set up as a physician. Why not? He had always been interested in the body and having talked to many quacks had learned the secrets of making lotions and potions.

Arriving in England, he first retrieved his fortune from the wood and made up his mind that he would stay in Kent. He found a suitable village and calling himself Aylmer practised there as a doctor. His charm of manner and his undoubted good looks soon made him popular and he was amazed how easily he slipped into his chosen profession.

Fortune smiled on him for in due course he was called in to attend the master of the manor house and the treatment was successful so the family there believed he was a very clever doctor. He was invited to dine and became a special friend of the young man of the house. He had certainly moved up in the social scale since his days as scullion to the Dacres.

As the months passed his connection with the gentry had an effect on him. He spoke like them, acted like them and as he was assiduous in his study of them and determination to be accepted, he passed unquestionably as one of them.

A Squire from Tandridge in Surrey was visiting at the Manor for a week or so and the doctor was invited to the house.

It so happened that the Squire had a beautiful daughter and no sooner had the self-styled Dr Aylmer set eyes on her than he determined to marry her. What a different proposition from the little Dacre serving-maid! He knew how to charm her and because he was considered to be a man of standing the Squire could see no reason why there could not be a marriage between the worthy doctor and his daughter.

The marriage was celebrated. There was a handsome dowry for the bride and Jack Cade began to think that the best thing that had happened to him was to murder a girl in a shrubbery. If he had not he would still be there, perhaps married to her – which God forbid – or making a little money here and there. Ah, this was different. He had achieved an ambition. He had taken a big step up in the world.

He rather wished that he had kept the name of Mortimer. But perhaps he was wise to have changed. Such a name might have set people probing to discover his true origins.

For a year or so he lived quite contentedly with his new status, his new wife and the profession he had chosen. But there were one or two moments of uneasiness. One came with the arrival of a doctor friend of his wife's father who visited them and naturally expected there to be a mutual interest in medicine. It was occasions like this – when Cade experienced great apprehension – when he realised he could be exposed. And if he were? What if he were traced back to the Dacre household in Sussex?

He was not quite so contented. Moreover his nature was such that he was always seeking for some higher place.

There was a great deal of murmuring throughout the country. Taxes were extortionate and Kent seemed to have been selected for even greater hardship.

Jack had always liked to hear himself speak. He had never been at a loss for words. He found himself holding forth on the subject; he was invited into people's houses and he would talk there; and very soon people were coming to hear him speak. This delighted him. He was enchanted with his new role.

And when the Duke of Suffolk was murdered he declared that the King was hard on Kent because from Kent had come the ships which had intercepted him.

Memories of a certain Wat Tyler were revived. He had led the people to London in protest. He had failed, it was true, because King Richard had ridden out to Smithfield and Blackheath and confronted the rebels, promising them all sorts of concessions which he had no intention of complying with. Wat was only a tyler. Jack Aylmer, Cade or Mortimer, whatever anyone liked to call him, was very different.

Wat Tyler had begun his insurrection when he had murdered a tax collector who had insulted his daughter. Well, Jack Cade's adventure had begun with murder . . . of a different kind it was true, but there was a similarity.

But how different were these two men. Poor Wat was a humble tyler. Jack Cade was a man who had left his humble origins behind.

He knew something of politics. There was trouble in high places. The Queen was very unpopular. The King was weak. There was no heir to the throne and the Duke of York, though in Ireland, had a very strong claim. The House of York was ready to push the House of Lancaster from the throne.

And what of those who were in at the beginning to help? What of Jack Cade, Aylmer as he called himself? Why should he not take an active part in politics? It would be more interesting than administering to the sick in some remote country village.

Jack was impulsive by nature. He was soon preaching revolution.

'Let us gather together, my friends. Let us go to see the King as others in Kent once did before us. They failed. They had not our foresight. Wat Tyler was their leader . . . a man of strength and purpose but a tyler of no education. It will be different with us. We shall set out in a different fashion. We have a leader who can talk to the King when he comes face to face with him. You will have a leader from the royal house itself. Yes, my friends, my real name is Mortimer and I am a cousin of the Duke of York. We will work for my cousin. A strong man . . . a man more royal than the King for he is royal through his father and his mother. He will rule England and we will set aside this scholar with the French harlot who leads him in everything he does.'

It was fine inspiring talk and the people rallied to him. It was a new role for him, one he had secretly longed for. He was going to be a leader and when they succeeded and the Duke of York was on the throne he would be likely to remember all that he owed to the man who had begun it all.

By Whitsuntide they were ready to march, for Jack Cade had gathered together some twenty thousand men. They set out and reached Blackheath on the first day of June. There they encamped and staked the ground as though they were at war and expecting an attack, a trick Cade had learned during his experiences in France. They waited there, ready to march on London.

Meanwhile the King, hearing that rebels from Kent were encamped at Blackheath and remembering the story he had often heard of his ancestor Richard the Second, who as a boy faced the rebels and dispersed them, dissolved Parliament in Leicester where it was at that time and came with all speed to London.

He was not a young boy as Richard had been; he hated bloodshed. He did not want to have to ride out with an army to subdue these people, so on his arrival in London he sent a deputation to Blackheath to learn the grievances which had brought the men to London.

Jack was prepared. They had heard that the whole of Kent was to be destroyed and made into a forest as reprisals for the death of Suffolk. The common people had not chosen the ships which had been sent to intercept the Duke. They knew nothing of such matters and would not suffer for them. The King surrounded himself with low men of whom the people did not approve whereas lords of his blood were put away from his presence. They were referring to the Duke of York who had been sent out to Ireland and with whom Cade wished to be allied. People were not paid for stuff and purveyance taken into the King's household. Chiefly of course the people of Kent were incensed by the heavy taxation which was laid upon them. They wanted reforms. They also wanted the King to avoid the progeny of all those in sympathy with the Duke of Suffolk and take about his person the true lord that is York lately exiled by Suffolk, the Dukes of Buckingham, Exeter and Norfolk. They wanted those who had murdered the Duke of Gloucester punished. The duchies of Normandy, Gascony, Guienne, Anjou and Maine had been lost through traitors. All extortions of the common people must be stopped.

Henry listened to these complaints with close attention. He could understand that the people were angry because they had been heavily taxed but the accusations against Suffolk and his friends angered him. The chief of these had been the Queen and he could see in this criticisms of her.

He gave orders that all loyal servants of the King and country should unite against the rebels.

Knowing that if the King's army came against them they would be defeated, Cade gave orders that they retreat to Sevenoaks. There they encamped while the King's army advanced.

Henry made the mistake of sending out a small detachment under the Stafford brothers – Sir Humphrey and William. The result was triumph for the rebels. Both Staffords were slain and the rest of the detachment retreated to Blackheath where the King had his men.

Cade was delighted. He was proving himself to be a born leader. His force was well ordered; what he had learned in France stood him in good stead; he was a brilliant soldier. From the slain Sir Humphrey he took his spurs, his splendid armour, his brigandine of small plates and rings fastened by leather, his salade helmet which rested entirely on his head and was not attached to the rest of the body armour. The top had a crest which swept in a long tail at the back. Arrayed in these Jack felt the nobleman whom he had always longed to be.

The fine armour and his success elated Jack to such an extent that he believed himself to be a great leader. He saw himself rising to power and becoming chief adviser to the new King who would of course be the Duke of York, raised to the throne by the courage and brilliance of Jack Cade.

'We are kinsmen,' he could hear the Duke saying. 'You shall be my chancellor.'

To have been victorious in battle against the King's forces was triumph indeed.

The King was most disturbed. This was indeed a rebellion. It was verging on civil war. His ministers did not like the mood of the people generally. What was happening in Kent today would be happening in the rest of the country tomorrow.

Perhaps they should placate the insurgents.

'Forsooth, I agree,' cried Henry. 'There must be no more bloodshed. Let us parley with these men. Who is this man Mortimer?'

'He is a kinsman of the Duke of York, so he says,' was the answer. They were all of the opinion that the Duke of York from Ireland was behind this revolt. It was reasonable enough. The King was weak; the Queen was hated and there was no heir, and the Duke of York did have a claim to the throne.

Yes, they were of the opinion that this revolt should not be allowed to spread, so they would parley with the rebels.

The fact that the King was ready to do this inspired Jack with new confidence.

'It is for us to make terms,' he cried. 'We will see what the response is to that.'

One of the most hated men was Lord Say, the Treasurer, whose duty it was to make the extortionate demands which had aroused the wrath of the people. That he did not keep the money for himself but raised it for the country's needs was beside the point. He raised the money; he made the demands; he was to blame. Lord Say's was a name which was reviled throughout the country.

'We shall refuse to treat with the King until Lord Say is placed in custody,' said Jack.

'That is easy,' said the King, 'and we must do it. We must prevent further trouble at all cost. Say can be committed to the Tower for the time being. He need only remain there until this is over. It may be the safest place for him.'

So Lord Say went to the Tower; the King and his army returned to London, and after a day or so Henry was deluded into thinking that if he did not take the rebels seriously they would disperse and go back to their business in the country.

He himself left for Kenilworth.

No sooner had he left than Jack marched his army into the capital.

It was a great day for Jack when he rode into the City. There was no resistance at all. People came out of their houses and cheered him. Street vendors and apprentices were all there to give them a welcome. For them it was like a day of a fair – a holiday.

But Jack was serious. He saw himself at the height of power even beyond his own dreams. He struck his sword on the street cobbles and cried aloud: 'Now is Mortimer lord of this city.'

He kept his men in order. There was to be no stealing from the houses, no raping of the girls and women. This was their own fair city of London and those who succeeded must not offend the Londoners. 'We must have them on our side,' he said, 'working for us.'

It was true that up to this time the Londoners thought it was all something of a joke. They were not averse to seeing the King discountenanced because they knew that would upset the Queen far more than it did him. No, this was amusing, rather like a royal wedding or a coronation . . . not to be taken too seriously though.

They very soon saw it in a different light.

Jack and his men spent the night at Southwark after setting guards in the city to keep the peace. The next day however he came back into the city and took up his place at the Guildhall.

He then sent some of his men to the Tower with instructions to bring Lord Say to him.

The bewildered Treasurer was brought into the hall and when he saw who his judges were to be, he tried to explain that what had been done had been by order of those above him.

Jack Cade would have none of this. He was determined to show these people that he was in command.

'You condemn me,' said Lord Say, 'but you cannot do that. I demand to be tried by my peers.'

'It is not for you to make demands,' said Jack. 'You stand condemned. You are guilty of crimes against the people. Make your peace with God.'

Nor was he allowed time to do that. Jack himself led the procession to the standard in the Chepe and there they cut off Lord Say's head.

The head was held high that all the people gathered there might see it.

'Here is the head of a traitor to the people,' said the executioner.

Then the people of London knew that Jack Cade's rebellion was no game to make a day's holiday.

That was not enough. Lord Say's son-in-law, William Crowmer, who was the Sheriff of Kent, was captured and dragged to the Chepe. His head was placed on a pole and it was lifted high until it was side by side with that of Lord Say. Those who carried the poles laughed and joked as they brought the two heads together and made it appear that they kissed.

'A pair of rogues,' shouted the men of Kent. 'So may they all perish.'

The citizens of London had grown grave.

They did not like those who came uninvited and made free with their city.

Jack had gone back to Southwark after the executions gloating on his success but was soon to discover that his optimism was a little premature. When he returned to London the next day he found that the citizens had risen against him. It was no longer a joke. They would not have him dictating the law in their city and when it came to sentencing people to death and actually carrying out the sentence without trial and without time for the prisoner to be shriven, that was entirely unacceptable. If such conduct was permissible it would only be among Londoners.

Before he had retired to Kenilworth the King had left a certain Matthew Gough in charge of the Tower of London and with the Mayor, Gough called on the citizens to defend their city. The response was immediate and when Jack with his army came to cross the Bridge he was met by a sturdy force. Cade's army was the stronger and during the fighting Matthew Gough was killed. Jack had taken the opportunity to storm the King's Bench and the Marshalsea prison and the prisoners he released fought for him.

They battled fiercely but the Londoners were defending their city and the conflict raged all through the night. By the morning both sides were exhausted and readily agreed that there should be a truce which should last some hours.

The Archbishop of York, John Kemp, who was also the Chancellor, old and infirm as he was, had stayed in London and had had no desire to retreat to Kenilworth with the King. John Stafford, the Archbishop of Canterbury, was also in London and the two decided that it was their task and their duty to disperse the rebels and prevent any further bloodshed.

They sent for William Waynflete, the Bishop of Winchester, who happened to be at Haliwell, a priory in Shoreditch, at the time and the three churchmen met for a council in the Tower of London.

'These rebellions can be dangerous,' said Archbishop

Kemp. 'One hasty action could spark off a civil war. On the other hand the right action at the right moment could put an end to the rebellion. King Richard did it with Wat Tyler but I would not wish to make false promises to these rebels.'

'There is one thing we can offer them,' said the Bishop of Winchester, 'and that is free pardons. There must be some of them who are growing uneasy. If we offer to let them go peacefully back to their homes and assure them that there will be no reprisals against them, they might well decide that is the best plan of action for them.'

'Will the King agree?' asked Kemp.

The Bishop of Winchester snapped his fingers.

'The King has chosen to retreat. I do not think we should ask his advice on this matter. There would not be time to in any case. What do you say that we offer these rogues pardon on condition that they go quietly to their homes?'

The three of them agreed that if they could end the rebellion promptly that would be the best course possible, and it was accordingly arranged that Jack should have a meeting with the Bishop of Winchester at St Margaret's Church, Southwark.

Jack was realising that to go on could mean disaster. He had collected a large quantity of booty which if he could get it safely away would keep him in comfort for the rest of his life. If it ended now at this point he could come out of the adventure very profitably. He could return to his country home something of a hero.

Yes, he agreed, for a free pardon he would disband his army of rebels and they would return home.

The Bishop went back to the Archbishops in triumph. The affair was concluded amicably. It was shameful that men should be able to rise and cause so much damage and then be given a free pardon but sometimes expediency was necessary.

Pardons were accordingly issued – two of them – one for the rebels and another for their leader in the name of Mortimer.

Jack stayed in Southwark. He had a little job to do. He must gather together all the goods he had pillaged, hire a barge and get them all sent away by water. He was delighted with his acquisitions and gloated over them as he carefully packed them and got them into the barge.

As soon as they were safely away he himself would be gone and then he would like to lose himself. Those who had been robbed of their possessions might be watchful for him. Well, he had called himself Mortimer for the purposes of the insurrection. He could change that now and go back to Aylmer. Although as Aylmer he had raised the rebels; and to return to Cade might stir memories in the Dacre country. Perhaps he needed a new name but he did not want to leave his comfortable life with the daughter of the Squire of Tandridge.

He was glad of a few days to ponder his next move.

The barge was ready to leave for Rochester by next day's tide. He would return to his lodging and prepare to leave with it.

As he turned away from the river a man sitting idly there called to him: 'Good day.'

He answered genially and the man went on: 'Have you heard the news about Mortimer?'

Jack was almost amused to hear stories about himself. He found it extremely gratifying to consider what a mark he had made.

'No,' he said, 'what's the latest?'

'Well, seemingly he's no more Mortimer than I am.'

'How do you know?'

'Well, they've traced him see. Mortimer . . . that be a very grand name and the family says to themselves "Now who is he who claims to be one of us?" Seems he had no right . . . no right at all.'

Jack was beginning to feel very uneasy.

'What are they doing about it?'

'Well, as I heard it, it seems they've given a pardon to this Mortimer and if he's not Mortimer, well then there's no pardon for him, is there? I tell you this. They're on the look-out for him. They say he's Jack Cade . . . a bit of a rogue by all accounts. They'll get him; and I wouldn't care to be in his boots when they do.'

What good fortune to have talked to this man! To have heard what he did. That it was accurate he had no doubt. The man had even mentioned his own name.

So they were looking for him. There would be no pardon for him if they caught him. They always liked to get the leaders.

He was in imminent danger.

He would not go back to his lodging. He would stay on board the barge and at the very first moment he would be away.

He lay among his precious goods. He should never have called himself Mortimer. It was his pride again. But he should not blame his pride. It was that which had brought him as far as he had come. He was born lucky. Surely luck wouldn't desert him now.

It would be a traitor's death for him if he was caught. His pardon meant nothing. That was for Mortimer and he was no Mortimer. They would seize any pretext for getting him. He might have had to swing on a rope for the girl he had killed at Dacre's but this last adventure it would be hanging, drawing and quartering, a fate enough to strike terror into the boldest heart.

But good fortune had always been on his side. He trusted it would now.

It seemed it might for at midnight he was able to start his journey to Rochester.

He could have left his booty but he could not bring himself to do that. He would store it somewhere and it would always be there waiting for the time when he would be free to enjoy it.

It seemed that fortune was favouring him again. He reached Rochester safely and put his booty into a house which had been recommended to him and where he knew that for a considerable payment – which he could well afford – it would be safe until he came to take it away.

While he was trying to work out some plan there was a proclamation throughout the town. A reward of one thousand marks was offered to anyone who could bring Jack Cade alive or dead to the King.

So it really was known who he was. They would realise now that the leader of the rebellion was the murderer from Sussex.

He should have been content with the life he had built up as Aylmer. Why had he not realised that? All that precious booty would be lost to him if he were not careful.

He could not stay in Rochester. Without delay he must disguise himself and get as far away as possible. He saw that it might be necessary to start afresh as an entirely new personality. Indeed that seemed the only possible way. He had done it before as Aylmer and with outstanding success. Why should he not succeed again? And he would have his store in Rochester to come back to when everything had blown over.

The first necessity was Escape.

Disguising himself as an old pedlar he left Rochester and went across country towards Lewes in Sussex.

There was one man who had sworn to bring Jack Cade to justice. This was Alexander Iden, a squire of Kent who had become Sheriff after Jack Cade had murdered his predecessor William Crowmer.

He went to Southwark where he asked many questions of those who had seen and known Jack Cade. The trail led him to Rochester. Jack Cade had disappeared, he was told. Someone remembered seeing a pedlar who had looked a little like him.

A pedlar. It was a disguise which had been used many times before. Alexander Iden would work on the assumption that Cade, disguised as a pedlar, was making his way into hiding.

Iden was indefatigable. He was determined to get Crowmer's murderer and as he proceeded through the countryside he was certain that he was on the trail.

Meanwhile Jack continued his journey. He would make for the coast. Perhaps it would be wise to leave the country. There were not so many ships leaving for France now. The war was petering out in defeat for the English. But he could probably get across on some pretext. He had absolute faith in himself.

There would be no mercy for him if he were caught. They would discover that he was the murderer of the serving girl at Dacre. Not that that would be so serious a crime as leading a rebellion and executing important men like Lord Say and Crowmer.

His situation was indeed desperate. He was afraid to present himself at the inns now. He knew they were looking for him. Too many people would be after that thousand marks reward.

He skirted Heathfield in Sussex. He did not want to go right into the town. That could be too dangerous now. He came to a large garden, part of a big estate. It was quiet and peaceful there. There was an extensive orchard where he could make a comfortable bed and be off at dawn.

As he was settling down to sleep he thought he heard a rustle among the trees, a footstep on the grass. A stone rattled as though someone had dislodged it when walking. He had become very sensitive to such sounds.

He started up.

Someone was there. The figure of a man loomed up among the trees.

Cade was on his feet in an instant.

'What are you doing here?' asked the man.

'No harm,' replied Jack. 'Just seeking somewhere to spend the night.'

'This is a private orchard.'

'I'm sorry, my lord, if I've trespassed. It was just a place for a poor man to lay his head till morning. I meant no harm.'

'You have done great harm, Jack Cade,' said the man, 'and I have come to take you to justice.'

Jack sprang on Alexander Iden and they fought desperately for a few moments. Jack was strong but Alexander was armed. Jack lay on the ground groaning and Alexander leaned over him. 'It is no use,' he said. 'It is over for you, Jack Cade.'

He lifted Jack onto his horse and took him back to Heathfield.

While he acquired a cart in which he placed him, Jack was only half-conscious but he did know he was captured.

Alexander Iden explained to the astonished innkeeper who

supplied the cart and horses: 'This is Jack Cade and I am taking him to London.'

'Poor fellow,' said the innkeeper, 'rogue though he was. I wouldn't be in his shoes.'

'He won't be in them much longer.'

'Nay, it will be the end for him. Why can't folks stay quiet in the station to which they've been called?'

Alexander did not answer that. He wanted to get to London as fast as possible.

Jack lay in the cart. He scarcely felt the jolting. Now and then he would come back to consciousness, and remember.

It was all over then. It was finished. He was finished.

Not that, he thought. Anything but that.

He was lucky. He died on the way to London.

Alexander took him to the White Hart Inn in Southwark where he had stayed.

'That's him all right,' said the hostess. 'No doubt of that. That's Jack Cade. I'd know him anywhere.'

He was taken to the King's Bench prison until it was decided what should be done.

Then they took him out and cut off his head. His body was cut into quarters and that all might witness what happened to those who thought it a good idea to rebel against the King, it was placed on a hurdle and trundled through the streets with his head resting between his breasts. From the King's Bench to Southwark and over London Bridge to Newgate . . . the scene of his brief glory.

The parts of his body were displayed in prominent places in Blackheath, Gloucester, Salisbury and Norwich.

That is the end of Jack Cade's Rebellion, said the people. But it was not exactly so.

In calling himself Mortimer he had implicated the Duke of York; who was too important and too ambitious a man to let it be thought that he had been associated with an adventurer like Jack Cade.

Chapter VIII

IN THE TEMPLE GARDENS

From Dublin Castle Richard Duke of York was watching events in England with great attention. As soon as any messages arrived he scoured their contents for news of the rebellion.

This Jack Cade – impudently calling himself Mortimer – had arisen. With what purpose? he asked Cecily, his clever and most forceful wife.

Because, was the answer, the country was ripe for rebellion. The King was no King. He was tolerated because rumour had endowed him with a certain saintliness. His great delight was in building colleges and attending churches. Laudable in a priest but hardly suitable for a king.

'Sometimes I think Fate likes to play a joke on us. It selects the most unlikely man to wear the crown when . . .'

'When there are those with as much righ . . . some would say more . . . to wear it,' finished Cecily who did not believe in diplomacy.

Her husband, this great Duke of York, had far more right to the crown than Henry of Lancaster and what a King he would make!

'Henry is heading for disaster,' went on the Duke.

'Greatly aided by that little virago from Anjou.'

'And my lord Somerset.'

'Do you think the rumours about him and the Queen are true?'

'I know not, my love, but it serves the lady right that they are circulated against her. She is too affectionate to her friends and too vindictive to those whom she dislikes.'

'I fear we fit into the second category,' said Cecily.

'Rather rejoice in it. The day will come . . .'

'It may well,' answered Cecily. 'It is a pity that they banished you to this God-forsaken place.'

'Knowing, of course, that we shall never have peace with the Irish. The Irish are a versatile people. They love many things but what they love beyond everything is discord. They are born with the desire to fight. You can see it in the babies even.'

'I always thought it would be a good plan to leave them to fight among themselves.'

'That, my love, is what I am considering doing.'

She waited. Richard always talked to her of his plans and listened to her advice. He appreciated her. She had earned the nickname of Proud Cis and she definitely deserved it. She was no brainless female fit only for the bearing of children – although she was quite good at that too. She came of a fruitful family. She was one of the Nevilles and her mother had been Joan Beaufort, daughter of John of Gaunt and Catherine Swynford. So she was royal – for the Beauforts had been legitimised and she could not forget it. Her mother had borne ten children of whom she was the youngest; and before he had married her mother her father had sired eight children on his first wife, the daughter of the Earl of Stafford.

We have reason to be ambitious, thought Cecily. Our children have royal blood from both parents.

Richard was steeped in royalty. He was descended from Edward the Third by both parents. His father had been the second son of Edmund of Langley who had been Edward the Third's fifth son; and his mother was a daughter of Roger Mortimer, a grandson of Lionel Duke of Clarence, second son of Edward the Third, Lionel's daughter Philippa having married Edmund Mortimer the third Earl of March. Lionel had been older than John of Gaunt so if Henry the Fourth had not usurped the throne from Richard the Second, Richard Duke of York would certainly have come before the present King.

It was a fact to be proud of. It was something they would never forget and since this affair of Jack Cade, Richard had been thinking a great deal about it.

Clearly the people of England were not satisfied with their King and consequently the Duke of York was feared in some circles which was why he had been sent to Ireland. And what was more clear than anything was that the time might be getting ripe when something could be done about ridding the country of an incompetent ruler and replacing him by someone who could rule well — and in any case had more right to.

Cecily followed his thoughts.

Richard went on: 'It would be advisable for me to return to England to clear myself of this suspicion which Jack Cade has aroused against me.'

'The rogue! To dare to call himself a Mortimer.'

'Rogue indeed but a shrewd one. The name of Mortimer would bring many to his banner.'

'Because they would think that you were behind the rising.'

'It might well be. So you see, my dear, I must go home to face my accusers.'

Cecily nodded sagely.

'I am of the opinion, my lady, that that will not inconvenience you greatly.'

'I shall welcome it. I long to see the shores of England once more. It will be good for George. Poor little mite. He has never seen his native land.'

'I doubt he will notice where he is.'

'Even babies would detest this country.'

'Then I am to take it that you will rejoice to return to England.'

'You may indeed.'

'There might be difficulties . . .'

'You mean the King will be suspicious of you. Poor fool. Has he the wits to be suspicious of anyone?'

'Don't underrate him. He is simply not fitted to be a King. He is quite a scholar, I believe. He loves his books.'

'Books don't hold kingdoms together,' said Cecily scornfully. Then she added: 'I look forward to seeing the children.'

They had a full nursery. There was Anne aged eleven, Edward aged eight, Edmund seven, Elizabeth six, Margaret four, and little George who had been born in Ireland. A pleasant family and what one would expect of a daughter of a very fruitful mother. There had been sorrows in the family. Three little boys – Henry, William and John – had not survived their infancy. But they had three left to them which was comforting for it was good to have boys. The joy of Cecily's life was Edward – her eldest boy since the death of little Henry; and Edward seemed to be growing into a true Plantagenet. He was going to be very tall; there were signs of that already. He had the strong blond looks of his ancestors. He was remarkably like Edward the First; and that was a good sign. He was lively, demanding his own way, excelling at outdoor exercises and charming all the servants. A worthy successor to his father – and who knows, wondered ambitious Cecily, what his father would have to leave him when the time came.

Richard nodded. He too was eager for a sight of the children.

'So,' said Cecily, 'we are to return to England.'

'How soon can you be ready?' asked the Duke.

'I can be ready as soon as you give the order to leave.'

They laughed together. He could read the exhilaration in her eyes; she could see the dreams in his. Who knew, they might be going home to fight for the crown.

Edmund Beaufort, Duke of Somerset was riding through the streets of London towards the palace of Westminster. He was the most unpopular man in England and he was on his way to see the most unpopular woman. He hated the mob. Unthinking idiots, he grumbled to himself. They judged a man by his victories and his defeats. It never occurred to them to consider extraneous circumstances. How could any general succeed in France at this time? Everything was against him. Charles of France – that weak and ineffectual Dauphin – had suddenly shaken himself out of his torpor and was roaring like a lion. The

English had lost heart since Joan of Arc had appeared to tell them that Heaven was on the side of the French. It was all hopeless. Somerset wanted to shake the dust of France off his feet for ever.

He had returned not exactly in disgrace but somewhere near it. He had been obliged to relinquish Rouen and that was tantamount to losing Normandy. He was blamed for the disasters of the last few years. Bedford was dead; Gloucester was dead . . . though Gloucester had not helped them to success . . . but now people were talking of him as though he were a martyr. They believed he had been murdered and they accused Margaret of having a hand in that.

Margaret it seemed was his one friend, an important one it was true for Henry relied on her completely and he obeyed her wishes in every respect. So if he had only one friend yet she did happen to be the most powerful in the Kingdom.

It will blow over, he thought, unless of course this rumour about York is true.

Margaret was delighted when she heard he had come. Somerset was a true friend as the Suffolks had been. She was sad thinking of Suffolk, that dear man who had come to France and brought her to England and had been so kind to her. And Alice too . . . poor broken-hearted Alice. It infuriated Margaret to think of the dastardly way they had murdered Suffolk. She could grow white with anger at the thought and could only be appeased by telling herself what she would do to those who had murdered her dear friend if ever she got the chance.

Henry was so mild of course. She had had great difficulty in persuading him to allow harsh sentences to be passed on those who had been caught taking part in the Jack Cade rebellion. It was true they had been given pardons. That was the rabble, the mob, who followed blindly. It was the leaders who had to be severely punished. She was sorry Jack Cade had not been brought before his judges alive. Henry shuddered at the thought of bloodshed. He really was becoming more and more aloof from life. He wanted to be alone with his books and the time he spent on his knees made her wonder whether his brain was softening. There was one virtue in all this, it did give her a free hand. He rarely questioned anything she did but when it came to punishment he did raise a feeble voice and utter the only oath he used, which was 'By St John' and if he were greatly put out he would mutter 'Forsooth and forsooth'.

Henry lived like a recluse and a very pious one at that. He did not dress like a King but like a townsman with a round cape and a long cloak of drab colour; he refused to wear the fashionable long pointed shoes and wore the round ones which countrymen wore. When he had to be attired for State occasions he wore a hair shirt under the glittering robes. Margaret herself loved to be arrayed in splendid garments. Of course she did. Had she not suffered poverty all her life before she came to England and was she not the Queen? Moreover she was beautiful and naturally she wanted to make the most of her charms.

Henry wanted nothing for himself but he gave freely to others. He never wanted to punish evil doers – even robbers and such malefactors. He found excuses for them. It was very benevolent but it did nothing to deter the criminals. The fact was that he was a good man; he would have been at home in a monastery and it was a pity fate had set him on a throne.

He was at this time taking a great interest in his half-brothers, the Tudor children. He himself would supervise their education and make sure that they were provided for. 'It is what my mother would have wished, God rest her soul,' he declared. She had lived with Owen and he remembered Owen with affection. Owen was still somewhere in Wales. His mother and Owen might not have been married but, as he said to Margaret, that was no fault of the children.

Margaret shrugged her shoulders. The Tudors were of no interest to her. She had to concern herself with governing the realm, for it was becoming increasingly obvious to her that Henry was incapable of doing that.

Yet the people loved him. Everything that went wrong in the nation's affairs was blamed on others – and particularly on the Queen.

They hated her and with every month that hatred grew.

The English were losing their French possessions to the French – and she was French. They looked for scapegoats. They had had Suffolk but they were not satisfied. They wanted others and their thoughts had come to rest on Margaret.

Who had given Maine to the French? they demanded. Who had betrayed the armies? Margaret. Of course she had. She was not working for England. She was working for her father, René of Anjou, and her uncle Charles, the King of France. What had happened to the Duke of Gloucester? He had died mysteriously when he had been arrested on the way to Bury. She had had a hand in that.

So there she was. The French spy in their midst, the murderess, the arrogant little Queen who ruled the poor saintly King who was too virtuous himself to see sin in others.

The rumour had started that she was a bastard and not the daughter of René of Anjou. What had her relationship with Suffolk been? It was useless for anyone to point out that Suffolk had been an old man and that Margaret had been on terms of great friendship with his wife. They wanted her to be not only illegitimate but immoral and they were going to do their best to make others accept this view. She was certainly the most unpopular woman in England.

She received Somerset with a show of affection. She never sought to hide the love she bore her friends any more than she did her hatred towards her enemies. Margaret prided herself on her honesty and nothing should curb it, no matter how the display of it might wound others.

'My lady,' said Somerset kneeling, 'you sent for me.'

'Rise, Edmund,' she said. 'It is good to see you. At least I have a friend in you.'

'Until the end of my days.'

'Edmund, there are disturbing rumours. Is it true York has left Ireland?'

'I believe it to be so.'

'For what purpose? Has this anything to do with Jack Cade?'

'I fear it may have.'

'Cade called himself Mortimer but it has been proved he had no connection with the Mortimers.'

'I would not be so sure of that.'

'Then if it was so York is a traitor to the King.'

'York is an ambitious man.'

'We did well to send him to Ireland. He has no right to return without our permission.'

'What does the King say to this?'

'The King!' Margaret's lips curled. 'He says that York has been in Ireland, has proved himself a good administrator.'

'All the more reason why he should be kept there.'

'That's what I tell Henry. But you say York is already on his way over.'

'That is my information.'

'Do you think he will make trouble?'

'I think he is coming to prove that he had no part in the Cade rebellion. That would suggest he comes to assure you and the King of his loyalty.'

'He had better,' replied Margaret grimly. 'I will take you to the King. He is very kindly disposed towards you, Edmund.'

'For which I believe I have to thank your good grace.'

'Henry is always ready to love my friends,' she answered complacently.

It was true. He doted on her. Nothing would ever mean so much to Margaret as her royalty, and although sometimes she forgot that Henry had bestowed it on her, she was fond of him. Secretly she rejoiced in his weakness which enabled her to develop her strength. She never had to fight Henry and never found it difficult to impose her views on him; she might have had to persuade him at times, but that had always been easy. He was delighted that he had acquired such a beautiful wife who could take her place in public affairs – in fact take his place, so that he could often elude that which was distasteful to him. She was always gentle with him for the reason that he never gave her cause to be otherwise. He was not demanding in any way. He was very grateful for Margaret and he thought her interest in those about her was wonderful. She had arranged several marriages for the women of her household.

If she liked them she liked them a good deal and brought those tremendous energies of hers to work for what she considered their good. She would naturally be offended if they did not agree with her and sometimes rebelled against the plans she made for them. She could become angry then, and a friend could become an enemy. She would do a great deal for her friends but she never allowed an enemy to be unaware of her resentment.

It was amazing how much force, energy and passion were contained in that small body.

Henry received Somerset with affection. Margaret was fond of him and had made Henry see what a good servant he was in spite of the unkind things which were said about him in almost every quarter.

'We must support our friends,' said Margaret; and he agreed with her.

'My lord Somerset is a little disturbed about the news of York,' said Margaret. 'He has no right to leave Ireland without permission from you.'

'He has done very well there,' said Henry, 'and I do not think he was very eager to go.'

'Of course he was not,' cried Margaret. 'He wanted to be here. He liked to keep his eyes on the crown.'

'He has been a good servant to it,' ventured Henry.

'He will be a good servant for just as long as it suits him.'

'It suits all of us to serve the crown,' replied Henry placidly.

'It depends in what manner,' replied Margaret shortly. 'My lord Somerset comes here to warn us of York's coming.'

'Oh, we will see him when he arrives. He will bring us news of Ireland.'

Margaret raised her eyes to the ceiling in some exasperation.

The gesture implied that it was useless to attempt to talk to the King.

It would be up to her . . . and Somerset . . . to act whenever York presented himself.

Richard knew that he was coming into trouble. He had two very good excuses for returning to England. One was that if he were to keep order in Ireland money must be sent to him. This had not been done. The other was that accusations which had been made against him as the man behind Jack Cade's rebellion must be refuted.

He was in need of money. Although he was the greatest landowner in England his income was not enough for the upkeep of his vast estates, and since he had not been paid for his work in Ireland, he must come home to sort out his affairs. But chiefly of course it was to quell these suspicions of his being behind the uprisings. At least both these were good enough reasons. Another was too dangerous to discuss with anyone but Cecily.

'The King manages to retain a certain popularity but will he continue to do so when the affairs of the country go from bad to worse?' he asked her. 'The whole of our French possessions – or almost all – are lost. During the last reign we were the rulers of that country; now we have nothing . . . not even that which is our rightful inheritance. The people will turn against Henry. They are already against his wife. Somerset is un-popular. And then . . :'

'And then,' went on Cecily, 'it will be your turn. They cannot get a son.' Fruitful Cecily was scornful. 'I should not be surprised if Henry is impotent. No son . . . a virago of a French wife and a King who finds it hard to say boo to a goose. It won't last, Richard. Oh no, it can't last.'

'So think I. The people want a strong man . . . who is yet through his birth fit to be their King.'

'Closer to royal Plantagenet than Henry himself,' added Cecily.

Yes, Cecily knew that he was returning not only to see to his estates, not only to vindicate himself but with a very brilliant prospect in his mind which could leap to glory.

They set sail from Ireland and landed in Wales where friends awaited to tell him that the Queen was denouncing him as a traitor. It seemed they were not unaware of the reasoning behind his actions.

Very well, he would go to London and with feigned humility assure them that he had no knowledge of the Jack Cade rebellion, which was true. If he had meant to set an insurrection in progress he would not have used a rogue like Jack Cade for the purpose. He wondered what the mood of the country was and his instincts told him that the time was not yet ripe.

Henry still retained a certain popularity; there was the hope that Margaret would produce an heir; as for the unpopularity of the Queen, queens had often been unpopular and it would be unwise to put too much stress on the people's suspicions of this one.

As he began to march towards London men joined him. They wanted a strong King and they were alarmed at the loss of the French possessions and the influence of the Queen.

Richard's spirits were rising particularly when he heard that William Tresham who had been Speaker of the House of Commons was on his way to meet him. Tresham's differences with Suffolk had deprived him of his post. He had turned against the Court party led by Margaret and now clearly saw that there was a chance of the Duke of York's becoming a power in the land.

It was obvious that when he had heard of York's landing he had decided to join him. What could be a better indication of the support Richard would get from those who were dissatisfied with the present regime?

Alas, a great disappointment was to follow for Tresham never reached him. He was intercepted by Edmund Grey, Lord Grey de Ruthin, in Northamptonshire and in the encounter was slain.

So, thought Richard, although there would be some to support him, there would be powerful men against him. He would have to go warily.

He had one strong ally in the Duke of Norfolk. Even before the news of York's return Norfolk had expressed his dissatisfaction with the King's – or rather the Queen's – rule and had summoned certain knights and squires down to his castle of Framlingham to discuss this matter.

As soon as he heard that York was in England he set out to meet him and they met at Bury where they immediately went into a conference together.

Nothing was said about York's claim to the throne. That was too dangerous a matter and Richard had to feel his way very carefully. He had encountered certain opposition and it was clear that the nobility had not exactly rallied to his banner. He would therefore intimate that all he wanted was reforms. He and Norfolk were joined by the Earl of Oxford and Lord Scales. There would be a meeting of Parliament shortly and they decided together who should be the knights of the shire for Norfolk.

So far so good. Men were rallying round York and he sent

messages ahead asking all those who wished him well to join him. By the time they reached London he had with him four thousand armed men.

He was easily able to overcome the attempt to keep him from the King's presence and forcing his way in he confronted Henry, when he knelt with a humility which Henry was greatly relieved to see. York was his kinsman. He meant no harm, he was sure. He bade him rise and state why he had come in this manner.

'My lord King,' said York. 'I come to ask for justice . . . nothing more. I have not been paid for my work in Ireland and I find it impossible to continue there. I have heard that there have been lies uttered against me in regard to the rogue Jack Cade and I come to assure you that this man was a stranger to me. I never knew his name until after his death and I deplore his treachery towards yourself as every right-thinking man in England must do.'

'I believe you,' said Henry. 'Why, dear cousin, you are my friend, I know. We were much disturbed by this matter and have never believed you had a part in it.'

York took the King's hand and kissed it.

'Then my lord, these matters will be dealt with in Parliament.'

'They must be indeed, and dear cousin, remember that when you come with an army there will be those to oppose you. That is natural, eh? But to me you come in peace and as you so rightly say these matters must be settled by Parliament.'

'My lord, perhaps you will appoint a council.'

'I will indeed.'

'And in view of my position I should be a member of that council.'

'So it shall be,' said the King.

York bowed, well pleased. It was easy to deal with Henry. All he wanted was peace.

Inside the Temple in London where a meeting had been held between certain members of the Parliament to discuss the losses in France it had grown unbearably hot and the meeting had broken up with acrimony on both sides, chiefly between the Duke of Somerset and the Earl of Warwick.

Somerset was blamed by Warwick for the disastrous losses in France and Warwick was of the opinion that a man who had brought such ill fortune to his country should be impeached.

Both men were of overbearing natures. Both considered themselves of rare importance. Edmund Beaufort, Duke of Somerset, had the support of the Queen and through her that of the King. Moreover he was royal. His grandfather was John of Gaunt and if his father had had to be legitimised he was still royal. In his youth he had won brilliant victories in France; he had been known as one of the greatest commanders. Was it his fault if the whole battle front had changed, if some blight had settled on the English armies? He was beginning to believe that those were right who thought Joan of Arc had really been sent from Heaven, and Somerset was not going to be blamed for what was inevitable. Of course he had failed in France. No one could have succeeded in such circumstances. Secretly he believed that if Henry died – and Henry was sickly and without heirs – there was no sign of one after all these years – he, Somerset, would have good claim to the throne.

The Earl of Warwick was watching him intently as though reading his thoughts.

Warwick, thought Somerset. Who was Warwick? Of very little importance before he had had his first stroke of luck in marrying Anne Beauchamp, daughter of the Earl of Warwick. Salisbury's son who had married the only daughter of Richard Beauchamp and inherited her father's vast lands and title of Earl of Warwick! Strangely enough he and Somerset were related because Warwick's grandmother had been Joan Beaufort, daughter of John of Gaunt.

These entwined branches sprang from many trees. Warwick's aunt Cecily had married the Duke of York, and Warwick was allying himself more and more with York.

The real enemy, Somerset believed, was the Duke of York. Yes, York was determined to destroy him. Somerset knew where York's thoughts were moving. He saw himself as heir to the throne. Sickly Henry, childless, and an unpopular Queen meant that eyes were all turned on the next claimant.

It could be York. Some would say he was the most likely. But Somerset was not without his supporters.

As they walked out into the Temple gardens for a breath of fresh air the scent of the roses was everywhere. They had been well tended and grew in profusion on either side of the path and the gardener had arranged them so that red were on one side, white on the other.

Warwick approached Somerset and there was no mistaking the hostility in his eyes.

'My lord,' said Warwick, 'you should count yourself fortunate that you walk freely in these gardens.'

'I understand you not, my lord,' retorted Somerset.

'Ours is a sad country these days, my lord. How long ago is

it since the streets of this city were ringing with triumphant bells and there were processions there to celebrate our victories?'

'You would know that, my lord Warwick, as well as I and I cannot think why you should ask such a question of me.'

'Of whom else should I ask it, since you are the author of our troubles?'

'You go too far.'

'I will go as far as I consider seemly.'

People were beginning to gather round sensing a growing excitement. A quarrel between two of the mightiest nobles in the country.

Somerset's hand was on his sword. He was notoriously quick-tempered. The Duke of Buckingham caught at his sleeve to restrain him. Warwick looked him steadily in the eyes.

'My lord,' said Warwick, 'I see plans in your eyes.'

There was no mistaking his meaning. Somerset felt an uneasiness creeping over him.

'I am loyal to the King,' he cried. 'I am his servant as long as he honours me with his commands.'

'We are all good servants of the King and this realm,' retorted Warwick. 'But methinks, lord Somerset, that there is one who comes before you in his closeness to the King.'

'So you are for York, are you, Warwick? You have decided to take sides in this quarrel you seek to ferment.'

'It is not of my fermenting but when there are those who concern themselves with great projects it is the duty of all honourable men to support that which is right.'

Somerset was seething with rage. He was alarmed. The country was against him. Unfairly they blamed him for defeats in France. He only had the support of the King and the Queen to rely on. But no, there were others. There must be some who did not want to see York rise to power.

He moved away from Buckingham's restraining hand and plucking one of the red roses, the symbol of the House of Lancaster since the days of Edmund, Earl of Lancaster and brother of Edward the First, he cried out: 'I pluck this red rose. The red rose of Lancaster. I am for Lancaster and the King.'

Warwick turned away and immediately picked a white rose – the symbol of York – the white rose worn by the Black Prince himself. He held the rose on high. 'I pluck this white rose,' he said. 'The white rose of York. Let every man among us choose his rose. Let him declare himself with these fair flowers. Then shall we know how we stand together.'

There was a shout of excitement as all began plucking the roses until the flower beds were completely denuded. Their cries filled the air.

'For York. For Lancaster.'

This was the prelude. The curtain was about to be raised on the wars of the roses.

The Duke of York had gone off to his castle of Fotheringay on the banks of the river Nen in Northamptonshire which had become a favourite seat of the House of York since Edmund Langley had taken possession of it. There he was joined by the Duke of Norfolk, the Earl of Salisbury and Salisbury's son Richard Neville, Earl of Warwick.

They had gathered together to plan how they should act at the forthcoming session of Parliament.

'The King cannot continue to reign unless he ceases to be guided by his wife,' declared Warwick.

Since the scene in the Temple gardens he had set himself up as an adviser to York on whose side he had now proclaimed himself so openly to be. York was a strong man he believed and what the country needed was a strong man.

'Poor Henry,' said York. ' 'Tis a pity he cannot go into a monastery. It would suit him better than his throne.'

'It may well be that in time he will,' added Warwick.

The others were silent. Warwick was perhaps being impulsive not in having such an opinion, but in voicing it.

'If the Queen were to have a child . . .' began Salisbury.

'My lord, do you think that possible?' asked York, desperately hoping to hear that it was not, for if Margaret did bear a child all their scheming would come to nothing.

'Hardly likely,' said Salisbury. 'Not after all this time. The King is too deeply concerned with his prayers and the Queen with being Queen. She divides her time between instructing her seamstress on the making of extravagant garments and arranging the marriages of her serving-women. The Queen is a meddler.'

'Better for her to meddle with her needlewomen and serving-wenches than with the affairs of this country,' put in Warwick.

'But she meddles in everything. And Somerset is her darling.'

'Do you think . . .?'

A fearful thought had come to York.

'I doubt it,' he said. 'Even Margaret would not go as far as to foist a bastard on the throne.'

'But Somerset – if he were the father – would salve his conscience by declaring – to himself of course – that it was a royal brat.'

'We go too far,' said Warwick. 'The Queen is not with child or likely to be, so we waste time in discussing who the father of a possible bastard might be. Let us give ourselves to matters of immediate concern. We must rid the country of Somerset. He should be impeached for what he has done in France.'

'The Queen will never agree to it.'

'It is a matter for the Parliament. What we shall aim for is to remove Somerset and set you, my lord York, up in his place. Protector of the realm to serve under the King, which means you will advise him, with the help of your ministers, and it may well be that we can snatch a little victory out of this morass of disaster and failure into which our once great country has fallen. We shall attend the Parliament wearing white roses. It will show clearly what our intentions are.'

'It is not easy to come by white roses at this time of year,' pointed out Norfolk.

'Then they should be fabricated in paper or whatever substance can be found. Let us keep to our symbol of the White Rose. All those for us shall wear it and you may be sure that our enemies will retaliate by flaunting the red rose of Lancaster. Then we shall know our friends . . . and our enemies.'

So they would go to the Parliament.

Margaret was furious when she heard that Richard of York had seen the King and that Henry had agreed to call a Parliament.

'That man is a traitor,' she cried. 'You know what he wants, don't you . . . he and that haughty wife of his? Do you know Proud Cis is already behaving as though she were a queen and that her women have to kneel to her?'

'She was always a proud woman.'

'It's because she is the daughter of that bastard Joan Beaufort,' went on Margaret.

Henry smiled at her affectionately. She had been so fond of that other bastard, Joan's brother, the Cardinal. Margaret was so fierce in her loyalties, her likes and dislikes, that she was not always logical.

'You mistake York,' he said. 'He has been wrongfully accused of complicity with Jack Cade. He wanted to be exonerated. That is all.'

'"That is all",' she mimicked. 'And wrongfully accused. He has not been wrongfully accused. You may depend upon it, Richard of York has his eyes on your crown.'

'How could he ever hope for that?' asked Henry, his eyes wide. 'I am the son of the King. I have worn my crown almost since I was in my cradle.'

Margaret looked at him in exasperation. Would he never learn? Could he not see evil when it was creeping up on him and was all around him? What a fool he was to think that the whole world was intent on good and every man as saintly as himself. It was well for him that he had a strong woman to look after him.

'At the Parliament,' she said, 'the supporters of York will wear white roses in their hats or on their sleeves.'

'The white rose is of course the symbol of York and has been for some time.'

'They wear them in defiance. Have you forgotten that scene in the Temple Gardens?'

'I did hear of it,' said Henry.

'Don't you see it was significant. It was like a declaration of war.'

'My dear Margaret, there is no war. There will be no war.

Those who wear the white rose are proud of it because it has been their symbol for so many years.'

It was useless to talk to him, to try to make him understand.

'Very well,' she said. 'Let them wear their white roses. We shall wear the red rose of Lancaster and show them that our red rose will never give way to the white rose of York.'

She would wear a red rose in her hair. Henry should wear one on his cloak. There should be a finer array of red roses than of white.

So at the fateful meeting of the Parliament were sown the seeds which were to develop into a bloody war – red rose against white rose – and change the course of history.

Both colours were well represented. Already men were straining to get at each other. They jostled one another, sought a pretext to fight.

It was an uneasy occasion.

Margaret was unaware of it as, looking very beautiful with the red rose in her hair, she listened to the ceremony of Parliament, during which it was agreed that the Duke of York should be recognised as heir to the throne should the King die without heirs.

The white rose faction seemed delighted with this and the Parliament broke up peacefully.

In the York apartments Cicely declared herself satisfied with the proceedings. 'The people will not endure foolish Henry and proud Margaret for long,' she cried. 'Speed the day when they put a real King on the throne.'

Her fond eyes were on her husband. Of course Richard should be king!

As for Margaret, she was incensed. The impudence of York! Heir to the throne indeed. Oh, if only she could get a child!

In the meantime Henry must keep his hold on the affection of his people.

'We will do some pilgrimages,' she said. Yes, that was it. They would make progress through the country. The people loved to see the King; and she would appear among them sumptuously gowned, looking beautiful, and she would try to hide her impatience with the stupid people and be so gracious that they all thought her the loveliest creature they had ever seen.

Yes, that was it. They should show themselves to the people. There was nothing the people liked better.

❁ Chapter IX ❁

THE KING'S MADNESS

Richard was frustrated almost beyond endurance. The hardest task a man of ambition could be called upon to do was to wait. Yet wait he must. That the opportunity would come he was sure; and to strike prematurely would be to ruin his hopes. So there was nothing he could do but retire from court and bide his time.

It was nearly two years since that Parliament when the hostile wearers of red and white roses had faced each other. That could so easily have developed into conflict which would have been unwise and have achieved nothing.

He had suffered a certain temptation then. There were so many who recognised the incompetence of Somerset's rule, the domination of the Queen over the King, and who looked upon Somerset and Margaret as two wicked conspirators. But it was not the moment. It would have been a reckless gamble which might have resulted in the end of hope.

Looking back he now began to wonder whether he had been too cautious. When the people had rioted in Westminster after that memorable Parliament they had shouted for Somerset's blood. They would have murdered him if they had caught him.

Yes, and made a martyr of him. That was not the way. Somerset should be tried and his crimes and failures made clear to everyone. The people blamed him for the failure in France and a gang of soldiers returned from the wars surrounded his house in Blackfriars and would have murdered him there and then had he not been rescued.

Some thought it ironical that his rescuers should be the Duke of York with his ally Devonshire. But it was all part of a strategy. Richard was anxious that all should realise that the last thing he wanted was to create conflict in the country. He was all for law and order. He wanted Somerset to be impeached, he wanted him to stand his trial, yes. What he did not want was for him to be murdered by the mob.

Together he and Devonshire had rescued Somerset and taken him to the Tower. Not as a prisoner, Richard was eager to stress, but for his own safety. He was eager to make a good impression on the people; and if ever he found government in his hands the last thing he wanted was to have come to it through the mob.

He was a cautious man and he soon realised that the King with Margaret behind him was too strong on his throne to be lightly overturned. The Commons might support York but the Lords certainly did not. He knew that the best thing he could do was retire quietly for a while and bide his time.

He retired to the Welsh border where he was by no means inactive. He was persuading his friends to stand with him; making them see that there could be no prosperity for England while she was ruled by the Queen and Somerset, a man who had failed dismally in France and was now doing the same in England. Were they going to stand by and see the decline of their country or were they going to be rid of this feeble House of Lancaster and set up that which had more right to be there and had the will and the power to govern – the Royal House of York?

The King was growing more feeble; the Queen more arrogant and Somerset more ineffectual. Moreover it was clear that the King could not beget a child.

'The time must come when change is inevitable,' said the Duke of York, and yet he knew that the moment had not yet come.

There had been a series of progresses through the country. Margaret enjoyed them; Henry tolerated them for her sake and because the Earl of Somerset thought it pleased the people. It was certainly a mixed blessing to the hosts of the royal party and those who were given the honour of entertaining them certainly had to count the costs. If the party stayed for more than a few days bankruptcy could stare the host in the face, for to provide the quantities of food that had to be supplied to the King's travelling retinue could be ruinous.

But how Margaret enjoyed those journeys. Seated on her horse or carried in her litter, brilliantly attired, she felt a Queen indeed. She had come a long way from the days of poverty when she had been forced to seek a refuge with her grandmother. That grandmother would have offered all kinds of advice now, she knew. But Margaret was determined to enjoy her triumphs. The King admired her. Her exquisite clothes were commented on wherever she went. She knew she was very beautiful with her royal crown set on her golden hair which she wore flowing about her shoulders to show it in all its beauty. Beneath her purple cloak fastened with bands of gold and precious gems, her cote-hardi would fit her beautiful figure to perfection and it would be made of the richest materials and adorned with glittering jewels. She always liked her emblem to be prominent everywhere – not only in her dress but wherever they went. People no longer carried daisies as they had out of compliment to her when she had first arrived in the country; but at the great houses she would be gratified to see the flower prominently displayed.

It was a pity Henry did not pay more attention to his dress. It was difficult to make him wear the correct garments even for State occasions.

At least he admired his wife and in his eyes she could do no wrong; and if the people showed little enthusiasm for her – and indeed sometimes betrayed a definite dislike – she cared nothing for them. She had complete faith in her ability to command Henry and as Henry was the King that meant she ruled England to a large extent.

She was determined to honour the Earl of Somerset and her hatred of the Duke of York was deep. She enjoyed reviling him; she revelled in her hatred. She thought that if he would only go far enough she would have his head on London Bridge.

One cold March day she was at her writing-table. She was trying to make a match for one of her serving-women. She so much enjoyed matchmaking and she found the very man for her woman. She would break the good news to them, get them married and perhaps attend the christening of the first child.

She had several protégées for whom she had made marriages.

She loved to dabble in their affairs, to watch over them, to listen to their troubles and to follow the course of their lives. When they had children she was pleased but often a little envious. It did not seem right that the common people should be able to bear children while those to whom children were of the utmost importance remained barren.

Neither she nor Henry were passionately interested in the act of procreation. It was to them both a necessary duty, but she was growing rather disheartened. It was nine years and in spite of their dutiful efforts there was still no sign of a child. If she could have a son what a joy that would be. York would be silenced for ever.

As she rose from her writing-table she wondered whether to summon her woman and tell her the good news. 'You are to be married,' she would tell the astonished girl; and she hoped she would be suitably grateful.

She sent for the woman. While she was talking to her one of her attendants came in to say that a messenger had arrived and was asking for an audience with her.

She dismissed the woman and said she would deal with her affairs later. In the meantime she would receive the messenger.

She was delighted to see that he came from her father, but when she looked into his face she realised at once that it was not good news.

'My lady,' he said bowing low, 'I come from the King of Sicily your noble father. Here are letters for you but he said it might be better if I prepared you for the news.'

'Then do so,' she commanded.

'Your noble mother the lady Isabelle is very ill.'

Margaret looked steadily at the messenger. 'Do you mean she is dead?' she asked.

'My lady, I fear so.'

She nodded. 'Give me the letters,' she said. 'Then go to the kitchen where they will refresh you after your journey.'

She took the letters from the messenger and saw that they

were indeed in her father's hand. She glanced through them. She would read them thoroughly later.

Her mother dead. She could scarcely believe it. Not that strong, vital woman.

Memories crowded into her mind. She remembered her mother more from her very early days. She would never forget that journey to the French court when Agnès Sorel had accompanied them.

Agnès . . . beautiful Agnès, beloved of a King.

She rose from her writing-table and as she did so she felt suddenly weak and dizzy. She clutched it for support and then slid back into her chair.

One of the women was running to her. Vaguely she heard her exclamation of alarm.

When she awoke she was resting on her bed and the doctors were there.

They were not sure, they told her. But there were signs. There was a possibility.

'I am pregnant,' she whispered.

'My lady,' was the answer, 'it could well be so.'

She felt bewildered. Coming so soon on the shock of her mother's death she could scarcely grasp it. Death on one hand and the possibility of birth – glorious birth – on the other. No wonder she felt bemused.

She must not become overexcited. She must wait until she could be certain before she told Henry.

There came a day when she was sure. She hurried to Henry and embraced him. He smiled gently at her.

'It would seem that you have heard good news,' he said.

'The best possible news,' she told him. 'It has happened at last. Henry, I am with child.'

'Forsooth and forsooth,' he cried. 'Can it really be so?'

'I believe it to be so. The doctors do also.'

'So long we have waited. So much effort . . .'

'Nevertheless it is true. I am going to have a child. Think what this will mean. Think of York's face when he hears of it. What use for him to flaunt his white rose now? This will change everything.'

'If the child is a boy,' began Henry.

'It will be a boy,' cried Margaret. 'It *must* be a boy.'

She was right. York was stunned when he heard the news. If this child were a healthy boy it would destroy his hopes. A son . . . after nine years! But it was not born yet. It might never be and if it were a girl that would not be so dangerous, but a boy would be disaster.

'Do you think it can be true?' he asked Cecily.

'I will believe it when I see the child,' she retorted.

'It is possible, of course. Perhaps it is just a rumour. I can't believe that just at this time.'

'You don't think it is someone else's?'

'Somerset's you mean?'

'Can it be Henry's? They say he is getting more and more feeble.'

'He certainly is not interested in women. He has never had a mistress and I believe he has had to force himself to sleep with the Queen.'

Lusty Cecily laughed aloud. Then she said seriously: 'The Queen is capable of anything, I do believe.'

'We must wait in patience. For one thing the rumour may not be true, for another the child might not live.'

'And if it does, Richard, and if it is a boy?'

'Then it may be necessary to take the crown by force,' answered Richard grimly.

'So thought I at the time when there was that hostility in the Temple Gardens between the wearers of the white and red roses.'

'Civil war is the last thing I want.'

'But the alternative . . . ?'

'If we cannot settle by peaceful means then we shall have to resort to arms.'

Cecily nodded. 'They are laughing, these Lancastrians, at their good fortune.'

'They may not be laughing for long,' answered Richard.

Henry was pleased with life. He refused to see the trouble all about him. Somerset fretted about York and declared that he was fomenting trouble. Henry did not believe him really. Henry liked to feel that men were good though now and then a little misguided perhaps, but he could not accept the fact that his kinsman of York meant any harm to him. Margaret, of course, agreed with Somerset. She was always telling him that he must not be so gentle, so ready to believe the good in everyone. Margaret was so fierce at times – only because she was fond of him, of course, and cared so much about the prosperity of the country.

This summer they were taking a long progress through the land. Henry liked to visit the monasteries and abbeys and colleges as he passed through the countryside and promised himself that he would build more. He was glad that they were getting out of France. Let others deplore their losses if they would; he thought that when they no longer had anything to fight for in France, it would be so much the better.

He felt rather strange now and then, so listless that all he wanted to do was to be alone with his books. Then he would sometimes find himself half asleep in the middle of his reading. Sometimes he would awaken with a start and wonder where he was and for some time be unable to recall.

He was delighted to see Margaret so contented now that she was to have a child. It was what she had desired more than anything.

'At least now,' she said, 'they won't be able to criticise me for my barrenness.'

He tried to tell her that they were not really criticising her. They were merely anxious for there to be an heir to the throne. It was love of the country that made them sad about there not being one. Now it would be very different.

They were at Clarendon in the New Forest. Margaret was happy here. She loved to hunt but she was dispensing with that pleasure now for she was six months pregnant and growing larger every day. Some of the wise old women said that the way she carried the child indicated that it was a boy.

How contented they would be if that were so. But a child of either sex would be welcome. It would at least show that they could get children. Although of course everyone would be wanting a boy.

Well, they were at peace here at Clarendon. Henry had been feeling very tired of late. The long day's riding had been more exhausting than usual. They would stay a little while at Clarendon.

The next morning when his attendants came to his bed-chamber they found him lying very still, his eyes wide open, staring ahead of him. He did not seem to see them. When they spoke to him, he did not answer. He lay very quietly and did not seem to be able to move his limbs.

They went in consternation to the Queen, knowing that she would be angry if not informed at once of the King's strangeness.

She stared at him lying there supine on the bed. He looked different somehow – like a corpse.

She took his hand. It fell from hers without Henry's seeming to be aware of it. He did not appear to see her. He just lay – unseeing, unhearing, unthinking.

'Call the doctors,' commanded the Queen.

They came but they could neither make him see nor hear. He responded in no way.

'What is it?' demanded the Queen impatiently.

'It would seem that the King has lost his reason.'

Margaret stood up, her hands on her body. She could feel the child moving. The King losing his reason. What nonsense! She must send for Somerset at once.

She faced the doctors. 'Say nothing of this . . . as yet,' she commanded. 'This may pass. We do not know yet what ails the King, but I do not wish to let loose disturbing rumours.' The doctors said that they would say nothing.

Somerset came riding with all speed to Clarendon and Margaret at once took him to see the King who was still in a form of coma, although he appeared to be conscious. His eyes were open; he was breathing; but apart from that he might have had no life at all.

'Edmund, my dear friend,' she cried, 'what calamity is it that has fallen on us?'

'The King, the doctors appear to think, has lost his reason.'

'I fear that may be so. But there is a possibility that he will recover.'

Somerset nodded. 'It came upon him suddenly. It may well be that it will depart in the same way.'

'And in the meantime?'

Somerset said: 'We should wait a while. Let no one know of this until we are sure what it means.'

She nodded. 'So thought I. I have commanded the doctors to say nothing.'

'That is well, but there are spies everywhere, you know. The servants . . .'

'I think I can trust them.'

'You can never trust servants, dear lady. However we must hope that nothing of this reaches the ears of the people until we understand what it is and plan what we can do about it.'

'My child is due in three months.'

'If we can keep this quiet until the child is born . . . and if the child is a prince . . .'

'Oh, Edmund, how glad I am that we think alike. We will wait until the child is born and by that time Henry may have recovered. But what can this condition mean?'

'I fear he may be losing his reason.'

She looked at him in horror.

'You know who his mother was. That means that he could, I suppose, take after his grandfather.'

'The mad King of France! I have heard gruesome tales of him.'

'He was of a different temperament from Henry. Henry is so gentle, so peace-loving. The malady – if it be the same – has affected him differently. It has just robbed him of his senses.

Charles the Sixth was a raving lunatic at times violent, wreaking havoc wherever he was so that none dared go near him.'

'Pray God it does not come to that.'

'Not with gentle Henry. But it is a calamity none the less. All we can do is wait. We do not want this to come to York's ears.'

'God forbid. He would want to set himself up as Protector or Regent or some such post before we could plan anything.'

'York must not know. It may well be that it is a temporary stage. How long has he been like this?'

'Since his attendants went to his bedchamber and found him so only a few days ago.'

'We will wait then. Keep the matter as secret as possible and you should make your way to Westminster where the child should be born. You cannot remain at Clarendon. That would most certainly give rise to gossip.'

'It will not be easy to convey him to Westminster without its being noticed that there is something strange about him.'

'We will do it as best we can and I suggest that you begin to make the move as soon as possible.'

'I will do it, and I thank God that you are beside me.'

Margaret lay in her bedchamber in Westminster awaiting the birth of the child. This should have been the happiest time of her life and instead it was fraught with uneasiness.

In nearly three months Henry's condition had changed little. He could move his limbs now; he could eat; he slept; but he did not speak and he was completely unaware of what was going on around him. She had tried to speak to him about the child and he, who had been so overjoyed at the prospect of becoming a father, clearly did not know what she was talking about.

She had summoned the doctors William Hacliff, Robert Warren and William Marschall to his bedside because there were none in England to equal them for skill, but they shook their heads and conferred together. The King had lost his reason, they had to admit. The malady could have descended from his grandfather even though it had attacked him in a different form. They were with him constantly. They concocted syrups and potions, baths, fomentations and plasters. The King took them all patiently and lay or sat quietly saying nothing, hearing nothing and not responding in any way.

She knew there were wild rumours for it was quite impossible to keep the secret. Soon the true state of affairs would have to be divulged for many of the rumours were more horrific than the reality.

The doctors had said she most certainly must not fret. Her big task now was to produce a healthy child. It was unfortunate that this should have happened at this time of all times, but she must think of her all-important task.

They were right, of course. She must purge her mind of all anxiety. She must not think beyond the birth. Nothing must go wrong with that. She wondered how much of what was happening had reached the ears of the Duke of York.

Then her pains had started. Her women were with her, and at last after hours of agony she heard the cry of a child.

So prepared was she for misfortune that she could scarcely believe the truth when they told her that she had a boy – a beautiful, healthy boy.

She lay still rejoicing; and after a while they came and laid him in her arms.

❁ ❁ ❁

Somerset came to see her with the Duchess. They expressed their delight in the child and the Duchess walked round the bedchamber with him in her arms.

'But he is beautiful!' she cried. 'He looks the true son of a King.'

'The people will be pleased,' said Margaret.

'We will have the christening and purification as soon as possible,' said Somerset. 'Have you decided on a name for the child?'

'I have indeed,' replied Margaret. 'He was born on St Edward the Confessor's day, and Edward is a good name, is it not, for a King?'

'One of the best,' said the Duchess.

The Duke said: 'The people loved two of the Edwards. The second they despised. But I think they will like the name for when they think of Edward they think of Longshanks and his grandson Edward the Third. Yes, Edward is a good name.'

'York's eldest is Edward,' the Duchess reminded them.

'I know,' said the Queen, 'and by all accounts every inch a Plantagenet. Is he really as tall as they say he is?'

'He is a fine-looking young fellow – fair and tall and, young as he is, a favourite of the women. At least that's what I hear.'

'A curse on him,' said Margaret lightly. 'But why do we talk of that Edward when we have this little one here?' She turned to the Duke. 'I wonder if the sight of him might move Henry.'

'If anything could it would be the child,' said Somerset.

Margaret nodded. She was half fearful for something told her that Henry would not even know his own child.

There was no time for resting on her triumph.

Everyone would know now that there was something very wrong with the King if he did not appear at the christening of his son.

So it was proclaimed that the King was ill but the truth could not for long be withheld.

The christening ceremony was splendid. A costly chrisom was provided for the baby – richly embroidered in exquisitely coloured silks and studded with pearls and rich gems, but lined with linen so that the child's delicate skin should not be scratched. There were twenty yards of cloth of gold needed to decorate the font and Margaret's own churching-robe contained five hundred and forty sables. The cost of this was over five hundred pounds.

Margaret tried hard to live for just that day and refused to look ahead. It was not easy. The dark clouds were gathering.

❀ ❀ ❀

'So,' said York, 'the Queen has a son. Whose son? Not that idiot's surely! I believe him to be impotent. In such case how is it that our beautiful Queen produces a child?'

'Whom do you suspect?' asked Warwick.

'She is on very intimate terms with Somerset.'

'He is rather old.'

'But capable of begetting a child.'

'She is friendly with Buckingham.'

'Ah, she has her friends. But there must be a Regency, a protector of some sort now. Henry is incapable of governing.'

'It is true,' said Warwick. 'And you, my lord, should be our Protector. As the next in line of succession – recently displaced by this little Prince – it is your due.'

'So I thought,' said York. 'A Parliament must be called without delay.'

After her ceremonial churching which was attended by twenty-five of the highest ladies in the land including ten Duchesses, Margaret had left for Windsor. She had decided that it would be best for the King to stay there for a while where he could be free from too much exposure. She knew of course that the rumours were thick in the air and that very soon there would be some decision made as to who was to rule the country. As Queen she believed she should and she was going to fight for the position.

In the meantime she prayed for Henry's return to sanity, but he still showed no sign of having the least idea where he was.

Surely the child would awaken something in him?

Young Edward was dressed in his magnificent christening robe and Margaret put him into the arms of the Duke of Buckingham. With Somerset on one side of her the three of them went into the King's bedchamber.

He was seated in a chair, his plain unkingly clothes hanging loosely on him, his hands dangling at his sides and he was staring listlessly in front of him.

Margaret went forward and knelt at his feet.

'Henry, Henry, it is I, Margaret, your wife. You know me. You must know me.'

He stared over her head and she felt a great urge to shake him.

'Henry,' she cried sharply. 'You know me. You *must* know me.'

There was still no response.

'We have a child,' she cried. 'A son. It is what we wanted. More than anything we wanted this son. The people are delighted. They are calling for him . . . and for you. You must rouse yourself.'

There was no flicker of intelligence in those lack-lustre eyes.

She returned to Buckingham.

'Bring the baby,' she said.

Buckingham came forward. He held the baby out to Henry, but Henry just sat there, mute and unaware.

It was well known that the King was incapable of governing and that he suffered from some strange illness. They did not call it madness but people were talking of his French grandfather and everyone had heard what had happened to him.

So while the King remained thus there would have to be a Protector of the Realm, a King's Lieutenant, someone who could stand at the head of affairs until the King recovered.

As the Queen, it is my place to act for the King, thought Margaret. Her mother and grandmother had done so when the occasion arose, and she could see no reason why she should not do the same.

Matters drifted on. Christmas came and still no decision had been made and Henry remained in his strange state, unaware of anything that was going on around him.

Margaret, after having consulted with Somerset and Buckingham, decided to take matters into her own hands. With their help she prepared a bill setting out what she considered her rights.

She wanted to rule the country in Henry's name. She would be the one to appoint whom she chose to the important posts in the government; she should have power to bestow bishoprics on members of the clergy; and she should be assigned what was necessary to keep her, the King and the little Prince in the state due to them.

Parliament pretended to consider. They were delighted by the birth of the Prince but they were certainly not going to place more power in the hands of Margaret whom many held responsible for the disasters in France. Somerset was unpopular; he was allied with the Queen. It was decided therefore that the task must fall to one who was near to the throne and at the same time a strong man who was capable of governing: the Duke of York.

Here was triumph. Proud Cis was beside herself. She gathered her children and while she held young Richard in her arms – he was only a year old – she told them how their great father, who should really be King, was now head of the country.

'We must make sure that he remains so,' she said and her words were directed in particular to her tall, twelve-year-old son – handsome Plantagenet in looks, already earning a reputation for wildness – the son of whom she was most proud.

Edward declared he was ready to fight for his father's rights and the Duke laid his hand on his shoulder and said, 'When the time comes, my son. When the time comes.'

And it would come. They were all sure of that.

The Queen was furious. They had slighted her. She was the Queen; she had produced the heir to the throne. The Regency should have been hers.

The Duke of York wanted to play the game with caution. He declared to the Parliament that he accepted office only because he considered it his duty to do so. The King must know that – as soon as he returned to health – he, York, would stand aside.

As a man who believed he would one day be King he wanted to show his determination to uphold law and order. Kings could not rule satisfactorily without that, and he had made up his mind that one day he was going to rule.

He appointed his brother-in-law Richard, Earl of Salisbury, Chancellor. He would surround himself with friends in high places and the first thing to do was to be rid of Somerset, who was impeached and sent to the Tower.

It was hardly likely that his enemies would stand aside and allow York to rule in peace and it was soon necessary for him to march to the North and suppress disturbances there where certain noblemen led by the Duke of Exeter had raised their standards against him.

During those months of his Protectorate York showed himself to be the strong man the country needed. He was cautious and well aware that there was a great deal of support throughout the country for the Lancastrians. The King was the King and the people were fond of him – imbecile though he might be. There were many stories in circulation about his clemency and his gentleness. 'Poor Henry!' they said. His Queen was a virago. She was French; she was extravagant; she ruled the King; but still she was the mother of the heir to the throne. York knew that the time had not come to make the great bid. In the meantime he contented himself in governing the country, which all had to admit he did with more skill than his predecessors. He had captured Exeter, and Somerset was his prisoner, but he brought neither of them to trial. He was not sure what effect that would have on the people.

Meanwhile Margaret, secretly furious that she had been

passed over as the Regent, saw clearly that if she was to keep her power it could only be done through the King. Henry was her salvation. He would do as she said. All her strength had come through him. If he remained in this state of idiocy that would be the end of her hopes to rule.

Henry must get well.

With characteristic energy she set about the task of nursing him back to health. In the first place she believed that he could never get well while he was at the centre of affairs in Westminster where there were too many people visiting him and too much talk about his condition. People would keep on talking of his grandfather and expecting him to go raving mad at any moment.

It was not like that. She thought she was beginning to understand what might have happened. Henry had never wanted to be a king; that office on which men like York – and even Somerset – cast covetous eyes was a penance to Henry. He hated the ceremonies, the conflicts, the desire to maintain his position; even the progresses through the country which he seemed to think were the answer to all evils were not so very agreeable to him. As Margaret saw it a resentment against a fate which had made him the King had culminated in this complete collapse, this shutting off of responsibility, this rejection of a crown.

Of one thing she was certain – the potions, the syrups and the fomentations were not what was needed at all. It was Henry's mind which had deserted him; his body was not really sick.

She had found a new doctor, a certain William Hately, and he agreed with her theories.

'Get the King away,' he had said. 'Take him to some quiet

seat where there can be an atmosphere of peace about him. He may be susceptible to conflict around him. We cannot know that.'

'You mean take him to some place where the people are loyal to him. Where there would be no room for his enemies. My dear doctor, it is not always easy to know who are one's friends, who one's enemies.'

'There are parts of the country which are firmly loyal to the King and who tolerate the Duke of York only because he stands in the King's place while the King is indisposed.'

'He was always rather fond of Coventry. He has had a more loyal welcome there than anywhere. He was interested in the building of St Mary's Hall and took great pleasure from the tapestry there.'

'Let us try it, my lady. It may not help but we must try everything.'

'We will go to our castle of Coventry,' said the Queen.

She would be glad to get away, to devote herself entirely to the needs of the King. She knew it was useless to try to fight York at this time. Somerset was in the Tower and York's strong yet restrained government was having its effect. The fact that men like Somerset and Exeter were under restraint and had not been executed showed a tolerance in the Duke of York which pleased the people. They were already beginning to trust him.

As soon as the King is well that shall be an end of York, Margaret promised herself.

And that brought her back to the great need of the moment: the recovery of the King.

They travelled to Coventry, the King in his litter. On the Queen's orders they took the byways and avoided the towns but they could not make a secret entry into Coventry and the people of that city came out to cheer them as they passed through. The King lay still and silent in his litter with Margaret riding beside him, gorgeously apparelled as became a Queen. She it was who acknowledged the cheers of the crowd, though she knew those cheers were for the King and not for her. Never mind. They were for the Lancastrian cause and that was what was important.

Coventry, in the county of Warwickshire, was almost in the centre of England and took its name from a convent which had once stood on the site and had been founded as long ago as the days of King Canute. It was destroyed by the traitor Edric in the year 1016 before the coming of the Normans. However Earl Leofric and his wife Lady Godiva founded a Benedictine monastery on the spot and richly endowed it. It was at that time that the town began to prosper. The castle was built and was in the possession of the Lords of Chester. The city had been walled in at the time of Edward the Second and had six gates and several strong towers. The castle had eventually passed into the hands of the Black Prince and it became one of his favourite residences.

It seemed a very suitable place to bring the King and, if it were possible, nurse him back to health there.

The days passed quietly. Margaret spent a great deal of time with the King. She talked to him although he did not hear her, but William Hately believed that there was a possibility that one day he might. The worst thing, said the doctor, was to treat him as though he were an imbecile.

'His senses are clearly there,' he insisted. 'They are slumbering. It is for us to awaken them and we shall only do that by gentle methods.'

He was astonished and so were others to see how Margaret adapted herself to life at Coventry. She who had been so forceful, so ready to state her views, so determined that they should be acted on, was now playing the role of nurse and mother, dividing her time between her husband and her son, trying to arouse the shrunken mind of one and to assist the expanding one of the other.

It did not occur to them at that time that this was a further indication of her character. She was bent on one purpose: to nurse the King back to health that he might take his place in affairs again and she rule through him since they would not allow her to without him.

But it was more than that. There was a tenderness in Margaret. Faithful as she was to her friends, so was she to her husband. Her affection for him was firm; he had brought her out of France where she was of little importance and had made her a Queen. He loved her; he listened to her; he adored her. She was not going to forget that. She loved him and as Margaret could never do anything by halves, she loved him deeply; during that period her devotion was entirely for her husband and son. For Henry her emotions were loving and protective; for her son something like adoration and intense possessiveness.

It was a great task she had set herself; and she was determined to do everything in her power to make it succeed.

It was galling to learn that York was making a success of his task. He had now been appointed Protector and Defender of the Realm and Church and Principal Councillor of the King.

Margaret looked ahead to a future which could be gloomy if the King continued in his present state. There was no suggestion in the declaration that York was regarded as King;

and as soon as Henry recovered, or the Prince came of age, his authority would cease, but it infuriated her to think that he would have control over that precious infant in the cradle.

But not yet. The boy was too young and she was determined to bring Henry back to sanity.

The months passed. The wearisome task went on. Sometimes Henry raised a hand and that would send her hopes soaring. At others when she fed him he seemed to show a little interest in the food. Once she thought his eyes followed her as she crossed the room. That was a great advance. Then for days he would lapse into complete immobility again and she despaired.

Little Edward was her salvation. She spent a great deal of time with him. When he smiled at her a great tenderness welled up in her and she held him so tightly to her that he whimpered to be free. He was beautiful; he was her compensation; each day her maternal love seemed to strengthen. Everything . . . yes everything was worth while . . . while she had her baby.

Christmas was approaching. Henry had been in this state for more than a year. It was a long time since she had brought him to Coventry. William Hately was her great comfort. I shall never forget what he has done for me . . . and for Henry, she promised herself. When she despaired William Hately would have some hope to offer. When he thought he detected a change in the King, they would watch for it together.

'Sometimes I think you are as much my physician as the King's,' she told him.

It was a few days before Christmas. Margaret went into the King's room. Her heart leaped for the King smiled at her.

'Margaret,' he said, and held out his hand.

She went on her knees by his bed. She could not bring

herself to look at him. She feared she had imagined she had heard his voice. She believed that this must be some dream.

She felt his fingers on her hair.

'Margaret,' he said. 'My Queen Margaret.'

She lifted her face. She could not see him clearly for her tears were blinding her.

Then she said in a small choked voice: 'Henry . . . Henry, you are going to get well.'

She could not wait for more. Her emotions, which she had kept so long in check, were breaking free. She went into her room and for the first time for months she wept.

Margaret went to William Hately. She looked at him in bewilderment.

'I know,' he told her. 'I have seen the King.'

'He is well. He is recovered. He is himself again.'

'My lady, let us go gently with him. His mind will be delicate as yet. It has been dormant so long.'

'You are right,' she said. 'We must go carefully. What of our baby? He has not seen him yet.'

'Wait awhile. He is as a man coming out of a long sleep. Let him awake slowly. It is best for him. Do not let us overburden his mind with any matter which could distress him.'

'Our child would delight him.'

'It is true but it would remind him that there is the heir to the throne. I think we should not let him think of his kingly duties as yet.'

Margaret was ready to follow the doctor's advice.

'At least,' went on William Hately, 'let us wait a few days. Let us see what this cure really means.'

So they waited. Margaret sat with him. He talked a little and then slept for long periods. Margaret was terrified when he fell into one of these long sleeps that when he awakened he would be as before.

But this was not so. He continued to improve.

He knew that it was Christmas.

'At Christmas,' he said, 'it is my custom to send an offering to the shrine of St Edward the Confessor.'

'Yes, I know,' said Margaret. 'He was always your model. You always said that you would rather be like him than any of your great warrior ancestors.'

'I did and I meant it. And I would send to Canterbury to the shrine of St Thomas à Becket.'

'Your wishes shall be carried out. I shall see to that.'

He took her hand and kissed it.

Christmas was celebrated quietly at Coventry Castle but there was a great hope in Margaret's heart. The long months of anxiety were at an end.

She and the doctor decided that the time might be ripe to present Henry with his son.

She carried the Prince into his bedchamber and held him out to Henry.

'Henry,' she said, 'this is our son.'

He looked from her to the baby and memory came back to him. Yes, she had been pregnant before the darkness descended on him. That was long ago. This child was now a year old.

'Our child, our Prince,' he said wonderingly.

'The same, my love,' said Margaret, her emotion threatening once more to overcome her.

'What did you call him?' asked Henry.

'Edward. I thought it was a good name. I thought the people would like it.'

'I like it,' said Henry.

Then he put the palms of his hands together and began to pray.

Young Edward looked at him wonderingly and was not sure whether he liked him. He turned to his mother and looked as though he were about to cry until the jewelled necklace she was wearing caught his eyes. He seized it and so great was his interest in that that tears were avoided on his first meeting with his father.

Afterwards Margaret sat with Henry and he told her that he remembered nothing of what had happened since his illness overtook him. He had not been aware of anyone or anything.

'I have been with you these many months,' she told him. 'I have nursed you myself. I did not trust anyone else.'

She did not explain what was happening immediately. On the advice of William Hately she would do so gradually.

York was in control. The people seemed to like him. He had established a certain order throughout the country. Their dear friends Somerset and Exeter were captives.

'They must be released,' said the King.

'It is the first thing we shall do when we are in command again. We shall dismiss York and his friends and bring back our own.'

Henry looked a little tired and closed his eyes. William Hately said: 'Do not talk too much of State affairs to him. Let it come gradually. He has recovered but he is still weak.'

Let him recover gradually!

Impatient as she was for action, Margaret could see the wisdom of that. For the moment the affairs of the country must remain in York's hands, but not for long . . .

Bishop Waynflete and the Prior of St John's came to Coventry to see the King.

He was delighted to receive them and he was happy praying with them.

He has not changed, thought Margaret.

Soon we must leave Coventry. Soon we shall take over the reins of government.

That was a happy Christmastime. Every day Henry showed some improvement and began to take an interest in his surroundings.

The choice of Coventry had been a wise one for it had always been a favourite of his. He wanted to visit the churches of the town. There were three which had been standing there for years. Henry delighted in them, particularly that of St Michael which had been built long ago in the reign of the first Henry and had been given to the monks of Coventry by Earl Randulph. Then there was St Mary's Hall which he himself had built. It had an intricately carved roof with figures which were almost grotesque, a minstrels' gallery and an armoury. The enormous glass windows were a treasure in themselves. Henry delighted in it and his enthusiasm showed from his eyes as he talked of it with Margaret. In this hall was a tapestry which Henry had ordered to be made and which had been hung only a few years previously. It was thirty feet by ten and Henry had helped to design it. The colours, he pointed out, showed what advances had been made in dyeing and they really were exquisite.

It was wonderful to see his excitement over these things, but Margaret wished he could be equally so with regard to State matters. He did not seem to wish to discuss those. Whenever such questions were brought up, a film would come over his eyes and he would put his hand to his head as though he were tired. It was too dangerous as yet to insist for Margaret had a horror of his lapsing once more into that lethargy which bordered on idiocy.

What she would have to do was to bring his friends to him. Let him talk to them. Let him see that he was loved by many. Then they would set about ousting arrogant York from the Protectorate and bringing Somerset back.

One day there were visitors at the castle and Margaret received them warmly for she knew very well that there could not be stronger supporters of the Lancastrian cause. Their prosperity would most certainly depend on it, and that was the best reliance one could have on friends. A cynical observation, some might say, but it was nevertheless true and even if there was real regard it must be strengthened by expediency.

The visitors were brought in to the King and when he saw them his pleasure was obvious.

'Can it really be . . . Owen?' said Henry.

Owen Tudor was on his knees before the King.

'Your servant,' he said.

'Owen Tudor.' The King's eyes were glazed with emotion. 'I remember you well, Owen.'

'My lord, your mother and I talked so much of you, thought so much of you . . . When we were together . . . before they parted us we used to say how happy we could have been if you were with us.'

'Yes, I should have been happy too. I remember being impressed by you all and feeling a certain longing and a resentment, too, because I was the son of a King. Oh, Owen, how good it is to see you and recall those days when you taught me to ride my pony. I fear I was a timid pupil.'

'My lord, you were a good pupil. You listened to your teacher which is what few do.'

'My mother, Owen . . . Oh, that was a tragedy.'

'I think she could not endure the breaking up of our happy home.'

'Oh, it was cruel, cruel . . . And you went away to Wales. How fared you, Owen?'

'Well enough . . . in my native Wales. You were good to us, my lord. You never forgot us.'

'I did very little, Owen, for my stepfather and my half-brothers. Tell me, how are they?'

'If you would wish it you may see for yourself. Two of them are here in Coventry awaiting your permission to present themselves.'

'Awaiting my permission! My own brothers! Let them be brought to me without delay. But there are more than two.'

'My youngest son Owen has become a monk.'

'Ah, fortunate man. Where is he?'

'In Westminster.'

'I well remember him. And your daughter?'

'Jacina is growing up. She will be of marriageable age very soon.'

'We will find a husband for her. The Queen loves to arrange these marriages. Do I speak truth, my love?'

'It is a pleasure to set young people together. They should all marry young. That is my view. Then they should have children . . . lots of them.'

'Yes,' said Henry tenderly. 'Margaret is the Court's match-maker.'

'My eldest, your half-brother Edmund, will ask of you permission to marry. He is in love with the niece of the Duke of Somerset.'

'Margaret Beaufort! She is a much sought after little girl. I remember the Duke of Suffolk wanted her for his son.'

'I think she would be inclined to take Edmund . . . if you would consider it. After all, Edmund has royal blood through his mother.'

'I have no doubt that the Queen will arrange that matter. Now send my brothers to me. I would see them.'

'They want to assure you of their devotion. If ever you should need them, they are at your service.'

Owen knew that the Queen was watching him closely. The King might not want to think of the possibility of war but it was there and the Queen knew exactly what he meant.

When the two young men were brought to the King he received them with emotion. His half-brothers – Edmund and Jasper Tudor. They reminded him so much of their mother – who was Henry's mother too – and he was glad that he was related so closely to them.

They were a handsome pair – a few years younger than Henry who was at this time thirty-three years of age. Edmund must be about twenty-five and Jasper twenty-three or -four. They both had reason to be grateful to Henry who had made sure that they were adequately educated, first by the Abbess of Barking and later they had been put in the care of priests. Moreover Henry had bestowed titles on them – Edmund was the Earl of Richmond and Jasper the Earl of Pembroke. He would have given the youngest, Owen, a title if he had not gone into a monastery. The most fortunate of them all, in Henry's opinion.

Margaret eyed the three men with approval. Firm strong supporters of Lancaster and held together by ties of kinship.

Henry was happy to drop all ceremony and to talk to his stepfather and his brothers as equals. They talked for a while of the old days, which was sad because they must think of the death of Katherine their mother.

'How happy she would have been if she could be here with us thus,' said Owen.

'She sees us from Heaven,' answered Henry.

'There is one matter which grieves us all very much,' Edmund told him. 'It is the scandal which has been spoken about our mother and the slurs that are cast on us . . .'

'They call us bastards,' said Jasper.

Owen said: 'There was a marriage, my lord. I assure you there was. It took place just before Edmund's birth but when he was born I and your mother were married.'

Henry looked at Margaret, who said, 'There could be a declaration in Parliament. Why not? It has been done before. Why, Margaret Beaufort herself comes of a line which began as a bastard sprig and it was long after the birth of the Beauforts that John of Gaunt legitimised them. I see no reason why there should not be a declaration in Parliament.'

'We shall see to it,' said Henry.

Margaret rejoiced. It was the first time he had mentioned sitting with a Parliament.

There was no doubt that the Tudors' visit had done some good.

When they had left after giving a firm indication of their loyalty to Henry and Lancaster, Margaret talked of them to the King.

'They are fine men . . . all of them. Owen is getting old of course but you need strong men like Edmund and Jasper.'

'Owen did not seem to me an old man but I believe he was the same age as my mother and she was twenty-one when I was born.'

'I would trust them all to serve you well,' said Margaret, 'and that makes me warm towards them. I will arrange a marriage for the girl and I see no reason why Edmund should not have Margaret Beaufort.'

'Then, my love,' said Henry, 'if you decide it shall be so, it will be.'

There could no longer be any delay. Henry was weak still but Margaret insisted that he should be taken to the House of Lords and when he arrived there he dissolved Parliament.

The reign of the Duke of York was at an end. The King was returned and York had known his power was of a temporary nature.

It was unfortunate for the King and Margaret that York's period of supremacy had been long enough to show the people that he was a good ruler. Law and order had been restored to the country and York's rule had been seen to be just and firm.

Now it was over, but York would not lightly relinquish what he had cherished so much and for which he had an undoubted aptitude. Yet he must. He had taken on the Protectorate on the understanding that he must give it up as soon as the King was well.

The first act of the King's – or rather Margaret's – was to get Somerset released from the Tower. Shortly afterwards Exeter followed him.

Margaret now reinstated Somerset and he was the most important man in the country under the King.

There was of course a fierce hatred between Somerset and York. Somerset would never forgive York for imprisoning him; and York despised Somerset and wondered whether he ought to have taken advantage of the situation and finished him altogether.

The feud between those two was irreconcilable and would only end with the death of one of them.

Meanwhile Margaret was revelling in the return to power. She indulged in her favourite pastime of matchmaking. Margaret Beaufort was married to Edmund Tudor and for Jacina she found Lord Grey de Wilton.

She was delighted with her efforts and she knew that if they were needed the Tudors would be on Henry's side.

✿ Chapter X ✿

AT ST ALBANS

The Duke of York was angry. Everything had been changing; events had been falling into place; he had been achieving success; he had shown the people that he had the gifts of a ruler and then . . . the King recovered.

'And how far has he recovered?' he demanded of Cecily.

'He's likely to go toppling over into idiocy again.'

'Not that we wish him ill,' added the Duke.

Cecily pressed her lips tightly together. She wished him ill. She wished he would go back to his madness.

'But,' went on the Duke, 'when I had a comparatively free hand I felt I was getting things in order.'

'You were, and if the people had any sense they would make you King.'

'They always have such a respect for a crowned King,' said York.

Cecily was silent seeing herself and Richard being crowned in Westminster Abbey. That was how it should be. They both had royal blood and Richard had more right to the crown than Henry.

'What now?' she asked.

'Salisbury and Warwick will be with us shortly. We shall decide then.'

He was right. It was not long before Salisbury and Warwick arrived.

They were as resentful as York himself.

'What will happen now?' they cried.

'Disaster for the country,' answered York.

They were silent. The Great Seal had been taken from Salisbury and given to Bourchier, the Archbishop of Canterbury. The Governorship of Calais had been taken from York and given to Somerset. It was the last straw when Somerset had called a Council at Westminster which neither York, Warwick nor Salisbury were invited to attend.

'Somerset is at the root of all the trouble,' declared York. 'But for him, I should have remained at my post.'

'Do not forget that the Queen stands beside him.'

'The Queen and Somerset are our enemies, true,' agreed York. 'Aye, and the enemies of England.'

'They must be curbed,' said Warwick.

'How?' asked Salisbury.

The Duke of York was thoughtful. Then he said slowly: 'Everything we have worked for in the last year is wasted. It might never have happened. We cannot blame the King. He never wanted to take a hand in State affairs before his illness and now . . . it is clear that he wants to be guided. He is the figurehead but he wants a strong man to decide for him.'

'And Somerset has taken the role,' said Salisbury.

'My lords,' cried York, 'Somerset is our enemy. We must rid ourselves of Somerset. That is all I ask. The King is King . . . the crowned King. I do not want to displace him.

But he is unfit to rule and if we are going to save this country from its enemies and bring it prosperity we must have strong rule.'

The others were in agreement with that.

'And how shall we enforce it?' asked Warwick.

'We must prepare ourselves for conflict.'

'You mean fight? Civil war?'

'We shall not be fighting against the King. I want to make that understood. We shall march. Show our strength and demand the removal of Somerset.'

Warwick was watching York steadily. 'It is the only way,' he said. 'This has been brewing since that scene in Temple Gardens. It had to come to a head. It could be war.'

'It must not come to that,' insisted York.

'A war of the red and white roses,' said Salisbury.

'I want no war,' went on York.

'I want Somerset removed from power, the Queen to realise that she cannot rule us, and a good strong government to take over until the King recovers full sanity or the Prince of Wales is old enough to rule.'

'It shall be our task to bring about that happy state,' said Salisbury.

At Westminster the King and Margaret heard that York had gathered together an army, that he had been joined by Warwick and Salisbury, and was preparing to march south.

Somerset had hurried to them to tell them the news. The light of battle was in his eyes. He was thinking that perhaps here was the opportunity to settle for ever with his enemy of York.

The King was distressed. 'Marching!' he cried. 'What does he want to march for?'

The Queen tried to hide her exasperation. When would Henry realise that everyone was not kind and gentle like himself?

She burst out: 'Because he sees himself as King. He wants to put you from the throne and take it for himself.'

'No, no, my dear lady, York does not mean that. He is angry because he was not asked to the Council. Perhaps, my dear Edmund, we should have included him.'

'Nay, nay, my lord,' soothed Somerset. 'The Queen knows that we have to be watchful of your enemies.'

'So he is marching south,' said Margaret.

'I daresay he hopes to reach London.'

Margaret understood. York was popular in London. During his Protectorate trade had flourished. Trade was all these merchants thought about. London would be for York and she knew what the Londoners could be like when aroused. They were an army in themselves.

'What we shall have to do,' said Somerset, 'is march north to meet them.'

Henry frowned but he was too tired to raise objections, and clearly Margaret agreed with Somerset.

'My lord,' said Somerset, 'you should march with your army.'

Henry was very sorrowful but he made no protests.

'Oh God,' thought Margaret, 'I would I were a man. I would be there at the head of my army. I would bring this traitor York to justice.'

She realised she could not march with the army.

She said quietly: 'I will take the Prince to Greenwich.' She turned to Somerset. 'There I shall eagerly await the news. I must know at once when the traitor York is in your hands.'

'You shall hear with all speed, my lady,' Somerset promised.

'I trust it may be soon.'

Her mouth had hardened, and she clenched her hands as she thought what punishment she would inflict on this man who had dared to challenge the crown.

Beside the Duke of York rode his eldest son Edward. The boy was thirteen, young perhaps to ride out in what could well become a battle, but Edward was a precocious boy and had been from his early childhood. A son to be proud of, thought York – with a great deal of his mother in him. And best of all he had those fair, handsome Plantagenet looks. He was a little wild, but only as boys should be, even at his age casting a speculative eye on the women and his father had heard that he had already indulged in a few adventures. Over young, perhaps. But in such times a boy must grow up quickly.

He was proud of young Edward. He wanted him to understand the position. He talked to him as they rode along.

He trusted there would be no conflict, he said. What they really wanted to do was show strength and by so doing remind their enemies that they could be a force to be reckoned with. 'If we can drive that home without bloodshed, so much the better,' he said.

Edward listened. He believed his father should be King. His mother had said so often enough. Edward admired his father almost to idolatry, and to be riding beside him on an occasion like this filled him with pride. Secretly he hoped there would be a battle. He wanted to distinguish himself, to make his father proud of him.

'The King is ill advised,' went on York. 'The Queen is against us and she works with the Duke of Somerset who has done great harm to this country.'

Edward listened avidly. He hoped he would come face to face with the Duke of Somerset. He would cut off his head with his sword and present that head to his father.

'Always remember,' said the Duke, 'never to indulge in battle unless it is the last resort.'

'Yes, my lord,' said Edward, still dreaming of Somerset's head.

The Duke was dismayed when he heard that the King was marching north at the head of an army to meet him. This was the doing of Somerset and the Queen. Henry would never willingly have ridden out to battle.

The Duke discussed with Warwick and Salisbury what should be done.

'There will be bloodshed if the armies clash,' said York. 'This will be the opening battle of a civil war. The King does not want that any more than we do.'

'Somerset wants it. The Queen wants it.'

'Somerset knows that we are going to ask the King to hand him over to us. He must be impeached. We have to save the country. That is all we ask. Then we shall form a Council and rule under the King.'

'The Queen won't give up her favourite and Somerset will certainly do everything to prevent himself falling into our hands.'

'I want to let the King know that this is no battle against

him. It is no fight for the crown. I want him to know that we are loyal subjects, devoted to the welfare of our country and because of this we cannot stand aside and allow it to be ruined.'

By the time they had reached the Hertfordshire town of Ware Richard had made up his mind that he must let the King know his true intentions. When a subject – and such a subject – set himself at the head of what could be called a small army it might well seem that he was intent on making war.

The King must understand.

He wrote to Henry. He explained clearly that he had not wavered in his loyalty to him. His grievance was that he had been excluded from the government by the Duke of Somerset who had charges to answer for. Every man who rode with him was loyal to the King.

He called one of his trusted messengers to him and gave him a letter.

'Ride with all speed,' he said. 'It is imperative that the King reads this before another day has passed.'

York was confident that Henry would be only too delighted to call off any confrontation.

The messenger rode off and very shortly came to the royal camp.

He immediately disclosed the fact that he came on an urgent message from the Duke of York and he had a letter which he wished to deliver into the King's hands.

He was immediately conducted to the royal tent. The King was sleeping but a man who was clearly a very noble lord came to ask his business.

'I come with an important letter for the King from my

master the Duke of York. It is to be delivered into the King's hands.'

'Give me the letter and I will make sure that it is given to the King as soon as he awakes.'

'Thank you, my lord.'

'And I will give orders that you are given safe conduct back to Ware.'

The messenger was grateful and retired, his duty as he thought accomplished.

He did not know that the man who had intercepted the letter was Somerset himself.

A stroke of luck, thought the Duke. Who knew what the King would do on receipt of a letter like this? But perhaps one did know. He would say, 'Welcome, my dear cousin of York. Let us forget our grievances . . .' and before long York would have a place on the Council.

'Never, while I have a say in matters!' murmured Somerset.

He broke the seals and read the letter. So York had no quarrel with the King! He was a loyal subject! He did not want to usurp the throne. He wanted to serve under the King. But there was a note of warning however. A happy state of peace could only be achieved if certain people were delivered up for judgement.

'Indeed I see your game, master York. You will be a good subject if the King will hand me over to you and your friends. And what for, eh? No, thank you. My head is too useful to me for me to wish to be parted from it.'

He held York's letter in the flame of a flare.

The King should never know it had been sent.

So the King had ignored his letter. Very well, there was nothing more to be done but try to settle this matter by force of arms.

News came that the King had set out with an army and had halted at Watford.

'We will try once more,' said York. 'If we fight we have started a war. It is worth another effort. But Henry must understand that Somerset must be delivered up to face the judgement of his peers.'

'Deliver up those whom we accuse, my lord,' wrote York. 'When you have done this you will be served as our most rightful King. We cannot give way now until we have them. We shall fight and either get them or die in the attempt.'

Somerset was with the King when he received the letter for he had been unable to intercept it this time. The King grew pale.

'What do they mean, Edmund? They want you, of course. What can we say to them?'

'My lord will not be dictated to by rebel subjects.'

'I must not be. I think I had better see York. It would be easier to talk.'

'My lord, it would be useless. Let me draft a reply for you. I will say that you resent York's overbearing tones and perhaps that will bring him to his senses.'

'Yes, we must bring him to his senses. Do that, Edmund.'

Edmund's reply to York was not quite what the King had intended.

'I shall know what traitors dare be so bold as to array my people in my own land. I shall destroy them . . . every mother's son, for they are traitors to me and to England. Rather than give up any lord that is here with me, I shall this day myself live or die.'

When York read this he was astounded. It was so unlike the King who had always shuddered at the thought of bloodshed and had once made his servants remove the decaying quarters of a traitor which were being displayed in the city of London. He was telling them that they were traitors and what their fate would be if they fell into his hands.

He showed the reply to Warwick.

'There is only one course open to us,' said Warwick. 'We must fight.'

'Then let us give our thoughts to the battle since the King has decided it must be. First we will show the King's letter to every captain. He will fight the better for it since he will know what his fate will be if he is captured.'

The letter was duly shown and the whole army knew what fate would await them if they did not achieve victory. There was not a man among them who was not prepared to fight for he was not only fighting for a cause but for his own life.

York surveyed his army philosophically. It was five thousand strong, larger than that of the King, but the King had trained men among his. Victory would not come easily.

News came that the royalist army was making for the town of St Albans so the Yorkists must get there with all speed. Whoever was first would be able to choose the position and position was all important.

York had divided his army into three sections – one led by himself, one by Salisbury and the other by Warwick. Warwick was in the centre with Captain Robert Ogle and six hundred men.

About the town was a ditch and this was surmounted by a fence of stakes. The Lancastrians, having arrived first, had immediately taken up the best position behind these palisades and it was clear they had the advantage. Salisbury and York rushed into the attack but despite continued assaults they could not break through the fences.

The hopes of the Lancastrians were high. They were trained men of the King's army and York's followers were merely men with more desire to right what they considered wrongs than skill in military matters.

Seeing that his allies were in difficulties Warwick came forward to their defence but in doing so he perceived that there was one section of the palisades which was not defended. His task had been to wait and come to the aid of either York or Salisbury but he decided to ignore that. He saw an opportunity and he seized it.

He gave the order for his men to make for the undefended palisade while his archers protected them with a stream of arrows. Sir Robert Ogle led them over the ditch and the palisades and then on into the town while cries of 'A Warwick! A Warwick!' filled the air.

Within a short time Warwick's standard, planted over the town, struck terror into the Lancastrians. York saw it and exulted.

He shouted to his men. They were going to join the brave Warwick.

Now Warwick could attack the Lancastrians from the rear and by this time York and Salisbury were attacking in front. Through Warwick's prompt action the Lancastrians had lost their advantage and were sandwiched disastrously between the enemy forces.

In the streets of the city the fighting was fierce. Through Shropshire and Cock Lanes to St Peter's and Holwell Street the battle cries rang out.

'Attack the lords,' shouted Warwick. 'Spare the commoners.'

Perhaps the warning was not necessary. It was the lords who could not elude their pursuers so encumbered were they by their armour. The foot soldiers and archers in their leather jerkins were far more mobile.

Warwick paused by the Castle Inn in St Peter's Street and stared at the figure there on the ground.

'By God,' he cried. 'I believe it is.'

The battle was well nigh done. A resounding victory for York. And there dead beneath the sign of the Castle Inn lay Somerset . . .

The matter is resolved, thought Warwick.

Henry was most distressed. He hated bloodshed. It was tragic that these matters could not be solved in a peaceful manner.

He knew that Somerset hated York. York had shown himself so clearly to be his enemy. York was determined to end Somerset's rule and Somerset was determined to do the same for York. Henry was very fond of Somerset and so was Margaret. He quite liked York, too. Oh dear, why would they not resolve their differences in peace?

And here they were in St Albans. It was most uncomfortable and his forces were all at their posts under Somerset and he was with them . . . leading them, he supposed. He had no heart for battles.

And upon the opposite side was York with Salisbury and Warwick. They should all be friends.

The fighting had started. York had not a chance of success, Somerset had told him.

'I know, I know,' said Henry, 'but no more bloodshed than is necessary.'

'It shall be so, my lord,' said Somerset, the light of battle shining in his eyes.

Henry closed his. Buckingham was beside him. There was noise and shouting all about him. He hated to hear men and horses in distress. They were shouting for Warwick.

'God help us,' said Buckingham. 'Warwick has broken into the town.'

An arrow struck Buckingham at that moment and he fell to the ground. The King turned to him in consternation and as he did so an arrow caught him in the neck. He fell from his horse and lay on the ground bleeding profusely.

He saw that Buckingham's face was covered in blood.

'My poor friend,' he murmured; and then realised that his garments were soaked in his own blood.

Someone was standing over him.

'My lord . . .'

'York. Is it York?'

'You are wounded, my lord.' There was real consternation in his voice.

'Forsooth and forsooth,' said Henry.

York knelt down beside him.

'We are your loyal servants,' he said.

'Then stop this slaughter of my subjects.'

'It shall be done,' said York. 'The battle is over. Victory to the King's loyal subjects. This affray was necessary. My lord, we crave your forgiveness for any inconvenience caused to you.'

'War is senseless,' said the King.

''Tis so, my lord; we would have preferred to have settled in peaceful talk.'

'I bear you no ill will,' said the King. 'But stop this fighting. Attend to the wounded. Let us have done with war.'

Henry was aware of others surrounding him and he allowed himself to be lifted into a litter. He was escorted to the Abbey by York, Salisbury and Warwick and there his wound was dressed. It was an ugly one but not likely to be fatal.

When he learned of Somerset's death he was overcome by grief. He was further grieved when he heard how many of his friends had died. Lord Clifford, Lord Northumberland, and Buckingham's son. The Earl of Dorset, son and heir of Somerset, was so badly wounded that he had to be carried away in a cart.

'Forsooth and forsooth,' muttered the King.

It was necessary for him to ride with them to London, York told him, that the people might see that there was no rift between them.

What could Henry do?

The victory was York's.

In great suspense Margaret waited at Greenwich for news of the Battle of St Albans.

When she saw messengers approaching she hurried down to meet them demanding: 'What news?'

She did not have to wait to be told. She could see it in their faces.

Somerset slain. The King wounded!

That frightened her. How? Where? How badly?

An arrow in his neck! Oh, the traitors. What she would do to them if ever they came into her hands!

But the King. How ill? This was enough to send him into a stupor again.

They were marching to London. The King with York, Salisbury and Warwick, that trio of traitors. He came as their prisoner, did he? No. They treated him as their King. They were most insistent. They had no quarrel with the King. Somerset was dead. Their mission was achieved.

How sad it was to lose friends. She thought of good Suffolk and poor Alice's suffering. And now Edmund was slain too. And his son taken away, that beautiful young man nothing but a wreck now to be carried away in a cart. She could not have borne it but for the burning anger within her. It was only the thought that one day she would take such fearful revenge that they would wish they had never been born.

Hatred superseded grief. She would fight them. She would turn their victories into bitter humiliating defeat.

She went to the royal nursery. Little Edward was sleeping peacefully, but she picked him up and held him tightly to her.

One day, my love, you will be a King. Pray God you are a stronger one than your father.

The child began to whimper, angry at being disturbed in his sleep. But she would not let him go. She sat on a stool and rocked him to and fro.

He was her hope. She was going to fight for him, and one day . . . one day she would have York's head on a pike.

She put the baby into his cradle. Then she went to her apartments. She would eat nothing. She sat staring straight ahead; and thus she remained for several hours during which none of her women dared approach her.

There was a Parliament of course, attended by the King with York in command.

Margaret considered she was publicly insulted, for it was stated that the government as managed by the Queen, the Duke of Somerset and their party had been an oppression and injustice to the country.

At Greenwich Margaret gave vent to her fury, but to what avail? The King was petitioned to appoint the Duke of York as Protector of the Realm and Henry agreed.

He could do nothing else, Margaret knew. York had him in his power. Oh, but one day . . . one day . . .

At least they had not made a prisoner of him. They continued to pay lip-service to him. They declared that he was the true King and that they had no wish but to serve him and the country.

Fools, to believe them, thought Margaret. There is one thing York wants and that is the crown.

Then she heard that she, with the Prince, was to go to Hertford where the King would join her. There were signs that his distressing malady was returning.

So he came to her to be nursed back to health. The arrow wound was not serious and was healing now. But he was ill, there was no doubt of that. He did not sink into a complete torpor as he had before. He would talk a little and read a good deal. But there was no doubt that his mind was failing.

'There is nowhere he would rather be than in the Queen's loving hands,' said York.

So they were together; and she was touched by the sight of him. He was delighted to be with her and his son.

'This is peace,' he said.

❁ Chapter XI ❁

LOVE DAY

Margaret had a strong purpose now. Revenge on her enemies. She was going to destroy those three men, York, Salisbury and Warwick. They were her enemies as Gloucester had never been, and she would not rest until she had had her revenge on them. This was something she could not do alone. She realised this. If the King lost his reason completely or died she would be desperately alone with a son to fight for and without adequate means to do so. She needed Henry, a sane Henry, but not too strong because he must be guided by her.

She was going to make the crown safe for her son.

Henry's state of health gave her great cause for alarm. He must not be allowed to drift into that torpor which amounted to idiocy. She was prepared now. She would recall William Hately and together they would bring Henry back to health, for Hately's sensible advice had worked wonders before and it still would, she was sure.

She sought to interest Henry in their child. The little boy was very useful. His charming ways enchanted all, and Margaret was more passionately devoted to him every day, loving him with all the fierceness of her nature. Nobody was going to take the crown away from him.

So she needed Henry, a live, sane Henry.

Once more she devoted her days to the care of these two. She discussed with William Hately the best course of action and because of Henry's passionate love of music, on the doctor's advice she sent her sheriffs out into the country to look for musicians. She thought young ones would interest the King because he so much enjoyed encouraging the young.

'Go into the villages and hamlets,' she said. 'Search out boys with talent. Let them know that if they want to become musicians there is a place for them at Court. They will be paid good wages and will never want.'

When the boys began to arrive Henry showed an interest in them and their studies. He had always believed in teaching and bringing out the abilities of any who possessed them. There was no doubt that this had been an excellent idea.

There were some who wanted to go into the Church. Henry had a special interest in these. He promised to advance them and did so, and took a great interest in their progress. Margaret moved to Greenwich to be nearer London – but not too near for the Londoners were ardent Yorkists, and she was anxious not to attract too much attention to herself and the King at this stage. It was important, she felt, to lull the Yorkists into a sense of security. Let them think they were in command. So they were, but not for long, she promised herself.

She rejoiced in Henry's definite recovery, slow though it was. People were drifting to Greenwich. There were the sons of fathers who had been slain at St Albans. They thirsted for revenge with a passion which almost matched Margaret's. She encouraged them. One day it will be a different story, she told them in fervour. It will be for us to command them. And then it will be to the Tower in preparation for the scaffold for some.

York, Warwick and Salisbury, they haunted her dreams.

The day will come, she promised herself. And then no mercy. She found pleasure in inventing torments for them. Henry would have been horrified if he knew what was in her mind. He had always been squeamish. Perhaps that was why he had all but lost his throne.

Never mind. He was a good and loving man. He would obey his wife. And then when her son was of age he would be a fine strong King, for she would bring him up to be just that.

In the meantime it was a matter of treading warily – which was very difficult for a woman of her temperament. But she was doing well.

In Greenwich they talked constantly of the day when they would be strong enough to defeat York.

'We'll have his head on London Bridge, never fear,' said Margaret. 'But not a word of this before the King. The King is a saint. He would die himself rather than shed anyone's blood. That is why he needs us . . . to help him govern.'

They were beginning to see in Margaret a leader. It was incongruous that this small woman with the dainty hands and the long fair hair and the eyes which flashed blue fire when she talked of what was in store for her enemies should be the one to lead them. But such was the power of her resolution, such her eloquence, such her burning determination that they were beginning to accept her.

Henry the new Duke of Somerset had recovered from his wounds and was constantly at her side. She was going to put him in his father's place as soon as possible. It was the least she could do for dear Edmund; but apart from that she loved the new Duke for himself. He was her ardent supporter and like her he thirsted for revenge.

There were three who were very welcome at Greenwich; Henry's stepfather, Owen Tudor, and his half-brothers, Edmund and Jasper. Henry was always delighted to see them and would be happy recalling the days when he was a little boy and Owen Tudor had taught him to ride.

But the Tudors did not come merely to talk of old times with Henry. They were staunchly for the Lancastrian cause. They were strong men – all three of them, ready to face hardship, ready to risk their lives; and for the sake of Katherine, beloved wife to one and mother to the other two, they were firmly behind Henry.

They were pleasant days for Henry who was ignorant of the revengeful plans. He did not want to think of that fearful time in St Albans. The wound on his neck had proved to be slight and he could not bear to think of poor dear Somerset lying dead under that inn sign. He never wanted to go near St Albans again. He just wanted to forget the horrible sounds and sights of war.

'Forsooth and forsooth,' he muttered to himself. 'Why do men make war when all know we are always better off without it?'

Let York be protector of the realm. Why not? It was what York wanted; it stopped war. A number of the people wanted it. They said York managed very well and as long as he went on doing so there need be no trouble. York had been most respectful to him and he had stressed the fact that he regarded him as the sole King of the realm. It was only because he needed to recover from his illness – which had been aggravated by events in St Albans – that York was installed as Protector. It was only a temporary measure.

But Henry was very happy for it to continue.

So he listened to the music played by the boys who had been brought in to be taught and gently remonstrated with them when they did not play correctly. He loved to hear them and they loved to play for him.

Then there were those who wanted to go on pilgrimages to holy shrines. They came and discussed their projects with the King. He delighted to hear them. He himself would like to go on a pilgrimage.

'That might be an excellent idea,' said Margaret. They would travel through the country and the people would be delighted to see them, particularly if they had the little Prince with them – their gentle King who wished no ill to any and their charming Prince who could always captivate with his innocent manners. And her . . . well, they might not like her so much. There was a good deal of prejudice to overcome. But they must applaud her devotion to her family.

This was not the time though. Margaret had other plans . . . just at first.

'When you are well enough,' she told Henry, 'we will make our pilgrimage.'

'I feel well now,' said Henry. 'Well enough to make a short journey.'

'We will see,' said Margaret.

Not yet, she thought secretly. Not until the people can see you as their ruler. Not until York is no longer Protector. In a little while perhaps, but not yet.

The visitors continued to come. Margaret held her secret meetings and the King listened to his music, discussed possible pilgrimages, spent a great deal of time with his confessor, prayed and meditated.

Alchemists came to him who believed that they could discover the philosopher's stone by which they could turn base metals into gold. 'It would be a miraculous discovery,' said Henry, thinking sadly of his depleted exchequer and how wonderful it would be if the country did not have to inflict such heavy taxation on its subjects.

He would visit the royal laboratories and spend hours with the alchemists. They arrived at Greenwich from all over the country. The were all on the verge of discovering the secret formula; but none of them ever found it.

And so the King's days passed pleasantly, while the Queen gathered about her a formidable force.

The King's health was greatly improved but he was easily tired and there was no doubt that the battle of St Albans had had some effect on him. However he was well enough to take to the saddle; his mind was clear; and although he would never be robust, he was in good health.

The time had come, thought Margaret.

She did not discuss the next step with Henry. She wanted to present it to him as the considered opinion not only of herself but his friends.

Young Henry Beaufort, son of Edmund and now himself Duke of Somerset, was a bright young man of about nineteen or twenty. Understandably, he hated York with a venom equalling that of the Queen. 'It is York's contention that he is only Protector of the Realm during the King's indisposition,' said young Somerset. 'If the King is no longer indisposed there is now no need for York to hold that position. It seems, my lady, that all we have to do is announce that the King is well.'

Margaret was thoughtful. That was as it might be. But there would be fierce opposition, she knew. York, Warwick and

Salisbury had gathered their troops and come to oppose Henry.

'It was done with speed and shrewdness,' she reminded them.

With the Lancastrian lords they discussed how the desired effect should be brought about. York was not in London at the time. He must be kept in the dark as to the King's progress. If he knew that Henry was recovering he would be on the spot.

'We must choose our time with care,' said Owen Tudor.

Jasper thought that the King should go unexpectedly to one of the sessions of Parliament over which York and his immediate cronies did not preside, and make the announcement that he was now well and capable of taking over the government of the country.

'It is the way,' said Margaret. 'Now we have to persuade the King.'

That was not quite so easy. Henry enjoyed his life at Greenwich. He loved his music, his conversations with those who were almost as religious as himself; he loved the company of his son and he was grateful that he had a Queen who could care for him and keep unpleasant business away from him.

She reminded him gently that he was the son of a King; he had been a King since he was nine months old and the people wanted him. It was time now to take on his duties. She would be beside him, always ready to help him. He need have no fear.

It was a cold February day; the Duke of York was in the North and Warwick was in Calais for he had been given the important Governorship of that town when York had become Protector. As for the chief members of the York faction, they were all on their estates in various parts of the country.

The King rode up from Greenwich to Westminster, Margaret beside him.

He went into the House of Lords.

The assembled company, not knowing that he had left Greenwich, was astounded to see him enter thus ceremoniously.

The King stood before them, seeming in amazingly good health.

'My lords,' he said, as they had decided he should, 'you see me, by the blessing of God, in good health. I do not think my kingdom now needs a Protector. I request your permission to resume the reins of government.'

The Lords rose as one and cheered him.

He was well. He was the King. It was his place to govern.

❀ ❀ ❀

It had been completely successful. Margaret was gleeful. 'You see, all we need is a firm hand. Our first act must be to notify the Duke of York that he is no longer Protector of this realm as it was unanimously agreed by the Lords that he cease to hold this office.'

Now they could get to work. York could do nothing. His men were scattered and the same applied to Salisbury. Warwick was in Calais so was not of immediate concern.

The Parliament had agreed that York's services were no longer required. The King could not be turned out of his office. He claimed it. He was well now.

Henry was King again.

The King's chief adviser should be the young Duke of Somerset. There were raised eyebrows at that. Henry Beaufort was loyal enough, but he lacked experience and his father could hardly have been called a success in the later years of his life. It was the conflict between York and Somerset which was at the root of the trouble. But Margaret, fierce in her loyalties, was scarcely shrewd in her judgement. She wanted to show this young man her compassion for the death of his beloved father; she wanted to reward him for his friendship to her. Her emotions told her that this should be his reward; she did not pause to consider the wisdom of the move.

Henry wanted to bestow the seals on his good friend William Waynflete, Bishop of Winchester and Margaret saw no reason why Henry should not be indulged in this. Waynflete was a good Lancastrian – not fiercely against the Duke of York it was true, but believing firmly that Henry was the rightful King and should be supported for this reason. He and Henry had had many a happy hour together, discussing theology and architecture. Waynflete had often accompanied the King to Eton and King's College and had a great interest in them.

Yes, Waynflete was the man.

The changes were completed before York could do anything about it and there was consternation in Sandal Castle near Wakefield when the news was brought to York.

His resignation demanded! It was hardly necessary. He was already deprived of his post. The King was now well enough to resume his duties.

It was a complete surprise.

The family clustered round him. Edward wanted his father to tell him exactly what had happened. He wanted to set out right away and force another battle on the King. Edmund, his brother and younger by a year, was eager to hear more of the details. George was trying to imitate Edward and talking of battle and little Richard toddled up to try and understand what all the excitement was about. Even the little girls were listening.

Cecily was furious. 'This is that woman's doing,' she said.

Edward nodded. All the children knew that 'that woman' was the Queen and that she was very wicked. George said that she had come from France riding on a broomstick and it was only because she was a witch that she had been able to marry the King. When Elizabeth had asked Edward if this were true he had shrugged it aside impatiently.

'When they say she's a witch,' he explained, 'that just means that she's artful and wicked and cruel and ought to be destroyed.'

The Duke of York said: 'Of course it is her doing. Henry never has the wit to do anything alone.'

The children were overawed. Their father was speaking of the King and only their father could speak thus of the King. Everyone else had to be very careful. This was because their father really should have been King and that was what all the trouble was about.

Even the little ones wore their white roses and they always kept their eyes open for anyone wearing a red rose; if they saw anyone – though they rarely did in Yorkshire and anywhere near them, wherever they were – Edward and Edmund always wanted to kill them.

'When shall we be marching down south?' asked Edward. He would be rather sorry to go because there was a certain serving-woman in whom he was interested. She was old – by his standards – but he did not mind that any more than she minded his youth. She had so much to teach him; he enjoyed his lessons with her and did not want to break them off . . . even for a battle.

'I don't think we shall be,' said the Duke thoughtfully.

'You mean you are going to stand by and let that woman treat you like that?' cried Cecily.

'My dear, we do not want civil war.'

'You were the victor at St Albans. That should have been an end of it.'

'I believe it should. But rest assured, Cis, there will be no end to conflict while the Queen holds sway over the King.'

'What nonsense! You have shown you are more fit to rule than Henry.'

'I think the people know that. They will remember . . . when the time comes. But that time is not yet.'

It was not long before Salisbury arrived. He had heard the news too.

'What does it mean?' he asked.

'That the King is in better health. He must be, to have presented himself to the Parliament. He is King once more which means that I am no longer Protector.'

'And what do you propose to do about it?'

'Nothing,' said York. 'Remain here in the country . . . and wait.'

Salisbury was in complete agreement. 'And wait,' he said, but there was something ominous in the words.

Margaret was gratified when York made no attempt to dispute the fact that it was the King's right to rule and that he was fit to do so.

'He knows when he is beaten,' she remarked to young Somerset. 'Though he is wrong if he thinks I shall ever forget what he has done. I shall remind Henry – for he is apt to forget

– that whatever York says, he took up arms against his King at St Albans.'

'We shall have the traitor's head yet,' Somerset promised her.

'I am determined on it. York need not think that all is forgotten and forgiven. That shall never be. I am going to discover the mood of the country and I shall take Henry and the Prince on a long progress. I want the people to see their King, that he is well and that he is able to rule them. He is never averse to these journeys and if he can visit the churches and the monasteries, he will be happy. The people like that too. It pleases them that they have a saintly and virtuous King.'

It was agreed that such a progress would be beneficial to the Lancastrian cause and the Queen would be able to assess what support she could rely on. She dreamed of leading a triumphant army against York.

With characteristic energy she set about planning the tour. They would ride slowly through the country, pausing at great manor houses and castles on their way where they would stay a few days and let the people see them. They would make their way to Coventry which had always been a loyal city. And when the time had come . . . when the country was behind her she would strike.

So the progress began. The King was sincerely welcomed; the little Prince was cheered wherever they went; and if the greeting for Margaret was less exuberant, she could bear that. These people would understand in the end, she promised herself.

They came to Coventry and there held Court. The ladies of the castle worked a tapestry in honour of the visit. It was beautiful and depicted Margaret at prayer in a head-dress decorated with pearls and a yellow brocaded dress edged with ermine. The King was shown beside her and the tapestry was hung in St Mary's Hall as a token of the town's loyal regard for its sovereigns.

While they were at Coventry Margaret advised the King to send for York, Salisbury and Warwick to come to them there. They all declined, sensing trouble. How could they go, asked York, without taking an armed force with them? And if they did that it would not look as though they came in peace. Salisbury agreed with him. As for Warwick, he was too busy in Calais where his duties would not allow him to leave.

'They are afraid to come,' exulted Margaret, and from what was to be called the Safe Harbour of Coventry she went on with her plans.

❦ ❦ ❦

Steeped as she was in plots for revenge she could still spare time for romance. She liked to discuss her plans with Henry because he always agreed and smiled at her tenderly calling her the Royal Matchmaker.

'Well,' she said, 'now that dear Edmund has been murdered . . .' She always referred to Somerset's death in battle as murder and the murderer-in-chief as York — 'I feel it is my duty to look to the welfare of his sons.'

'I think you could have been said to have done that, Margaret,' replied the King.

'They are good boys. If Edmund had lived they would have been married by now.'

'I daresay they will in due course.'

'They should have the best possible matches and I think I have found the answer. The King of Scotland has two daughters. I thought it would be a good idea if they were married to Henry and his brother Edmund.'

'King's daughters!'

'Well, why not? The Beauforts are royal are they not? The family has been legitimised and they are in a direct line from John of Gaunt.'

'Yes, but what will James say . . . ?'

'James of Scotland could, I am sure, be persuaded. We owe it to Edmund, Henry, to look after his sons.'

'My dear Margaret, if this were acceptable to the King of Scotland I would raise no objection.'

'I should think not,' cried Margaret. 'Such marriages could bring us nothing but good.'

'I do not think the King of Scotland would agree.'

'He certainly cannot if he does not know what is proposed.'

'My dear, if it is your wish . . .'

'It is and it should be yours. Have you thought what these marriages could mean to *us*? There is always trouble on the Border. With Henry Beaufort up there and his brother with him, we should have friends, not enemies, in the Scots.'

'If it would mean peace, my dear lady, I would give every encouragement to it.'

Margaret was pleased. The King's approval was not necessary to her but she always felt that she liked to have it.

She set negotiations in motion. It was a disappointment that there was a lukewarm response from the King of Scots which might well mean 'Don't meddle in these matters and keep your matchmaking schemes within the bounds of your own country.' If she was proposing a match with the Prince of Wales that would be another matter.

Margaret was obliged temporarily to shelve the matter.

There was something of great importance with which to occupy herself, and this she determined to carry on without consultation with Henry.

She had always kept in touch with her uncle the King of France and her father the titular King of Sicily and Naples. If René was rather frivolous, the King of France was far from that. Margaret was eager to make the throne safe for Henry and she felt it could never be that while York lived. She would not be happy until she saw York's head displayed on some prominent edifice for all to witness his defeat and humiliation. Vengeance was like a burning fire within her which could only be doused by horrible death. It did not occur to her that for the Queen of England to indulge in correspondence with an enemy of England was more than incongruous. It could be construed as treachery and in view of her unpopularity, which was already overpowering, Margaret was playing a very dangerous game.

There was one whom Margaret hated almost as intensely as she did the Duke of York and that was the Earl of Warwick. It was Warwick's tactics which had achieved victory at St Albans for the Yorkists. He was as dangerous as York. The only difference was that he laid no claim to the throne.

Warwick – with characteristic shrewdness – had taken over the governorship of Calais, which some said was the most important port in Europe, and if it had not been quite that before, Warwick was certainly making it so now. He was turning himself into a kind of pirate king of the Channel, and making it impossible for French ships to pass through with safety.

Margaret had already written to her uncle explaining that she did not want Warwick back in England. He was too clever, too important to the Yorkist cause and while he was in Calais he was kept out of the way. Would the King harry the port a little, making Warwick's presence in Calais absolutely necessary to its safety? Threaten it. Make a determined set at it. At all costs keep Warwick out of England.

Again it did not occur to her that to ask an enemy of her country to attack one of its possessions was treachery of the worst kind. Margaret was single-minded. She wanted Henry safe on the throne and that could only be brought about by the death of York and she did not care what means she employed to bring that about.

Charles VII had changed since those days when as Dauphin he had listlessly allowed his country to slip out of his grasp. He was now reckoned to be the most astute monarch in Europe. He wanted to help his dear niece, he wrote, and he was authorising Pierre de Brézé, the Seneschal of Normandy, who had always been one of Margaret's devoted admirers, to prepare a fleet for the purpose of destroying Warwick's fleet and immobilising the port of Calais so that – so said the King of France – Warwick would be unable to use it for attacks on Margaret and Henry. He did not add that Calais was the town he most desired to get his hands on.

Margaret was delighted. Warwick would never be able to stand out against a French fleet.

It was summer when the fleet was ready. De Brézé sailed along the coast looking for Warwick's fleet. But a heavy mist fell and visibility was poor and there was no sign of Warwick and his ships. It was a pity, thought de Brézé, for he had sixty ships manned to the strength of four thousand and he contemplated an easy victory.

Land came into sight. He was puzzled. It could only be

England. He lay off the shore for a while and when the mist lifted a little he knew with certainty that he was close to the English coast.

He landed some of his men in a quiet bay and then sailed along until he came to the town of Sandwich.

He then set the rest ashore. The people of Sandwich were taken unaware. When they had first seen the ships they had thought they were Warwick's and were prepared to give them a good welcome, for Warwick was regarded as a hero in Kent.

The raid was successful – from the French point of view – and de Brézé sailed away with booty and prisoners from whose families he hoped to collect considerable ransoms.

When it was discovered that the Queen had actually requested the help of the French – for there were spies in the royal household and Margaret, who was impulsive in her actions, was also careless and some of the correspondence between her and the King of France had been intercepted – the hatred towards her intensified. She was a traitor. She was fighting for the French against the English. Their own Queen. They had never liked her. Now a wave of hatred spread through the country and nowhere was this stronger than in the county of Kent and the city of London. They blamed her for the raid on Sandwich. They blamed her for loss of trade which upset the Londoners particularly.

Margaret's little scheme to immobilise Calais had failed dismally and had moreover harmed her reputation irreparably.

Henry was most upset and realised that Margaret, in her enthusiasm, had done a great deal of harm. He tried to explain to her and for the first time she understood that he could be firm.

He was after all the King; there were times when his royalty seemed important to him. 'I am the King,' he would gently remind those who sought to override him – even Margaret.

'This warring can bring us no good,' he declared with a certain strength. 'I am eager to put an end to it.'

'You never will while York lives,' said Margaret grimly.

'Margaret, I want no more killing, no more strife. York has a right to his opinions. He never wanted to take my place. He has said so.'

'Said so,' cried Margaret. 'You would heed the word of a traitor.'

'He is no traitor! Think of his conduct after St Albans. He came to me, wounded as I was, and knelt before me. He could easily have killed me then.'

Margaret covered her face with her hands in exasperation.

Henry gently withdrew them. She looked into his face and saw a purpose there.

He will have to have his way, she thought; he is the King and now he is remembering it.

She listened to what he had to propose. He was going to call all the nobles to London; York, Warwick, Salisbury and with them lords like Northumberland, Egremont and Clifford who held grievances against them for the blood that was shed at St Albans.

'Do you want fighting in the streets of London?'

'No,' said Henry sternly. 'That I shall forbid. These men are going to take each other's hands in friendship. I shall command them to do so. I am the King.'

Margaret was astounded. She had never seen Henry look like that before.

Henry had realised that the path Margaret was taking would lead to civil war. She had made herself very unpopular and there were no cheers in the streets for her though they came readily enough for the Prince and Henry himself. But there was uneasy silence in the crowd when Margaret appeared. Henry feared that it could well develop into something very unpleasant and even Margaret's life might be in danger.

He must put a stop to this conflict. He must bring about some understanding with the Yorkists. He believed in his heart that they did not want war any more than he did. It was only people who thought as Margaret did who were so thirsting for revenge that they would plunge the country into bloodshed to get it.

He decided in a desperate effort to make peace between them to summon all the leading nobles to Westminster. When they arrived they caused great consternation to the Londoners who wanted no battles fought on their precious territory. If the rival factions wanted to fight, they said, let them go somewhere else to do it.

The Yorkists were arriving in strength. Salisbury had with him five hundred men and he lodged with them in Fleet Street, and it was not long afterwards when the Duke of York came in to Baynard's Castle with some four or five hundred.

Sir Geoffrey Boleyn, the Lord Mayor of London, was disturbed and ordered the city's guards to watch over the property of the London merchants; he set patrols to march through the streets after dark and there was an air of tension throughout the city.

Margaret thought the King should never have attempted to call the nobles together; they would never agree; moreover the promises of the Yorkists she was sure could not be relied on. Secretly she did not want peace. She wanted revenge on York and she could not get that very easily unless there was war.

Then the loyal Lancastrians began to arrive. There were the young lords sporting their red roses led by three, all of whom had lost their fathers in the battle of St Albans – Clifford, Egremont and Northumberland, every one of them seeking an eye for an eye. Bloodshed in their eyes could only satisfy for bloodshed.

The tension increased when Warwick, the hero of Calais, arrived in the city with six hundred trained soldiers.

Henry arranged a meeting which was to be presided over by Bishop Waynflete and Thomas Bourchier, the Archbishop of Canterbury.

The King had previously had a meeting with York, Salisbury and Warwick and was pleased to find how conciliatory they were. York insisted that civil war was the last thing he wanted. He had felt it necessary that the late Duke of Somerset should be removed from his post and it was for this reason that he had been marching to London when the affray at St Albans had broken out. It was unfortunate that the King had been wounded and that Somerset had been killed. He was sorry too for those young lords whose fathers had been slain and could understand their grief and anger at their losses.

'Perhaps it would be well if you showed that you truly regretted this affray,' suggested Henry. 'How would you feel about building a chapel at St Albans . . . on the site of the battle? Masses could be said there for the souls of those men who had died there.'

The three men considered this and said they would be delighted to build a chapel for such purpose.

'Then I think we are making some progress,' said Henry delightedly. 'But a little more may be demanded.'

'What do you suggest, my lord?' asked York.

'I think if there was financial recompense to those families who have suffered we might get them to agree to keep the peace. Certain sums are due to you – to you, my lord Warwick, for the governorship of Calais and to you, my lord Duke, for your services as Protector. Suppose these sums were diverted to the Duchess of Somerset, to young Clifford and Egremont and others who have suffered losses.'

York, Warwick and Salisbury said that they would like a little time to consider this.

'Not too long,' Henry warned them. 'The people are restive and want a declaration of peace between you all as soon as it can be arranged.'

York laughed when he was alone with his friends.

'The chapel . . . yes, we can do that,' he said. 'That is a small matter. The money . . . ? Well, when were you last paid, Warwick?'

'I never have received a groat.'

'Nor have I. So let us most magnanimously offer to these families that which would most likely never have come to us. Let us have our wages diverted to them. They can wait for them . . . just as we did . . . and I doubt they ever see the colour of the money.'

Henry was delighted. 'You see,' he said to Margaret, 'how simple it is when you make the right approach. People are at heart good, but they get carried away by their passions. If only they would pause and commune with God.'

With the Yorkists being so ready to agree to a peace there was nothing the Lancastrians could do but accept.

'There shall be a thanksgiving service at St Paul's,' announced Henry with gratification.

'And do you believe these Yorkists?' asked Margaret with scorn in her voice.

'I believe they want peace. York is a good man. I know him well. He is a close kinsman, remember. He really wants what is best for this country.'

'Not forgetting the House of York,' added Margaret.

'We all want to see our families well cared for.'

'But fortunately all do not want to wear the crown.'

'York does not think of that. He is a good man, I swear, Margaret.'

'Oh, Henry, you are so easily deceived. And Warwick. He is the most dangerous of them all. He is the sly one. He has wormed his way into the people's affections. They cheer him wherever he goes. They think he is wonderful because he performs piracy on the high seas.'

'He attacks only the French who are making things uncomfortable for him in Calais.'

'He should never be at Calais. He should be removed from that post. Henry, you could give it to young Somerset. It would show how sorry we are that his father was killed in our service.'

'Somerset is too young for the task.'

'How old is Warwick?'

'He must be nearly thirty.'

'Not so much older than Somerset.'

'It is not only a question of age, my dear. Warwick has shown himself to be a great leader.'

'He has shown himself to be a pirate. But I know the English love pirates.'

'The English love law and order as do all sensible people. No, it would be wrong to take the governorship of Calais away from Warwick. The people would be angry. They idolise him in the south-east. They say when he rides up from Sandwich to London they run out to cheer him and throw flowers at him.'

'All the more reason why he should be deprived of that post.'

'But he has excelled in it, and you know how the people feel about de Brézé's raid on Sandwich.'

It was dangerous ground. She had erred badly over that, they said. They blamed her, although she had never asked that the English mainland should be attacked.

However, with unaccustomed firmness Henry made it clear that the governorship of Calais should not be taken away from Warwick, and the citizens of London, who shortly before had been apprehensive, were delighted that there was to be a ceremony. The King had decided on the Feast of the Annunciation and it was to be a day of public thanksgiving. Enemies would enter the cathedral as friends – hand in hand – and they would all give thanks to God for this day.

There was a grand procession through the streets. The Duke of Somerset and the Earl of Salisbury – sworn enemies until this day – headed the procession; and behind them came the Duke of Exeter with Warwick. Henry followed in all his royal robes which he so hated to wear but he had his hair shirt underneath them and hoped that the discomfort would offset the extravagant splendour in the eyes of the Almighty. Behind the King was Margaret with the Duke of York. They held hands as they walked. She found it very hard to hide her disgust at the procedure. To walk thus with her greatest enemy, holding his hand when it was his head she wanted and that on a pike, was nauseating. She had almost refused to do it but remembering what had happened at Sandwich and the new mood of the King, she felt she could hardly refuse. But she was not York's friend and never would be.

York however was pretending to be on terms of great friendship. Could he really want peace? Had he really given up his ambitions to wear the crown?

She could not believe it.

The whole thing was a farce.

It pleased Henry, though. Poor simple soul, he believed these people when they said there should be peace. He used himself as a pattern and seemed to think that everyone had the same motives, and was as direct and honest as himself. Poor foolish Henry! How he needed a woman to look after him. And this new mood was faintly alarming.

So they went into the cathedral and the service began.

Afterwards there were bonfires in the streets and the people danced merrily round them. Troubles were all over, they believed. The enemies were now friends. Recompense had been made to those who had suffered.

It was called Love Day. The day when the wearers of the red and white roses became friends.

Chapter XII

THE KING-MAKER

Henry was delighted to receive Jasper Tudor, the Earl of Pembroke, who was in good spirits. His brother Edmund, Earl of Richmond – a title, like that of Jasper, owed to the goodwill of the King, for if he had not recognised them they would have no titles and very few possessions – was unable to attend.

He had not been well of late. If he had he would have hastened to tell the King of his good fortune. His wife, Margaret Beaufort, whom the King had so obligingly arranged for him to marry, was pregnant and there was great joy in the family. Jasper was unmarried and Owen was a monk so it was gratifying to know that there would be an addition to the family.

'It is wonderful news,' cried Henry, always delighted in other people's good fortune. 'And how is Margaret?'

'Margaret is well and so much looking forward to the event.'

'She is a little young to bear a child.'

'She is not quite fourteen,' said Jasper. 'Young, yes, but she is mature enough. They are very happy together and this child will bless their union. My father, I and our sister are full of delight. We hope for a boy, of course.'

'I understand that but I doubt not you will be grateful for whatever the Lord sends you.'

'Indeed yes. Margaret is young. It is good that she has proved so soon that she is fruitful.'

When Jasper had left, Henry told the Queen the good news. Margaret could understand their delight in the coming of a child. She herself had waited a long time and now her boy was the joy of her life. She was a little irritated by the Tudors though because some of the titles Henry had bestowed on them had been taken from her. The Pembroke estates in particular had at first been assigned to her and she had not at all liked giving them up for Jasper. Having had little in her youth and been the daughter of a man who was constantly in debt she cherished her possessions with something like fanaticism. Still, the Lancastrian cause needed men like the Tudors. All their blessings came from Henry, their benefactor as well as their half-brother, and so she did not openly show her resentment over the Pembroke estates, but welcomed the Tudors whenever they came to Court. She showed an interest in their affairs, and now rejoiced with Henry in their good fortune.

'I trust all will go well with Margaret,' said Henry. 'She is really nothing but a child herself.'

'She will be all right,' said Margaret lightly. Other people's difficulties were always light-weight in her opinion.

Henry said: 'I have asked to have news of the birth as soon as it happens.'

'Well, we shall expect messengers from Wales with the good news.'

It was a grey November day when the messengers came. They clearly did not bring good news.

When Henry heard they had arrived he was filled with

apprehension. It was not yet time for the birth, for he had understood it was to be in January.

It was Owen Tudor himself who came. Bad news indeed.

'My dear Owen,' cried the King, 'what is it? Not Margaret? Oh, I feared she was too young.'

'Margaret is sick with sorrow, my lord.' Owen seemed unable to go on.

'My dear Owen,' began the King, 'she is young . . . There will be more.'

Owen shook his head. 'It is my son, your half-brother . . . Edmund.'

'Edmund? What of Edmund?'

'He is dead, my lord.'

'Dead? Edmund? But how . . . ? Killed . . . ? Murdered?'

'Nay, my lord. It was some malady. It attacked him suddenly and . . .'

'But he is so young.'

'Twenty-six, my lord.' Owen turned away. He was remembering the day Katherine had told him that she was going to have a child and how their delight had mingled with their apprehension when they had arranged for the reluctant priest to marry them. It was all long ago . . . twenty-six years . . . those happy days which he often looked back to. He remembered so much of them . . . the quietness of life at Hadham; the peace of the gardens . . . the happiness of obscurity. What fools they had been — what idyllic fools, to think that a Queen could ever be left in peace.

'My dear Owen, this is such sorrow. I will pray for his soul. Poor Edmund. And poor Margaret.'

'The child is due in two months' time.'

'Yes, I know. I trust this will do no damage.'

'Jasper has taken charge of her. That is why he is not here with me. He has taken her to Pembroke Castle. He will keep her there until the child is born.'

'Jasper is a good man.'

'He was devoted to his brother. We are a devoted family, my lord.'

'I thank God for it.'

'There is nothing we can do now but wait for the birth of the child.'

'Go back now to Pembroke, Owen. Convey my regrets to Margaret. Tell her my thoughts are with her and I shall remember her in my prayers.'

'That will comfort her, I know.'

After Owen had left Henry thought a great deal about the sad young girl who was about to become a mother. He mentioned her in his prayers whenever he prayed and as he was constantly engaged in prayer that meant very frequently.

Poor young girl, he thought. But Jasper is a good man. He will look after the child for the sake of his brother if nothing else.

It was January when the news came from Pembroke.

It was good news this time. Margaret had been safely delivered of a boy.

Owen himself rode over soon after the messenger had brought the news and Henry received him with open arms and embraced him warmly.

'So you are a grandfather, eh, Owen?'

'I am proud to be,' said Owen.

'It is the best news. Margaret has come through safely in spite of her youth and the terrible shock she has suffered.'

'And the child is a fine healthy boy.'

'God has sent him to comfort her.'

'She is happy in the child, and she has been most touched by your concern for her. I have given her all your tender loving messages and I am sure they were of great help. She wanted only one name for the child. It is Henry.'

The King laughed. 'So he is my namesake. God bless little Henry Tudor.'

Ever since the Love Day celebration Margaret had been very restive. Considering her present situation and consulting with her closest adherents, those nobles whom she thought of as the leaders of the Court party such as young Somerset, Egremont, Clifford, Northumberland, Exeter and Rivers, she had come to the conclusion that Warwick was an even greater enemy than York.

There was some charismatic aura about Richard Neville, Earl of Warwick. He was the sort of man whom nature seemed to have destined to play an important part in the affairs of a nation. Who was he? In the first place son of the Earl of Salisbury, and he would have been of no great importance while his father lived. But what should he do but marry Anne Beauchamp, daughter of the Earl of Warwick. Yet at the time of the marriage two lives stood between him and possession of the Warwick title and the vast estates that went with it. Nature conveniently removed those obstacles and on the death of the Earl, Richard Neville took the title.

It was not only good fortune that he possessed. He had not only strength, ruthlessness, love of adventure; he was a man to mould affairs. It was a pity that he had allied himself with York instead of standing by his King.

Since he had taken the governorship of Calais he had become a menace to the French; and while he was in possession of Calais, it was considerably to York's advantage.

Margaret was angry. She had wanted young Somerset to have Calais. She had pleaded with Henry to give it to him, but Henry, in this new found strength of his, was stubbornly refusing to accede to her wishes.

'It would never do, Margaret,' he said. 'The people have a fondness for Warwick. They think of him as a hero in the south-east of the country.'

'He is nothing but a pirate. He brings us into disrepute with the French.'

'My dear, the French are not exactly friendly with us, are they? Oh, I know they are your people and you love them, which is natural. I would not expect that to be otherwise. But you must remember that you are English now and it is in our successes that you must rejoice.'

'In Warwick's? In your enemy's?'

'But he is one of our great Earls. He walked with Exeter in the procession. There was amity between us.'

Oh, what was the use of talking to Henry! Some might say that the French were acting as privateers in the Channel and that Warwick was merely retaliating. It might be pointed out that in the last years the high seas had become profitable for pirates and that Warwick was taking his share and not leaving all the pickings to the French. Margaret would not listen. She hated Warwick – even more than she hated York – and she wanted Calais for Somerset. She wanted to make sure that that important town was not in the hands of her enemies.

An opportunity came which she seized eagerly. It was not Margaret's way to consider the advantages and disadvantages of a situation. She was entirely optimistic when an idea occurred to her and impatient with any who might try to point out flaws in the arrangements she planned.

Warwick had gone too far in his latest exploit. He had intercepted ships carrying cargo from Lübeck. It was a very different matter intercepting ships from France with whom the country had been on terms of war for so long, but there was an agreement between Lübeck and England which had been made only two years before. To intercept and carry off these ships was therefore a flagrant violation of that treaty.

Margaret immediately called her friends together and made sure that Henry was not present and knew nothing of the meeting.

'This is outrageous,' she cried, her eyes flashing and gleaming with triumph. 'But it delivers Warwick into our hands. I shall call together a council which will be headed by you, my lord Rivers, and others we shall appoint, and the Earl of Warwick shall be commanded to relinquish his post. As it will be offered to you, my lord Somerset, it might be well if you did not attend the first meeting of the Council. This is going to be the end of Warwick's power in Calais.'

It was an easy matter to get the Council to agree for they were all members of the Court party, all adherents of Lancaster, all against York, and in great delight Margaret sent an embassy to Calais, informing Warwick that he was to relinquish his post forthwith as it had been unanimously decided that in view of the Lübeck action, he was no longer fitted to hold it.

Warwick's answer was what might have been expected.

'It was the Parliament who appointed me. I shall certainly not resign unless on order from Parliament. I take no heed of inner councils which lack parliamentary authority.'

Margaret fumed with rage. The Parliament would not agree to force him to resign, she knew. They considered what the effect of his resignation would be on the people of London and the south-east who had grown rich while he was governor of Calais. They said he made the Channel safe for English shipping; they liked their buccaneer. It appealed to them to think of his terrorising the old enemy the French; the booty he captured was sent over to England and that was enriching the land.

Somerset had done nothing to recommend himself except ingratiate himself with the Queen and that went against him with quite a number of people.

Once again Warwick had flouted her. But she saw a glimmer of hope.

Warwick was coming over to England – no doubt to harangue the Parliament and tell them he was the best man for Calais and if they wanted to see England triumphant in France again they needed men such as he was.

Margaret would not see the truth of this. But Warwick was an enemy and she wanted to destroy him.

It was not impossible. She wondered who to take into her confidence. It must appear natural of course. There were continual quarrels between the wearers of the red and white roses and these often resulted in bloodshed. A brawl between them would not seem of any special significance, but if such a brawl occurred in a certain place and Warwick was there and he was slain . . . it would be difficult to attach blame to anyone, least of all the Queen.

Warwick would be at Westminster. He was coming to explain to the Council the position at Calais; to tell them what a fine fellow he was, of course, thought Margaret. Well, while he was at Westminster Hall there should be a quarrel between Warwick's retainers and those of the royal household. Warwick should be brought hurrying from the council chamber and there must be those waiting for him. They must fall upon him, kill him and then mingle in the general affray.

It seemed comparatively simple to Margaret. Then with Warwick out of the way York would have lost his most powerful friend. York without Warwick was far less formidable than he was at the moment. Warwick had the south-east of the country with him and he was fast becoming known as a hero, one of those men who went into battle carrying the certainty of victory with them like a flag.

The day was set. Margaret was waiting in an atmosphere of increasing tension for news to reach her of her enemy's death.

Warwick arrived at Westminster Hall with his retinue prominently displaying his badge of the Ragged Staff which was recognised all over the country and being applauded wherever it was seen.

He left his men in the hall while he went along into the council chamber. He had not been there for more than five or six minutes when the fighting broke out in the hall. One of the King's men had jostled a bearer of the Ragged Staff; muttering disparaging remarks against Warwick.

Warwick's men hit out at the King's man who immediately brought out a dagger. It was the cue. The royal servants were prepared to do the Queen's bidding and in a matter of seconds the brawl had started. Warwick's men were taken a little by surprise. Although they were prepared for insults they had not thought it would be as deadly as it was proving to be. They rushed at the assailants crying 'A Warwick! A Warwick!'

Warwick himself hearing the turmoil came rushing out of the council chamber as Margaret had guessed he would.

It was the sign. Those who were ready to kill him dashed forward. But he was too quick for them and while he parried the blow he was surrounded by his own men, for they had realised almost at once that this was no ordinary brawl. This was an attempt to assassinate their leader. They would defend him with their lives and this they proceeded to do.

Warwick, bold adventurer that he was, saw at once that he was in a very dangerous position. His men were outnumbered and the purpose of this affray was to kill him. His only hope lay in escape. His well-trained men grasped the situation immediately. They cut a path through the shouting royalists and Warwick hurried through it. Several of his men guarded him while he with a few friends made his way out of the hall.

There was not a moment to lose. Even the gallant men of the Ragged Staff could not hold the royalists off indefinitely. Warwick's barges were at the river's edge and he — and a few friends — rushed to them and were on their way up river when their pursuers howling with frustrated rage came dashing down to the water's edge.

'We must make for Sandwich with all speed,' said the Earl. 'I shall return to Calais at once. I see I am unsafe here. The Queen has decided to murder me.'

Before he crossed, however, he sent messengers to his father Salisbury and to his uncle-in-law, the Duke of York, telling them of the assassination attempt and that he believed the Queen was responsible for it.

Warwick also sent messages to the Council which he had so hastily been forced to leave.

The Parliament had appointed him to Calais, he said. He would not give it up. He would abandon his estates in England rather.

Margaret was frustrated. Her scheme had failed; perhaps it had been clumsy, not well enough thought out; and now Warwick knew that there had been a plot to assassinate him and he would suspect the Queen was at the bottom of it.

Letters came to Calais from Salisbury and York telling Warwick that the Queen was preparing to attack. They believed that the plot against Warwick was the first step in her campaign. They would very soon be going into battle, for York had discovered that Margaret believed the King was popular enough to rally the people to his cause.

Warwick must return to England. They needed him.

Warwick considered this. Henry was useless in the role of King; more and more the real ruler would become Margaret. That would be disaster for England . . . and Warwick.

It was men such as Warwick who made Kings and Warwick had decided that York was the man to be King . . . York guided by Warwick.

He must leave Calais. He would take with him his trained men of the Ragged Staff to seek victory in the war against the Lancastrians.

Warwick rode through England from Sandwich to London in the style of a king. Everywhere the people of Kent came out to cheer him. They called him the Captain of Calais and he reminded them of the old days when England had kings worthy to lead them, when victory was the order of the day. Warwick was of that kind.

He knew it. He revelled in it. He thought: when the time comes I will make York a king.

His captains were led by Andrew Trollope and John Blount – two of the finest soldiers one could wish to meet who would serve him well, he believed, but they had implied with the utmost firmness that they would not take up arms against the King.

This was no conflict with the King, he had pointed out. This was a battle between certain noblemen. Henry was King – all accepted that. But the Queen chose his ministers; the Queen worked with the French against the English. What they had to do was to prevent that, to set up a council of ministers who would make sure that the best men ruled and the Queen was not allowed to pursue her treacherous way. All the captains saw the point of that and they were proud to march through the country flourishing the badge of the Ragged Staff.

Even so the people did not flock to march under his banner. They had had enough of war. They wanted no more, least of all civil war. Peace was what they wanted, peace and prosperity.

Sensing the mood of the Londoners, Warwick skirted the city and made for his home ground of Warwick. There he heard a sorry story. There had been raids by the Lancastrians. All over the country the people were taking sides and as a well-known supporter of his uncle-in-law York, his lands were considered fair game by the Lancastrians.

He was convinced that it was time to march against the Queen, and decided to make his way immediately to Ludlow where he would join York.

His father, the Earl of Salisbury, was in the meantime on the road to Ludlow and with him were his two sons, Sir John and Thomas Neville. As they were approaching Blore Heath to their great consternation they saw in the distance an armed force advancing towards them. It was too late to turn back. They had been seen, and within a very short time it became clear that they were about to encounter Lancastrians on the march.

Salisbury was greatly outnumbered.

'We'll beat them, never fear,' said John Neville. 'One of us is as good as three of them.'

It was the old cry of those who were going into battle against great odds. Salisbury did not like it. But there was no help for it. They must stand and fight.

The battle was swift and bloody. Men were dying all around. The Yorkists fought so fiercely that they were able to hold their ground against superior numbers until nightfall and then there was such confusion that Salisbury and those of his men who had come through the encounter were able to get away, which they thought the wisest course of action. It was with great sorrow that Salisbury learned that his two sons had been captured. They had been over bold, it seemed, in pursuing the enemy.

The fortunes of war, thought Salisbury ruefully; but at least he had escaped to ride on to Ludlow.

He would carry the news that the country was rising and taking sides.

Warwick arrived at Ludlow soon after his father. He too had encountered a hostile force. This was led by the Duke of Somerset but Warwick, seeing that they could be grossly outnumbered if they paused to fight and being sure that he could be of more use to the cause alive, gave the order to fly as they could and thus they avoided an encounter.

It was disconcerting to hear that his father had had a similar adventure and that his two brothers, John and Thomas, were in the hands of the enemy.

York greeted them with the utmost warmth and Cecily made them very welcome. She knew that Warwick was the brightest star of the Yorkist party for his reputation since he had gone to Calais had increased tremendously. He was reckoned to be the most outstanding man in the country. Cecily took note of such things.

York's eldest son, Edward Earl of March, was fascinated by Warwick, and clearly proud of the family connection. It seemed to young Edward that Warwick embodied all the virtues of manhood. Edward was seventeen now, even more handsome than he had been as a boy; he had already topped six feet and was still growing. He was strong, full of vigour and determined on success, and Warwick liked the look of him as much as Edward liked Warwick. His brother Edmund, Earl of Rutland, younger by a year, lacked Edward's outstanding good looks and spirits, but he was a fine boy all the same. York should be proud of them – and clearly was.

Young Edward came to their conferences. He was all for going into the attack. Wild, of course, thought Warwick, but he was a bit that way himself. He was beginning to think that this young Edward might have qualities of leadership which were lacking in his father. Warwick mused that the Duke of York could have been King after the battle of St Albans, but he could never quite overcome his scruples. It showed a good and just nature perhaps, but there were moments when kings could not afford such luxuries.

Warwick rejoiced that York had a son, for if York were to fall in battle there would be someone very worthy indeed to step straight into his shoes.

It was disconcerting to discover that the Queen had gathered together a sizeable army. Even Warwick was dismayed to see by how many they would be outnumbered.

Young Edward was boastful, and said he was glad that there were so few of them against the enemy. He was trying to be another Henry the Fifth. Well, it was a good sign.

Moreover Margaret sent messengers into the Yorkist camp to tell the men that if any of them put down their arms they would be freely pardoned. This made York very uneasy for he knew that his followers while they deplored the state of the country and knew it came through bad government could not rid themselves of the belief that they were fighting against the King. It was amazing how Henry had managed to win their loyalty. They knew that he was a near saint; they knew of his love of prayer and learning. If only he had had the strength to govern, if only he had not been the tool of a ferocious Frenchwoman who had no judgement and was not above an act or two of treachery, they would never have thought of coming against him. They were not against *him*, they insisted. They were against the Queen and her advisers. If she would make York Protector again and Warwick was left to guard Calais for them they would be content.

But the Queen was stubborn; she would rather fight than work with York.

'Once again,' said York, 'I will send a message to the King as I did before the battle of St Albans. I will tell him that we are his loyal subjects, but there are certain matters which must be set right.'

The Lancastrian army was before Ludlow; they had camped to the south of the town in the fields which were watered by the river Teme. Margaret was in good spirits. She knew that the people wanted to be loyal to their King. She had men and arms but her greatest asset was Henry himself.

Though he hated battle so much she had insisted on his accompanying the army. He had been so reluctant that she had worked indefatigably, pointing out that he would be called a coward, that he would be failing in his duty if he did not ride with the army and confront those traitors York, Warwick and Salisbury.

She rode round the camp accompanied by the King. The news must spread to Ludlow Castle that the King was with them. Every Yorkist soldier must know that he was fighting against his King.

Once again she sent messages addressed to all the captains in the enemy's camp. 'The King is here before Ludlow. If you fight against his army you fight against him. Pause to think what this means. You will be traitors to your King. Come over to us now and there will be free pardons for all.'

It was clever.

Margaret was almost wild with joy when Captain Trollope, leading a company of Warwick's best troops from Calais, joined the Lancastrian army.

Trollope declared: 'I will never take up arms against my King.'

Margaret welcomed him warmly. He should have a command in her armies. She was certain now of victory.

There was gloom in Ludlow Castle. Defeat was staring them in the face. Even Warwick admitted it.

'I would have staked my life on Trollope,' he said. 'And it is not only him. He has taken some of my best men with him.

They are not fighting for Margaret, not for the Lancastrians. It is simply that they will not fight against the King. They are good men all of them. If the King had not been there . . .'

'But he is there,' said Salisbury, 'and what are we to do? We have a handful of men against a trained army. We will be overcome in an hour.'

Warwick nodded. 'Trollope knows our plans and our strength. It will be folly for us to stay here and be annihilated or worse still taken captive. There is one course open to us, as far as I can see. And that is flight, if we want to live to fight another day. We have been the victims of desertion. We were undermanned before. The Queen has reacted too quickly for us. I think the answer can only be flight. As soon as night falls we should leave without delay.'

York was thoughtful. He was thinking of his family. Salisbury understood.

'There is no other way, I fear,' he said. 'You will have to leave Cecily here with the younger children.'

'To leave them . . .'

'If you want to live, yes,' said Warwick. He was thinking York had not the makings of a great leader. He was thinking of his wife and young children when he should have been thinking of survival to live and fight another day.

'March and Rutland can come with us,' said Salisbury.

'There is no time to be lost,' added Warwick. 'As soon as night falls we must slip away.'

York saw at once that Warwick was right and it was easy to explain to Cecily because she too grasped the position.

'Warwick is wise,' she said. 'You must go . . . you, Edward and Edmund. The little ones will be safe with me. I am sure Henry won't let us be harmed.'

'I wouldn't trust Margaret.'

'Oh, she won't have time to think of me. God go with you.'

'I shall keep you informed and we shall be back.'

'Indeed you'll be back, and when you do you'll be victorious, I'm sure of that.'

Cecily was a strong woman; she would be able to care for herself and the children he was leaving behind.

Darkness was falling. There was not a moment to lose. He summoned his captains and told them that they could not possibly stand out against the mighty Lancastrian army which was gathered to confront them. The soldiers must get away and disperse. They would be in no danger. It was the leaders they were after.

York, Warwick and Salisbury with the young Earls of March and Rutland quietly made their way out of Ludlow. Through the night they rode heading towards Wales. There they decided to break up the party and as York still had connections in Ireland he would go there and stay until he could make plans for his return. He would take Rutland with him.

The others would go back to Calais. Edward was very eager to stay with Warwick. So he with Salisbury and Warwick made his way to the Devon coast where they hoped to find a ship to carry them across the Channel. It would have been too dangerous to attempt to sail from Sandwich or any of the ports in the south-east, for their enemies would surely be lying in wait for them guessing that Warwick would try to make his way back to Calais.

Edward enjoyed the adventure. His attachment to Warwick grew with every hour. Warwick was a hero. He was so resourceful, so strong, all that Edward himself would like to be.

There were some alarming moments during the journey. Warwick was certain that Margaret would have sent out warnings to all her friends in the country that they might keep a watchful eye for the fugitives. And if ever she had York, Warwick or Salisbury in her hands she would lose no time in getting rid of them. It would be certain death.

Warwick was watchful. On one or two occasions he was sure they came near to capture but in due course they came to Dynham Manor which was owned by John Dynham, a trusted Yorkist.

It was a great relief to sleep in a bed; to sit at a table and eat good food and to feel comparatively safe, but they could not linger, of course. They were close to the sea and the sooner they left England the better for them. It was a long journey across the water but they would be safer there than they were staying here where they might be discovered at any time. Guernsey belonged to Warwick, as a fief of the Crown, so he could make for Guernsey first and from there could find out what was happening in Calais and whether it would be safe to return there.

John Dynham was an ardent Yorkist. He would do everything he could to speed them on their way. At great risk he procured a boat with a party of fishermen to sail it to Guernsey. Meanwhile his wife kept them hidden.

In due course they sailed for Guernsey but they had not gone far when a storm arose. The fishermen were terrified.

Warwick shouted at them to stop their trembling and look to their tasks. 'Take the ship to Guernsey,' he cried. 'That is your duty.'

'Master,' said their spokesman, 'we be but poor fishermen. We know little of boats such as this. We'm never been near Guernsey in our lives.'

Warwick looked at the consternation of those about him and cried out: 'By God, I have not come so far to be lost at sea.'

Whereupon he seized the tiller and set the course westward.

He took the boat through the storm and they reached Guernsey in safety.

Edward watching thought: Warwick is a hero. I am going to be exactly like him.

In Guernsey they learned that Calais had remained loyal to Warwick and they immediately set sail. When they arrived Warwick was welcomed with acclaim. The people were with him to a man; but he sensed their uneasiness.

He explained this to Edward. He had taken to Edward. He was certain that here could be a future King. If York was not quite fit for the throne, this son of his would be. Warwick meant to create him in his own image. He was going to make a king of him – which Warwick intended to be himself, in all but name. There was that in his character which made him prefer the role of manipulator. Providing the puppets went his way, that was the role to have. Moreover he could hardly lay claim to the throne himself, and it was essential for a man to have that claim.

York had it. So had young Edward.

Warwick was supreme. Edward saw that clearly. Here he was after fleeing from his enemies, nothing left to him but this governorship of Calais which undoubtedly would be taken from him in a matter of weeks, yet he was jaunty and still sure of himself. There was something indestructible about him.

Edward wanted to be just like that.

Warwick admitted that they had suffered a defeat. War was like that. Up one day, down the next. It was the final battle that counted. And that was to come. They would now begin planning their return and Edward should see how it was done. He would learn what tactics to follow. How to play on men's emotions.

Warwick certainly knew how to do that. He only had to appear to be cheered and idolised. Edward listened to him talking to his men.

'Yes, we have lost this battle. Temporarily we are on the run. But look you, my friends, we have this port of Calais. It is the most important port in Europe. They will try to take it away from me, but are we going to allow that? Indeed we are not.'

The burghers of Calais pledged themselves to Warwick. They lent him the money he needed for his army. They put their faith in him, rather than a weak government from England headed by the Queen.

As he had expected the Queen immediately appointed the Duke of Somerset as Captain of Calais.

'He may come here,' said Warwick, 'but he will not land in Calais, I promise you that.'

Edward watched with growing excitement. He could scarcely tear himself from Warwick's side.

When Somerset's fleet appeared before Calais Warwick gave the order to let off the cannonade. Somerset, furious, could not return to England but he knew that it would be folly to attempt to land. He therefore turned aside and landed some way down the coast at Guisnes where he bribed the custodian of the castle and his men to allow him to take possession.

He had brought a considerable company of men with him, but the ships in which they sailed were manned by sailors of Kent. The men of Kent had always greatly admired Warwick.

He was their hero. They declared that the winds were blowing their ships off course. The same winds blew them into Calais harbour.

How Edward laughed when they arrived. Warwick went to greet them, his armour shining, looking like the hero of Legend.

There was feasting for these men but the soldiers they brought with them had a different reception. Many of these had at one time been Warwick's adherents under the command of Trollope and had deserted to the Lancastrians at Ludlow.

They were despatched to dungeons.

'Always show strength,' he told Edward. 'These men have deserted. The rest of them are honest King's men.'

Edward listened avidly as he addressed them.

He gave the honest King's men free choice. He would welcome them to his service but only if they wished to come. They could speak honestly. They need have no fear of that. Honesty was a quality he respected. It was only traitors who would suffer under his hands.

Many were bemused by him. It was the effect Warwick had on men, Edward was realising more every day.

The ranks of his troops were considerably increased.

Even so, many of the soldiers declared they were the King's servants and wished to serve only under him.

'Very good,' said Warwick. 'You are loyal soldiers. You shall be sent back to England.'

He was just; he was a shining example. Edward was not the only one who thought he resembled a god.

After he had commanded that those who had deserted him should be executed, he sent a sly message to the Duke of Somerset fretting at Guisnes.

'I must thank you, my lord, for your very excellent stores. I have found them of the utmost use in my cause.'

No, one defeat could not be the end of a man like Warwick. The red rose had but temporarily triumphed over the white.

Warwick was looking ahead. Life was an exciting game and the best of all was making Kings. He had lost his confidence in the Duke of York, but not in York's eldest son. Edward Earl of March had the makings of a King. Those masculine blond looks of his were pure Plantagenet. The boy was springing up. He was now all of six feet four inches. In an assembly he towered above the rest. The eyes of women followed him. Instil wisdom into that handsome head and he would have a King indeed.

He took the young March into his confidence. He explained his actions when it was wise to do so. He did not tell him that he was supplanting his father in Warwick's mind. That he had decided to mould a different model; to attach his strings to a new puppet.

Edward was scarcely puppet material. A strong man he would be, with a will of his own – and all the better for that. Warwick wanted to set his mind working in the right direction.

There was promise in the air. Every little circumstance must be made use of; and if the débâcle at Ludlow had helped him to know a little more of the Duke of York and incline him slightly away from him, so much the better.

He would not so much support York as the reform of Parliament. One thing was certain, Henry needed guidance; the Queen's rule – and that was really what the country was getting – was disastrous. Margaret would never understand the

English people, she had no notion that if she was going to rule she must have their consent to do so. She must have their respect and approval. They might be subjects but they were of a nature to choose their ruler. If they did not like the one providence had given them, they would change him. They had done so before and they would do so again.

And if the Duke of York did not quite fit into Warwick's conception of what a King should be, the Earl of March – with Warwick behind him – did.

As Warwick pointed out to Edward, timing was important. It was the most important thing of all. One week could mean success, a week later defeat. They had been routed; they had fled to Calais, but look how fortune was beginning to smile on them.

Their adherents were increasing every day. The great Duke of Burgundy was smiling on them. *He* did not mind that there were raids on the French King's ships. As long as Warwick did no harm to Burgundy he could do what he liked to France. Burgundy saw in Warwick a kindred spirit. He was amused by the manner in which the Earl, by holding the port of Calais, was dominating the seas.

'We must strike soon,' Warwick told Edward. 'The moment is becoming ripe. We should not delay too long for as I told you everything can change between one sunrise and sunset. You see, we have news from Kent as to how Somerset is fitting out ships in Sandwich to come against us, for I have my friends in Kent who keep me informed of every move. If we went to Sandwich we could take the town easily. My friends of Kent would rally to the banner of the Ragged Staff.'

It was amusing and added to Warwick's prestige when one January night news came that Somerset was ready to sail.

Warwick lost no time. He sent out a fleet of his own led by Sir John Wenlock and John Dynham to take them by surprise. This they did, capturing all the ships which were in port and at the same time landing in the town and arresting Lord Rivers and Sir Anthony Woodville in their beds. What was so gratifying was that the townsfolk rallied to help Warwick – which, said he, was the best sign of all.

When they arrived in Calais, Lord Rivers and Anthony Woodville were imprisoned.

'It is only necessary to execute men who can be dangerous to you,' he explained to Edward. 'To kill these two would bring us nothing but the animosity of their families. They are too weak to harm us. It is well to let them live. And if they escape to serve the Queen again, that matters little. They do more harm than good to her cause.'

There was perpetual activity at Calais. By night the ships brought stores and ammunition into the harbour from England. Warwick heard with delight that the men of Kent were waiting to flock to his banner when he came. The government in England was proving itself to be incompetent; the Queen was imposing her will on her chosen ministers and she did not understand the English and every day she earned their dislike a little more.

'The time has come,' said Warwick, 'to consult with your father. We must go to Ireland. There are matters to be discussed which cannot be done by messengers.'

'The English fleet will never let us get there,' said Edward.

'That is not the way I expect to hear you talk, my lord. We are going to get there despite any fleet that any country could put on the sea.'

Edward said that of course they would. He just thought that

Exeter and Somerset would put everything they had into stopping them.

They set out for Ireland and reached that country without mishap. The Duke had established himself in Ireland. He was a born administrator and just as the English had profited from his rule, so had the Irish. They recognised this and showed their appreciation by allowing him to rule in peace.

But the Duke's heart was in England. He wanted news of Cecily and the younger children. He said he and Rutland were eager to go home, and he was delighted to see Edward growing into such a fine specimen of manhood and was sure he could have no better tutor than Warwick.

For eight weeks, they discussed the situation; they made plans, exchanged ideas and decided on their strategy. Warwick then thought that it was time he returned to Calais where he would make his final preparations.

Edward took a fond farewell of his father and prepared to leave with Warwick.

'It won't be long now,' said the Duke. 'We shall all be together soon.'

Edward glowed with the anticipation of seeing his father King of England. How proud his mother would be. She could play the Queen in earnest then. He would be the heir to the throne and that was a dazzling prospect. Rutland and young George and Richard would be princes. They would be greatly excited by that.

In the meantime the kingdom had to be won. They had to drive that virago of Anjou back to her native country. They had to make poor old Henry see that he was unfit to wear the crown.

It was Edward who first sighted Exeter's fleet off the coast of Devon. There would be a mighty battle now and Warwick was not equipped for a fight, but there was no help for it.

'This day,' cried Warwick, 'we shall show our true mettle. Here we are a small force and before us lies the might of Exeter's fleet. We'll not flinch. We fight for the right and always remember that I have not been beaten yet and one of us is worth ten of them. That makes the numbers right. But we have valour and ingenuity which is unknown to them. Come, my lads, serve me well and I promise you victory.'

It was like a miracle. Exeter was turning away. He was not going to fight. Warwick laughed aloud. He guessed what had happened.

The seamen doubtless came from Kent or the south-east. Warwick was their idol. They would refuse to fight against him. Not only from affection and admiration but because they believed he had some divine quality and to fight against that was like pitting mortal strength against the gods.

Laughing with glee Warwick came safely into Calais.

During the feverish preparations at Calais Francesco dei Coppini arrived in the town.

He was an Italian Bishop who had been ostensibly sent to England on command of the new Pope Pius II but was in fact a secret agent for the Duke of Milan. His mission was said to be to raise money to fight the Turks. He had believed that as this would be a kind of crusade against the infidel it would find favour with the King of England.

However, discovering that one of his aims was political and in some measure aimed against France, Margaret would not receive him; moreover she prevented his seeing Henry.

Warwick, who knew what had happened, decided that since Coppini had been snubbed by Margaret it would be a good idea to cultivate him, to make much of him and thus give his own campaign a religious flavour, as though it had been approved by the Pope.

Warwick was a little impatient with the pious talk of his guest but he assured him that he had no intention of displacing Henry; all he wanted to do was reform the government, to dismiss those men who were ruining the country, and curb the activities of the Queen. When Coppini saw the fleet Warwick had amassed and listened to his eloquence he was sure that the expedition would be successful and as Margaret had not been friendly to him, he would give the enterprise his blessing and even sail with it. So he was there when, in the pelting summer rain, Warwick landed at Sandwich, where he was greeted like a king; within a short time he was marching on to Canterbury where he paused only to pay homage and ask the blessing at the tomb of St Thomas à Becket.

Then he began to journey on to London.

Warwick never lost sight of the importance of the people. It was in this that he differed from Margaret. She considered their approval a trivial matter while to Warwick it was all important. London greeted him with warmth and his brother George, who was the Bishop of Exeter, came forward to embrace him and give him the blessing of the Church. So much had Warwick's force swollen as he marched through England that it was now nearly forty thousand strong.

There must be a service at St Paul's, which all the leaders would attend, and at St Paul's Cross Warwick addressed the multitude.

'We have been called traitors,' he cried. 'We are no traitors. We are the King's liege men and we are come to declare our innocence to the King or die on the field. All of us here will swear on the cross of St Thomas of Canterbury that we are doing nothing which could conflict with our allegiance to the King.'

The crowd roared its approval. 'The King, the King.' And then: 'Down with the Queen.'

They understood. They would not be governed by a foreign woman. They wanted good government, such as York had shown he could administer, but under the King. They wanted an end to Margaret's favourites.

Coppini spoke to the multitude. The King must not remain blind to his country's needs. The Yorkists had right on their side. There must be sweet reason. The King must listen to the Duke of York and to the Earls of Warwick and Salisbury. They came with good sound sense. Those who stood with them would receive special pardons for their sins. Those who stood against them were defying God's will.

Warwick saw that it had indeed been a wise move to ingratiate himself with Coppini. The people were religious and superstitious and Coppini, he gleefully told Edward, was as good as a thousand men.

Warwick sent another message to the King as he came near to Northampton. Coppini meanwhile went among the ranks stressing the fact that if they served the great Earl of Warwick they would be granted absolution of their sins. He was sorry for the Lancastrians. They faced excommunication.

The spirits of the men were high. They could serve their earthly hero Warwick and at the same time earn the good graces of Heaven.

Victory must be certain in such a case.

❀ ❀ ❀

The King's forces had been drawn up in the fields with their faces turned away from the River Nene; they were close to Delapré Abbey, busily occupying themselves digging trenches and getting the guns in their correct positions.

The King was restive. He hated war. He was glad though that Margaret was not here. She was not far away in Coventry with young Edward but at least she would be out of the battle. Margaret alarmed him; she would ride with the men like a general. Had she been here she would have been stalking through the camp, haranguing the soldiers, behaving in a way which did not exactly endear her to them. But she never understood that. She thought they were there because it was their duty to fight for their King. It was, but Henry had always understood that they needed to respect and admire that King before they could be asked to fight for him.

Warwick, now the seasoned warrior and constantly on the alert to seize the advantage, spread out his forces facing the enemy. Salisbury was in London. York had not yet arrived, so he appointed Edward to lead one wing and Thomas Fauconberg the other. He trusted Fauconberg entirely. He was connected by blood being the bastard of Warwick's kinsman William Neville. Even at this stage Warwick sent messages into the enemy's lines exhorting them to parley rather than fight. Let the King come forward to speak with Warwick. That was all he asked, but he was determined to speak with the King or die.

He was very much aware that if this battle ensued he would be fighting the King and he wanted no charges of treachery against him.

The battle was short. The rain began to pelt down and the

King's cannon was useless. Warwick's instructions were always: 'Attack the leaders and the lords, leave the commoners.' It had proved wise on other occasions and it did now on this one. Buckingham, Egremont and Shrewsbury all lay dead on the field.

It was victory for Warwick.

The first action Warwick took when he knew that the battle was won was to seek out the King.

Henry was found sitting passively in his tent. He was not so concerned by the fact that he had lost the battle as that so much blood had been shed.

Warwick with March and the Bastard of Fauconberg went on to their knees and swore allegiance to him. They wanted to assure him that he was still their King.

'It would not seem you regard me as such,' said Henry mildly, 'when you bring a force of arms against me.'

'My lord,' said Warwick, 'not against you. Never against you.'

'To be against my armies is to be against me.'

'My lord, all we seek is justice. The people know that. Give us a chance to state our views to the Parliament.'

'Every man should be permitted to state his view and so shall he in my kingdom if my will be done.'

Warwick was not displeased. Here was another puppet for the master to handle.

For three days he kept Henry at Northampton and then took him to London, treating him all the time with the respect which was due to his rank.

Through the streets of London they paraded, Warwick

going before the King bareheaded and carrying the sword of state.

All was well, said the people. Warwick was in command as they all knew he must be and at the same time he was the King's very good subject. It was a happy compromise.

The Queen had disappeared. Some said she had fled to Scotland. Good riddance was the general comment. Now the King, helped by Warwick and the Duke of York, could rule wisely.

Henry stayed at Eltham and then went to Greenwich. He spent his time waiting for the Parliament to be called in hunting for exercise, reading and listening to music. Secretly he was rather pleased that Margaret was not with him. He loved her of course, as a man should his wife; she was beautiful and eager for his welfare – he knew all that, but he wished she were a little less eager for it. He wished she would leave him alone to go his own way. It was pleasant enough when he had strong men to help him govern. He was rather fond of York who was after all a kinsman, and it was quite true that he was descended from both branches of the family and one of them was in fact nearer to the crown than Henry's own.

Then York arrived in England and for the first time actually claimed the throne.

That caused something of a turmoil and many of the lords were indignant. But Henry could see the point of the argument. He had always been a King for as long as he could remember and could not imagine anything else, and oddly he would be loth to give up the crown, burdensome as it was. On the other hand it was true that York had a claim . . .

When it was suggested that he should continue to wear the

crown throughout his lifetime and then let it go to York he agreed.

Margaret would have been furious. What of their son? she would have wanted to know.

Poor boy, he would be happier without a crown. Crowns were no guarantee of happiness. Rather they were the source of sorrow and heartbreak.

Yes, he would agree that York was to take the throne on his death. That was the solution which would put an end to these senseless sheddings of blood.

News came that Margaret who had fled to the North had gathered an army and was marching south.

The King shook his head in sorrow. York, taking Rutland with him, marched north to meet the Queen; and Warwick with Edward stayed on in London, intending to spend Christmas with Henry.

✤ Chapter XIII ✤

THE PAPER CROWN

When Margaret heard of the defeat at Northampton she ground her teeth with rage. If she could only get York in her power – and most of all Warwick – she would not hesitate to have their heads. That was what she longed for more than anything.

But there was much to be done; she must not waste her energies on fruitless fantasies of what she would do with her enemies. She had her boy to consider. Edward was seven years old. He had been constantly in her care and she would not let him escape from it. She was going to be sure that he did not grow up to be like his father.

There had been a time when she had asked Somerset if it would be possible to have Henry deposed and his son crowned King. Somerset had advised her not to mention such a matter to anyone else. It might be construed as treason.

Treason! When she made a reasonable suggestion that her poor ineffectual husband – who was capable of madness in any case – should stand aside for her young and beautiful son who would one day inherit the throne?

But she did recognise the fact that she ought to take care, so that matter had gone no farther.

She had said goodbye to Henry at Coventry and left him to join the army at Northampton while she went on to Eccleshill in Staffordshire. As soon as he had defeated the Yorkists she would join the King.

It was to Eccleshill that the messengers came.

Defeat. Débâcle. A battle which was almost over before it had begun.

And what of her? Here she was not far off and she was the one they hated. She was the one they wanted to get into their power. She, the Queen . . . and her precious son the Prince of Wales.

'There is no time to be lost,' she said. 'We must leave at once.'

She sent for Edward and told him.

'But where shall we go, my dear lady?' asked Edward.

'We shall go to our true friends. I know there are some in this country we can trust. And if there are not enough of them, we shall go to our country's enemies. They will assist us for their own sake.'

Edward looked bewildered. Poor child, he was too young to understand what a world he had been born into. But he was a Prince, the heir to the throne and Margaret was going to fight with all the strength of which she was capable to make sure that he was not cheated out of that.

Summoning her servants she prepared to leave at once and they were soon on the road to Malpas. Margaret failed completely to understand the effect her arrogance had on her followers. Interested as she was in her women's love affairs and having a genuine concern for their welfare, she could never forget that she was the Queen; and she would be amazed if they did not immediately fall in with her wishes. There had been two main influences in her youth and they were the domination of her mother and grandmother and the feckless poverty of her father. She had seen the power of feminine rule. She was determined to emulate her grandmother and mother and equally determined to cling to the high position she had acquired; if she could prevent it, she was never going to live as she had in her childhood with poverty and the fear that everything the family had would be lost to them.

Now that the King had suffered a major defeat and was in the hands of his enemies who would assuredly bend him to their will, her servants asked themselves why they should have to be treated as being so inferior by a woman who first of all could well find her power cut off and secondly was a foreigner who did not understand English ways.

So on the flight from Eccleshill there was a certain amount of murmuring of which Margaret was oblivious – but if she had been aware of it would have taken little heed.

They had come to a wood and as she entered it Margaret felt a shudder of apprehension. It was merely because it was late afternoon, the wood seemed so quiet and the trees made it dark.

She looked with concern at the saddle horses which carried her precious belongings, the jewels which represented so much money, the fine garments which she loved. They were a small band and a lonely one.

She had just turned to give an order to hurry when out of the woods came a band of men. She recognised the livery of one of the nobles and with sinking heart she believed that these were Lord Stanley's men and he was a firm Yorkist supporter.

The men stood a little distance from her.

Margaret, fearless as ever, rode ahead of the company.

'Good day to you,' she said. 'You are not attempting to impede our progress, I hope.'

The arrogant tone betrayed her.

'You are the Queen,' said the leader of the men.

'You appear to have forgotten that,' she answered coolly.

'Nay, we were expecting you to come this way. We had news of your arrival.'

'You have come to join me?'

The men laughed.

'Go to it,' shouted their leader.

'Ay, John Cleger, we will!' shouted the others.

To Margaret's horror she saw that they were making for the saddle horses and some of them had begun to unstrap the baggage.

'Stop them!' she cried. 'Why are you standing there, you oafs?'

It was a fearsome moment for her own men were standing by not attempting to stop the robbers. Then she saw a few of them go over to the saddle horses.

'Do your duty,' she cried. 'Kill these robbers.'

One of the robbers came over to her and the Prince who was beside her.

'We want the horses,' he said. 'Better dismount, lady. You and the boy.'

'How dare you talk to your Queen in such a way!'

'I reckon you'm not that now, lady, or if you are it won't be for much longer. Get down, boy.'

Edward watching his mother, remembering her instructions that he must be brave, sat his horse looking straight ahead of him.

The robber seized him and dragged him to the ground. Margaret cried out, and leaping out of the saddle went immediately to her son.

'It's all right, lady. I wanted your horses, that's all. As fine a pair as I ever saw.'

This was nightmare. She gripped her son's shoulder and held him close to her. The robbers and her own servants were quarrelling over the contents of the saddle bags.

Her jewels! Her beautiful clothes! All lost!

One of them turned and looked in her direction. She did not like what she saw. What would they do when they had everything she had? She knew. Instinct told her. She had identified them as Stanley's men. Her own had deserted her for the sake of getting a share in the booty. Every one of them should die the traitor's death if they were ever brought to justice and they knew it.

They would prevent that at all costs and there was one way of doing it.

She knew that these men would have no compunction in killing her and the Prince.

She drew her son closer to her. It was characteristic of Margaret that she should think of his safety before her own. In her turbulent heart this boy had first place. He was her beloved son for whom she had waited so long; she would fight for him with every spark of strength she possessed. She would die for him if need be. She was fond of the King but she despised him. She wanted to care for him and govern him. It was possible that she wanted to govern this boy too. But she wanted him to grow up strong, not like his father. And now he was in acute danger. She knew that neither of them would be allowed to leave this scene alive if those wicked men could help it.

Keeping her eyes on them she withdrew a little into the trees. She must not go too openly. She must tread cautiously. If she could get one of the horses . . . but that was impossible, they would see her mounting.

Edward was looking at her with eyes that were full of hope. She was there. The mother who seemed to him invincible. He knew they were in danger but he believed that no one could ever stand up for long against his mother.

The men were still wrangling over the jewels. How long would it last? The moment of doom was getting nearer and nearer.

'Lady . . .' It was a soft voice in the trees.

She was alert. A young boy looked at her from behind the trunk of a tree.

'I have a horse here. I know a way through the woods . . . a special way. I could take you and the Prince . . .'

Who was this boy? She did not know. In any case he looked very young and could not do her the harm these men could.

'How . . .' she began.

'Let the Prince come first,' he said.

'Edward,' she whispered. 'Go!'

She could stand there watching the robbers while Edward might well slip into the trees unseen. He went, accustomed to obeying his mother without question.

Her heart was beating wildly. She kept her eyes on the men. They were not watching her. They thought it would be quite impossible for her to leave without a horse and if she attempted to mount and her son with her they would immediately be aware of it.

'Now, lady . . .'

She was in the trees. Edward was already mounted. Hastily

the boy helped her to get up beside him. Then he was up and they were off.

They had gone a little way through the trees when she heard the shout.

She clung to the boy and Edward clung to her; her lips were moving in prayer.

The boy was right. He knew the woods far better than the robbers or her own servants could. In any case those men would rather lose the Queen and the Prince than the contents of the saddle bags.

So they rode on, all through the rest of the day and the night.

The boy told her that he was fourteen years old, and had always wanted to serve the King and the Queen. His name was John Combe and he lived in Amesbury. He had been riding through the woods when he saw the robbers and realised what was happening.

His eyes shone with devotion and loyalty. 'It was my chance, my lady, to do you good service. I thank God for it.'

'You are a good boy and you shall not be forgotten for what you have done this day.'

Nor should he be. Margaret was as fierce in her devotion to her friends as she was in her hatred of her enemies.

'There are many who lurk in the woods to rob, my lady,' he told her. 'I am ever watchful when I am there. But I have my secret ways through. It is easy to be lost there. The trees are like a maze.'

'I thank God that you came when you did. You have saved the life of your Queen and your future King.'

The boy was clearly quite moved, so was Margaret and all through that arduous journey she marvelled at the fortuitous appearance of John Combe. She had told him that she wanted to go to Wales.

'That is a journey through mountainous country, my lady.'

'Nevertheless I have loyal friends there, and that is where I must go.'

John Combe then turned the horse westward and they rode on.

It was easier when he was able to acquire two more horses and they could dispense with the need to ride all three on one.

Even so the journey was long and had it not been for the ingenuity of the boy they would have been lost.

What joy it was when they came in sight of Harlech Castle.

Margaret was very happy with her reception. Warmly she told of John Combe's courage and skill in bringing her and the Prince out of an acutely dangerous situation. It was not long before she was joined by Owen Tudor.

She had been right to come here. There was strength in these Tudors. It was a great tragedy that Edmund had died but Jasper soon joined them and he gave a good account of how young Henry was living in Pembroke Castle with his mother.

'A bright child, my lady,' he told her. 'A Tudor every inch of him and a touch of his royal grandmother without a doubt.'

Margaret had only a little patience to spare for young Henry Tudor. She wanted to know what help she could get here in Wales.

They understood at once.

Owen said: 'Jasper has a great fondness for his nephew, my lady. You would think the boy was his own son.' And then he went on to discuss what troops they could muster and what would be the best plan for taking an army into England.

'The victory was Warwick's, I'll trow,' said Owen.

'Warwick is the one whom we have to battle with. York is a good administrator but I believe he lacks that which a leader needs.'

They were a little outspoken, these Tudors. No one could lack that quality more than the present King. Ah, but the King had a Queen.

It was to the Queen that the Lancastrians would have to look in the future.

❦ ❦ ❦

She was desperate. She needed help. Henry had deserted her, his wife, and what was worse their son, so she believed. He had promised the throne to York when he died. There could not be a worse betrayal.

Everything depended on her. The King of France had always been fond of her. Some might have thought he was attached to her because of the good she could bring to France, but Margaret was guileless in such matters. Most of her difficulties throughout her life had come from her habit of judging everyone by herself and believing they would act in such a way because she would.

Now her fierce energies were concentrated on her son, and she would use any method to regain the promise of a crown which Henry had so wantonly thrown away to their enemies.

Why should not the King of France help her? That he would for a consideration she was sure. With help from France she could defeat Warwick, York, Salisbury, the whole lot of them. But Charles of France would want a very big prize to supply the sort of help she needed. What was the biggest plum she could offer?

Even as the idea had struck her she turned away from it. It

would be a little too daring. But suppose she said to Charles: 'Help me to defeat Warwick and make the crown of England safe for Edward and I will give you Calais.'

Calais! That port so dear to the heart of Warwick and the English people! That centre of trade right on the edge of the continent of Europe! Calais was of the utmost importance to the prosperity of England. Wool, leather, tin and lead were all sent to Calais to be sold into Burgundy. In Calais these goods were taxed and sorted. For trade and for defence Calais was essential to England. The French could not attack it without first coming through Burgundy to do so and as the King of France was on uneasy terms with the Duke of Burgundy, Calais was comparatively safe. Warwick as Captain of Calais had shown its worth. Calais had made it possible for him to increase his power. It seemed likely that Charles of France would do a great deal for Calais.

And yet without help how could she defeat her enemies? How could she make the crown safe for her son?

Calais. She dreamed of it.

She sent a messenger with a tentative suggestion to her old friend and supporter Pierre de Brézé.

While she was in Wales the Duke of Exeter arrived. He had fled from the battlefield, lucky to be alive. But he was determined to fight on and he believed that he could rally men to his banner in the North of England.

'It is help we need,' said Margaret. 'We want to overwhelm them with our strength. If my good uncle the King of France would only come to my aid . . .'

She thought of the message she had sent to Brézé. She eagerly awaited the response and every morning when she awoke it was with the word Calais on her lips. Sometimes she was appalled by what she had done; and yet she knew that if she had the chance to go back she would do it again.

With the Tudors raising an army in Wales and Exeter going to the North, the scene was hopeful. But what she must do was outnumber Warwick and York; she must meet strength with greater strength; she must let the men know that if certain people in England were determined to destroy her, she had friends in other places.

They would hate to lose Calais; but better that than that young Edward, Prince of Wales, should lose his throne.

She decided that she would go to Scotland and seek help there. A ship was found for her and on a cold December day she set sail from Wales with her son.

The weather was even more bleak when she arrived in Edinburgh, but the warm welcome of the Queen Dowager, Mary of Gueldres, gave Margaret new hope. The late King's sister had been the Dauphiness of France and Margaret had known her in the past. She felt therefore that she was going among friends.

If she could prevail upon Mary of Gueldres to give her help that, with whatever the King of France would send her, would enable her to swell her armies to such an extent that the Yorkists would soon be fleeing before them.

Mary of Gueldres it was true had her own problems at this time. Her husband, James the Second, had been killed in battle, for he had taken advantage of the defeat of Northampton to attack the old enemy; and now Mary was acting as regent for her nine-year-old son. However, she showed sympathy for Margaret's troubles and, needing Margaret's help almost as much as Margaret needed hers, it seemed likely that they might strike a bargain.

A reply had come from Pierre de Brézé. He could not believe he had read her hints correctly. Did she really mean that in exchange for help from France she would give up Calais? Did she realise what this would mean to her cause? The English would never forgive her. If she did this she would see what their actions would be when they heard it. Oh yes, the King of France would be delighted; there was nothing she could offer him more to his taste, but Pierre was her good friend and he wanted her to think very earnestly of this matter before she committed herself to an act which would set the English crying for her blood.

She was half relieved, half angry.

I will do it, she thought. Brézé is too weak.

But that was unfair. He had shown himself a good friend to her. Their relationship had been an almost tender one. He admired her strength and her beauty and in a way was in love with her. His thoughts were for what would benefit her most.

For the time being she would shelve the matter and turn her attention to Mary of Gueldres.

Mary was sorry for her. She wanted to be of help; but naturally she must not be foolish, when her own position was so precarious. It was always dangerous when a King died leaving a young heir – a minor who must be surrounded by those who wished to govern for him.

In Lincluden Abbey where Mary had given Margaret apartments, the two women talked and bargained together – Margaret with a kind of feverish intensity, Mary more coldly, calculating each step before she made it, in contrast to Margaret's impetuosity.

There was a fellow feeling between them. Both had young sons to protect. Mary was without a husband it was true but

Margaret felt that hers could sometimes be an encumbrance rather than an asset.

'It is only temporary help I need,' Margaret explained fervently. 'Once I have regained what is mine everything shall be repaid.'

'I know it,' replied Mary, 'but conflicts go on for years before they are resolved and I have dificulties here. We have very unruly nobles in Scotland.'

'They could not be more so than those of England. I often wish I could get rid of them all.'

'Ah, we have to take care that they do not get rid of us.'

'You and I should make a bargain. We should help each other. My dear cousin, give me men, give me arms and let our children marry. Let that be the bond between us. Your little Mary could be my Edward's bride.'

It was tempting. The daughter of a Scottish king was not as desirable a *parti* as some might be. Her father was dead, her mother was struggling to keep the throne safe for her son – and if Margaret succeeded in defeating the rebels Edward would one day be King and little Mary of Scotland Queen of England.

It was a golden prospect if only the war could be won, if Edward was not to be ousted from the throne; but it seemed very likely that he would be, since after Northampton, Richard of York had been declared heir to the throne on the death of Henry.

Mary of Gueldres hesitated.

She knew how desperate Margaret was. She knew that she would do almost anything for help. She would consider nothing too high a price to be paid for what she wanted.

Mary of Gueldres said: 'For myself I would agree willingly to this marriage, but it is those about me . . . I fear before they would be willing to help they would want something more . . .'

'What?' cried Margaret. 'Tell me what?'

'Berwick,' said Mary quietly.

Berwick! That border town which was so important to the English.

Well, she had been ready to give Calais. Why hesitate at Berwick?

'Very well,' she said. 'Berwick shall be yours . . . in exchange for an army which will help me destroy these rebels.'

Cecily Duchess of York had arrived in London in great style with three of her children – her daughter Margaret and her two youngest sons George and Richard.

They must all behave with the utmost dignity, she had told them. Their behaviour was of the utmost importance because they had become Princes. They had always been of the highest in the land – but then so had others; now they had stepped up with their father who when the King died would be King in his place. As for their brother Edward – anyone must realise just by looking at him that he was surely born for a crown.

Edward was the children's god. He was always so dazzling to look at and stories of his adventures reached them; he was a great soldier, a great adventurer and he never seemed out of temper. He would be King one day, their mother told them, but not yet praise God because their noble father came first.

The Duke was coming from Ireland to join them and when he arrived it would be a great day of rejoicing for everybody. Cecily decided that it would be fitting for her to go to meet him and therefore the children would be left behind in the mansion in Southwark where they had been living since they came to London.

'Your brother Edward will come often to see you,' she told them. 'But you must not expect too much attention from him. He has great affairs with which to concern himself and he will spend much time with the great Earl of Warwick. If the Earl should come here, make sure you treat him with the correct respect. Edward will notice if you don't.'

They did not believe their big handsome brother would trouble very much about that. Life was exciting. And when their father came to London he would go to Parliament and after that nobody would be able to say they were not Princes.

The days passed. The children went riding through the city but they were too young to notice the tension in the streets. Northampton might have been a resounding victory but there were many lords who supported the red rose of Lancaster and when a King was in conflict with certain members of the nobility and when new rulers were going to replace old there was always acute danger. It was true that Henry was not fit to govern; it was true that many hated the Queen; but there was a young Prince at present with his mother and to accept the Duke of York in his place did not please everybody.

That the Duke and Duchess of York already regarded themselves as the rulers was obvious. When the Duchess had left London on her way to meet her husband she had travelled in a chariot decorated with blue velvet and drawn by four pairs of the finest horses. Margaret of Anjou had never travelled more royally. The Duke was a more able administrator than Henry, that was true; but it seemed that Proud Cis would be every bit as overbearing as Margaret.

In due course York came riding into London. With Cecily in her velvet-covered chariot it was a very grand procession, but there was a notable lack of enthusiasm among the people.

The Duke cared nothing for that. He lost no time in present-ing himself to the Parliament and on his way there had one of his men ride ahead of him carrying a sword – a custom which implied that he was already the King.

The people watched in silence and later, when presenting himself in Parliament, he insisted on the lords listening to an account of his pedigree which showed that he had more right to the throne than Henry. Henry's grandfather had usurped the throne, he declared. Others had come before him. Therefore he, York, was the rightful King.

There was great consternation throughout the House and the lords were uncertain how to act. They accepted the pedigree, on the other hand Henry was their crowned King. At length one of them suggested that as the matter was so complicated it should be put before judges. It was a matter of law and for them to decide.

When York returned to Southwark it was to find Warwick there with Edward.

They immediately retired to an apartment where the three of them might talk in earnest.

It was clear that Warwick did not approve of York's action in going to the Parliament. 'The time is not ripe,' said Warwick; and he was regretting that York stood before his son. How much easier it would be to handle Edward!

'We have delayed long enough,' said York. 'It is time we let the people see what we stand for. We want Henry deposed and we have to let Margaret know that she has not a chance.'

'It's true,' said Warwick, 'but we should tread with more care. There is hostile feeling all around us, and it will need little to turn that into active support for Henry.'

'Henry is hopeless and all know it.'

'He still retains their affection. Well, we have gone so far, we must see what the judges make of it.'

The judges very quickly let them know. 'This matter is too difficult for us to decide,' was their verdict. 'It is above our knowledge of the law and learning.'

It was fortunate that Warwick's brother, George Neville, had been made Chancellor. He declared that it was clear that the King's health prevented him from ruling. Let the decision remain to let him wear the crown until he died and then let it go to York.

There were some who thought this would shorten Henry's life because there would most certainly be those who would want to be rid of him.

George Neville then said that if Henry died mysteriously they would not rest until they had found his murderer and no matter how high in the land that person was he should suffer the traitor's death. Moreover, the Duke of York was considerably older than Henry. It seemed very likely that Henry would live longer.

So it was stated that York was officially to be declared heir to the throne.

When Henry was approached he buried his head in his hands. 'I only ask to be left in peace,' he said.

'The Duke of York and his heirs will have the throne after you.'

'Yes, yes,' said the King wearily.

They were amazed. Had he forgotten the boy of whom he and Margaret had been so proud?

'I want peace,' cried Henry. 'My country wants peace. Forsooth and forsooth, let us have peace and pay the price for it if we must.'

343

So York was declared heir to the throne. But there was no rejoicing in the streets.

Warwick shook his head apprehensively. 'It was wrong. The people don't like it. One always needs the people with one particularly in a situation like this which could be unpopular. No, you should not have done this. You should have waited until by very force of arms we could have deposed Henry and set you up.'

'I agree with that,' said Edward.

York looked sadly at his eldest son. Edward seemed to be all Warwick's now. Rutland was his dear faithful son. Rutland would never question any moves he made.

Even as they talked together messengers were arriving. Margaret was gathering forces. She had the Tudors building up an army in Wales. Exeter was doing the same in the North as she herself was in Scotland.

'No time for complacency,' said Warwick. 'Edward and I will remain in London to keep watch over the King and build up an army. You should go to York and muster as many men as you can. We may have to fight. It is hardly likely that Margaret will quietly accept this.'

The Duke of York agreed and left London for Yorkshire where he would amass an army to fight with him and retain his new title.

Christmas would soon come. Through the cold winds of winter York marched with his men. He would do little until the spring; it was never wise to make battle in the depths of winter.

He did not believe Henry would live long. There might be some who would make it their duty to see that he did not. And then . . . the crown would be his. Edward would be a worthy heir for all that he had become Warwick's man rather than his father's. Never mind. They were all on the same side and Edward was a son to be proud of.

They had come to the town of Worksop and as they were marching out of the town they were unaware of the ambush and Somerset's troops were upon them before they could make ready to return the attack.

The fighting was fierce and the losses on both sides great.

They must get to York, thought the Duke. They must get to the castle of Sandal at least. That was within a mile or so of Wakefield.

He rallied his forces and cried out to them that they must leave the field and make with all speed for Sandal.

He was relieved when the grey stone castle rose up before him, a mighty fortress on the left bank of the River Calder.

He glanced at his son Rutland who was riding beside him. His favourite of late, one who had adhered to his father and resisted the wiles of the hero Warwick. Foolish to feel that envy but under Warwick's influence Edward had changed towards him. They had been critical of him in London; they had made him feel that he was no longer the leader. Warwick was like that. Whenever he was present, one felt that though he might not be in command in the flesh he was in spirit.

'We will show them, my son,' he said to Rutland.

'We will, Father,' replied the boy.

They had not realised the size of the army which was approaching. Exeter with Clifford had done well in raising such an army for Margaret.

Salisbury who had accompanied them said that they were

safe in the castle. He had sent messengers to Warwick and Edward to let them know how things stood. They need not worry. They could hold out until Warwick or Edward came to relieve them.

The Duke was frustrated. To be besieged in a castle waiting for Warwick and his son, it was too much to be borne. They criticised him enough already.

It was all very well to wait. He could imagine the day Warwick arrived, scattering the enemy, proudly riding into the city; and there would be Edward beside him, admiring, hanging on his words, pitying his father because he had had the ill luck – mismanagement they might say – to get himself besieged in Sandal Castle.

'I shall not wait for relief,' said York. 'I shall go out among them. I shall reduce their ranks. I will cripple this army so that it cannot come against me again.'

'Is this wise?' asked Salisbury. 'We are outnumbered.'

'We are not outclassed,' said the Duke. 'I can fight battles without Warwick and my eldest son.'

' 'Tis so,' agreed Salisbury. 'But their help would be useful.'

'Where are the enemy now?'

'Encamped at Wakefield.'

'A mile or so away. Then we will prepare to attack.'

Thus was fought the battle of Wakefield. It was folly from the start to have attempted it. The Yorkists were completely out-numbered. Many were slain on that field including the Duke of York and his son Rutland.

It was with great exultation that the Lancastrians discovered the dead body of the Duke. They cut off his head and sent it to

York to be stuck on the walls of the city and someone had placed a paper crown on his head.

Salisbury was captured but they would not allow him to live. He was too dangerous. His head was displayed on the walls of York beside that of his friend and ally.

It was defeat. York was dead. When Margaret heard the news she was almost wild with joy.

'The tide has turned,' she cried. 'This is our greatest victory. We are going to win back what is ours and the fate of every traitor in England shall be as that of the Duke of York.'

Chapter XIV

MARGARET'S TRIUMPH

Edward was at Gloucester when he heard the news of his father's defeat and death. He was completely stunned. He could not believe this was possible. He stared blankly at the messenger and then a terrible grief overcame him.

He wanted to be alone, to think of his father. He had always admired him so much, always looked up to him, seen him as a King, invincible. And now . . . defeated . . . dead, and his head on the walls of York surmounted by a paper crown. The ultimate mockery.

A great rage overtook him then. Those who had jeered at his father should pay dearly for their mirth.

'What are we doing waiting here?' he cried. 'We must march . . . march against them. We must inflict such slaughter upon them that they scream for mercy.'

He thought of Warwick, his hero. Where was he now? Still in London. Warwick would say: Be calm. Do not scream Revenge! just for the sake of revenge. Let it be revenge tempered with reason. They shall pay, yes, but in a manner best suited to our cause.

He thought of his mother, proud Cis, who was certain that before long she would be Queen of England and the boys too . . . the Princes. And what of Rutland? . . . dead with his father. Father and brother slain on one field. He could almost hear the quiet tones of Warwick: 'Alas, my lord, that is war.'

Then the understanding came to him in a blinding realisation of what this would mean to him. When he contemplated it he could for a few moments, in spite of his grief, think of nothing else.

He, Edward, no longer merely Earl of March but Duke of York, could be King of England.

That was something to fight for . . . to live for. My God, he thought, they will not long be laughing at my father's head. King Edward! It would come. Something within himself assured him of that.

Even as he mourned several of his friends came to him to tell him that they could no longer stay in Gloucester. They were Humphrey Stafford, Walter Devereux and Devereux' son-in-law Herbert of Raglan.

They knew he was staggering under the terrible blow the revelation of his father's death had been; they were aware that the defeat at Wakefield was the most significant setback the Yorkists had suffered as yet – but the result of it was to place a heavy burden on Edward's young shoulders and into their manner there had crept a certain respect which had not been there before.

Even through his grief Edward was aware of it and exulted in it.

'Friends have come in with news from the Marches,' said Devereux. 'Jasper Tudor is in England and has brought with him French Bretons and Irish, enemies all. He is preparing to march against us. And Margaret when she hears of what has happened at Wakefield will be marching south.'

'Let them come,' cried Edward. 'The sooner the better. Praise God we have an army of stalwart men. I yearn for battle. I swear by God it will not be long before the blood of my father and my brother is avenged.'

'Amen,' murmured the others.

'Then why do we wait? Let us prepare now to march.'

Edward's mood communicated itself to all those about him. Men looked at him and saw in him the leader which his father had never somehow managed to be. Edward was so tall, so handsome, so Plantagenet, that men said it was as though Edward Longshanks walked again. He looked invincible. The determination to avenge his father was clear to all who beheld him.

He halted his army at Wigmore where he had his own castle. Here he saw that the men were adequately lodged and fed. They would go into battle fighting fit; and the memory of Wakefield was with them every inch of the way.

Between the valleys of Brecon and Hay came Jasper Tudor, with his father, Owen Tudor, riding beside him. This was a great day for the House of Lancaster. The Duke of York was dead. What better news could there be? The throne had been saved for Owen Tudor's stepson Henry. Owen was confident that now the Yorkists would accept defeat.

'There is still Edward of York,' Jasper reminded him.

'A braggart boy.'

Jasper was not so sanguinary. He had seen Edward. There was a certain regality about him. 'He has the look of a King.' he said.

'Oh, you are bemused by the height of him, by those golden good looks. I've heard they'll be the death of him. He is too fond of good living.'

'Kings often are,' said Jasper.

'Jasper, my son, what has possessed you this day? I tell you we are riding high. Imagine that head on the walls of York. A paper crown, ha ha.'

'I am imagining it,' said Jasper. 'I doubt not Edward is too.'

'It will unnerve the boy,' said Owen.

Jasper did not answer. He marvelled at his father. He was a man of great charm and good looks, a man who walked through life without seeing the dangers. Perhaps that was what had brought him through a dangerous marriage with a Queen, which had endured for several years, escape from the Tower, and living a dangerous life in the Welsh mountains to serve his half-brother. Sometimes it seemed to Jasper that Owen Tudor did not see the realities of life. Fortune had favoured him, had brought him through danger time and time again so that he believed she always would.

The two armies were close now. Edward had the advantage because he knew the ground so well and he was impelled by such an urgent desire for revenge that he knew he could not fail.

He was going to avenge his father or die in the attempt; and he was as certain in his own heart that he was going to live to be King of England.

He had decided that the battle should take place at Mortimer's Cross and there he camped his army round about the village of Kingsland.

It was Candlemas Day and about ten o'clock in the morning when there was a sudden shout from one of the soldiers. He was standing as though struck dumb, staring up at the sky. Everyone looked up and there was a shocked and terrible silence. Above them was not one sun but three. None of them had ever seen such a rare phenomenon as a parhelion before, and they did not know that it was caused by the formation of ice or snow crystals in the atmosphere and being hexagonal in shape produced a double refraction which took the form of a halo.

More and more men came out to gaze up at the sky and when Edward came out and looked he was filled with dismay but even more so to see the effect it was having on his men. He looked up defiantly to the sky.

'Yes,' he cried, 'it is an omen. It indicates that the Trinity is with us, God the Father, God the Son and the Holy Ghost will be beside us this day.'

It was amazing how words spoken by a strong man in such tones of authority could have such an effect on an army. They now looked up at the sky and they marvelled. Edward had convinced them that there would be victory this day.

Jasper's troops had arrived and the battle began. Edward was in the thick of it, remembering all that he had learned from his father and particularly from Warwick. 'The Trinity is with us,' he cried. 'Revenge for Wakefield.'

He had taken on a new stature. He was the King already. It was as though Edward Longshanks had come back to earth. The result seemed inevitable. They were gaining ascendancy over the enemy.

'Spare the commoners, kill the leaders,' he cried. Warwick had taught him that. It was the leaders they must rout out.

Jasper was dismayed. He could see defeat staring them in

the face. This Edward was a new leader to conjure with. He had ceased to be a boy when his father died.

The Earl of Wiltshire was beside Jasper. 'It is time to get away . . .' cried the Earl. 'It is either flight or death. Come . . . if you want to live to fight another day. There'll be no mercy for us if we are captured.'

It was true. All hope was gone. The battle of Mortimer Cross had been fought and won by Edward and the Yorkists.

'Where is my father?' said Jasper.

'He will defend himself. He always had the luck.'

'I would like to know that he is safe.'

'You cannot turn back. Come, Jasper, is it to be retreat and fight another day for us or certain death?'

Jasper saw the wisdom of flight. His father would take care of himself.

At that moment when Jasper with Wiltshire was riding with all speed into the Welsh mountains, Owen Tudor was surrounded by soldiers. His horse had been wounded and was lying beside him, and Owen knew that this time his luck had failed him.

He was brought to Edward, who studied him sardonically.

'Well, Owen Tudor, you have not been so fortunate this time!'

Owen smiled that smile which was still attractive enough to charm. 'My lord, the fortunes of war are unpredictable.'

'Perhaps your fate is far from unpredictable.'

Owen felt a tremor of dismay. Was Edward telling him that he would have his head?

'You took up arms against my father,' said Edward.

'My lord, I took up arms for my brother, the King.'

'Ah, Tudor, you are very proud of the connection.'

'My lord, are you not proud of your connections with Kings? Is that not what this war is all about?'

'It is to set the rightful King on the throne and to put an end to bad government.'

'And to uphold the rights of the true King.'

Owen was too sure of himself.

'Take him away,' said Edward.

They marched to Hereford where the people gave a welcome to the victorious army. People came out of their houses to see Edward of whom they had heard so much. How the women loved him! He exulted in their admiration. They wanted a King like him – a virile adventurer, a handsome charmer; they might admire Henry for a saint but he was not the man to enchant them.

They would give up Henry tomorrow – these people of Hereford – for the sake of this tall, handsome Plantagenet King.

The prisoners marched with them. He noticed the looks which Owen Tudor attracted. He had an indefinable charm which was there even though he had left his youth behind him. He must have been an extremely handsome man for Queen Katherine to forget her royalty for him.

But it must be the end of him. There should be no mercy shown to any of those who had stood against the White Rose of York.

He himself would witness the execution and when it was done there should be fresh heads to set on the walls of York and those already there should be taken down and most reverently buried.

Owen did not believe that he was going to die. He knew that the people were gathering in the market square. He knew that they had been promised a spectacle. But he believed something would happen at the last moment to save him. It always had. He had lived a charmed life ever since Queen Katherine had noticed him in her household and had fallen in love with him. The memory of those days would live with him for ever. Sometimes he believed that Katherine watched over him from Heaven . . . him and their children. Those long days of secret happiness now seemed as real as they ever had.

He had never ceased to love her. He had worshipped her, revered her and had taught their children to do the same. Edmund was dead now, but how proud she would have been of little Henry, her grandson! Owen had taught the child to love her too.

Oh Katherine, he thought, I cannot die yet. There is much to be done. Something will happen at the last moment. I shall go out there to my execution but there will be some miracle. I know it.

The crowds were filling the square. So it had got as far as that. Something will happen, he thought. My time has not yet come.

He was led out into the square with others. There was a hush in the crowd when they saw him. They knew him well. He was the romantic Owen Tudor who had married Queen Katherine, who had loved her and sired her children and in the end she had been snatched from him and died of a broken heart, they said, for love of him.

The women were sad. He was a romantic figure even now that he had lost his youth.

One came forward and cried in a shrill voice: 'Save Owen Tudor. He is too beautiful to die.'

She was dragged away – poor mad creature, they said.

Even now he could not believe it. Even though he saw the block and the axe and the executioner standing there.

Something will happen. There will be a sign from Heaven. Edward is just allowing this to happen to show me how near I came to losing my head.

There would be a messenger. Stop the execution of Owen Tudor. It would be romantic, dramatic as his life had been since he loved Katherine the Queen.

They were urging him forward. He was now stepping up to the block.

Hurry, hurry or they would be too late.

But no one was coming. There was no one to save Owen Tudor now. He must accept his fate. At last it had come then. Someone had put up a hand and torn off the collar of his red velvet doublet. Now there was no help for it. He must lay his head on the block.

He smiled whimsically at the crowd on whom a great silence had fallen.

'Ah, my friends,' he said in a firm voice. 'This head which you will now see placed on this block at one time was wont to lie in the lap of Queen Katherine.'

The silence was deep. He was urged forward. Then quietly, realising that this was indeed the end, he laid his head on the block.

'So he is dead,' said Edward. 'So perish all traitors. Though he was a man who supported what he believed to be right. No matter. He fought on the wrong side and at Mortimer's Cross he met his deserts. Let his head be placed on the Market Cross that all may see it.'

So that head which he had in his last breath boasted had rested in Queen Katherine's lap was placed on the Market Cross. In the morning people were surprised for they found the mad woman they had seen on the previous day seated at the foot of the cross. She had combed Owen's hair and washed the blood from his face and about the Cross she had set up a hundred lighted candles while she chanted prayers for his soul.

'There was a man who attracted women to him,' said Edward musingly. He did himself, but perhaps differently. He wondered fleetingly who would light candles to his memory. But he had his whole life before him and it would be glorious.

He ordered that the woman should not be turned away and the candles should be left burning.

Let Owen go out as he had lived . . . romantically. He could rejoice in the end of the Tudor but there was still Jasper and he was a man to reckon with.

He was sorry Jasper had escaped. Never mind, one day he would have Jasper's head where it belonged and that would be the end of these upstart Tudors.

He remembered fleetingly that there was another – a child somewhere. Yes, he had heard of a young Henry Tudor. A baby . . . nothing more.

He must get Jasper and when he had he could forget that there was a little Henry Tudor somewhere in Wales.

Margaret was marching down from the North. She had a mighty army with her. It was true they were undisciplined and that they followed her not so much because they believed in her cause but because she had promised them they would be allowed to loot the towns through which they passed; to march with Margaret meant for Scotsmen that with luck they could carry off a good deal of English valuables over the Border when the fighting was over.

It was the only way that Margaret could amass an army and she had never been very scrupulous about the means.

With her was her little son, Edward – eight years old now and on whom all her hope rested. She was going to bring him up to be a man; he must not be weak and vacillating like his father, but able to win his rights and hold them.

There might be some who criticised her for taking a child with her at such times. But he was going to learn how to fight from childhood; he was going to be a great and ruthless King, for Margaret was sure that ruthlessness was necessary to rule well.

She kept him with her. She taught him herself. He was the whole meaning of life to her; she had long ago decided that Henry could never be made into the man she wanted. Therefore it would have to be Edward. Henry was now in the hands of her enemies. That was not such a tragedy as it would have been but for Edward. Edward was the important one; he was her future King; and he was also her very own child. Dearly she loved him; everything she did was for his sake.

So began her march south.

'Sooner or later,' she told the little Prince, 'we shall come face to face with the armies of the Duke of York or the Earl of Warwick and when we do we shall give battle and we shall win . . . win . . . win . . .'

'Win,' cried the young Prince firmly as she had taught him.

She caught him to her and held him fast. She was a demonstrative mother. 'And one day there will be a crown on this little head, I promise you. Even though the wicked Duke of York will try to snatch it from you.'

Little Edward cried: 'He never shall!' just as she had taught him, and he touched the silk red rose which was sewn into his tunic.

He rode beside her at the head of the army and he looked all the time for the spies of the wicked Duke of York and those of the equally wicked Earl of Warwick.

The people in the towns were hostile as they came south. How dared the foreign woman bring with her this band of ruffians who looked on the spoils they could collect from the towns and the villages as fair game. The trouble was that when the looting started beggars and vagabonds came in from all over the country to join in.

Margaret had never lost the talent for turning the people against her.

Meanwhile as far south as London there was anxiety and when Warwick set out with an army many joined him. Warwick took the King with him; he was anxious to show that he was still Henry's loyal servant. It had always been his cry that it was not the crown he wanted to take; he merely wanted to make sure that the country was well governed. He accepted Henry as the rightful King but on his death the Duke of York should be the King. That seemed to him reasonable and there were a great many who were ready to agree with him.

The weather was bitter. It was not the time of year for fighting. Alas, that was something Warwick could not choose; but if the weather was bad for him it would be equally so for his enemies and this was time for a decisive battle.

It was the twelfth day of February when he rode out of London. He had a worthy army behind him and the goodwill of the people of the capital. Rumours had reached London as they had other cities of the conduct of hordes of looters and spoilers who made up Margaret's army and the merchants were terrified that they might invade the city. Their goodwill went with Warwick's disciplined men and Warwick knew it.

He was full of confidence as he rode north. With him were the Duke of Norfolk, the Earl of Arundel, Lords Montague and Bonvile, Sir Thomas Kyriell and Captain Lovelace, a gentleman from Kent who had been captured at Wakefield and had managed to escape. This last was an excellent soldier and Warwick put him in charge of some of his best troops.

He had new weapons with which he hoped to strike terror into his enemies. There were firearms which could shoot lead bullets, and something called wildfire which was calculated to strike terror into all who beheld it. It was cloth dipped into an inflammable mixture which was lighted and attached to arrows; when the arrows with the wildfire attached to them were shot into the enemy's ranks they should cause the worst kind of panic for they would ignite anything they touched.

At St Albans Warwick called a halt. He had chosen this for the site of the battle. It was at St Albans that he had on a previous occasion won great success. Looking back he realised that before that famous battle he had been of little account. It was at St Albans he had proved his worth. St Albans had brought him good fortune once. It would do so again.

It was always an advantage to choose the battleground, and he was sure he knew which way Margaret was coming and he spread his forces out so that both roads from Luton might be blocked.

She was some way off and he had several days' grace; he would spend them in constructing defences. He was superbly equipped. His bowmen had shields of a kind which had never been used before; they opened while the archers shot their arrows and then closed again; these shields were studded with nails so that if the enemy rushed forward to attack they could be thrown down to trip up men and horses and break their legs. Traps were set across the ground.

Warwick congratulated himself and his friends on their magnificent preparations and assured them that the battle would be over before it had begun.

'Look to the King,' he said. 'He will not wish to be in the thick of the battle but it would be well to guard him. I do not think he will attempt to escape but you, Bonvile, will keep close to him and someone else must join you.'

Sir Thomas Kyriell volunteered to do so and Warwick said that there could not be a better choice.

'Lovelace, I am putting you in charge of the right flank.'

Lovelace nodded. He hoped he did not show how uneasy he was. He was in a dilemma. His position was not a very happy one. He had not escaped from Wakefield as he had said he had. It was rather different. He had been released on a condition. He had no wish to be a spy. It was not his role at all. He was a soldier. But when faced with torture and horrible death he had had to make a choice.

'You may return to Warwick's army,' he was told. 'You will lead his men; but in truth you will be working for us. You will send messages to us as to where his strength and weakness lie; you will let us know his plans . . .'

He wished he had not agreed. He wished he had accepted death and honour. But it was hard on a man.

So here he was in Warwick's army, enjoying Warwick's trust. Well hardly enjoying it . . . wishing with all his might that he had never been captured at Wakefield.

But perhaps he was unduly worried. Warwick was going to

win this battle; and if he did, why should he worry about what Margaret and her captains could do to him? After the resounding victory that Warwick would surely achieve there would be nothing to worry about.

Warwick would succeed. He must succeed. He must so completely rout the enemy that Lovelace would never have to worry because he had failed to play a double game.

Henry's tent had been pitched under a tree and Lord Bonvile and Sir Thomas Kyriell were with him.

'Never fear,' Lord Bonvile promised him, 'we shall not leave you. We shall be beside you while the battle rages.'

'Battles,' murmured Henry, 'I would there need never be more battles. Of what use is this bloodshed? Have I not promised that York shall have the crown on my death? Oh shame on them, shame on them, so to treat the Lord's anointed.'

'It is the Queen, my lord, who will not agree to the people's wishes. She will take the crown for her son.'

The King shook his head and mumbled. Bonvile and Kyriell exchanged glances. It was strange that the King should be ready to pass over his son. Could it really be that Edward was not his child and he knew it? Or was it simply that Henry was ready to make any sacrifice for the sake of peace?

One thing was clear. It was only necessary to look at the King to understand why this war had to be. He was unfit to rule; and when there was a claimant who looked like Edward Longshanks and who acted like him – then clearly that claimant was meant to be King.

Almost as soon as the battle began Warwick realised his mistake. His defences on which he had spent so much time and on which victory depended were useless. Margaret was not coming in by either of the roads he had imagined. She was going to strike his army on the undefended north-west front. This meant that his men would be facing the bitter wind while the enemy would have it at their backs.

Another point which he had overlooked was the size of Margaret's army; it was not quite double his own but nearly so; not a decisive factor certainly, but in view of the layout of the land and the position which had been forced upon him it could prove disastrous.

It began to snow and the wind blew the snow into his men's faces; the wildfire, to which they were not accustomed, was worse than a failure; it reacted against them. When they shot it forward the wind cruelly blew it back; and they were the ones who suffered from the deadly weapon.

The nets and traps which he had set up were useless; and the Lancastrians were smashing into his defences. It was becoming clear that all his skill and all his ingenuity could not save him. The men were quick to see that they were losing the day.

Lovelace saw it. He had his own life to save and there was only one way he could do so.

He shouted an order to the troop of men under his command and they galloped after him right into the Lancastrian forces shouting: 'A Henry. Margaret the Queen for ever.'

Margaret was exultant. The battle had been all but won, but Lovelace had added the final touch.

Warwick was in retreat. The first battle of St Albans had been a disaster for her; the second was triumph.

In his tent, guarded by Lord Bonvile and Sir Thomas Kyriell, Henry sat praying silently. All about him were the sounds of war. He was deeply distressed. He prayed for death – his own death for it seemed to him that there was nothing in life but continual conflict. If he were dead Edward of York would be King and perhaps there would be peace. But no, Margaret would never stand aside and let them take the crown from their son. That was what this was all about.

Sir Thomas was whispering to Lord Bonvile: 'We should go now. Our friends are leaving the field.'

Lord Bonvile hesitated. 'Who will guard the King?'

'None will harm him. Margaret would not want that.'

'Who will know that he is the King?'

Henry heard them whispering. 'You are planning to leave me,' he said.

'My lord, our army is all but defeated. If we stay here we shall assuredly be killed.'

'Nay. I will protect you. You have protected me and I will protect you.'

The two men exchanged glances. It was their duty to stay with the King. Warwick had commanded them so that he would be protected from any of the soldiers from either side who might seek to murder and rob him. When the looting began it was not easy to restrain them. If the King were left alone in his tent and discovered there he would very likely be murdered.

'Then, my lord,' said Bonvile, 'we will stay.'

The battle was won. The enemy were in flight. Margaret was triumphant. She embraced her son and cried out: 'We have defeated them. We will drive them from this land. This is the end of York and Warwick. Perhaps they will see this now. Let us thank God for this victory. But we shall not rest on it, my son. No, no, now we should go to London. We shall proclaim you heir to the crown. I shall be Regent until you are old enough.'

'My lady,' said the Prince, 'what of my father?'

'They have your father with them. Pray God he is safe. Everything is changed now. This is victory, my son.'

Lord Clifford came into the tent. He was clearly excited.

'My lady, we have found the King. His servant Howe is without. He has been sent here by Lord Bonvile.'

'Bring Howe to me without delay.'

The King's servant was on his knees before the Queen.

'My lady, I can take you to his tent. He is guarded by Lord Bonvile and Sir Thomas Kyriell.'

'Traitors,' she cried. 'They have always been my enemies.'

'They have guarded the King and saved him from the soldiers who might have harmed him, my lady. The King has promised them mercy for their services.'

'Take me to him . . . at once,' commanded the Queen.

Henry staggered to his feet.

'Margaret,' he cried.

She ran to him and embraced him. 'Thank God you are alive. Oh, Henry . . . it has been so many months . . . But it is over now.'

'Margaret, to see you like this . . .'

'Victorious,' she cried. 'Our enemies in flight!'

'Now there must be peace.'

'Peace when we have what we want. See here is your son. Edward, your father.'

Henry embraced his son and there were tears in his eyes as he contemplated the boy.

Margaret was surveying Sir Thomas Kyriell and Lord Bonvile who had stood back while the reunion was going on.

Her expression hardened. These men were the enemy. They had fought with Yorkists against their King.

'My lord Clifford,' she said, 'call guards and put these men under arrest.'

Lord Bonvile said: 'The King has promised us free pardon.'

She ignored him.

'My lord,' began Bonvile, appealing to Henry.

Henry said: 'Yes, these men were my good friends. They stayed with me when they might have escaped. I have promised them their freedom.'

The Queen nodded. 'Even so, we must put them under restraint.'

The guards came in and took Lord Bonvile and Sir Thomas away.

'Now,' said Margaret smiling, 'you should reward those who have served you well. First your son. You must bestow a knighthood on him; and there are others who have served our cause with extreme gallantry. Will you, my lord, at this very moment honour those whom I shall have brought to you?'

'Willingly,' said the King.

Henry was resting in his tent. He was very feeble still and he needed rest if he was to endure the journey to London which it seemed necessary to endure. Margaret knew that what she must do was march to London, take the capital and set up the King in his rightful place so that he could rule and all should know that he had a strong heir to follow him. The proclamation which had decreed that Henry should rule as long as he lived and then be followed by the Duke of York must be overruled and declared null and void.

She was glad of the King's weakness for that gave her the chance to do what she had intended to do, and from the moment she had set foot in his tent she had known that if the King had been aware of that he would have tried to prevent her.

She had set up a court room and in it was the block and the executioner with his axe; beside her on a dais sat her son.

Sir Thomas Kyriell and Lord Bonvile were brought in. They had fought with the enemy; they had brought their men to serve against the King. They were traitors to the anointed. And what was the fate of traitors? Death was the answer.

'The King promised us pardon if we stayed to guard him,' said Lord Bonvile.

'There is no pardon for traitors,' said the Queen coldly. 'You shall reap your rewards, my lord. Justice shall be done.'

She turned to her son. 'What punishment shall be meted out to these two traitors, my son?'

Well primed and eager to show he had learned his lessons well, the Prince cried out: 'They should lose their heads.'

The Queen smiled. 'Judgement has been given,' she said. 'Let the sentence be carried out without delay.'

The Prince looked on wide-eyed as the two dignified men were led to the executioner's block. He saw the blood gush forth as their heads rolled away from their bodies.

Margaret saw that he neither shuddered nor turned away. She was pleased with him. She was sure he would not grow up to be like his father.

Chapter XV

THE FATEFUL DECISION

'This,' said Margaret, 'should be the beginning of the end. We have trounced the great Warwick. What is the victory at Mortimer Cross now? It is for us to march to London to show the people the King and to tell them the war is over. The enemy is defeated.'

It was the answer. But the Earls of Pembroke and Wiltshire were thoughtful. Margaret's army consisted of the roughest men; a great many of them were mercenaries; they were fighting this war not for a cause but because of the booty. They were dreaded and hated throughout the country.

The troops of York and Warwick were of a different calibre. They were fighting because they believed they needed a strong King and Henry was not suited to the role. They had merely wanted him to reign with strong men to guide him and after his death for York to take the throne. York had convinced many of them that he had the greater claim in any case.

The people of London would never open their gates to Margaret's army. One did not have to think very deeply to imagine the pillage that would take place if the richest city in the kingdom was thrown open to the marauders. London had its own troops. It would never allow Margaret's rabble to enter.

There was discussion and argument. Margaret began to see the point. There would be opposition and London had decided the fate of several kings.

Perhaps she was not strong enough. Perhaps now that she had shown she could win battles she would lure different kinds of men to her banner. Perhaps she would not have to rely on these mercenaries collected for her by her very good friends.

When Jasper added his voice to the others she was inclined to sway towards their view. In the meantime she remained at St Albans.

Warwick rode at the head of his defeated army. The débâcle at St Albans had been a humiliating experience. Looking back he could see where it had gone wrong. There had been too much preparation and it had all been of no avail – frustrated by the simplest of strategy. The battle had not taken place facing the direction he had intended it should. It all depended on that – and the defection of Lovelace. Who would have believed it of the man? Whom could one trust? Men changed sides as easily as they changed their boots.

And now? Well, he had been in worse trouble. All was not lost. He must join up with Edward. The young man would be in good spirits, flushed with the success of Mortimer's Cross. Together they would form a considerable army; and his men would merge with the victorious and forget their defeat.

He sent scouts ahead to make contact with Edward and as he marched he made his plans.

He had lost his figurehead. He no longer had the King. He could not say that he was the King's servant when the King now marched with the enemy. Of what use was the King when he was not a figurehead? Poor Henry, he was too supine to be anything else.

'Forsooth and forsooth,' said Warwick, imitating the King's own oath, 'since I do not hold him, I must needs do without him.'

He was in good spirits when in the town of Burford he made contact with Edward and his army.

They embraced. Then Edward looked about him.

'Where is the King?' he asked.

'Right before me,' answered Warwick.

Edward looked bewildered.

'You are now the King,' said Warwick.

Edward stared at him; and then his face was illumined by a smile. He began to laugh.

'There is little time to be lost. We will rest here and I will tell you what happens next.'

So they rested, for that night only. There must be no delay.

'It is imperative that we reach London before Margaret,' said Warwick. 'The people of London will not let her in. They do not trust her armies. They will welcome us to protect the city and that is what we will promise to do and then my friend . . . and then . . . we will present them with their new king Edward – the fourth of that name. I know it will succeed.'

'I will make it succeed,' said Edward.

And Warwick glowed with satisfaction. This would be the cleverest move of his life. Out of defeat he would snatch victory.

London was in turmoil. News of the Yorkist defeat had reached it and the citizens feared that now Margaret's army would descend upon them. Councils were hastily called to discuss the best move.

Proud Cis was terrified for her two sons George and Richard. She was full of foreboding. The death of her husband and son had filled her with melancholy. She had been so certain that she was almost Queen of England. She worried constantly about Edward's safety. If she lost him all her hopes would be centred in George and Richard.

She said a fond farewell to them and sent them off to the Low Countries and settled down in Southwark to await the worst. Meanwhile the magistrates had decided that they would be unable to keep out the Queen's army and must try to make terms, perhaps placate them; in any case keep them from the looting they had previously indulged in. Houses and shops were hastily boarded up and people began to arm themselves.

There were messages from Margaret; she needed food and money for her army and demanded that London supply them. The mayor and the aldermen set about collecting this. When news came that many of the rough Northerners had tired of waiting at St Albans and had deserted, wandering back to the North and looking for loot as they went, the Londoners were delighted.

They decided to do a little looting themselves and took the food and money which the Mayor and the aldermen had collected for the Queen.

It was a great day when scouts from Warwick rode into the

city. He, with the Duke of York, was on his way and they asked nothing of the Londoners but to be allowed to protect the city from the rough mercenaries many of whom comprised the Lancastrian army. If the city would open its gates, the Earl of Warwick, with the Duke of York, would march in and drive out all those who came to destroy it.

There was rejoicing through the city and when the united armies of Warwick and York appeared the gates were thrown open and the people came out to greet them. An orderly army rode in. Though half the size of Margaret's it had won the most important battle of all without fighting.

When, still at St Albans, Margaret heard the news of York's and Warwick's arrival in London, she realised she had lost the great opportunity of a lifetime. She should have dismissed her rabble army and marched into the capital with the King and her faithful knights. There were enough of them and they were gallant men who believed in the cause. But Warwick had forestalled her and London looked upon him and the handsome Edward as their saviours.

The time was ripe. Warwick saw that and he believed that in all affairs time was the important factor. Margaret had been victorious at St Albans but she had succeeded with a band of ruffians, foreigners most of them, and she had made the fatal mistake of not coming with the King to London. Now the loss of the battle of St Albans did not matter. Margaret had played into their hands and Warwick was not the man to lose such an opportunity.

He summoned the Yorkist peers to Barnard Castle, one of the homes of the House of York, and there he set out before them what they must do. It was fortunate that among those present was George Neville, Warwick's younger brother and loyal adherent, Archbishop of York and Chancellor of England.

'There is no time to lose,' said Warwick. 'London is ready to receive Edward and what London does today the rest of the country will do tomorrow. I'll swear that if Edward were proclaimed King at Paul's Cross the people would cheer themselves hoarse and be ready to uphold him.'

'I believe it would be so,' said George Neville.

Edward's eyes were shining. This was success *now*. He had believed he would eventually attain the crown but he had not conceived that it could be so suddenly, particularly after Warwick's defeat at St Albans.

But Warwick was a wizard. He was one of those sorcerers who could turn defeat into victory.

The first step, said Warwick, would be for George to preach a sermon in some popular place . . . say St George's Fields. There he would tell the people that Edward was their true King by descent. He was closer to Edward the Third than Henry was. He would remind the people that the son of John of Gaunt had usurped the throne from the son of the Black Prince but there was a line closer than that of John of Gaunt.

Then he could tell them that Henry, saint though he was, was unfit to rule. Let them go into new fields where the white rose flourished. George knew how to play on their feelings, how to rouse them to a frenzied desire to see the handsome young scion of the house of York in the position which was his by right.

'I would not have the people believe that it is merely the Nevilles who would take the crown from Henry and pass it to Edward,' said Warwick. 'The people of London must be with us. You can win them, George, with your tongue which can be as mighty as our swords, I trow, and more persuasive.'

George Neville was determined to prove his worth. He preached the sermon of his lifetime and from the first he had the people with him.

'My lords and ladies. You have seen what happens when we have a weak King ruling over us. The country is at the mercy of war. Instead of revelling in the simple joys of our firesides we are the victims of despair. Our homes are destroyed, our women ravaged. Englishmen are fighting Englishmen. This is no way to live, my friends. But what can we do to put an end to it? What could we do to find ourselves walking in a new vineyard? We could do it. In this very month of March we could make a gay garden with this fair white rose and herb the Earl of March. Think of him. Is he not every inch a king? Is he not the living image of his great ancestor, that one whom, in the excess of affection, was known as Edward Longshanks. He even bears the same name – the same long shanks, the same fair looks, the same devotion to his country and his subjects. King Henry is a good man, none deny it. But you know, my friends, that he is not strong in the head. You know that in the past he has been hid away for his weakness. Friends, do you want a King of feeble mind to rule over you? Do you want a King who is a captive to his foreign wife? Do you want Queen Margaret to rule over you?'

'Nay,' cried the crowd with fervour. 'Never.'

'I hear you. I hear you well and my friends I know your good sense. Then if you will not have Queen Margaret will you take King Edward?'

The shouts filled the air. There was not a nay among them.

'Edward,' they chanted. 'Edward for King.'

Warwick was gleeful. It was more successful than he had thought possible. George had preached the sermon of his life and they would be talking of it in the city for weeks to come . . . years to come mayhap. Because there was going to be change. Edward was to be crowned King.

Warwick went with all speed to Barnard Castle where Edward was waiting to hear the result of the meeting in the Fields.

'We will strike now,' cried Warwick. 'We must get this matter settled immediately before anything can happen to stop it. I shall issue a proclamation for Wednesday. I shall summon the people to Paul's Cross and there you shall be proclaimed the King.'

To his great joy everything went as he had planned it. Edward was proclaimed at Paul's Cross and went immediately to Westminster Hall. He seated himself on the marble chair. He had become Edward the Fourth.

How the people loved him – particularly the women. They leaned from their windows to throw spring flowers down at him as he passed by. He had a smile for all and especially warm ones for the women. Even at such a time he could show his appreciation of them. They had heard tales of his amorous adventures which made them giggle indulgently. Very different from Pious Henry, they commented.

'Ah, but Edward is a man.'

That was it. They loved him. It was great Plantagenet again. A return to the blond giants who had figured in the stories their mothers had heard from their mothers.

There would be no more wars; peace for ever; and a strong King to keep law and order while he supplied them with tales of his romantic adventures.

London loved Edward. London made him the King; and the rest of the country must needs accept him.

Warwick looked on with satisfaction. He was now the power behind the throne, the King-Maker.

He called a council at Barnard Castle.

'We must not allow this success to blind us to reality,' he said. 'There is a large Lancastrian army in the North to be dealt with. The King is with it and that means we cannot sit back and enjoy this situation in which by skill and diplomacy we have placed ourselves.'

Warwick paused and looked at Edward. He hoped the young King realised that when he said we have placed ourselves he really meant I have placed us.

With that easy grace which was almost as much a part of his charm as his outstanding good looks, Edward said: 'Richard, my dear friend, may I lose my crown if I ever forget one part of your efforts in placing it on my head.'

Warwick was satisfied.

'You are worthy to wear it,' he said. 'Worthier than even your father would have been. I doubt not that if you and I stand together we shall remain firm until every one of our enemies is defeated.'

'So be it,' said Edward.

It was like a bond between them which could only be broken by death.

'Now,' said Warwick, 'there is work to be done. The people are with us. We have to rout the Lancastrians. I shall not rest happy until Henry is in our hands . . . Margaret too. That woman is the source of all our troubles.'

'Then,' said Edward, 'we shall gather together an army and march in pursuit of Margaret.'

It was not difficult. Men rallied to Edward's banner. It was understood that the end of the war was in sight. They had a new King. He was the sort who would bring victory first and then prosperity.

Edward was exultant. The role of King suited him; but he was not more satisfied than Warwick. Warwick saw in Edward the perfect figurehead, the beautiful young man with the right appearance, the right manners, all that people looked for in a king; self-indulgent, yes, but that was all to the good because it would leave the actual ruling of the country to Warwick. Warwick would be the power behind the throne; Warwick the ruler of England; they would call Edward King but it was the King-Maker who would govern.

It was very satisfactory – the more so because of the defeat at St Albans. If he could snatch victory from that débâcle, he was capable of anything.

He had strengthened his position. In all important places were his men. Brother George was the Chancellor; he would see that the Parliament did what Warwick wanted it to; his brother John, Lord Montague, would go with him to control the armies when they travelled north. Hastings, Herbert, Stafford, Wenlock . . . they all recognised the genius of Warwick and wanted to be reckoned as his friends.

It was a happy day when he had brought the new King to London and Margaret had decided that she would be too unwelcome there to attempt to enter.

Fortune favoured the bold – indeed it did. And here he was in that position on which he had set his sights from the very first battle of St Albans.

He had power in his grasp. He must hold tightly to it; and he could not be sure of it until Henry was again a prisoner and Margaret was with him.

Therefore there was no time for rejoicing. They must set out for the North and not rest until they had vanquished Margaret's army.

Bitterly Margaret considered what had happened. What folly to have allowed Warwick and Edward to go to London. She had always hated the Londoners because they had hated her. And they had cheered for Edward and Warwick. They had dared call Edward their King.

Henry was with her. He was praying all the time. He was so weary of the wars, he told her. Would they never stop? He would do anything . . . anything to make them . . . give them what they wanted, anything.

'Forsooth and forsooth, what life is this for us!'

'We have our son to think of,' Margaret told him fiercely. 'Have you forgotten that?'

'He will be happier in some quiet place,' said the King, 'far away from conflict.'

'He is not like you,' retorted Margaret. 'My son was born to be King.'

Henry sighed. He was so weary. Margaret could not sit quietly; she would find such comfort in prayer, he told her.

She paced up and down – over to the window, straining to see if a messenger was coming, then back to the fire, standing there staring into the embers, seeing Edward proclaimed by the treacherous Londoners . . . Edward in battle . . . the battle which was now taking place.

She was kept informed. No sooner had Edward declared

himself King than he prepared for the march to the North. He was determined to destroy her and her armies.

'Nay, my lord,' she thought fiercely, 'it is I who will destroy you.'

It was Palm Sunday. Henry would not go with the army. 'This is a time for prayer,' he said. 'We should be kneeling together, those men of York and those of Lancaster. They should ask for God's help to solve their differences.'

Margaret was contemptuous. 'Meanwhile they should rely on their archers. If prayers were effective surely you would be the greatest king on earth.'

Henry shook his head sadly. Margaret spoke vehemently. He would never be able to make her understand his feelings.

'It may be,' she went on, 'that God will be with us this day. He was at St Albans. Then the snow worked to our advantage . . . not theirs. It blew in their faces and sent their wicked wildfire back into their ranks. The elements were with us then. Pray God they will be now.' She walked up and down the room. 'How dare they! We defeated them at St Albans. We brought you back to us. It was a great victory. How could they have marched into London and proclaimed Edward King!'

'They did it,' said Henry.

'And they shall pay for it,' replied Margaret. 'How I wish I were with the army now. I should love to see the enemy destroyed. Nothing will satisfy me until I have Warwick's head on London Bridge . . . yes, London Bridge where they are so fond of him. As for Edward . . . *King* Edward. I wonder how he would fancy a paper crown like his father's.'

'I beg you do not talk so,' said the King. 'How happy I should be if we could settle this grievous matter in a friendly way.'

Oh, he was useless. She thanked God for her son. Without him life would be meaningless. Edward, dear Edward, he possessed the same name as the usurper. Edward, a King's name, she had thought. And now *that* Edward dared call himself King.

Her rage threatened to choke her. Oh God, she prayed, send me news of victory quickly.

The snow was falling. It was bitterly cold. The snow had helped them at St Albans. She could laugh aloud to think of how Warwick had so cleverly – as he thought – placed himself and then found that he had his men in the face of the wind.

What was happening now? The armies would be meeting . . .

Messengers at last. She hurried down to meet them.

'What news? What news?'

'The battle rages, my lady. They are at Towton. There was a skirmish at Ferrybridge. The enemy were at Pontefract and tried to secure passage across the Aire at Ferrybridge. Your army under Lord Clifford defeated them and slew their leader, Lord Fitzwalter.'

'Oh God be praised.'

'But they crossed farther down the river at Castleford, my lady.'

'God curse them.'

'And now they do battle at Towton.'

'How goes the battle?'

The messenger paused and Margaret felt cold fear grip her.

'It is early to say, my lady. The weather is bad. The snow is falling.'

'Pray God he sends it in the traitors' faces as he did at St Albans.'

The messenger was silent.

'If you have nothing more to tell me you may go to the kitchens for refreshment.'

'Thank you, my lady,' said the messenger. He was glad to escape. He would not envy the one who must bring bad news to the Queen.

The suspense continued. It was unbearable. She sent for her son that he might share her vigil. She could not bear to see the King on his knees in prayer. He looked so frail, so ineffectual. He should have been there with his troops. His presence would have had its effect on them. What a King who could not fight because it was Holy Week!

The hours were passing. Still no news. The wind was howling about the castle walls. Margaret could not tear herself away from the window.

And at last news came.

That it was bad news was clear to her. She listened in horror to the tale the messenger had to tell.

The two armies had met at Towton which was a village not far from Tadcaster and the battle had been going on for ten hours. Lord Clifford after his brave defence at Ferrybridge had been slain. Many of the Lancastrian nobles who had not fallen in battle had been taken prisoner, Devonshire and Wiltshire among them.

The battle of Towton had been fought and won by the Yorkists; and the King and the Queen were in imminent danger.

Margaret was stunned with grief. What could she do? One thing was certain: she could not remain here to let herself be taken with the King and their son.

She must fly with all speed.

She went to the King. He was on his knees still.

'Rise,' she said imperiously. 'There is no time for dallying. We must prepare to leave at once. There has been disaster at Towton. We have to get away before they come for us.'

'The battle is over then . . .'

'Over and lost. We are leaving at once. Delay could be the end of us. That is not yet.'

Her spirits were reviving. This was not the end of Margaret of Anjou. There had been disasters before, and always she had come out of them. She would win through yet. Was she going to be beaten by one single battle?

What of St Albans? The glory of that had still not died.

She would win through yet. But she must live to do so. She must keep the King with her. And while she had her dear son Edward to fight for, she would go on. She would win in time. Not all of Warwick's skill, nor all of Edward of York's charm would prevent her from putting the rightful king on the throne.

'Where can we go?' said Henry.

She hesitated only for a moment.

'We have good friends in the North,' she said. 'The North has always been with us. It is those perfidious Londoners who are against us. Never mind. They shall pay for their treachery. We will go to our good friends. We will go to Scotland.'

Edward rode into York with Warwick beside him. As he looked up at the walls he saw the heads of his father, his brother and his uncle and sadness overcame his triumph, but it was soon replaced by fury. His first act would be to remove those heads and give them a decent burial. Others should replace them. They would not be difficult to find.

Into York in triumph – King of England. It was what his father would have wished.

Margaret in flight; her armies in disorder. A new reign had begun.

🏵 Chapter XVI 🏵

THE WAITING YEARS

The years were taking their toll. She was no longer the young and beautiful Queen whose dainty looks belied her urgent determination. But nothing the years could do to her could subdue her spirit. Perhaps if it had not been for Edward — her darling, her beloved, her precious son — she would have given up. She had long decided that Henry was of no use in her ambitions. Strangely enough she still retained a lingering fondness for him. She thought of him often and wondered what was happening to him. He would never be able to fend for himself.

It was years since she had seen him. Edward was a young man now. He was devoted to her as she was to him and through all their adventures they kept their eyes on the goal. Something within her would not let her give up hope.

At first when they had flown from York and come to Scotland craving hospitality from Mary of Gueldres she had believed that in a short time they would return to England. It would be amusing if not tragic how people's affection for them flickered and wavered according to their prospects. Edward the Fourth was crowned; the people of the South wanted him as their King. The North was more faithful to Henry though. It was amazing what a hold such a weak man could have on their affections. But he was useless to fight. She often told herself that if he had appeared at Towton at the head of his troops instead of spending the day on his knees because it was Palm Sunday, there might have been a different result to that battle – and that would have meant a complete reversal of their fortunes.

Well, it had not turned out to be so and here she was an exile in France ... waiting ... waiting for the moment which she still believed would come.

When they had arrived in Scotland straight from York at that terrible time they had found it necessary to keep the promise she had made to surrender Berwick to the Scots. Of course, the English hated her for that. She knew of course that they would consider it treason. But she had been forced to find a refuge for them. She had the King and the heir to the throne to consider. Berwick was surely a small price to pay for their safety.

She had quickly realised that her only hope lay with her native land, with her own people. She would go to France, she told Henry. She would muster help. Then with an army behind her she would come back. Pierre de Brézé would help. She would rally their loyal supporters in the North and they would march against the usurper.

Henry had shaken his head in sorrow. He wanted only to live in peace.

But her indomitable spirit would not be stilled. For the first time she had parted from her son. What an agony that had been! Every day she had been uneasy, wondering what was happening to him. She had made up her mind that once they were together again they should never more be parted.

It was hard to come as a suppliant. She had so looked

forward to reunion with her father and how warmly he had greeted her! He had changed little; he was still the same optimistic failure. Margaret's mother had died some nine years before and he had married again. He was absorbed by his young wife, Jeanne de Laval, and it very soon became clear to Margaret that although her father would give lavish entertainments for her which he could ill afford, he was not really interested in helping her regain the throne. A glazed look would come into his eyes when she broached the matter. He agreed that it was a fearful thing which had happened, and Edward of York was a traitor who should pay for his wickedness with his head. Words . . . all words. But of course what she should have expected of René.

It was a pleasure to see her sister Yolande yet sad to hear from her the account of their mother's death. Yolande and her husband Ferri de Vaudémont had nursed Isabelle through a long illness. 'It was terrible to see her suffering,' said Yolande. 'You were spared that, Margaret.'

For a few days they were inseparable, recalling old days – such as they could remember – but after a while Margaret realised how far she and her sister had grown apart. Yolande thought her obsessed by revenge and overbearing, and Ferri agreed with his wife. After all, Yolande had not been brought up by that forceful grandmother.

There had been another blow. Margaret's uncle, the King of France, had died. He had always been fond of Margaret and she had been relying on that tenderness. Now that the Dauphin Louis was the King, it was a different matter. Louis was artful, already earning the nickname of The Spider; he was not so enamoured of his cousin as his father had been and was certainly not going to put himself out to help her.

There had been one faithful friend, Pierre de Brézé. Ah, Pierre. He had been her constant friend; he had always had such a regard for her that she sometimes thought he was in love with her. He had changed . . . not in his regard for her, but he had suffered a short term of imprisonment in the Château of Loches, for on the death of King Charles, Louis had remembered old scores and attempted to settle them. Fortunately for Pierre and Margaret he had quickly been released.

Louis had not shown any animosity to Margaret. In fact he had greeted her with a show of affection, calling her cousin, and giving entertainments for her at his court; but as Pierre had warned her, one could not be sure of Louis. His methods were secretive.

It had been a great joy when Jasper Tudor had arrived in France with Sir John Fortescue who had been another faithful friend. Negotiations had then begun with Louis who made it clear that if Pierre de Brézé was to help Margaret there must naturally be some compensation. Louis knew exactly what he wanted. Calais. The transfer had been hinted at before; now he wanted Margaret to complete documents which would give that important town to him.

There had been long consultation and expressions of apprehension from Jasper and John Fortescue who knew that if Margaret signed Calais away the English would never forgive her. She must not, said Jasper. But, Margaret had reasoned, what did it matter? Calais was in the hands of the English; Warwick was the captain still; she might sign it away but that would not necessarily give it to the French. The situation was desperate for they could do nothing without the help of France.

Finally she agreed that when the Lancastrians recovered Calais, Jasper should immediately be made captain. Louis would lend her twenty thousand livres and if that sum was not repaid immediately Calais would be his.

It was the best bargain Louis could get and he was sure in due course Calais would be his.

She would never forget that cold October day when she sailed from Harfleur with fifty ships and the two thousand men whom Louis had allowed her to raise. She had believed up till then that all she had to do was land. Alas, it was not so. Ill luck dogged her. Although she did manage to land at Tynemouth people did not come flocking to her banner and she quickly realised that survival meant sailing with all speed for Scotland. Greater ill fortune awaited her; her ships were lost – money, supplies, everything. Men were drowned and some washed ashore to give themselves up to Edward's men.

She and Pierre managed to reach Berwick where she was greeted with the news that Edward was marching north.

That was not all. The Scots were less inclined to offer hospitality now. Berwick was in their hands. What else had she to surrender to them and make their help worthwhile? Mary of Gueldres wanted to be friendly; she was sorry for Margaret, but what could she do? She had difficulties of her own.

News came from France that Louis was no longer so friendly. The Duke of Burgundy had made it clear to the King of France that he did not approve of his supporting Margaret's cause. Edward was King and seemed firm on the throne; trade between Burgundy and England was important. The Duke could make trouble in France if the King persisted in his policies against Edward in Margaret's favour.

Louis was wily. He wanted no trouble at this time with

Burgundy so he made it clear that no more help could come from him.

It seemed that God had deserted her. Her only joy was in her son. He was so delighted to be with her. He was growing up and she promised herself that when he was a man everything would be different, for her troops would then have a leader whom they could follow. She was sure that her Edward would possess all those virtues which were necessary in a leader. It was said that the usurper, that other Edward, had them; but everyone knew what a wild life he led; the wives of the London merchants were not safe from his lechery. What was maddening was that when people talked of it they did so with a twinkle in their eyes as though this was some virtue. It was because he was said to be so charming and handsome to look at. As if they could be an excuse for his monstrous behaviour! But sometimes it seemed to Margaret that they were bemused by him. It would not always be so, but in the meantime her Edward was but a boy and there was a crown to be won.

There had been a brief moment of hope when de Brézé had marched with her into England and captured Alnwick Castle. But how short-lived that triumph had been. The Earl of Warwick had come marching north and within a lamentably short time had recaptured the castle and she had been forced to retreat in haste, her army in disorder. It was at this time that one of the most terrifying moments of her life had occurred. She had been with Edward alone in the forest, lost for the moment. She kept Edward with her always and at such times would never allow him out of her sight. She had known that some of her friends were not far off but temporarily she had lost her way. The trees were so thick. They all looked alike and she was not sure which way to turn. And as she stood there holding her son's hand tightly in her own, from among the trees there appeared the most hideous man she had ever seen. Perhaps it was some fearful disease which had enlarged his features; he seemed enormous, and he was quite terrifying.

Edward had shrunk near to her and she had put a protective arm about him. The touch of her own son gave her an even greater courage than was usually hers, though she had never been easily afraid and had always trusted in her own powers of survival.

He was a robber, this creature, an outlaw . . . living apart from his fellows, bearing a grudge against them for making him an outcast because of his grotesque appearance. He approached, a knife in his hands.

She dared not show her fear. She had to protect her son. Instead of retreating, she held Edward firmly by the hand and approached the robber.

'My friend,' she said, 'this is the son of your King. We are lost in the forest. We are in retreat from our enemies. I know you will save him.'

The robber had paused. That he was astonished was clear. He must have been startled to find himself face to face with the Queen.

He stammered: 'You place yourself in danger wandering through these woods.'

'That we know, and we do it because there is nothing else left to us.'

'If you go on you will be captured by soldiers. The woods are full of them.'

'I know,' said Margaret.

'Would you trust me?'

She looked at him fearlessly. 'I would,' she answered.

'Then follow me.'

She had done so fearlessly because oddly enough she did trust this man, robber that he was. In time they had come to a cave. He went into it, giving a low whistle as he did so, and within a few moments a woman had appeared. She stared at Margaret and the Prince and Margaret said: 'Good day to you, my friend.'

'It's the Queen and her Prince,' said the man.

'What'll she be wanting with us?' asked the woman.

'Shelter and a hiding-place from her enemies.'

The woman nodded.

There were sounds in the woods. Yorkist soldiers were at hand. What would they not give to capture the Queen and the Prince? They should not! She would risk anything rather than fall into their hands. Better be robbed of everything she possessed. Not that she had much.

So she and Edward had entered the cave. The home of the robber and his wife was divided into two apartments. One of these they gave up to Margaret and her son, and for two days she and Edward had stayed there; they had eaten with the robber and his wife until that time when the robber came in to report that it would be safe for her to emerge.

How strange that helpers appeared in unexpected places. The outlaw had taken her to her friends and she had parted with him with tears of gratitude in her eyes. She had little to give him, she told him, but she would never forget him. She could give him only a ring in exchange for his services.

'Of all I have lost,' she told Brézé, with whom she was delighted and greatly relieved to be reunited, 'I regret nothing so much as being unable to reward in a manner suited to their deserts those who are of service to me.'

They had found their way back to Scotland, but what a cool reception she had received there. It was as though everyone but herself considered her cause to be hopeless. Being unwelcome in Scotland, what was she to do?

Brézé advised her that she should return to France. There surely she would find more sympathy than anywhere else. Her father must help her; and the Duke of Burgundy could, she believed, be persuaded to do so.

She said goodbye to Henry. He was bewildered, scarcely aware of what was happening. He reiterated that he wanted only to be left in peace with his books and his prayers.

Exasperated, but in a somewhat tender manner, she had taken her leave of him. 'I shall get help,' she had said. 'It is the only way.'

He had nodded, scarcely listening.

So she sailed once more for France with Pierre and his son Jacques, with Exeter and Sir John Fortescue, those faithful few whom she could trust. And this time with her was Prince Edward. She was never going to be separated from her son again.

Looking back she saw that in her determination she had followed will o' the wisps – any little lights in the darkness which might offer some hope. She should have known that the wily Duke of Burgundy would not want to help a cause which he, like so many, thought to be a lost one.

But leaving Scotland, where could they go? Her hope had been the Duke of Burgundy. Brézé did not think that they could look for much help there but she was adamant, for if not to Burgundy, where else? Louis had shown her that he was not inclined to help.

She had very little money; she must get a loan quickly. They could not afford to waste time so as soon as she landed at Sluys she sent a message to the Duke of Burgundy telling him where she was and asking to be received by him without delay.

The Duke was astounded and dismayed. He had no wish to see her. The position with the King of France was delicate; he knew that Louis was watching him more closely and that Edward, backed by Warwick, was becoming a power to be reckoned with.

He immediately sent Philippe Pot, one of his most reliable followers and a man of immense tact and diplomatic talents, to Margaret with the message that the Duke was unable to receive her at this time because of pressing duties.

Margaret had snapped her fingers at such limp excuses and retorted that she came from King Henry of England and she was determined to see the Duke.

'My lady,' said the diplomatic Philippe Pot, 'do you realise the hazards of the journey? To meet the Duke you would have to pass close to Calais. It would be known that you were travelling there and your enemies would make every possible effort to capture you.'

Of course she had brushed aside his warnings. He should know better than to tell Margaret of Anjou what she must or must not do, and even the great Duke of Burgundy discovered that he would have to do as she wished.

But though she had forced herself into his presence in such a manner that his natural gallantry would not allow him to repulse, she was quickly made to realise that there was little he would do to help her. He managed to intimate that although he was happy to receive her, the King of France was not very pleased that she should be his guest.

How humiliating! A Queen of England to be so treated! To make her feel again and again that her presence was unwanted. They all seemed to have accepted Edward as King of England and showed clearly they had no wish to be embroiled in her quarrels.

There was nowhere she could turn; Scotland, France, Burgundy; she was an embarrassment to them all.

A message came from her father. She must retire for a while to his estates in Bar. There she could live quietly while she decided what she would do.

And so to this little town of St Michiel she had come. She could not be more isolated. The town seemed to be cut off from the world. There was peace there, but when had she ever wanted peace? She knew the countryside well because she had been born not very far away at Pont-à-Mousson. She remembered the days of her childhood when she had ridden along the banks of the Moselle.

René had given her a small pension. She was grateful for she knew that he would have had to borrow to provide it. It was not much, but adequate for her to rent a house and form a little court there. But even he had little time to worry about her and her affairs. He was absorbed by his pretty young wife and he had always been a man to live for the moment and it would be a somewhat self-indulgent moment at that.

So here she was in the little walled town living the life of an impoverished gentlewoman and yet somehow maintaining what appeared to be a court. She would be ever grateful to her friends and in particular to Pierre de Brézé and Sir John Fortescue. Pierre had spent the larger part of his fortune in her service and his admiration and devotion was a constant prop to her in all her troubles; as for Sir John she knew he was ready to follow her whither her ill fortune led her. What especially endeared him to her was his devotion to the Prince. Being a scholar himself – judge and lawyer – he was well equipped to undertake the Prince's education and this he did. For the Prince he had written *De Laudibus Legum Angliae*, a work which explained the Constitution of England and royal behaviour, because he feared – he had secretly confided to Margaret – that the Prince was more interested in martial excellences than in learning.

And so the years were passing. The Prince was growing up and was a source of great joy to Margaret. He was the very reason for living as far as she was concerned. He was devoted to her and as he grew older he realised more and more all that she had done and was doing was for him.

Secretly he despised his father, but that only made his love for his mother more intense.

Watching events – as far as was possible in her remote village – looking after her son and seeing Sir John train him for kingship was her delight in those years. She never doubted – nor did Sir John – that one day Edward would be King of England.

Seasons came and seasons went . . . seven years passed by while Edward of York remained King of England and Margaret waited.

Meanwhile Henry had fared even worse than Margaret. After Hexham he had become a fugitive, escaping capture so narrowly that his pages and his very cap of state had fallen into the enemy's hands. He had flown from the battle with a few of his followers . . . riding through the night . . . anywhere.

He had his friends though. The North was faithful. There were many who believed that the anointed King was the true King and any who replaced him, however strong, whatever his claim, was the usurper. There was many a manor house to offer hospitality where he could rest and be fed and treated as a King. But after one or two narrow escapes when someone had betrayed him he would have to move on. There were many who wished to help him but who were afraid to do so, for King Edward would have little mercy on any whom he considered to be traitors and to harbour King Henry would be called a deed of treachery to Edward.

He was a fugitive. He marvelled. He who had been a King in his cradle was now pursued through his kingdom by one of his subjects. If only he could be left alone to pray, to meditate, to read his holy books, he would not care who ruled the kingdom. He just wanted peace.

But he did not think he would get that if they captured him.

At some of the houses where he was given hospitality he had stayed in more prosperous days during his progresses through England. He remembered the ceremony of welcome when all the servants were overawed and deeply respectful. How different it was now when he must creep in – very often be given a small room which his host would say was safe.

All he wanted was just enough room to kneel and pray to God and perhaps a pallet on which to lie for a few hours of necessary sleep.

One night they came to Crackenthorpe near Appleby in Westmorland. Riding through the night, they had passed a monastery. Henry had looked at it with eyes of longing. What would he not have given to be one of those happy monks. Fate had been cruel to make him a King.

John Machell, the owner of the manor of Crackenthorpe, came out to the courtyard after one of Henry's friends had gone into the house to tell him he had visitors.

Taking the King's hand John Machell kissed it assuring him of his loyal service at all times.

'This is the time we need it, John,' said Henry. 'We are worn out with travelling. Can you give us a bed for the night?'

'My lord, my house is at your service.'

'Nay, nay John, that would not do. What comment there would be. Your King comes as a fugitive. There is another who calls himself King in England now.'

John Machell said there was one King as far as he was concerned and he would serve that King with his life.

'There is need for caution,' he was told.

He realised that and was persuaded to let his household believe that some travellers on their way to York were spending the night at the house.

There was a fine chamber for Henry. He sank to his knees and remained there for a long time. Food was sent to his apartment and he found great rest and comfort in the house of John Machell at Crackenthorpe.

He was able to rest there for a few days and then John noticed that one of the servants was regarding the King in a rather curious manner and he knew that it was time for him to move on.

He had an idea. The Abbot of the nearby monastery was known to him, and he believed him to be one who deplored the usurpation of the throne and was a true Lancastrian.

'I will go to see him,' he said. 'Stay quietly in your chamber but be ready to leave if there should be any alarm. There may be people here who would betray you to the enemy. I will be back before nightfall.'

When he returned he was excited. He believed he had something to say which would give the King great pleasure.

His friend the Abbot had given him a monk's habit. He suggested that at dawn the King and his friends leave the house. When they had gone a little way the King could change into the habit. He could then leave his friends and present himself to the Abbot. The Abbot would know who he was but no one else would. The Abbot would naturally offer hospitality and perhaps he could mingle with the monks and live as one of them.

Nothing could have delighted Henry more. He was all eagerness; his friends had never seen him so enthusiastic and ready to embrace a plan.

All went well. He arrived at the monastery, was welcomed by the Abbot and took his place with the monks.

He had not been wrong. This was the life for him. He fitted into it with ease. He lived by the bells. The silence preserved in the monastery was helpful to him and made it easier for him to hide his identity; and as he had often lived like a monk, no one would have guessed he was not one.

A few months passed in this happy state but as it was supposed that he was on a visit from another monastery he could not stay too long.

The Abbot however could warn an Abbot of another monastery of the King's coming and he could rest there for another short period before he passed on.

Henry was happy to do this. He left the monastery with many protestations of gratitude; and then began his wandering life. He realised that none of his sojourns could be long but when he felt the walls of a monastery close about him, when he was in his austere cell he was happier than he had ever been anywhere else.

'If I could have chosen this life,' he said, 'I should have been a happy man.'

The time was passing. Sometimes he thought of Margaret in France and Edward who was growing into a man. They seemed far away. Perhaps in his heart he did not want Margaret to come back. He did not want the conflict to start again.

At length he came to what was known as the Religious House of Whalley in Ribblesdale and here he found refuge as he had in other places of this kind. Eagerly he embraced the life; praying, working in the fields, whatever it was he was happy doing it. Sometimes he completely forgot that other life of ceremonies and arduous duties which he had never felt fit to perform.

'Oh God,' he prayed, 'I thank Thee for bringing me to this rest. If it be Thy Will let me spend the rest of my days in such good life.'

Alas for Henry, his prayers were not to be answered.

Beside the religious house of Whalley was Waddington Hall and when Dr Manning, Dean of Windsor, was visiting there he asked the honour of the King's company. Henry accepted the invitation and set out in his monk's robes for the Hall.

Had he been more observant he would have noticed that for some days one of the monks had been taking a great interest in him. The eyes of this monk were always on him, but Henry had not noticed this. The fact was that the monk was becoming more and more convinced of Henry's identity, and it occurred to him that if the visiting monk were indeed the one-time King this fact should be made known to those it might interest. The country had been for some years under the rule of Edward the Fourth and no one was going to deny that life had not improved considerably. The French woman was heartily disliked throughout the country and there were constant rumours that she was awaiting an opportunity to return. If this were so this monk was playing a part. He was in hiding waiting for the time when his virago of a wife returned to plunge England into war again.

The monk was now certain that the man he was watching was Henry. He went to Sir John Tempest to whom Waddington Hall belonged. Sir John, with his son-in-law Thomas Talbot, was immediately determined to act. If this monk were indeed the King in disguise, there would be a good reward for his apprehension, moreover it was for the good of the country to have him under surveillance, they assured themselves. He was coming to Waddington Hall that he might converse with the Dean in their dining-hall. They must act promptly. They did not wish to be accused of complicity in any plots to restore Henry to the throne. It was so easy to be caught up in these matters, so easy for innocent men to be called traitors.

So Sir John Tempest with his son-in-law, Thomas Talbot, and Sir James Harrington, who lived at Brierley near Barnsley and was a man who had been to Court, put their heads together. They would take the King while he sat at dinner in Waddington Hall and from there transport him to London, sending messengers on to King Edward and the Earl of Warwick telling them what they had done. They had no doubt that they would be rewarded for their loyalty and prompt action.

Thus while Henry sat at dinner in earnest conversation with the Dean, some of the servants noticed a commotion without. There was one man who had served the King since his escape from Hexham and he had always regarded the King's safety as being entrusted to him. Alert for danger he scented it immediately and even as the King was eating his frugal meal he was beside him.

'My lord,' he said, 'there is no time for anything but escape. We have been betrayed.'

The Dean rose hastily. The King less so. Sometimes he felt, If they will take me, let them!

But the life of late lived in monasteries and holy places had been good. He did not want to give that up for some prison somewhere where these blessings might be denied him.

'We should leave . . . just as we are . . .' said his faithful servant. 'Even now we may be too late.'

Rising from the table Henry allowed himself to be almost dragged from the hall. It was dark outside. 'We must make for the woods,' Henry was told.

The trees grew thickly in the woods. 'Perhaps we could wait here until morning,' said Henry.

His servant shook his head. 'Nay. They will be after us. You may depend upon that. We must get as far as we can. Perhaps we could make our way to Bolton Hall.'

Bolton Hall was owned by Sir Ralph Pudsey who had already proved himself a loyal servant of the King.

'Let us do that,' said Henry.

They had come to the river Ribble across which were stepping stones.

'We will cross by the Bungerley Stones,' his servant told him and as Henry attempted to do so there was a shout close by.'Here they are,' cried Thomas Talbot. 'They did not get far.'

Henry stared with dismay. His enemies were upon him. As

they crowded about him he lifted his head and demanded what they wanted of their King.

'We must take you to King Edward, sir,' said Talbot. 'He wants to know where you are.'

'It is a sorry state of affairs when the anointed King is treated thus by his subjects.'

The men were silent. They felt overawed. But they were determined to present their quarry to King Edward.

It was depressing riding south. They did not show him the respect due to their King. He looked back with longing to those days he had spent in seclusion. Oh for the peace of the holy life! Oh for the comfort of prayer!

They had come to Islington and there waiting for him, having been advised of his arrival, was the Earl of Warwick displaying the Ragged Staff and riding like a king so that an observer must have thought their roles reversed. It is he who comes as a king, thought Henry. But then he is a maker and unmaker of kings. He has made Edward as surely as he has unmade me.

'Well met, my lord,' said Warwick.

'Is it so? You see your King in humble fashion.'

'I rejoice to see you, none the less. But you are King no more. Edward is our King.'

'My father reigned as a King and so did my grandfather. I was a King in my cradle. Yet you have decided that I am no King.'

'Edward is our King now. You are his prisoner. You must make ready to go to the Tower.'

'And you must do with me what you will.'

'I doubt harm will come to you if you keep your place.'

'My place, ah! That is the sorry question. I was anointed King and I think I and others in this realm know my place.'

Warwick gave orders that Henry's legs should be bound under his horse with leather thongs. They put a straw hat on his head and thus he rode into the City of London.

London was for Edward. Edward had brought prosperity to the country; Edward knew how to rule; he had driven the Angevin virago out of the country. So they came out to watch Henry, pale, aloof and unkingly. How different from handsome Edward, all smiles and bonhomie, throwing his glances up at the pretty women who leaned out of the windows to cheer for him.

Henry rode forward looking ahead as though not caring what they thought of him. They had never hated him as they did his foreign wife. She was the one who had been the cause of all their troubles, but Henry had allowed her to be as she was. Henry was weak; Edward was strong. The Londoners did not have to ponder long to find out where their allegiance lay.

Some were silent; some jeered. They wished him no harm though. Poor Henry.

So he came to his room in the Tower.

Mildly he remonstrated with those who called him impostor.

'My father was King of this realm,' he repeated, 'and peacefully he possessed the crown for the whole of his life. His father, my grandfather was King before him. And I as a boy, crowned almost in his cradle, was accepted as King by the whole realm and wore the crown for nearly forty years, every lord swearing homage to me as they had done to my father.'

His jailors remonstrated with him. He must be quiet. Good Edward was on the throne and was going to stay there.

It was a sad day for Henry when he had been captured. He did not see Edward, Warwick or any of the noblemen; he was left to guards.

There were many of them who thought themselves mighty to have charge of a King and be able to treat him as inferior to themselves.

Sometimes they struck him when he did not answer readily. 'Speak up, man,' they would shout; and marvel that they had struck a king, for King he was, though brought low. It was true that he had been anointed and crowned a King. And there they were with him at their mercy.

He rarely protested. When he did it would be to utter mildly: 'Forsooth and forsooth, you do foully to smite a King anointed thus.'

His very meekness irritated them. If he had attempted to fight back they would have respected him more. But his manner invited their curses and neglect. They did not care what they gave him to eat and brought the remains of their dinners for him. It seemed a great joke to them. They would not bring him changes of clothes; his hair grew long; he was getting very thin and turned away from the scraps they brought him.

It would have been kinder to have taken him out to the Green and chopped off his head, thought some of the guards. But Edward was too clever for that. He was not going to have it said that he murdered the King. He had come to the throne through right of succession and conquest. Not murder. Besides there was a Prince in France and a forceful woman who might at any time raise her head.

No, the King's blood must not be on his hands. If he died a natural death so much the better. There would be one of them out of the way. But Edward agreed with Warwick, there must be no hint of murder.

So while Margaret waited in St Michiel for an answer to her prayers, Henry languished in the Tower, dirty, unkempt, insulted, often hungry and thirsty, finding comfort only in prayer.

❀ Chapter XVII ❀

THE QUARREL

At this time Richard Neville, Earl of Warwick was at the height of his powers. None could deny — perhaps not even Edward the King himself — that Warwick was the most important man in the kingdom. He was indeed the King-Maker. Edward could never have attained the crown but for Warwick; and had Warwick decided to throw in his lot with Henry, Henry would be on the throne at this time.

Life had been good to him, he conceded. Not in bringing him into the world with a fortune in his grasp; that had not been so. True he was the son of the Earl of Salisbury but his great fortune had not come from his birth.

No, life had smiled on him when he had married Anne Beauchamp, only daughter of Richard Beauchamp, Earl of Warwick, although at that time he had no notion of what great good fortune that was. At the time of his marriage two lives had stood between him and the vast Beauchamp inheritance. Anne's brother Henry, heir of Warwick, died leaving only a daughter as his heiress and two years after her father's death this child died. Anne was sole heiress and so everything passed to her husband, who had become Earl of Warwick and the richest nobleman in the country.

Anne had brought him a great deal but there was one thing she had failed in. He had no son. He had his two girls, Isabel and Anne – delightful creatures, but girls. And Anne could bear him no more children. Well, she had made him rich and brought him a great title so he must be content, and his two girls would be the greatest heiresses in the Kingdom.

After the first battle of St Albans and his exploits in Calais he was accepted as one of the heroes of the age and he had become one of those legendary figures who cannot be suppressed. There might be the occasional setback . . . but there was nothing which could deter them for long. He could turn defeat into victory as he had after the second battle of St Albans. Who would have believed that after suffering such a defeat – one might say a débâcle – he would be riding into London and proclaiming a new King.

He had genius. There was no doubt about it. He knew it and in his cleverness had made others accept that fact.

He was the Lord of the Kingdom.

Edward would have given him any honour he needed. He only had to ask.

'What shall it be, Richard?' he had said. 'I owe so much to you.'

He had shrugged his shoulders. He could not be the King. But he was Warwick.

He said: 'I will be just Warwick. I think that is enough.'

Edward declared with ready satisfaction that it certainly was. No one in the kingdom should ever doubt what everyone owed to Warwick.

'Ah, my good friend, you are right. The name Warwick is as proud as any man could wish.'

Edward had that easy charm. He liked to leave things to Warwick. Warwick was shrewd; he had the people with him. But not so much as Edward had. How they loved that golden youth in whom the marks of debauchery had not yet begun to show, but they would, Warwick knew; none could live as Edward did and remain unscathed. The people thought it was manly. God forbid! But it was a change of course after the piety of Henry. It was surprising that though people admired piety and applauded it, they soon grew heartily sick of it; and when a libertine like Edward rode through their streets and eyed the merchants' wives and daughters the merchants seemed to like it.

There was no doubt that Edward possessed that indefinable quality called charm. That was all to the good. He was the best possible figurehead behind whom a King-Maker could work, as long as Edward did not forget that he owed his position to Warwick.

Often he told the King that he was not completely safe. True Margaret was on the continent and Henry in the Tower; but while Margaret lived they must be watchful. She had friends in France. Not only her father – poor ineffectual René, drooling over a young wife now . . . well, he would do that very well, Warwick was sure. They must not forget him though. He could be in a position to supply Margaret with the means to return. But the big menace was the King of France.

'He is not so fond of Margaret as his father was,' said Edward. 'I doubt he would want to be embroiled.'

'He would like to harass us . . . a pastime greatly loved by the French for as long as any of us can remember.'

'He would not want to go to war with us.'

'He might like to help Margaret to do so. The North is ready to rise with her. Don't forget they hid Henry all those years. He has friends up there. Edward, a marriage in the right quarter could do our cause all the good in the world.'

Edward nodded.

'Marriage with France,' went on Warwick tentatively.

'Indeed yes.' Edward was thinking of the most enchanting woman he had ever met. When he had been hunting she had suddenly appeared before him and throwing herself on her knees had begged him to restore her husband's estates. Edward had been amazed that one so young could be a widow. Her husband she told him had been killed at the second battle of St Albans.

Edward fell in love as rapidly and regularly as most people sat down to dinner; and because of his charm and royalty he could invariably dispense with the preliminaries of courtship. It had been different with the fair young widow. She was most elusive, so he was thinking of her and only half listening to Warwick. He knew Warwick was right, of course. He would have to marry and marry soon. He only hoped the French Princess was personable. He could not abide ugly women. But with his habitual easy-going temperament he shrugged all that aside. He would have to do his duty and that need not interfere with his enjoyment.

Warwick was saying something about negotiations with the King of France, talking a little smugly. Edward smiled inwardly. He believed Louis treated Warwick as an equal. It was amazing what store Warwick set on that.

'No honours,' he had said. 'It is enough to be Warwick.'

'Louis has changed his tune of late,' said Warwick complacently. 'He is aware of our strength.'

Warwick was smiling to himself. He meant *his* power. The wily King of France knew where the power in England lay. The man who had his respect was not so much the King as the King-Maker.

Oh yes, he could be proud. He certainly was at the pinnacle of power.

The King of France was indeed his friend. When his ambassador, Jean de Lannoy, arrived in England he had glittering prospects to lay before Warwick. He could work with Louis. There would be peace between their countries. They would stand against Burgundy; and they would be the firm allies which surely fortune had meant two such brilliant men to be.

And of course there should be a French marriage. Edward needed a wife. Perhaps, considered Louis, his daughter was too young. She needed more years to grow up. What of his wife's sister, Bona of Savoy?

This would be an excellent arrangement Warwick decided. He discussed it with his brother George.

'The King should settle into matrimony,' he said. 'It is very necessary for one of his temperament. He should be producing heirs instead of bastards.'

George said that this was certainly so but he wondered how the King would feel about the choice of bride. Since he had become a connoisseur of feminine charms he might be difficult to please.

'This is a marriage, George. No need for romance. Let the King marry and produce an heir. Who knows it might even sober him a little.'

George was in full agreement. It was an excellent idea to

make a marriage which would please the King of France and strengthen the friendship between their two countries.

Edward listening to the proposal displayed his usual tolerant charm.

'Can we trust Louis?' he asked.

'A marriage will bring us closer to him. When can one ever completely trust one's allies?'

'This Bona of Savoy . . .' mused Edward.

'A lovely creature by all accounts.'

'They always are,' said Edward. 'Oh well, I daresay she is fair enough.'

Warwick was pleased when he reported to George.

'He has given his promise?'

'He has not said in so many words that he will agree to the marriage, but he will. He will see the advantages. Edward is no fool. He loves his crown. He'll do everything he can to keep it.'

'Or let you keep it for him.'

'I think he is appreciative of what I have done.'

'I should hope so.'

'I knew when I made him King what to expect of Edward. I shall be with him shortly. He is pausing for a brief visit to Grafton Regis to stay with Lord Rivers and after that he will join me.'

'He seems to have become very fond of the Rivers.'

Warwick laughed. 'I believe his latest flame is Rivers' daughter. Woodville's widow.'

'A very comely woman, I believe.'

'So you have heard of her. My dear brother the King's path is strewn with comely women.'

It would not be difficult to persuade the King, he was sure. Oh, he was very sure of himself. Rising on the crest of the wave. Warwick supreme. There was no doubt that he was the power in the land. The King of France treated him as though he were royal; he corresponded with him — not with Edward. All over the world he was known as the ruler of England, the power behind the glittering figure of the King, they must deal with him if they wanted friendship with England. Who would be a King when one could be a King-Maker.

He had made sure that his family shared his prosperity. That was wisdom. When he needed support they were at hand to give it. George of course as Chancellor was rich and powerful. John was now Warden of the East Marches; his two sisters had married into influential families, one to William Lord Hastings who was one of the King's intimate friends and the other to Thomas Lord Stanley, member of a powerful northern family. He had scattered his influence. He believed that if he measured his possessions and his influence against those of the King he would be the richer.

And Edward was amenable. He seemed content to let Warwick rule. Even the King's licentious habits were in Warwick's favour. Better for the King to be so interested in the bed rather than politics. Not that Edward was a fool in those matters. There was strength in him and if he did not allow himself to be so often diverted by his pursuit of women he would have been a power to reckon with. So be grateful again, thought Warwick. All the same he must not allow Edward to become too friendly with men like Hastings, Stafford and Herbert. It would not do for him to get it into his head that he could do without Warwick. Not that he had, but he was growing up. It was easier to deal with a boy of seventeen than it was with a man rising into his twenties.

Edward was not a vindictive man. He could easily forgive his enemies; and one who had fought against him one year could become a friend the next. He was even ready to cultivate the young Duke of Somerset whose father had been one of the chief Lancastrians and Edward's greatest enemy.

'Unlike the scriptures I do not visit the sins of the fathers on the third and fourth generation,' said Edward. 'If a man likes to come to me and be my friend, I shall be ready to forget what his father has done.'

And he did attract men to him; that ease of manner, that charm, those outstanding good looks brought him admirers and friends as well as a host of mistresses.

He was becoming very fond of the Rivers family, Warwick noticed. Why, Warwick could not understand. Surely it was not because he had at one time taken a fancy to Rivers' daughter?

'If he is going to favour the families of his mistresses,' he joked to George, 'we shall have so many favoured ones in the land that favours will be the order of the day. But we must get him married. I shall get an answer from him at the very next council meeting.'

It was at this council meeting that Warwick received his first intimation that the relationship between himself and Edward had changed.

There were many of Edward's new and intimate friends present, and Warwick did not realise at first that they were there to rally round the King, who gave no indication to Warwick that anything had changed between them.

Everyone knew what hopes Warwick pinned on friendship with the King of France and how he prided himself on his ability to handle Louis. Therefore the first shock came when Edward declared that he did not trust Louis of France.

'We have heard from our good friend the Earl of Warwick,' said the King, 'that Louis is eager for an alliance with us. But it is a fact that Pierre de Brézé, who is Margaret of Anjou's warmest and most faithful supporter, is highly favoured at the Court of France.'

'This is not so,' cried Warwick. 'When Louis came to the throne Pierre de Brézé was imprisoned in Loches . . .'

'And quickly released,' retorted Edward. 'Moreover I have it from one of our French prisoners that Louis is plotting against us.'

'That is nonsense,' cried Warwick, shattered not so much by these accusations as by the fact that Edward had brought them up before the Council without first consulting him. 'I shall send a despatch to the King of France immediately informing him of the allegations which have been made against him and asking him to prove to you all that they are nonsense.'

He looked defiantly at the King who met his eyes with a smile as he said that as usual the Earl of Warwick had got to the root of the matter and if he thought that was the right action then so must it be.

Warwick breathed more freely. It was not really a revolt. It was just an opinion he had expressed. He had not meant to go against him deliberately.

'And now,' said Warwick, 'there is the question of the King's marriage. This must be settled. I hope very much that the King will agree with me.'

Again that charming, affable smile. 'I do, my lord. Indeed I do. Nothing would suit me better than to be married.'

'Your subjects will be delighted,' cried Warwick.

'It may be,' said the King, 'that my choice may not be to the liking of everyone present. No matter, I shall do as I like in this.'

'My lord,' said Warwick beaming with pleasure, 'tell us who is your chosen bride.'

He was certain now that all was well. He had discussed the marriage with Bona of Savoy, and Edward had understood what advantages it could bring.

Then Warwick could not believe he had heard correctly. Had the King gone mad?

He was saying: 'I have chosen my bride. She will be Elizabeth Woodville, daughter of Lord Rivers.'

A deep silence fell upon them. Warwick sat as though numb. At length George Neville spoke. 'The lady is virtuous and very beautiful, my lord,' he said, 'but is she not too far below you for marriage?'

'She is indeed virtuous and beautiful,' agreed the King. 'As for her lowly station, praise be to God that is a matter which can easily be remedied.'

George was trying to divine what his brother was thinking. He knew that he could have had no idea that the King was going to announce this.

He stammered: 'I know her mother was the Dowager Duchess of Bedford but she is not the daughter of a duke . . . nor an earl even. How would such a marriage be received, my lord? What would other rulers think?'

'They shall be at liberty to think what they will. I will have Elizabeth Woodville or no one.'

'My lord!' Everyone was intent on Warwick who had now risen to his feet. 'I know well your jovial nature. You are amusing yourself at our expense. You do not mean this, of course...'

Edward was still smiling but there was a strong note in his voice.

'I mean it,' he said. 'I mean it with all my heart. Stop your efforts to persuade me. In any case they are too late. Elizabeth Woodville and I were married at Grafton Regis...'

Warwick sank to his chair. He said nothing. The beats of his heart were like hammerstrokes. He could have struck that smiling, handsome face.

He said nothing, but he knew it was over.

The puppet had turned into a man and was no longer his to control.

When Warwick left the council chamber he had a great desire to be alone to think. In all his life he had never felt so shattered. That Edward had acted so was bad enough but it was some time since that May day at Grafton Regis and he had been keeping his marriage secret all this time... and meanwhile he, Warwick, had been negotiating with the King of France. Edward had humiliated him in the extreme. Not only had he broken free but he had actually kept this all important secret from the man who had made him.

Warwick was not sure how to act.

His brother George came to him in great anxiety. For some moments they looked at each other, unable to express their thoughts. George was very worried.

At length he said: 'What shall you do?'

'He is determined to act as he fancies. It is this woman. She must be a witch.'

'He is easily bewitched by women.'

'He has had so many he must feel very deeply to have been dragged into this by this one. Think what it means. He allowed me to negotiate with Louis while he was actually married. I shall be the laughing stock of all France and England.'

'Not you, brother. Louis will understand that we have a feckless stallion to deal with.'

'I shall never forget the way he stood there smiling at me . . . with that look in his eyes. "I will do what pleases me. I shall take no heed of the needs of my country, of the efforts the man who put the crown on my head made to do just that." Oh George, what base ingratitude!'

'Indeed it is so,' agreed George.

'And think of the implications.'

'I am thinking of that and wondering how you will act. Do you think it would be better to say nothing just at first? After all the deed is done. They are married. Nothing can change that . . . save divorce. You behaved with admirable calm at the Council.'

'I was shocked into silence.'

'That is not such a bad thing for it might have been dangerous for you to have spoken your thoughts.'

'By God if I had . . .'

'Yes . . . And we all were with you. This is an act of folly which I doubt not the King will learn to his cost and when he does it is to you he will turn, brother. He will wish that he had listened to you.'

Warwick was silent. George was right, of course. George had a clear, incisive mind. He would have to accept this low-born woman as the Queen. And in time it might well be that having seen his folly the King would turn back to him. He sighed deeply. Then he said: 'You are right, George. I must be calm. I must say nothing. I must appear to accept this woman as Queen.'

Thus when Edward came to him smiling as though there had been no rift between them he agreed to present the Queen to the lords in Reading Abbey.

'My brother Clarence will walk on one side of Elizabeth and you, Richard, on the other. That pleases me. My brother and my closest friend to welcome her. She will be so happy . . . and so shall I.'

Swallowing his rage, suppressing his rancour Warwick did it but it needed iron control of his feelings to perform the exercise with a good grace.

To keep up this attitude was easier to contemplate than to put into practice.

Elizabeth Woodville was an ambitious lady and she was surrounded by impecunious members of her family. She was determined to advance them and such was her power over the King that she had little difficulty in doing this.

Warwick was glad to see that many of the nobles were growing more and more disgruntled by the elevation of the Woodville family. The Queen married her sister Margaret to Lord Maltravers, son of the Earl of Arundel; her sister Mary was married to the son of Lord Herbert who was heir to the Pembroke title; and there was outraged indignation when her brother John, aged twenty, became betrothed to the Duchess of Norfolk who was nearly eighty years old.

It was easy to see the motives behind these marriages. No one could realise the tremendous importance of the right marriage more than Warwick. He owed his vast wealth and titles to his. He could see that in a short time the Woodvilles would be of greater importance than the Nevilles through these advantageous marriages.

The people did not like it. They deplored the marriage. Even the most humble in the land criticised the low birth of Elizabeth Woodville – which was amusing if it were not so very useful.

It began to dawn on Warwick that if he were not careful he would be ousted from the realms of power. All that he had done would be forgotten; there would be a new ruling family in the country – that of the Woodvilles.

The time had come for him to do some deep thinking. What did a King-Maker do when his puppet refused to respond to the strings? He found a new puppet.

It was an exciting project. There was another. At the moment he was a poor neglected prisoner in the Tower.

This needed a great deal of thought.

There came a day when he found himself face to face with Edward and because his plans were now taking real shape in his mind he no longer felt the need to cloak his feelings.

Edward noticed the strange brooding expression on his face and when he asked what ailed him, Warwick's rage broke out.

'Need you ask, my lord? I am suffering from a surfeit of disloyalty. I have given my life to what I believed was a good cause. I have squandered men and money in giving England a ruler whom I thought would serve her well. And what does he do? He makes a marriage which is suicide to his political advantage. He has destroyed the hope of an alliance with France. As for myself I have had indignity heaped upon me. While I was negotiating with the King of

France you, my lord, were making a mockery of those negotiations . . . of not only your faithful friend but the King of a powerful country. Do you wonder I am sick at heart?'

Edward expressed no surprise that he should be addressed in this manner by a subject. He had always recognised Warwick as a specially favoured one. He laid an arm about his shoulders.

'You distress yourself unnecessarily,' he said. 'I know the people don't like my marriage. But Elizabeth is different from all other women I have ever known . . . and I speak of one who knows the sex well. It was the only way, Richard. It was marriage or nothing . . .'

'And you were duped by that tale?'

'Oh come, she meant it. She was a virtuous widow.'

Warwick threw off the King's arm. 'It was an act of folly and I promise you it is one you will regret.'

He did not wait for more. He had made the break now. Affable as he was, Edward would not forget that scene in a hurry.

Now he would have to act, Warwick had decided, and he knew what he was going to do.

Warwick rode north to his castle of Middleham, his head teeming with plans. At Middleham were the King's brothers George and Richard. He had always been on very good terms with them. There could not be two brothers less alike. George, Duke of Clarence was vain, avaricious and selfish; he was easily swayed and Warwick had been able to win his friendship. The other, Richard, Duke of Gloucester, was a quiet, studious boy, rather delicate, and he had been brought up at Middleham and had formed a close friendship with Warwick's younger daughter Anne.

Therefore Warwick had the two Princes as he thought in his power. Clarence would be malleable; he was not so sure of Richard. The younger boy was passionately devoted to his brother Edward, and would not be easily persuaded that his own advantage might lie elsewhere. In fact Warwick was certain that Richard would stand by his brother no matter what happened.

Clarence on the other hand was disgruntled. He was old enough to see that the Woodvilles were fast becoming the most important family in the land and that was something he was not prepared to tolerate, for there was an arrogance about the new Queen's family which extended even to the King's brother.

So to Middleham where his two daughters, Isabel and Anne, with his wife were waiting to greet him.

Richard was there too, in the courtyard. The boy had grown since he had last seen him, though he was delicate still and one shoulder was higher than the other, though slightly so and almost imperceptible. Poor Richard, he lacked the outstanding good looks and physique of Edward, but that had not prevented his partaking in all the manly pastimes which were necessary for boys of his rank.

The Duke of Clarence was on his way, the Countess told him. He had sent heralds ahead to announce his coming as the Earl had expressed an urgent desire to see him.

Warwick embraced his family. He loved them with as much affection as he could spare from his ambitions. Naturally he had spent little time with them. He could never prevent himself regretting that he had no son; but the girls were pretty, charming and obedient. He must therefore be grateful for what he had.

Clarence arrived in rather flamboyant style, eager that none should forget he was brother to the King. Warwick greeted him with such respect that even Clarence was satisfied. He sat on the Earl's right hand at table. Warwick intimated that he wished to speak to the two Dukes alone as soon as the meal was concluded.

When the three of them were together in a small but private room Warwick looked very seriously from George to Richard and said that he had no doubt that they were as worried as he was by the manner in which the Woodvilles were behaving.

'Indeed yes I am!' cried Clarence. 'These marriages . . . this taking of power . . . and all by these upstarts.'

'I see you have a grasp of the situation,' said Warwick. 'The people are getting displeased. I do not think the King understands how angry the people are growing.'

'If the people are growing angry my brother the King would be aware of it,' said Richard gravely.

Ah, thought Warwick, be wary of Richard!

'Our brother is too busy with his woman,' said Clarence with a laugh.

'My lord, you speak truth. I fear this country will be at war again if we do not take heed. In fact I think it is time our King was taught a lesson.'

Richard had gone white. 'I will not remain here and listen to such lack of respect for the King.'

With that he walked out of the room.

'You mistake,' Warwick called after him. 'I love the King. I have served him with all I have . . .'

But Richard was gone.

Clarence shrugged his shoulders. 'He is very young,' he said. 'He worships Edward blindly. He even says he likes this marriage because it is what Edward wants.'

'It is true he is young,' said Warwick, 'and therefore you

and I need not concern ourselves with him yet. I am glad he has left us for now we can talk as men.'

Clarence smiled, well pleased. 'I knew you had something of importance to say to me.'

'Indeed I have. As you know, I have made your brother King of England.'

'I know you are called the King-Maker.'

'And rightly. It would seem, my lord, that if we allow matters to go on as they are you and I . . . and young Richard who will not listen . . . yet . . . will be the subjects of the Wood-villes, for all these marriages they are making are going to make them more powerful than any of us . . . even the King.'

'I'll not tolerate that.'

'I thought you would not.'

'What then?'

'Your brother is not so secure on the throne that he can afford such a marriage. There is one other . . .'

'Henry . . . poor old Henry . . . the prisoner in the Tower.'

'A figurehead, nothing more. And we would have an heir. Not Margaret's bastard . . . for bastard I believe him to be. Henry could never have begotten a son and she was friendly first with Suffolk and then with Somerset . . . There would be an heir . . .' Warwick was looking intently at Clarence, whose eyes widened as he grasped the Earl's meaning.

Clarence on the throne! Why not? He was Edward's brother and in fact if Edward did not produce a child he was next in line.

It was a glorious prospect.

'Well?' he said almost imperiously as though the crown was already on his head.

'The King of France would be our ally. It would be

423

necessary to get his help. We should also bring back Margaret to work for us . . .'

'With the Prince of Wales . . .'

'Why shouldn't they work for us? Although the people detest her they like to have everything in order. If we could bring out Henry and ride with him into battle . . . and bring Margaret and the so-called Prince back to England . . .'

Clarence's eyes sparkled. He loved intrigue and as he thought of the possibilities of this he was overcome by excitement. He had always been jealous of Edward. His mother, his father, everyone had marvelled at Edward's good looks and charm, and it had not been easy for one of Clarence's nature to have such a brother.

And now Edward had been a fool! He had married that low-born woman; he had offended Warwick and everyone knew that Warwick had put him on the throne. Edward had at last shown that he was not so clever. And Clarence was going to show that *he* was clever, very clever indeed.

Warwick was smiling. How easy it was. Henry would be much more malleable. Imagine Clarence on the throne! Still, it might never come to that.

Warwick went on: 'I have long known your regard for my elder daughter Isabel.'

Clarence was smiling secretly. It was so obvious. Cunning old Warwick. Make Clarence King and his daughter Isabel Queen.

'My lord,' he said, 'how well you have guessed my feelings. I have always had the highest regard for Isabel and of late my heart has become deeply involved.'

'I have been thinking that a match between you two would be a very desirable outcome for you both.'

'You have guessed my heart's desire.'
Warwick laid his hand on the young man's arm.
'Well, there will be work to be done first.'
'I can scarcely wait to begin,' answered Clarence.

🌺 Chapter XVIII 🌺

THE QUEEN'S GRIEF

There were important visitors at the castle of St Michiel. Prince Edward came in excitedly to tell his mother of their arrival. Life was so quiet in St Michiel. The Prince had longed for something to happen. His mother often said that one day they would go back to England to claim what was rightfully theirs and Sir John Fortescue was always keeping him to his lessons and impressing on him that a Prince born to be King must be skilled in book learning as well as martial arts.

But nothing happened. The years passed. He had been a child when he came here and now he was sixteen. It seemed he had spent all his life in this quiet castle where every day was exactly like the one which had gone before.

And now . . . messengers.

He was with his mother when the messengers were brought to her. He stood by her while she received the letters.

There were several of them. One bore the royal seal. There was another from his grandfather and one from his aunt as well.

How slowly his mother opened them. She was pretending

she was not excited for she must be since that letter was from the King of France.

She read it through.

'What does he say, dear lady?' begged the Prince.

Margaret smiled at her son's eagerness.

'The King commands us to go to Tours.'

'The King. To Tours! Oh, dear mother, when?'

'Very very soon. And now here is a letter from your grand-father.'

He looked over her shoulder and read that Margaret and the Prince should lose no time in coming to Tours. The King was eager to discuss the prospects of the House of Lancaster which it seemed were growing a little brighter.

Margaret stared ahead of her. What did this mean? What could have happened? It had seemed so long now since Edward had usurped the throne and sent her into exile and Henry to the Tower.

But since the King of France was involved this must be of some significance. Not that she dared hope for too much. Perhaps she had hoped too deeply in the past; when hope turned to disaster the bitterness was hard to bear.

There was a letter from her sister Yolande. She reiterated what her father had said. There were hopeful signs and they were excited, for certain things it seemed had happened in England which had changed the outlook. Yolande's husband Ferri — the Count of Vaudémont — joined his wishes with hers that Margaret would lose no time in coming to Tours.

It was indeed exciting. She had to admit it. Something important was about to happen.

'My dear mother, you have become young again,' said the Prince.

She put her arms about him and held him close to her, suffocatingly so. She was very demonstrative and sometimes her absolute devotion was an embarrassment to the Prince. He was devoted to her. He knew that he owed her a great deal and all her vehemence was for his sake. He had been brought up to realise that he was the rightful heir to the crown of England and that it was his mother's dearest hope that he should have it. Yes, she was wonderful, but he wished that she would not be quite so fierce in her displays of emotion.

He withdrew himself, smiling at her and kissing her cheek to show that he loved her even though he did not want to be suffocated.

'We will prepare to leave for Tours at once,' she said.

It was with great emotion that she was reunited with her family.

René was there with his pretty young wife and he and Margaret openly wept as they embraced.

'I am so happy at this change,' he said. 'I am sure, my dear daughter, that soon all is going to be well for you.'

Then she was embraced by Yolande and Ferri and when they were all presented to the Prince they remarked how grown he was, how tall, how good-looking.

'A King in very truth,' said René.

The King of France arrived and expressed himself deeply moved by the emotion he saw in this family reunion although no one believed that the Spider King of France could be moved for one instant for sentimental reasons.

Margaret was all eagerness to learn what this change in England was all about and when she was told of the quarrel between Edward of York and the Earl of Warwick she could only express the utmost delight. She was less happy when she learned that Warwick was on his way to France and was planning to visit her.

'I will never see that man,' she cried. 'He is responsible for all my troubles.'

'You must see him,' said her father. 'You must forget all that has gone before. In him could lie your salvation.'

'In that case I shall remain unsaved. I will not see a man who has called my son a bastard and thrown cruel slander on my honour.'

'My dear daughter, you must be reasonable.'

Margaret said there was no need of them to continue the conversation for she had made up her mind.

A few days passed during which René, Yolande and Ferri did all they could to persuade her. She was adamant.

'It is too much to ask. Moreover if he is ready to betray his friend Edward, whom he made King in name, how could I trust him?'

'Edward deceived him. You must take advantage of this quarrel between them.'

'I will have nothing to do with Warwick.'

René was a little impatient. The King of France was anxious for a rapprochement between Warwick and Margaret for it was very much to his advantage to make life uncomfortable for Edward.

'I will see that an understanding is brought about between these two,' said Louis. 'When Warwick arrives he shall be presented to me in Margaret's presence.'

And this was what happened.

The King of France greeted the Earl with warmth and then presented him to Margaret, who regarded him stonily.

'Nay, my lord,' she said ignoring Warwick and looking fixedly at Louis, 'in all respect to myself and honour to my son I cannot receive the Earl of Warwick.'

Louis was annoyed but could do nothing about it. He drew Warwick on one side.

'The lady has a violent temper,' he said. 'We shall have to find a means of placating it. When she realises what you can do for her and her son she will be more gracious.'

Yolande came to Margaret's private apartments to remonstrate with her.

'You were always stubborn,' she said. 'The King will be furious. What you did was tantamount to an insult to him.'

'In presenting that man to me he was insulting me.'

'You, my dear Margaret, are not the King of France!'

'Nay, but I am the Queen of England.'

'Some would say England has a Queen Elizabeth.'

Margaret had to restrain herself for she could have slapped her sister's face. Yolande and she had quickly discovered that their temperaments did not blend well together.

'I shall do what is right according to my own standards,' she snapped.

'And lose yourself a throne. *You* may do that but that you should prevent your son's taking what he has a right to is nothing but selfish.'

Yolande flounced out of the room but her remark had made more impression on Margaret than all the persuasion had done and very shortly afterwards she agreed to see Warwick.

It was not in her nature to make it easy for him. She intended that he should grovel before her, and Warwick, proud as he might be, was ready to go to great lengths to obtain what he wanted. Friendship with Margaret was essential to his

430

plans. Therefore this reconciliation must be brought about.

He tried to appeal to her common sense.

'I put Edward on the throne,' he said. 'It was a mistake. I should have given my allegiance to Henry. If I had what a different story we should have had to tell.'

'Indeed you have created much mischief,' retorted Margaret. 'You have been a traitor to the anointed King.'

'I was wrong and am now ready to repair my misdeeds. I shall now be Edward's foe as vehemently as I have been his friend. I was misled by what I believed to be his claim to the throne and because of the King's illness . . .'

She silenced him. She wanted no reference to Henry's weakness of mind.

'I see that what you did is unpardonable.'

'There is no sin on earth that cannot be pardoned by magnanimity and generosity of heart, my lady.'

All the time she was thinking what this man could do. He emanated power and strength. He was not called the King-Maker for nothing.

But she was not going to give way lightly. It was when the King of France appeared and with a certain humble grace begged her to pardon the Earl of Warwick that she at length agreed.

'It will be necessary for my son to do the same,' she said. 'I am not sure that he will agree.'

The King and Warwick exchanged smiles. Of course he would agree. He would do exactly what his mother told him to.

Louis expressed a wish that they should all travel to Angers where the Countess of Warwick and her younger daughter Anne would be waiting to receive them.

Margaret's spirits were uplifted. She had had to subdue her pride to agree to friendship with Warwick but she knew that she had to catch at anything that might help her regain the throne for her son. Warwick could do that. He was the one man in England who could. It was really a miraculous piece of good fortune that he had quarrelled with Edward. Yolande was right. She would have been a fool to let that pass just because of her stubborn pride.

And how good it was to ride in a procession again like a royal Queen. And Edward beside her. Growing up handsome, brave, a son to be proud of. Nearly eighteen years old now. Old enough to take the crown.

She had heard with some surprise that Warwick's elder daughter Isabel had married Clarence. Clever Warwick. He had somehow won Clarence to his side and no doubt the bribe of Warwick's vast wealth had worked with the young Duke. He was a traitor to his brother. It seemed to her the world was full of traitors.

It pointed to one factor. Events were moving. The period of stagnation was clearly coming to an end and no matter what had brought it about that was something for which she must rejoice.

The King of France rode beside her into Angers. She noticed that the people did not cheer vociferously. Louis lacked that appeal which she accepted grudgingly belonged to Edward of York. The Valois were not handsome as the Plantagenets had been. Appearances were important. She herself was still a beautiful woman in spite of the ravages of time and events. She noticed approving eyes on her dear son and that warmed her heart a little.

Louis was aware of it too for he commented on the Prince's royal appearance.

'A great joy to you, my lady,' he said.

'My only one for a long time,' replied Margaret.

'And what a blessing. He will soon be marrying I doubt not and then you will have your grandchildren.'

She was wary. This conversation was leading somewhere. The Spider King was not known to waste words in idle chatter.

'I believe the young Duke of Clarence is very happy in his marriage. Warwick's girls are beauties . . . moreover they are the richest heiresses in England.'

'That may be so and I wish Clarence joy of his marriage. I'll swear his brother does not feel the same pleasure in it as my lord Warwick appears to.'

'Ha!' Louis gave his short bark which was meant to be a laugh. 'Edward has been acting with great foolishness. That is not the way to hold a crown . . . especially when a man has no right to it. Warwick put it on his head and Warwick will take it off when the time comes . . . and put it where it belongs.'

'If justice prevails that is assuredly what will take place,' she said.

'And princes should marry young. The sooner they begin to produce heirs the better. Warwick has a charming young daughter. What a prize . . . a beautiful healthy young girl and a half share in the greatest estates in England.'

'I cannot believe, my lord, that you suggest that the Prince of Wales should marry Warwick's daughter.'

'It seems to me . . . and to others . . . an admirable solution to the problem of the Prince's marriage.'

'My lord, it is quite out of the question.'

'Oh surely not.'

'I have forgiven the Earl of Warwick his treatment of me and the King. It has cost me a great deal to do that. To allow

433

my son to marry his daughter is something I will not consider . . . not for one moment . . .'

Louis bowed his head and was silent. Indeed he was not one to waste words.

At Angers the Countess of Warwick was waiting with her young daughter. Anne Beauchamp was a pleasant creature. Poor woman, thought Margaret, married to a man like Warwick. What life had she had! But her real interest was for the girl. Comely, yes, rather delicately formed and dainty, of good manners and some beauty. If she had been the daughter of the King of France or the Duke of Burgundy instead of a mere Earl – and an old enemy at that – Margaret would have considered the girl a possible match.

There were fêtes and entertainments at Angers. Warwick submitted with as much patience as he could muster. So did Margaret. The Earl had a promise of help from Louis but he did not want to move until the time was ripe. His friends were amassing forces in England; his most important scheme was to land when Edward was in the North for Warwick had arranged with his brother-in-law Lord Fitzhugh to send out rumours of a rising in the North which would take Edward up there with an army. If he could land in the South, free Henry from the Tower and set him up as King, he would have an immediate advantage; Warwick's brother John had deliberately not joined with him for the reason that he could be more useful seeming to remain loyal to Edward, and when Edward was lured to the North John would at the right moment desert him and declare for Henry and Warwick would then be in a position to defeat Edward.

It was a clever plan and Warwick's strategy had always been more successful than his actual physical warfare.

He needed everything to fall into place. Margaret was a stubborn woman; he wished he could do without her. When he looked back he could see that had Henry had a different Queen he might not be in the Tower today.

But Margaret would not agree to a union between Edward and Anne. Meanwhile the two young people had met and clearly liked each other. Edward said he thought she was a delightful girl, not in the least bit like her father. There was no trace of arrogance about her.

'Nor should there be,' snapped Margaret. 'Who is she but the daughter of an upstart Earl who got his titles through his wife?'

'And became so powerful that he decided who should sit on the throne of England,' Edward reminded her.

Edward was beginning to have ideas of his own; and she could see that he liked the idea of marrying Anne Neville rather than having some foreign princess foisted on him.

René urged Margaret to agree to the marriage. She must accept the fact that Warwick was important to her. This was the best opportunity she had ever had. It was like a miracle that Warwick should have changed sides.

Yolande and her stepmother joined their voices to René's. Perhaps if they had not so earnestly tried to persuade her she might have agreed earlier.

The King of France talked to her too. She told him that there had been a suggestion that Edward marry the daughter of Edward the Fourth. 'Elizabeth of York is a baby about four or five years old,' Louis reminded her. 'She is too young, and would you marry your son to the daughter of your greatest enemy?'

'You are asking me to do just that.'

'So you regard Warwick as a greater enemy than the man who took the crown from your husband?'

'It was Warwick who took it.'

'All the more reason why you should rejoice that he has become your friend.'

She told herself that it was because her beloved son Edward liked the girl that she gave in. But it was not really that. She knew that her only hope of defeating Edward and putting Henry back on the throne was through Warwick.

So, just as she had agreed to make a pact of friendship with Warwick she now agreed that there should be a betrothal between his daughter and her son.

What intoxication to contemplate the future! Warwick was almost ready to strike. He was succeeding as he had known he would. Louis had promised him forty-six thousand crowns and two thousand French archers. Jasper Tudor had arrived in France; Jasper had never wavered in his loyalty to the Lancastrian cause and now that Warwick was with them his hopes were high. He had men whom he could trust waiting in Wales to fight for King Henry.

There were many conferences in which Warwick laid his plans before Margaret. She would never like him, of course; but she had to admire him. She often thought during those days of how differently everything might have turned out if he had been for them and not against them.

'The Prince of Wales shall be the Regent,' he had said. 'For he is of an age to govern and I doubt very much that the King will be well enough to do so after such a long incarceration.'

That suited Margaret. She would be at his side. She would

guide him. Oh how happy she would be to see her darling son preparing to govern his Kingdom!

Clarence would have his reward for turning against his brother. He should have all his brother's lands. Clarence was not sure that this was enough reward. He had had his eyes on the crown. But there was time. Who knew what the outcome of this would be and there might be a few battles to be fought.

As for Margaret she should have the care of the Prince's betrothed. She should teach Anne her ways and what would be expected of her as wife to the Prince of Wales. Margaret was delighted. She could not help but like the gentle Anne, and every day she was less against the match than she had previously been. She had made it clear that the marriage should not take place until Henry was on the throne, and to this Warwick had agreed.

Warwick left and sailed for Devonshire with Clarence, Jasper Tudor and the Earl of Oxford while Margaret settled down to wait. That was mid-September and it was not until October that the news came.

She could scarcely believe it. It had happened. She called the Prince to her; she embraced him with fervour.

'He has done it,' she said. 'God be thanked, Warwick has put Henry back on the throne.'

It had all gone according to plan. Edward had foolishly allowed himself to be lured to the North to quell the rising in answer to the call for help from John Neville.

No sooner was he there when Warwick landed. John Neville then called to his men and told them that they were now going to bring back the true King. In fact his brother was already engaged in doing this. They were tired of the growing arrogance of the Woodvilles and the new nobility which the Queen was creating. All those who agreed with him could follow him south to join the armies of the great Warwick. Warwick's name acted like magic.

'In the morning,' said Neville, 'we will take the King.'

Edward had some faithful servants and one of them immediately hurried to tell him what had happened. Edward was sitting at dinner when the servant arrived and realising his position decided that there was only one course open to him and that was flight.

'If we stay we shall be captured . . . and murdered I doubt not,' he said. 'Warwick will know better than to try to make a captive of me. We must get away . . . but only for a while.'

There were some eight hundred of them including Hastings and his young brother Richard. They rode to the coast and reached Lynn where they found ships to take them to Holland.

'Better to live to fight another day,' said Edward. 'I would never have believed this of Warwick.'

'A curse on him,' cried Richard. 'The traitor.'

'Nay, brother,' said Edward. 'He was a good friend to me. That is why I know he will be a good enemy. Our ways parted. He wanted to go on leading me and I am out of leading strings. I always liked Warwick. Methinks I always will.'

❁ ❁ ❁

Henry blinked at the men who stood before him. He thought he recognised them from the past. Was one Archbishop George Neville and the other Bishop Waynflete?

The two men stared at him in shocked silence. His hair was unkempt, his face and hands dirty. His clothes hung on him.

'He looked,' said the Archbishop afterwards to his brother the Earl, 'like a sack of wool ... a shadow ... and he was as mute as a crowned calf. He had no notion of why we had come. He was bemused and after a while we heard him murmuring "Forsooth and forsooth."'

'My lord,' said the Archbishop, 'we have come to take you from this place. Your loyal subject the Earl of Warwick ...'

Henry looked more bewildered. There was so much explaining to do. They must take him from the Tower, wash him, clothe him in garments suited to his rank and feed him.

They brought him quietly from the Tower and took him away by barge so that none of his subjects might see the wreck he had become.

When Warwick saw him he was horrified.

'How dared they treat a King so!' he cried.

He had forgotten that until recently he had been one of those responsible for Henry's captivity.

That was over now. Henry was going to be King. Edward had flown. His wife would be joining him and so would his son. He would be amazed to see the Prince – as handsome and fine an heir as ever was seen.

It took Henry a long time to grasp what was happening. He murmured prayers most of the time. There was no sign of rejoicing. It almost seemed that he would have preferred to stay where he was.

Margaret was jubilant. Edward in flight; Henry restored. It was a miracle. And Warwick had done it. She had to admit that. He was not called King-Maker for nothing. And if he would be loyal the future could be bright. She had been right to suppress her pride. And now nothing should stand in the way of Edward's marriage to Anne Neville. She owed that to

Warwick for she had promised that when Henry was restored to the throne the marriage should take place.

Now that promise must be kept.

It was a grand wedding. August had just come in and that was the best time for a wedding. So many of the festivities took place out of doors. The King of France was present. The wedding was almost as much of his making as it was Warwick's. He was delighted. He saw an end to his enemy, Edward of England. It was always comforting when other people fought one's battles and Warwick had done that for him. Therefore he was delighted to grace Warwick's daughter's wedding with his presence.

It was a joyful occasion and Margaret was happy. There was no friction even between her and Yolande. It was a most felicitous occasion and perhaps the most happy part of it was the obvious affection which was growing up between the handsome Prince and his charming bride.

And now to Paris with a guard of honour to escort them and in the capital city they must be given royal treatment because that was the King's express order. The streets were hung with tapestry and there was music everywhere.

Only one thing could delight Margaret more and that was to return to England and find a similar welcome awaiting her there.

So much time had to be spent at the various towns on her journey through France that it was February before she reached Harfleur and was ready to sail. Then the weather had turned rough, the wind was fierce and the waves pounded the shore, so that she was advised it would be folly to set sail. Impatiently she glowered at the sea. It was all important that she reach England. She wanted to see Henry; she wanted to show their son to him and the country. For days she waited and when the seas abated a little, in spite of warnings she insisted on setting out. Within a short time the ships were back in port. To go on, declared the captains, would mean to lose them.

Angry and frustrated, she raged against the elements and as soon as she felt the wind was subsiding a little she set sail again only to be driven back by fresh gales.

People were superstitious and they began to say she was not meant to return to England. This infuriated her and once more she set out and had to come back.

Now everyone was getting nervous except Margaret. She was going to brave the weather and had it not been that she feared to put her son's life in jeopardy she would have insisted on starting out again.

Then suddenly the wind dropped. Immediately they set sail and with much rejoicing and prayers of thanksgiving they arrived safely in Weymouth.

It was hardly to be expected that Edward would meekly give up the crown; he realised however that Warwick was a strong enemy and had no doubt decided, knowing him so well, what action he would take and be prepared for it.

However, he could not delay in Holland and accordingly embarked at Flushing on the second day of March in the company of his young brother Richard of Gloucester and Earl Rivers. The rough winds which had tormented Margaret were a source of annoyance to him also and his crossing was delayed for a few days and some time was lost before he came in sight of Cromer. Even then he knew it would be folly to land before he had discovered what sort of welcome he was going to meet so he sent a party ashore to test the political climate. They came back to say it was frigid and that they should not land so they went higher up the coast to Ravenspur. The people of that neighbourhood were no more pleased to see him than they had been at Cromer. They wanted no fighting on their land. They had the rightful King on the throne now and they were for Henry.

They must be told that he came only to claim his dukedom, he declared, and he went so far as to cause his men to wear the ostrich feather badge of the Prince of Wales.

Because they did this his army was allowed to land and the army reached York where their reception was a little more friendly being on Yorkist territory. He then proceeded to Wakefield where he was joined by friends and when he arrived in Oxford his ranks were considerably swelled and his spirits rose accordingly. In the town of Warwick Edward was greeted as King and was proclaimed in the square. Here he delivered a speech to the people and promised that if the Earl of Warwick would disband his army he should have a free pardon.

It was while he was in Warwick that messengers arrived in secret from his brother Clarence.

Clarence craved Edward's pardon and wanted to rejoin him. He was filled with remorse to think that he had gone over to Edward's enemy; and if only he could come back he would bring a considerable number of men with him.

Edward rejoiced. He would forgive his brother; and although he would not trust him again, he bore no rancour for he had never trusted Clarence as he had Richard, and had always known Clarence for what he was – feckless, avaricious, self-seeking. Still he was his brother.

Indeed, yes, Clarence should be forgiven.

Near Banbury his men came to a halt. The enemy was in the near vicinity. A party of soldiers came riding towards Edward's forces and Edward saw that their leader was Clarence who in truth had changed sides and brought his men, whom Warwick thought were with him, to fight for Edward.

This was good progress, thought Edward as he embraced his brother without a reproach. He merely told him that all was forgiven and he was glad to have him back on the side to which he belonged.

Clarence told him that Warwick would not listen to any terms. He had gone too far to turn back. Moreover he thought he was going to defeat Edward and continue in his role of King-Maker. He had decided that Henry was to be his puppet now since Edward had shown that he was not to be jerked into suitable action by Warwick.

And so they met at Barnet. Warwick had drawn his forces at Hadley Green just to the north of the city. He had chosen his position where the ground sloped and had so placed himself that he commanded a narrow bottleneck from which he calculated the enemy would have to emerge. Edward was not going to fall into such a trap and under cover of darkness moved his forces so that they were parallel and very close to those of Warwick. Warwick was soon to realise that his well-laid plan had failed and he was reminded of the disastrous defeat at the second battle of St Albans. A heavy mist enveloped the battlefield and it was difficult to see where the forces lay. This was equally frustrating to both sides and at first it seemed as though Warwick would be triumphant. On one side of Edward was his brother Richard and on the other Hastings; Clarence was fighting where they could keep an eye on him for Edward knew that if the battle went against him

Clarence would attempt to change sides again and such changes in the heat of battle often made the difference between victory and defeat.

The battle had started as soon as it was light at between four and five in the morning and because of the heavy mist at one time Warwick's followers were sending arrows into their own ranks. The battle swayed one way and another. Here were two men whose whole future hung in the balance and each was as determined as the other on victory.

'Curse the fog,' cried Warwick. He could not know what was happening in his flanks. Out of the mists he perceived the Yorkist banner perilously close and one of his men came riding up panting, to cry out that Exeter was being sorely pressed. Warwick sent reinforcements to the Duke and then the cry went up that Edward of York was in flight.

Triumph surged over Warwick. He was invincible. He was the maker of Kings. He could not fail.

But it appeared that Edward was merely retreating to prepare for the attack. Through the mist he swung in, forcing the Lancastrians backwards, and Montague's men were falling to the right and left as Edward hacked his way through their forces.

The fighting was fierce, the carnage terrible, and the cries of the wounded and dying horses filled the air. Where the mist had lifted a little, Warwick saw that his forces had dwindled and that the Yorkists were advancing on them.

He knew then that the battle of Barnet was lost to him. He did not despair. He was thinking of the second battle of St Albans. He had lost that battle and turned it into a victory.

But he must make good his retreat. He must live to fight another day. One battle did not win or lose a war.

444

He had his horse and while he had a horse he was safe. He saw that his men – those who could and were of the same opinion as himself – were preparing to escape. The enemy would be after him, he knew. Was it not he who had taught Edward to let the common soldiers go and attack the leaders?

Now was the time. He would make for the forest. It was not the end. Just another battle lost.

He would snatch victory out of defeat. Escape . . . get to London. An arrow whined past him. Another came and struck his horse. He stumbled to the ground; he was heavily encumbered by his armour.

He was staggering and trying to run when someone shouted: 'That's Warwick.'

They were after him. The enemy. They had surrounded him. Someone threw him to the ground. They lifted his visor.

''Tis true. ''Tis Warwick.'

No mercy for the leader. They were Yorkists – all of them, intoxicated with victory. They were all of them fighting for the honour of slaying the great Earl.

He saw the flash of the knife as it descended. Darkness was heralding the end.

Richard Neville would make no more Kings.

Edward refreshed himself and his men in the town of Barnet. They were weary, for the battle had lasted for three hours. Then he ordered that the wounded should be attended to.

So Warwick was dead. That saddened him. He had admired Warwick, had idolised him. He did not want him to die. It had grieved him that they were on opposing sides and if Warwick had lived he would have freely pardoned him.

He gave orders that Warwick's body must be exposed for the public to see so that none should say afterwards that the King-Maker still lived. Then after a few days he should be taken to Bisham Abbey and buried there with his family.

Margaret was awaiting news of the battle. She was certain that this was going to set Henry firmly on the throne. Edward would be Regent and she would be at his elbow.

It was a long time since she had been so happy.

Then she saw the messengers. They came slowly – not as bearers of good news should.

She hurried to meet them.

'God help me,' she cried, 'what has happened?'

The messengers could not speak for a few moments. They just stood there looking blankly at her.

Nor did she reprimand them. She knew.

'The Earl of Warwick has been killed,' they told her. 'His armies are in retreat. Edward of York has won the battle of Barnet.'

She swayed a little and sought to steady herself. She saw her son coming towards her.

'News?' he cried. 'Oh dear lady, what news?'

She turned to look at him and he saw the bleak despair in her white face.

He ran to her and put his arms about her. She said quietly: 'I think I am going to swoon. Let . . . me . . . Let me for a brief while shut this away from me.'

Then he knew.

He stared at her blankly and then he caught her before she fell.

Her mood of desperation did not last long. It was not the end. One battle did not make a war. They had been defeated before. Warwick was dead, it was true, but the Prince of Wales thank God had not been at Barnet. They would win through yet.

'Is this not how it has always been?' she demanded. 'Ever since the white rose started to fight against the red there have been victories and defeats. One battle cannot decide the war. We have lost Warwick but Warwick did not always win. We are here in England . . . The King is free. We are free. We shall go into battle again and win.'

Jasper Tudor came to her. They were not beaten yet, he said. The mist had beaten them at Barnet. They would win through yet. She must not despair. If she and her gallant son marched through the country they would bring the people rallying to their banner.

The Prince said that Jasper was right: they would go into action; and as she looked at her son a terrible fear came to her. What did she want most, this son of hers alive, vital, beautiful, the whole meaning of life to her, safe and well, or the possibility of a crown?

I dare not risk him, she thought. Warwick had died. Such a short time ago he had been so sure of success. He had not been young it was true, but death and he had seemed far apart and then suddenly on that bloody field it had claimed him.

'Edward,' she said, 'perhaps the time is not ripe. Let us go back to France. Let us wait there until we have such a mighty force that none can come against us.'

Edward looked at her in astonishment. 'Do I hear aright? Is this my warlike mother?'

For a moment she was no longer the battling Queen, she was just a woman vulnerable because of her fears for her son.

He understood; he took her into his arms. 'Dearest mother,' he said, 'I am going to put a crown on this head of yours ere long. You are going to be the recognised Queen of England. I promise you that.'

'I want only you . . . safe beside me.'

He stroked her hair and soothed her. 'Dear mother, remember you are the Queen. For years you have taught me where my duty lies. I shall go into battle, win my father's crown and we shall live together, you, he and I happily all through our days.'

'I am a foolish woman,' she said.

'Nay,' he answered. 'You are a great one. Never shall I forget what I owe you . . . I shall remember while there is life in my body.'

She knew that it would be folly to give up just because Warwick had died at Barnet. They had put too much faith in Warwick. They could succeed without him.

So they marched and so they came to Tewkesbury where Edward of York was waiting for them.

The ranks of the army were weary. They had marched seventy-three miles; they should turn away. They were in no fit state to fight. But Edward of York was there . . . waiting for them.

Margaret was uneasy. How many men in that field now would turn to the enemy if they thought the fight was lost? How many could she trust?

'Ride with me,' she said to Edward. 'I want them to see

us . . . to know how determined we are. I am going to tell them what rewards shall be there when this battle is won.'

So they rode together she and her noble son and because of the young man's belief in victory and the indomitable courage of the Queen, the spirits of the soldiers revived and they ceased to complain of their exhaustion and prepared themselves to do battle next day.

She was there when the battle started, and she quickly knew that her men were no match for the enemy. She greatly feared for her son and cursed herself for not insisting that they fly to France instead of engaging in such an unequal struggle.

'It must stop . . . stop . . .' she cried hysterically. 'Where is the Prince? Bring the Prince to me.'

She was half demented not only with exhaustion but with fear. Some of her bodyguard said that it would be better for her to leave the field. She would be needed after the battle was over.

'My son . . .' she murmured.

She was half fainting. These fainting fits were new to her. They were due to an excess of emotion she supposed, but when they were on her she was limp and helpless, so she allowed them to put her into her chariot and take her from the field.

Close by was a small convent and it was to this place that she was taken. Anne, her daughter-in-law, was already there and they sought to comfort each other.

Edward of York was certain of victory. Warwick was dead and he felt freed from a bondage from which previously he had been unable to escape. Warwick had meant so much to him; he had been his friend and mentor. He had loved him and in his heart continued to do so; but Edward was not a man who could be on leading strings for ever. He had had to break away. He had hoped – and believed – that in due course he and Warwick would overcome their differences, reach a new understanding and be friends again.

Now that was too late. He did not wish the young Prince of Wales to be killed on the field. Too many deaths were bad for a man; he did not want blood on his hands; and although he had not personally killed Warwick his death would be laid at his door.

He sent out an order. 'If Edward who calls himself Prince of Wales be captured, do not kill him. I promise a hundred pounds a year for life to the man who brings him to me and the Prince's life shall be spared.'

He could afford to be magnanimous. The battle was almost over and was an undoubted victory and Edward believed that after this there would be no more. He would be safe on the throne.

He saw a party of men coming towards him. They had a prisoner with them.

Edward stared in amazement for the prisoner was Prince Edward.

One of the captains, Sir Richard Crofts, was close, proud of having captured the Prince, and came to claim his reward.

Several were crowding round as the two Edwards faced each other.

The young Prince was arrogant, good-looking in a somewhat effeminate way. Edward of York towered above Edward of Lancaster.

Edward of York said: 'How dare you so presumptuously enter the field with your banners displayed against me, your King?'

The young Prince held his head high and retorted: 'I am

450

here to recover my father's crown and my own inheritance to which you have no right.'

Edward was incensed by those words. He had convinced himself that he had the greater claim, but this captive boy was telling him that he was the son of Henry the Sixth who had to be held captive because the man who had usurped his throne knew that the people were with him.

In a sudden rage he struck the young Prince in the face with his gauntlet.

Those about him saw in this a signal.

The Prince had insulted the King and the King wanted vengeance.

Six or seven of them moved in on him, their daggers raised.

Prince Edward gasped and as he fell to the ground his last thoughts were of his mother.

So there was nothing now to live for. She was in a state of daze. She did not hear what was said to her. She had only one wish and that was for death.

Her gentle daughter-in-law tried to comfort her; but she too was plunged into deepest melancholy. It had been a brief marriage but she and her Prince had begun to love each other.

'We must fly from here,' Margaret's friends had said. 'Edward will not rest until you are his prisoner.'

'I care not,' she answered.

'It is important. There is the King to think of.'

But she could think of nothing but her dead son.

They left – she and Anne – and it was inevitable that they should be captured sooner or later. They had no heart for the flight, no desire to survive.

They were taken at Coventry.

Edward had decided that she and Anne should travel together in the same chariot and take part in his triumphant procession through London. The people would see that they were his prisoners and that the war was over. Right had prevailed and the strong King was on the throne. The Londoners would welcome that. They had always been for Edward.

It might have been humiliating but she no longer cared. She could see nothing but Edward her son . . . Edward as a boy . . . growing up and Edward during those last meetings . . . How right she had been to suggest they go to France. It must have been some premonition.

And she had lost him . . . lost him. Why should she care that Edward of York sought to humiliate her before the people of London? She had never cared for them before.

So they were at the Tower. Henry was there in that one they called the Wakefield. Would she see him? She doubted it. They would not let them be together.

They separated her and Anne and sent them to different prisons in the Tower.

'Oh God,' she thought. 'You have deserted me. Why did you not let me persuade him to go to France? If only my son could be restored to me I would ask nothing more. Crowns . . . kingdoms . . . what do they matter to me now? If I could but live in peace with my dear son I would ask nothing more.'

The door was shut on her. There were guards outside.

Alone! A prisoner!

If I could but have my son back alive and well I would ask nothing more, she mourned.

Edward of York was flushed with triumph. The people of London welcomed his victory. This would mean peace and peace meant trade. The hated Margaret was in the Tower; the so-called Prince of Wales had been slain in battle; this was the end of the Lancastrian cause. The red rose was trampled in the mire and the white one was victorious.

'Let us have an end of wars,' said Edward. 'Let us seek to make our country great through peaceful means.'

His brother Richard listened to him, his admiration shining in his eyes.

Edward laid his hand on his arm. If only he could trust George as he could Richard.

As they sat at the table with their most trusted friends Edward talked of the future. 'The country is being crippled by wars. We have enough enemies overseas. They rejoice in the conflicts which torture our realm. There must be an end to them.'

There was agreement all round the table.

'Margaret is subdued at last. The death of her son has done more to bring her to reason than any battle could.'

'It is time she realised she has no chance of ousting you from the throne,' said Richard.

'She will never realise that . . . while Henry lives.'

There was a hushed silence round the table.

Henry rose from his knees. His long hair fell about his face and he pulled his tattered coat closer about him.

It was cold in the cell at night. The thick stone walls shut out the warmth of the day. Not that he noticed much. As long as he could pray and meditate and take comfort from the spiritual experience he could live.

The food they brought him was often inedible. He did not care very much. Occasionally he ate and that was enough to give him the strength to pray.

He went to his bed and lay down.

He found comfort in thinking of his beautiful colleges at Cambridge and Eton. He hoped the boys were managing to live in some comfort there. If he were stronger, if he were free he would like to build more colleges. That was the happiest time of his life when he had first married Margaret and they had had those meetings with the architects . . . Perhaps it would come again.

He did not want all the tribulations of kingship. He wanted peace. That time when he had been in the monastery in hiding . . . that had been a happy time. How he had loved to mingle with the monks, to sit at their table . . . to meditate and pray.

Someone was in the cell.

They did not usually come at this hour. There were several of them.

They were standing round the bed.

He knew suddenly that they were going to kill him.

He was murmuring something. One man leaned forward and heard him mutter: 'May God give you time for repentance whoever you are who lay your sacrilegious hands on your Lord's anointed.'

Then he thought: Into Heaven, O Lord, receive your servant.

Life was flowing out of him. It was not very difficult. He was so weak and fragile. He did not fight. Pillows over his face . . . and so drifting into eternity.

So King Henry was dead.

He had died of a broken heart, said Edward and his friends. It was reasonable. It was the end of hope for him. The battle of Tewkesbury lost. His son slain in battle. There had been nothing left for him to live for.

'Let his body be exposed and lie in St Paul's where all may see it,' commanded Edward. 'There will be people to say that he met his death by foul means. That is something we must avoid at all costs.'

He was right. People did say it. It was so strange that he should die on the very night when Edward entered London, when Margaret and Anne Neville should have been sent to the Tower.

Others – Yorkist supporters – said that it was precisely due to the shock of all that had happened that he had died.

The King, however – firm on the throne now – insisted that all honour should be done to Henry.

His body was taken by barge to Chertsey and with great respect buried in the lady chapel in the abbey there.

🌸 Chapter XIX 🌸

FINALE

The years were slipping past — the long, meaningless years. Life had been harsh to her, or was it as her sister Yolande had said that she had never understood how to live. Yolande was happy with Ferri and her children, never seeking to extend her ambitions. Yolande had never had any patience with her. Perhaps she should have listened to her sister.

It was all too late now, although they could have lived together. No, they would never live in harmony. Better to be lonely and at peace.

She supposed she could not complain of Edward's treatment. He was now securely on the throne, popular with the people, still possessed of that charm even though he had grown obese and was as lecherous in his maturity as he had been in his youth.

She recognised now that there was a kingliness about him which Henry had lacked. Poor ineffectual Henry! How ironical of fate to give *her* such a husband.

She had stayed in the Tower only a short time and she believed it was Queen Elizabeth Woodville who had prevailed on the King to make life easier for her so that she passed from the care of one great lady to another and spent her captivity as a guest in their stately homes. Then the King of France paid Edward a ransom for her and after five years of wandering captivity she sailed from Sandwich.

How strange it had been to say farewell to the land to which she had come full of hope and ambition all those years ago – it must have been thirty; and stranger still and sad to return to her native country.

Freedom. That was a wonderful feeling. For a brief period she had wondered whether she could start again; whether she could snatch something from the tumbled ruin of her life. She would go to Paris to thank Louis for helping her to return to her country and buying her freedom. When his reply came that he would not be in Paris and she would do well to go to her father, she understood.

She was of no importance now. Her husband was dead . . . murdered, she thought fiercely, and the name of Richard Duke of Gloucester had been mentioned in that connection. But it was Edward of course, Edward who had asked for his death . . . as Henry the Second had asked for that of Thomas à Becket.

But what did it all matter, now that her beautiful son was dead?

René had provided her with the Château de Reculée near Angers and here she lived in utter melancholy.

Yolande had said she must make a new life but she quarrelled continually with her sister, who did not understand what it meant to know that her husband had been murdered and the greatest tragedy possible had befallen her – she had lost her beloved son.

Nothing could comfort her. Even her beauty was lost, for continual weeping and the violence of her passions which she seemed to find some satisfaction in letting loose had made her hollow-eyed and worse still her skin had grown dry and so scaly that those about her believed she was suffering from a form of leprosy.

She would see no one. This was the final affliction for one who had been beautiful and accepted her beauty as a natural right.

Her father died and she felt then that she had lost everything she cared about.

She herself was only waiting for death.

Just after René had died she decided to make a pilgrimage to Dampierre and, heavily veiled to hide her disability, she set out.

She reached Dampierre and rested at the château there and while she was there she was overcome by such a lassitude that she could not rise from her bed.

'Praise God,' she said, 'I think I am done with my troubles.'

Her premonition proved correct. In the fifty-first year of her life, eleven years after the death of her son and husband, Margaret of Anjou closed her eyes for the last time.

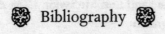 Bibliography

Aubrey, William Hickman Smith *National and Domestic History of England*

Bagley, J. J. *Margaret of Anjou, Queen of England*

Clive, Mary *This Sun of York: A Biography of Edward IV*

Costain, Thomas B. *The Last Plantagenets: The Pageant of England 1377—1485*

Green, John Richard *History of England*

Guizot, M. (Trans. by Robert Black) *History of France*

Haswell, Jock *The Ardent Queen. Margaret of Anjou and the Lancastrian Heritage*

Hume, David *History of England from the Invasion of Julius Caesar to the Revolution*

Kendall, Paul *Warwick, the Kingmaker*

Oman, Charles *Political History of England*

Oman, Charles *The History of the Art of War in the Middle Ages*

Oman, Charles *Warwick, the Kingmaker*

Ramsay, Sir James of Bamff *Genesis of Lancaster*

Ramsey, J. H. *Lancaster and York*

Ross, Charles *Edward IV*

Scofield, C. L. *The Life and Reign of Edward IV*

Stenton, D. M. *English Society in the Middle Ages*

Stephen, Sir Leslie and Lee, Sir Sydney *The Dictionary of National Biography*

Stratford, Laurence *Edward the Fourth*

Strickland, Agnes *The Lives of the Queens of England*

Timbs, John and Gunn, Alexander *Abbeys, Castles and Ancient Halls of England and Wales*

Vickers, K. H. *England in the Later Middle Ages*

Wade, John *British History*

The Plantagenet Prelude

When William X dies, the duchy of Aquitaine is left to his fifteen-year-old daughter, Eleanor. On his deathbed William promised her hand in marriage to the future King of France. Eleanor is determined to rule Aquitaine using her husband's power as King of France and, in the years to follow, she was to become one of history's most scandalous queens.

The Revolt of the Eaglets

Henry Plantagenet bestrode the throne of England like an aging eagle perching dangerously in the evening of his life. While his sons intrigue against him and each other, Henry's conscience leads him to make foolish political decisions. The old eagle is under constant attack from three of the eaglets he had nurtured, and a forth waits in the wings for the moment of utter defeat to pluck out his eyes . . .

The Heart of the Lion

At the age of thirty-two, Richard the Lionheart has finally succeeded Henry II to the English throne. Now he must fulfil his vow to his country to win back Jerusalem for the Christian world. Leaving England to begin his crusade, Richard's kingdom is left in the hands of his brother, John, who casts covetous eyes on the crown.

arrow books

Queen Jezebel

Jean Plaidy

The ageing Catherine de' Medici has arranged the marriage of her beautiful Catholic daughter Margot to the uncouth Huguenot King Henry of Navarre. Margot, still desperately in love with Henry de Guise, refuses to utter her vows. But even Catherine is unable to anticipate the carnage that this unholy union is to bring about . . .

In the midst of an August heatwave, tensions run high between the Catholic Parisians and the Huguenot wedding guests: Margot's marriage to Henry has not brought about the peace that King Francis longed for. Realising her weakening power over her sickly son, Catherine sets about persuading Francis of a Huguenot plot against his life. Overcome by fear, he agrees to a massacre that will rid France of its 'pestilential Huguenots for ever'. And so the carnival of butchery begins, marking years of terror and upheaval that will end in the demise of kings, and finally expose Catherine's lifetime of depraved scheming . . .

arrow books

ALSO AVAILABLE IN ARROW BY JEAN PLAIDY:
THE TUDOR SERIES

The Shadow of the Pomegranate

Jean Plaidy

Whilst the young King Henry VIII basks in the pageants and games of his glittering court, his doting queen's health and fortunes fade. Henry's affection for his older wife soon strays, and the neglected Katharine decides to use her power as queen to dangerous foreign advantage.

Overseas battles play on Henry's volatile temper, and his defeat in France has changed the good-natured boy Katharine loved into an infamously callous ruler. With no legitimate heir yet born, Katharine once again begins to fear for her future . . .

arrow books

ALSO AVAILABLE IN ARROW BY JEAN PLAIDY:
THE TUDOR SERIES

Uneasy Lies the Head

Jean Plaidy

In the aftermath of the bloody Wars of the Roses, Henry Tudor has seized the English crown, finally uniting the warring Houses of York and Lancaster through his marriage to Elizabeth of York.

But whilst Henry VII rules wisely and justly, he is haunted by Elizabeth's missing brothers; the infamous two Princes, their fate in the Tower for ever a shrouded secret. Then tragedy strikes at the heart of Henry's family, and it is against his own son that the widowed King must fight for a bride and his throne . . .

arrow books

The King's Secret Matter

Jean Plaidy

After twelve years of marriage, the once fortuitous union of Henry VIII and Katharine of Aragon has declined into a loveless stalemate. Their only child, Mary, is disregarded as a suitable heir, and Henry's need for a legitimate son to protect the Tudor throne has turned him into a callous and greatly feared ruler.

When the young and intriguing Anne Boleyn arrives from the French court, Henry is easily captivated by her dark beauty and bold spirit. But his desire to possess the wily girl leads to a deadly struggle of power that promises to tear apart the lives of Katharine and Mary, and forever change England's faith. . .

arrow books

ALSO AVAILABLE IN ARROW BY JEAN PLAIDY:
THE MEDICI SERIES

Madame Serpent

Broken-hearted, Catherine de' Medici arrives in Marseilles to marry Henry of Orléans, son of the King of France. But amid the glittering banquets of the most immoral court in sixteenth-century Europe, the reluctant bride changes into a passionate but unwanted wife who becomes dangerously occupied by a ruthless ambition destined to make her the most despised woman in France.

The Italian Woman

Jeanne of Navarre once dreamed of marrying Henry of Orléans, but years later she is instead still married to the dashing but politically inept Antoine de Bourbon, whilst the widowed Catherine has become the powerful mother of kings, who will do anything to see her beloved second son, Henry, rule France.

Queen Jezebel

The ageing Catherine de' Medici has arranged the marriage of her beautiful Catholic daughter Margot to the uncouth Huguenot King Henry of Navarre. But even Catherine is unable to anticipate the carnage that this unholy union is to bring about . . .

arrow books

ALSO AVAILABLE FROM ARROW BY JEAN PLAIDY
THE LUCREZIA BORGIA SERIES

Madonna of the Seven Hills
Jean Plaidy

In a castle in the mountains outside Rome, Lucrezia Borgia is born into history's most notorious family. Her father, who is to become Pope Alexander VI, receives his first daughter warmly, and her brothers, Cesare and Giovanni, are devoted to her. But on the corrupt and violent streets of the capital the Borgia family are feared, and Lucrezia's father causes scandal, living up to his reputation of 'most carnal man of his age'.

As Lucrezia matures into a beautiful young woman, her brothers are ever more protective and become fierce rivals for her attention. Amid glorious celebrations their father becomes Pope, and shortly after Lucrezia is married – but as Borgias the lives of the Pope's children are destined to be marred by scandal and tragedy, and it's a fate that Lucrezia cannot hope to escape . . .

arrow books

ALSO AVAILABLE FROM ARROW IN
THE LUCREZIA BORGIA SERIES:

Light on Lucrezia
Jean Plaidy

At just eighteen, Lucrezia Borgia, the alluring daughter of the
Pope, has already had her life touched by dishonour and tragic
loss. In the decadent society of fifteenth-century Rome, violence
is commonplace and scandal is never far from the infamous
Borgia family.

In the aftermath of her brother Giovanni's brutal murder,
Lucrezia knows she must build a life for herself if she is to break
away from the corrupt world her family is tied to. She hopes for
happiness with her husband Alfonso, but her brother Cesare is
determined to keep her near. Before long she is torn between
her deep love for her partner and her devotion to Cesare, a man
who has proved his brutal nature once and will not hesitate to
do so again . . .

arrow books